Scatter of Light

Book 5 of the Diamond City Magic Novels

by

Diana Pharaoh Francis

Bell Bridge Books

Other Bell Bridge Book titles from Diana Pharaoh Francis

The Diamond City Magic Novels

Trace of Magic

Edge of Dreams

Whisper of Shadows

Shades of Memory

Scatter of Light

Magicfall

The Witchkin Murders

The Crosspointe Chronicles

The Cipher

The Black Ship

The Turning Tide

The Hollow Crown coming soon

Bell Bridge Books
PO BOX 300921
Memphis, TN 38130
Print ISBN: 978-1-61026-179-1

Bell Bridge Books is an Imprint of BelleBooks, Inc.

We at BelleBooks enjoy hearing from readers.
Visit our websites
BelleBooks.com
BellBridgeBooks.com
ImaJinnBooks.com

10 9 8 7 6 5 4 3 2 1

Cover design: Debra Dixon
Interior design: Hank Smith

:Llse:01:

Dedication

To all that is precious in all of our lives;
may it grow and flourish in this time of turmoil.

Chapter 1

Riley

THEY SAY THERE'S no rest for the wicked. Turns out, there's no rest for the somewhat disreputable and slightly iniquitous, not to mention the totally exhausted and emotionally pancaked.

I had no idea how long I'd been asleep when pounding on the door sent me rocketing upright in bed. Clay Price, my boyfriend and love of my life, snatched a gun from under his pillow and shoved me behind him, all in one move.

I had no idea where the gun had come from, and to be fair, people meaning us harm weren't likely to be knocking. All the same, it wasn't like we'd fallen asleep anywhere safe. We were smack-dab in the middle of enemy territory, living on the edge of a very precarious alliance I'd made with a bunch of gangsters who could be the dictionary definition of wicked. Or evil. Or just fucking dangerous.

The pounding shook the door again, and both Price and I lunged out of bed. I made a face at the pile of urine, blood, vomit, and puke-covered rags that we'd been wearing when we got back from rescuing a bunch of hostages. That had been our side of the bargain with the Seedy Seven. They were the lieutenants of a Tyet mob boss named Savannah Morrell. After she'd died and I found myself and my family targeted by a variety of other baddies, I'd been forced to make a deal with them. They'd give me allegiance and the support to take over Savannah's criminal organization, and I'd get their family members back.

In a brilliantly sadistic move, Savannah had taken a family member from each of her lieutenants and held them hostage. If one stepped wrong, she'd maim or kill their loved ones. She'd kept them hidden, so when she was killed, the Seven were frantic to find them.

That fact gave me an ace in the hole.

I'm a tracer. One of the best. Everybody walks around spooling off a unique thread of colored light behind them that sticks to anything they touch. It's their trace and everybody's is unique. Eventually it fades, disappearing altogether when they die, or so the common thinking goes. Mostly because it's true for every other tracer I've ever heard of. Me, though, I'm a unicorn. Trace never fades for me, and I can even see the trace of dead people.

I'd tracked them to the middle of nowhere east of Denver, then Price, me, and a highly irritating FBI agent named Sandra Arnow had rescued them from Savannah's son, who'd taken charge of them and used his tinker powers to break, twist, and warp their bodies, healing them into shapes of horrid suffering as he went.

We'd finally gotten him under control and brought him and the hostages back, right into the middle of a Tyet war.

Price's brother, Gregg Touray, was one of those other evil Tyet lords who wanted to capture and use me to take over Diamond City. What passed for his heart was actually in the right place, which is to say he was driven to take control in order to destroy the other Tyets so people wouldn't have to live in constant fear. But the road to hell and all that and whatever his intentions, he didn't care who he had to hurt to get what he wanted. He saw it as a duty.

His small army of thugs had attacked Savannah's compound that my brothers Jamie and Leo, my sister Taylor, Dalton a frenemy with emphasis on enemy, my best friend Patti, and the Seedy Seven had taken as a base. They'd managed to keep Touray's army from overrunning the compound, but when we brought the hostages back, we'd had to force our way through enemy lines to get to safety.

With Price's elemental powers, we'd managed—barely—arriving just in time for Touray to jump out of one of the mansion's fourth-floor windows and pancake onto a Jeep's roof. His mind had been taken over by a brain-jockey—a powerful dreamer with the power to control and manipulate minds and memories. He'd managed to slip his mental leash long enough to try to commit suicide.

He was still alive, thanks to the healers who'd been standing by in the courtyard to help the hostages, but he remained in a coma. Price and I had stayed awake long enough to make sure he was on an even keel and then taken refuge in one of the many nearby bedrooms. After a shower that could have cooked lobsters, Price and I had crawled into bed. Our nap hadn't lasted nearly long enough, though the adrenaline shooting through my system helped fight off the grittiness of my eyes and made it slightly easier to resist gravity.

I reached for the still-damp towel I'd used after our shower. Price didn't bother with clothing. He stalked to the door and threw it wide, gun held at eye level. Old habits. He was a former cop and an enforcer for Touray's organization. He just assumed people were out to kill him. Unfortunately, he had a decent record of being right.

Taylor stood in the doorway, her body tense. Her gaze darted over Price who lowered his gun, and then she looked to me, still fumbling with the towel.

"There's a situation," she said, the words like bullets.

"Cass?"

"Gregg?"

Price and I spoke at the same time.

Taylor's expression hardened. I recognized the look. I wore it often enough. It was that mask you put on when you want to totally fall apart and couldn't afford to lose your shit, no matter how bad you hurt or how scared you were.

Neither Taylor nor I were particularly fond of Touray, but seeing Price suffering tore me up, and that tore up Taylor. Cass was another story. She'd been a friend of Price and Touray before I met her, and had quickly come to be one of my best friends. She'd saved my life more than once, and though I hated most dreamers, I trusted Cass like I trusted my family. In fact, as far as I was concerned, she'd become family. I was pretty sure Taylor felt the same. Worse, Touray's brain-jockey had used him to put the hit out on Cass.

We didn't know if she was still alive or not. I'd been too depleted to check, and now there was no time.

I stared at Taylor, heart in my throat. I grabbed Price's free hand and gripped it tight. He considered Cass a sister, too. If I was torn up, his brother's near death and Cass's unknown situation had shredded him to pieces.

I could see my sister trying to soften her expression, to no avail. She gave a negative jerk of her head.

"Still no word on Cass, and Touray's the same." She took a breath and looked back at me. "It's bad. Better come quick. The war room."

Her gaze switched to Price. "You should get your brother ready to move. We're going to have to bug out fast and soon." She shoved a fat shopping bag into his chest. "There's some clothes. Hopefully they fit. Don't take too long."

It wasn't until she left that I realized I didn't know where the hell this war room was. As big as this place was, I could easily get lost for days.

I jumped to my feet and headed to the bag, dumping it out onto the bed. We both quickly dressed in jeans, wool Henleys, and wool socks. Taylor had found me a bra and panties and a pair of boxer briefs for Price.

"I hate the idea of putting on these boots," I said, lip curling as I considered them. They were covered in blood and other body fluids and smelled bad.

"Beggars can't be choosers," Price said philosophically, reaching for his.

A knock sounded on the door. I pulled it open. Jamie stood on the other side, his long hair gleaming gold in the hallway lights. His expression was uncharacteristically serious, his brow furrowed, the corners of his mouth pulled down, his eyes diamond hard. He thrust another bag at me.

"Taylor sent me with these. You know where to go?"

"Not a clue. Taylor said the war room."

Jamie gave a short nod. "Hurry up then. I'll wait at the bottom of the big stairs. Take a left off this hallway. The next one will dump you out at the stairs."

He spun and jogged away. Foreboding curled in my chest. This was looking very bad.

"What the hell is going on?" I asked as I pulled two boot boxes out of the big bag. I passed Price his and dropped to the floor to pull mine on.

"Nothing good," Price said, stating the obvious as he laced up his hiking boots. "Waterproof and insulated. Nice."

"You could take your brother to my place," I said. "Unless you want to take him to one of his houses. He's going to need medical help. Maya can take care of his body, but he's going to need IVs to feed and hydrate him."

He stopped lacing to stare. "You barely trusted me to know where you live, and yet you'll let in Gregg and strange medical personnel? Are you sure?"

When I was a kid, my fucked-up father had tampered with my brain. He was a dreamer and—among other things—had programmed me not to trust people. I'd been paranoid about keeping where I lived secret. That, at least, had proved useful, especially now that we needed somewhere ultra-safe to hide Gregg until he was well.

"It's the best choice. Since almost nobody knows where it is, it's the safest place. You'll still want a guard for him twenty-four seven, just in case. Unless . . . are you going to stay with him?"

He shook his head. "I can help him better if I hunt down the brain-jockey. Killing him will free my brother."

"Will it?"

He gave me an odd glance. "Why do you say that?"

"A lot of spells survive their makers."

He shook his head. "This kind of spell is mostly a conduit from the jockey to the victim. It has to be reinforced regularly or it disintegrates. It's too much to hope that the jockey will just give up in the meantime. He'll be waiting and hoping Gregg wakes up. As it is, I'm willing to bet Gregg's keeping himself in a coma to keep from being this asshole's puppet. I don't know how long he'll be able to stay that way."

"You could ask Maya to keep him under," I said. "In case he can't do it himself."

"I might."

I stood, watching as he tucked his gun into the small of his back. "You should take him now. Use the tunnels. Hopefully everyone will be distracted by whatever's going on and won't try to follow."

He came to stand in front of me, his hands grasping mine. "Promise you won't go anywhere until I get back."

I chewed my lower lip, then shook my head. "I can't. Not without knowing what's happening."

His hands tightened, and his expression turned volcanic.

"I'll text you if I have to leave, and I won't go anywhere by myself," I assured him.

His mouth pulled into a tight frown. "Your available backup isn't exactly reassuring. Leo and Jamie are insane. They're just as likely to goad you into stupidity as stop you from attempting it."

He wasn't wrong. My brothers seemed to be missing that little voice of self-preservation in their heads that warned other people against suicidal risks. If they had a little voice, it was always goading them to greater demonstrations of stupidity.

"How about I promise not to take unnecessary risks?" It seemed like a decent compromise.

"That's just it, Riley. Your definition of necessary isn't the same as mine."

He wasn't wrong about that either. I made a face and pulled gently out of his grip. "I don't know what to say. We're between a rock and a hard place. You have to take care of Gregg, and I have to do whatever is necessary here. One thing is certain: we're wasting time we don't have."

Price thrust his fingers through his black hair. It was shaggy and hung well past his collar. "I know. I just wish you'd worry a little bit more about self-preservation."

"I'll be careful," I promised. "I'll keep Patti with me. She's reasonable and also scary." My best friend stood a little over five feet tall. She was a low-grade binder, but what she lacked in power, she made up in ingenuity. It was amazing what she could do against enemies. Stir in the fact that she had multiple black belts in a variety of combat styles, a take-no-shit attitude, and she wouldn't let me do anything too stupid, and Price didn't have a lot of reason to complain.

He sighed and nodded. "Fine. But keep me updated. As soon as I get Gregg set up, I'll come find you." He swept me up against him, giving me one of those devouring kisses that turned my bones to taffy.

He ended it far too soon. Both of stood back, panting.

"I love you," he said and then opened the door. "Let's go."

I dragged my fingers across his stomach as I passed, my throat tight. I knew this probably wasn't goodbye forever, but every time we separated, we took the chance it would be.

I felt Price watching me as I strode down the hallway. I didn't look back. I couldn't.

Chapter 2

Riley

THE MANSION sprawled out over several acres, and that was just the main building. The estate contained a bunch of outbuildings, gardens, stables, tennis courts, pools, and I didn't even know what else over at least four or five hundred acres. Savannah had been in the top one percent of the top one percent, aka filthy rich. Crime is lucrative, especially if you don't have anything resembling a conscience or empathy.

Following Jamie's directions, I turned left into the main corridor and broke into a jog. As he promised, it emptied onto a giant balcony overlooking the grand lobby. Jamie waited at the foot of the sweeping black marble stairway. I went down the right side, two steps at a time, falling in beside my brother as he strode across the vast space filled with enough furniture to be its own showroom.

He led me through the broad entry at the far end, then through a maze of corridors and smaller entertainment rooms, a massive ballroom, down a back stairway, and into yet another ballroom, this one about a third of the size of the first.

Giant TV screens ran in a line down the far wall with bank of computers just below. A bunch of tables and chairs cluttered the rest of the space. Despite containing a group of at least forty people, the room was quiet but for the man whose face filled every single one of the screens. I recognized him immediately: Senator Rice, hater of magic and mastermind behind most of the legislation designed to limit our rights. He'd have criminalized our existence if he could have gotten away with it.

He was talking, but the sound was off. He stood behind a lectern, wearing the sorrowful expression of a worried father, his brow furrowed. At the bottom of the screen in large white letters were an 800 number and a URL.

I always marveled at how benign he looked, like a high school band teacher or a librarian. His black hair was liberally frosted with gray. Cut short, it stuck out from his head in a short, textured crop, making him look younger than his sixtyish years. He wore blue horn-rimmed glasses, a charcoal suit jacket over a scarlet-on-scarlet embroidered vest, a pearl-gray shirt, and a charcoal bowtie featuring a sprinkle of tiny red stars.

Seeing Leo, Taylor, Dalton, Patti, and Arnow clustered with the Seedy Seven, Jamie and I went to join them. I could have cut the tension with a chainsaw.

Lewis Fineman stood nearest me. His soft belly contrasted sharply with his gimlet gaze. A little taller than me, he had a round face, his nut-brown skin ashen, his eyes sunken with heavy bags beneath them.

Beside him stood Laura Vasquez. If she lost any more weight, she'd risk getting lost in the couch cushions. Her skin had gone so pale it had a blue tinge, and without the bright-red lipstick she tended to wear, she looked like a walking corpse. With it she looked like a vampire, which was a kind of a walking corpse when you got right down to it.

At around fifty years old, Emerson Flanders—who was nearly as wide as he was tall without an ounce of fat on him—looked like he'd lost twenty pounds in the last couple of days. His expression beneath his full strawberry-blond beard was flat-out hostile, his pale-blue eyes bloodshot.

Tracey Erickson sat at a computer, his hair pulled back in a ponytail. He chewed his thumbnail as he tapped on the keyboard with his other hand. Gold sparks spattered off his fingertips like tiny sunbursts. His talent involved computers and electricity.

Beside him, Bob Wright stood ramrod straight. His navy silk suit was creased and rumpled, his red power tie pulled loose. His hair looked stringy and tangled, like he hadn't seen a shower or brush in days.

Ruth Blaine and Carter Matokai filled out the last two members of the Seedy Seven. Matokai had an inscrutable Mona Lisa look. He made a show of relaxing his body, but he couldn't seem to stop the pulsing flex of his jaw muscles.

Blaine looked like she'd stepped off the cover of *Vogue*. She wore a cream silk blouse with a pencil skirt and tall black pumps. She and I shared a voluptuous body type, but she had all the confidence of Cleopatra. Despite all that had happened, her expression showed no cracks of stress. I'd hate to have her across the table from me in a poker game.

I nudged in between Leo and Taylor. "What's going on?"

"Nothing good," Leo said. He bent forward and tapped one of the computer operators on the shoulder. "Start it over."

The screen blanked and then the Senator flashed into view again, this time with the volume turned up.

"Citizens of Diamond City," he said staring deeply into the camera. "Recently terrorists set seven bombs off in Diamond City, killing at least ninety-three people and injuring hundreds more. Some will never walk again. Many of you have lost sisters, mothers, daughters, brothers, sons, fathers, and friends.

"This is Theresa Johnson." A picture of a dark-haired girl around six years old popped up on the screen. She wore a puffy, red snow suit and posed beside a snowman, a broad smile plastered on her face.

"This is also Theresa Johnson." This picture show the same girl lying in the wreckage of a blown-up building, her hair and face charred, her hands outflung, her left leg ending at the knee in a bloody stump. Several someones gagged, and I swallowed bile, glad I hadn't eaten recently.

If Savannah weren't already dead, I'd gut her myself. She'd been blackmailing Price's brother to get her hands on the Kensington artifacts he had in his vault. To convince him, she'd set off a series of explosions in the city. The hell with any innocents who got caught up in the blasts.

When the city was very young, it had been a bloody, violent place—a lot worse, even, than today. On a crusade for peace, one of my ancestors—Zachary Kensington—had created a weapon. No one now remembers what it did, only that he and four other cardinal talents had used it to bring peace to Diamond City.

After that, Kensington had broken apart the pieces and hidden them, and people like Touray and Savannah had been searching for them ever since. Touray had obtained three, thanks to me. And he had a vial of Kensington's blood, which meant a tracer with the talent to see dead trace could find his workshop with all his notes. Thankfully, those four items were still safely ensconced in Touray's vault. I hoped to hell Touray never found the rest. No good could come of someone like him having that much power.

I yanked my meandering brain back to Senator Rice. I needed to concentrate if I was going to keep ahead of the game.

"Little Theresa had her whole life ahead her, only to have it ripped away because of Tyets run by those who practice magic and ravage the city like wolves. These people—no, not people. These are animals. These are monsters."

He slammed his fist into the top of the lectern, his eyes blazing with rage and hate. I was pretty sure he'd scripted the move.

"These demons can no longer be permitted to wreak havoc on innocent people—on families, on children. No more will they make war on the innocent people of this city!

"The president has mandated me to take control of the situation and eradicate the magical bloodsuckers who prey on you. You will no longer have to wonder if you will survive long enough to eat your dinner. You won't have to wonder whether you will be extorted or blackmailed on any given day. You will no longer wait to find out if a loved one will return home safely from the movie theater or the grocery store. I will make you safe. I guarantee it."

"Is he for real?" I asked, my stomach starting to churn. What did he mean: take control of the situation? What sort of powers had the president given him?

"It gets better," Jamie said through tight lips.

"The president has declared a state of emergency in Diamond City and given me all the resources necessary to cut the cancer from the city and return it to you, the human citizens.

"As of now, martial law is declared. Military personnel have set up checkpoints throughout the city and on all entrances and egresses. They will begin a dragnet to collect the magically infected and neutralize those with dangerous powers."

The camera narrowed on him. His expression subtly shifted, hardening with resolution.

"I know many of you have useful and harmless abilities that help your families and communities in many important ways. I assure you that you will not be targeted. We are interested in only those who threaten your safety and the safety of the city and this country, possibly even the world."

The senator leaned forward and dramatically swept off his glasses, staring intently into the camera, gesturing to punctuate his passionate words.

"I beg you—help me help you before it's too late. Come forward. Tell us what you know. Who scares you? Who threatens you? All information will be kept anonymous. No one will retaliate. Volunteering information will prove you are not only a hero but also a person of courage, generosity, and love for your families, your city, and your country."

He looked down, appearing to tear up. He swallowed jerkily and then looked back up at the camera. A less cynical person might think he actually meant it.

"I, too, have been faced with this difficult choice. In the end, my conscience would not let me risk my neighbors and friends. My comfort in turning in the dangerously talented comes from knowing that if they weren't corrupted by magic, they'd beg for my intervention to help. The actions you take now are as much for their own good as yours. This is no easy path to take, but I believe in your strength. I know that you will choose to do the right thing."

He straightened, wiping the crocodile tears from his eyes before sliding his glasses back into place. He cleared his throat, collecting himself.

"If that's a performance, he's a hell of an actor," Jamie murmured.

"He's a politician," Arnow responded acidly. "Acting and lying are what they do."

"He's very believable. Compelling even," I said, the churning in my gut turning to nausea.

The senator wasn't quite done.

"Call, text, email, or go to our website. You may also report any tips in person at any checkpoint or to any sweep officer. Again, your names will be kept confidential. You need have no fear of retaliation for your heroism as we work together to save your city. We are also offering a reward of one thousand dollars for every tip that leads to detainment."

He stood for a moment, his expression earnest, sorrowful, and fanatical, all at one time, and then the speech began all over again.

Someone killed the sound again.

"People won't fall for this, will they?" A techie sitting at one the tables turned to look at us. Her face was pale.

"A lot of people don't like the talented," said Taylor. "Hell, a lot of talented have been attacked by Tyets. Who knows how many might climb on the band-wagon?"

"Enough will," Arnow said. "You only need one asshole to point the finger at you. You don't even have to have talent for someone to turn you in. It's going to get ugly and fast."

"This is a fucking disaster," said Matokai. "He has to be stopped."

"How?" asked Vasquez. "He's got an army. Literally. Anything happens to him, more troops will descend on Diamond City, like a pack of wolves, and tear us to pieces."

"Change his mind," said Fineman. "Let a dreamer have a go at him."

"He'll be too well protected," Arnow said. "You won't get anybody close enough to him. Plus the man is paranoid. He'll have nulls and binders. No one is going to cast a spell anywhere near him."

I raised my brows at her in a silent question.

"Rumor mill," she said, interpreting my expression correctly. "Word is he even shits with half a dozen agents right outside the stall door. He's got a perimeter of at least a hundred feet that's a magical dead zone, plus a cadre of guerrilla agents outside of that with martial talents and magical weapons. He's better guarded than Fort Knox."

"Is Fort Knox even guarded that well?" Leo asked.

Arnow sliced him a cutting look.

"Isn't that a little hypocritical? Railing against the evils of magic while using it to guard himself?" asked Erickson.

Taylor rolled her eyes. "What turnip truck did you fall off of? He doesn't believe the shit he's spewing. This is a way to control who gets to use their talent and who doesn't. He'll be the czar of magic. If he says you can use it, you can. If he says you can't, you're fucked. Imagine what an ambitious guy could do with that kind of power."

A tempting thought occurred to me. I could turn Vernon in. That was my father. He'd returned to my life recently and had proceeded to both try to convince me that all the stuff he'd done in my head was for my own good, while at the same time attacking me on behalf of his boss, Jackson Tyrell. Tyrell pretended to be pure as snow but wasn't any better than Savannah. I could turn him in, too.

For a moment I let myself enjoy imagining all the things the senator might do to them.

In the end, though, I'd never be able to do it. As much as I hated them and thought they deserved it, turning them in felt a lot too much like joining the Nazis. In this case, the enemy of my enemy was not my friend.

Jamie rubbed his knuckles over his bristly jaw. He hadn't shaved in at least a few days. "Question is, what can we do to stop him? We don't have much time. He's moving fast. If we don't figure out how to back him off, we'll not only lose the city, we'll lose a hell of a lot of friends." He glanced at me, then at Taylor and Leo. "We can't let him get entrenched. As fast as he's moving, he could have half the city in custody by the end of the week."

"What do you mean, *as fast as he's moving?*"

"Tracey, put up what you found," Leo said, the flinty look in his eyes telling me I wasn't going to like what was coming.

Erickson tapped into his phone. Blue sparks flashed every time a finger hit the screen.

Senator Rice disappeared, and in his place we got a satellite shot of Diamond City and the caldera. The city had been built on three ledges stepping down the east side of the ancient volcano, with some of it spilling over onto the rim, which was where we stood now. The wealthier you were, the higher up you could afford to be. The Bottoms, down in the caldera's basin, was where the dregs of society went. An area of low rolling hills extended several miles to the north and east of the city. The forest had been cut away to allow for farms and the airport.

The image zoomed in with stomach-lurching speed, focusing on an area southeast of the airport. Snow had been bulldozed from the open fields to create a tall wall. Just inside, a fence of razor wire circled around. Nearly half the exposed land had been covered in long cement slabs, with more being poured into forms. The metal skeletons of several buildings had begun to grow up at one end. Hundreds of soldiers scuttled around, hauling building materials and driving heavy machinery.

"Is that what I think it is?" I whispered, hoping someone would tell me I was nuts.

"Depends. If you think Chuck E. Cheese is expanding into a game park, then no, you're wrong. If you think it's an internment camp for the magically talented, then I'd say you were dead on," drawled Bob Wright. His suit was creased, his necktie hanging loose. Like Jamie, he hadn't shaved in a couple of days.

"The explosions only just happened a few days ago. How could they get this much done in that time?"

"The senator is motivated," said Emerson Flanders, who was probably oldest of the Seedy Seven. He towered like a grizzly standing on its hind legs. "The president's given him carte blanche. He's also got a lot of pull in Washington, and no doubt with anti-magic organizations like the HFM."

"Humans First Movement. Like people with magical talent aren't humans," Patti sneered. "Those people are worse than Spanish Inquisitors."

"They are also extremely influential with a lot of money to throw around," Taylor said. "And they have a big membership. They do their best to scare everybody into believing we're out to get everybody. Take over the world. People buy it and blame us for every little thing that goes wrong. Flat tire? Cancer? Bad hair day? The talented are responsible."

"Jealous fuckers," said someone off to the right. I didn't see who.

"To be fair, it's not that they're entirely wrong," I said. "They have every right to be angry at the way they get treated by a lot of the talented community. They can't protect themselves, and the cops work for the Tyets who treat them like garbage."

A tight silence met my words, but no one argued.

"Motherfucker! There's another camp going up not far from this one. They've just finished clearing the land," Erickson said as he shifted the cameras.

"I hate to say it, but we might want to think about cutting our losses and getting out while we still can." Again from Flanders

I'd have agreed, except this was my town and I wasn't going anywhere. We might get out okay, but the rest of the magical population wasn't going to be so lucky, and I'd be damned if I'd just leave them to the senator's goons. Not if I could do something to stop this. Trouble was, I didn't know what I could do. The senator had an army and the law on his side. Fighting him head-on would come down to something like Ruby Ridge on a much bloodier scale. I didn't see any head-to-head scenario where we didn't lose.

Whatever we did would have to be guerilla-style.

"Getting out is going to be more difficult than you think," Jamie said, nudging Erickson's shoulder.

The images on the screens veered and split into four, each one focusing on the main exits out of the city. Every single one had been blocked, with soldiers manning the gates.

They stopped every car driving in or out. As we watched, they hauled a woman and two children out of a minivan at gunpoint and loaded them into the back of a semitrailer.

"Is that even legal?" I asked. Stupid question, really, which Jamie proceeded to point out.

"Who's going to stop them? As long as martial law rules, the senator can do as he pleases." The muscles in Jamie's jaw flexed and knotted as his mouth snapped shut. He gave me an expectant look, his crystal-blue eyes drilling into me.

I found that Leo and Taylor were looking at me, too. I suddenly felt a whole lot like Bambi surrounded by velociraptors. Only these velociraptors didn't want to eat me. Worse. They wanted me to tell them what to do.

I'd put myself in this role. I had decided to take control of my safety and the safety of everybody I cared about. I'd dragged them along—okay, it had been more like they'd galloped full tilt along with me—and whatever I decided we should do, they'd all be at risk.

I really hated being the leader. I didn't know how generals did it. How could they decide who to send into battle and where? How did they not drink themselves into oblivion to keep from worrying and feeling guilty with every drop of blood spent?

It all came down to necessity. We needed to act, and we needed to do it now or it would be too late. And like it or not, I was in charge of the resistance.

"All right, then," I said, sounding a lot more confident than I felt. My gaze gathered in the Seedy Seven and my team. "Let's find a private place to talk. The senator's coming for us. We've got to stop him, and I've got an idea how to do it."

Chapter 3

Riley

TAYLOR GUIDED us to a large dining room. Ornate crystal chandeliers glittered above a long table with enough chairs to seat thirty people with room to spare. A heavy white linen cloth draped the table, with each of the chairs swathed in the same cloth.

A floor-to-ceiling window looked out over an enclosed garden with a rocky waterfall and artfully arranged vines and flowers. Even in the dead of winter, the water burbled merrily and bright flowers dotted the greenery, reminding me that magic could do very good things as well as very bad.

I waited as the Seedy Seven marched in with grim expressions and talking low amongst themselves. Plotting, I was sure. After came my family, my best friend Patti, FBI agent Sandra Arnow, and Dalton—my father's former henchman and now our . . .

I didn't know what they hell he was, except he clearly had a thing for Taylor, watching her all the time like a spider waiting for a bug to land in his web. I hadn't asked her what she thought about that. I didn't think she knew, especially after Touray had laid a kiss on her that had apparently melted her panties. What's a girl to do when she's attracted to unscrupulous and dangerous men who've done some seriously bad things and who are about as trustworthy as rattlesnakes?

I'd have told her to run for the hills or lock herself in a steel room, but Taylor didn't run from anything. And even if she did, Touray was a traveller. He could find her anywhere—if and when he came out of his coma—and Dalton could walk through walls, making locked doors useless. Anyway, I'd thought Price was a bad guy, too, so I wasn't going to judge her if she decided one of them was good enough for her.

I grabbed Patti and my brothers and pulled them aside, speaking to them in a hushed voice.

"Can you three go tell Price about the senator? And then go with him to take Touray to my place? Patti, after that, I want you to collect Ben and his family and your cousins, and bring them back there, too.

"Jamie and Leo, I want you to see what you can do about making more space in the Burrows for more people, and then see what food and supplies you can bring in. Use the underground, not the front way. The senator's likely to be using satellites to track movements."

I sounded paranoid, but at the moment, paranoia sounded better than getting caught by the senator's troops.

"There's a lot of smoke from the bombs and fires," Leo said. "Probably enough cover not to have to worry about satellite tracking. Yet, anyway."

"Do what you think works best," I said.

Patti eyed me, her gaze narrowed. "You're not just trying to get us out of the way so you can go all Lone Ranger, are you?"

I grimaced. Next time Price worried about leaving me and whether I'd be careful enough if he wasn't around, I'd remind him that Patti was always on the job. "Not this time. Anyway, Taylor would break my knees before she let me try."

One of Patti's dark brows lifted skeptically, her arms folding as she kicked out a foot, the epitome of belligerent righteousness. "Better not. You try that shit anymore, and I swear to God I'll pull your lungs out through your nose and stuff them up your ass. Taylor can break your knees after I get done with you."

"Noted," I said, the corner of my mouth lifting.

"How crazy is this plan you have cooking in your pea brain?" Leo asked, looking more like a kid at Christmas than someone about to go to war.

I fought the urge to roll my eyes. Price was right to think they'd egg me on to greater heights of stupidity. Both of my brothers had a bizarre notion of fun. Daredevils, both of them, and very creative in their risk-taking.

"The truth? It's totally bonkers, and I wouldn't exactly call it a plan at this point. I'm totally open to a sane alternative." I didn't have a lot of hope, though.

"All of you better get going. I'll meet you there as soon as I can. We're not going to have a lot of time to stop the senator before things really go to hell."

"One of these days I'll be interested in hearing your definition of hell," Jamie said. "Because from where I'm standing, our asses are getting toasted."

"Grab your asbestos underwear. It's going to get a lot hotter."

I wasn't just doing the Eeyore-pessimism thing. I'd seen a lot of really awful stuff in my life. One thing I'd learned was if a situation could get worse, it would, and it always could. I had already imagined where this martial law and concentration camp shit was going, and it looked a whole lot like gas-chamber showers and mass graves.

Lots of people thought that sort of thing couldn't happen here in the US, but they were wrong. The near total congressional and senatorial support for the *Rice Act* that essentially took all rights from magic-wielders demonstrated that. So did Senator Rice's huge popularity among the plain-vanilla humans. They treated him like the second coming of Christ and that's what worried me so much.

Nobody was going to stop him from doing anything he wanted to do. In fact, they'd cheer him on. We were all that stood between him and slavery for the talented of Diamond City.

"At least we'll be warm," Leo said with a rakish grin. He gave me a quick hug, as did Patti and Jamie, and then the trio headed off.

After they'd gone, I sat at the head of the table. The Seedy Seven gathered at the far end with a lengthy no-man's land of table between us. Taylor and Arnow sat to either side of me with Dalton taking up a position just inside the door, arms crossed.

Dressed head to toe in black, he just needed a scythe to complete his reaper look. Strands of black hair escaped from the long ponytail running down to the middle of his back. With his darker skin, slashing black eyebrows, hawk nose, and sharply drawn bone structure, I'd assumed he was Native American, or maybe he'd descended from the Incas or Aztecs. He certainly had the right look. He reminded me of a panther, endlessly patient as he waited for the right moment to make the kill.

Make that a robot panther straight out of *Westworld*. His eye-mods gleamed silver, making him look inhuman. I wondered what he saw. I knew he could see different things depending on what mode he used. Silver seemed to be his norm.

I sat down, deciding to act like I was in charge, which, if the Seedy Seven went by our agreement, I was. Lewis Fineman sat opposite me at the other end, a clear statement that he meant to renege on our deal.

Not today, asshole.

My chin jutted. I'd spent most of my life hiding in the shadows staying under the radar of Tyet lords who wanted to force me to work for them. Coming out of the shadows to sit in this seat felt a whole lot like suicide, but at the same time, anger pounded inside me like a tribal war drum. I was tired of hiding, tired of letting others dictate my life. It was time to go on the offense. Time to be the change I wanted to see in the world. And that started right here, right now.

Fineman eyed me, and I had the impression of a crocodile peering up out of the water, lying patiently in wait for prey to wander too close. I gave him a slight nod. Challenge accepted. His brows rose, and he gave a slight dip of his head as if to say, "Give it your best." He clearly didn't think my best would be anywhere good enough. He was about to receive a shock.

Once everyone had taken a seat, Dalton swung the door shut and I started talking before Fineman could start spouting off.

"To recap," I said. "Senator Rice has declared martial law."

Wright made an irritated sound and opened his mouth. I cut him off.

"This changes our priorities." I made a point of saying *our*. "Specifically, if we don't find a way to get rid of him, we'll lose the city, many friends and family members, and we may end up in one of his internment camps. We can't assassinate him or conduct an overt war, or we'll see a hell of a lot more soldiers pour into the city and it will just get worse. We also don't have much time. He'll solidify his hold within a week at the rate he's going and we'll be up shit creek without a rubber ducky."

Taylor nodded at the timeline. She'd flown missions in Afghanistan and many other places for a variety of mercenary companies. She was more than a little acquainted with how fast the military could take down a city, particularly if many of its inhabitants welcomed them.

Several of the Seedy Seven also nodded, including Fineman. Points for me.

"Leaving the city now will be difficult, but not impossible. I'm sure you've all got a rabbit hole somewhere for just this sort of event. However, you'll lose everything here."

"Sounds like you've got another idea in mind," Flanders said, the words rasping like they had to struggle out of his throat.

"I do." It was a long shot. The chances of success were slim and none, but I couldn't think of anything better, and I wasn't running. I didn't have anywhere to go, and I wouldn't be able to live with myself if I didn't try to keep the talented of the city safe from the Senator's *cure*.

"We can't fight the senator head-on, so we have to end run him."

"How?" That was Vasquez. Her dark eyes had a sharp glint. Her fingers curled, her long red nails curving into talons. She was ready to kill someone. All she wanted from me was to point her in the right direction, and if I didn't, she'd go hunting on her own.

My solution was not going to make her at all happy. Not her, not any of them. In fact, they were going to think I was insane. Which, to be fair, I couldn't blame them for.

"The Kensington artifacts."

My words fell like pebbles into tar. In what seemed to be slow motion, the Seedy Seven stared, sneered, and then turned to look at Fineman, clearly dismissing me. They didn't even bother to argue. They'd given me a shot and I'd given them insanity, so they were regrouping.

On my way into the room, I'd made sure to pick up each of their traces. Now I reached into the spirit realm to gather them in my hand. A good hard tug would get their attention.

Instantly my bones ached, the deathly cold running up my arm to my shoulder and spreading tentacles through my chest. I gasped, my lungs spasming. I'd never had the cold affect me so hard and fast. Sleep had restored a little energy, but clearly I needed more rest and recuperation, neither of which I was going to get anytime soon. Story of my life.

I pinched my lips together as I swept the seven trace threads into my grasp and drew back out of the spirit realm.

Or started to. Two spectral hands grasped my wrist and yanked. I pitched sideways into glacial night.

I sprawled onto nothing. There was no floor, just a thickening in the air that halted my fall. It took me a second to get my bearings as I twisted upright. Or what felt like upright. Who really knew?

Brilliant streamers of trace spooled away in every direction, coiling, looping, weaving in and out in a brilliant tapestry against a vast darkness. My attention quickly zoomed in on the hands holding me. My mother. A ghost.

"There's little time. There are things you need to know, and I can no longer wait for you to come to me."

The reproof in her tone didn't escape me. If I weren't turning into a block of ice, I'd have flushed hot and red from guilt. I should have found a way to visit her before. Maybe after my stepmother Mel had been killed and Price was hanging by a thread, his power out of control and his brother kidnapped. Or maybe after I'd been captured and imprisoned by a drug lord. Or possibly after I'd survived an FBI assault that left me shredded from flying glass, only to be followed by a battle with five Tyet lords. I could have made time, surely.

I decided that saying so would only piss my mother's ghost off, and really, it's not like she had any idea what had been happening to me.

"Better hurry. I can't last long." Nobody could, but I was run down and my power ran through me like acid.

"What's wrong?"

I shook my head. "Tell me what you need to." *As fast as you can.* I didn't say that either.

"You must not trust your father."

That was her big news? "I know."

She shook her head, glaring at me. A wave of glacial cold rolled off of her, somehow colder than the spirit realm itself. How was that possible?

"You don't know. You think he's predictable in his ambition and ruthlessness. But you're wrong."

I'd gone past the point of feeling achy cold, and now I'd begun to numb up. My teeth chattered and flakes of ice clustered on my eyelashes, scraped off my eyes when I blinked.

"I don't understand. What are you trying to tell me?"

"I suspected for awhile now, but I didn't know for sure, not until Mel came."

Like she'd come on a vacation. Mel had *died*.

"Mel?" I croaked.

"The changes a dreamer makes to your mind will fade after death. It can drive you insane—when all your memories and knowledge turn inside out and nothing makes sense." She waved a ghostly hand. "That doesn't matter. Your father made changes to her mind. Like he did with you. But she's been remembering and now it's certain."

A searing pain burned in my chest where my heart lived, sending tentacles of fire up my shoulder, slipping around my throat and driving down through my arms. I felt my heart stutter. I needed to go. Now. Or I wasn't going to be able to leave.

Still—

I needed to hear the rest.

"What's . . . certain?" I gasped the words between fast, panting breaths. My head spun, and bright splotches blurred my vision. Could I even pull myself back to the living world at this point?

"He's got a brain-jockey in his head. Now go. Your body is suffering. You can't be here any longer."

She shoved at me, her own considerable tracer power swelling to thrust me out of the spirit realm.

I collapsed to the floor and what happened next was a blur. Loud voices, movement around me, pushing and pulling, dull pressure on my chest, and pain. So much pain. I couldn't move, could barely breathe.

My mother's words jack-hammered at my brain.

Vernon had a brain-jockey. Just like Touray.

The ramifications were too many to even begin to understand, but the big one kept flashing in my head like a giant neon light: *My father might not have been responsible for what he'd done to me.*

I hated that hope uncoiled inside me. Maybe my father *hadn't* had a choice in the things he'd done to me; maybe he was a victim—and unwitting puppet— not a sociopathic monster.

A white-hot needle inserted itself in my left eye, thrusting through and puncturing deep into my brain. My spine arched up off the floor as I convulsed. My hands flopped at the ends of my arms, my heels drummed the ground, my body twisting in violent revolt against the invader.

I had no weapons to fight with. Even if I could focus, even if I wasn't worn threadbare, overloaded, overextended and completely out of gas, this unrelenting assault would have pierced through all my defenses. But I was all of those things, and I couldn't have fought off a baby, much less a dreamer.

The mental harpoon penetrated deeper. Terror filled my lungs, making it impossible to breathe. Was this a brain-jockey taking over my mind?

The pain grew exponentially, and the violence of my body's rejection spiked with it.

I couldn't say what happened next. The needle struck something inside me, and my body froze. Electricity zinged outward along every nerve before coruscating through my skin.

"Shit! She's not breathing!"

"Get Maya. Go!"

"I don't feel a pulse."

"Is she paralyzed?"

The frantic voices ping-ponged around me, and I could feel hands touching me, pushing at me, at my chest, but it was like I was encased in rubber and all their touches were distant and vague.

Riley?

My name sounded inside my head, shaky and weak. Cass. Hope and relief swirled in my chest.

Can you hear me?

If I could have moved, I'd have been nodding frantically. *Where are you? Are you okay?*

I don't have much time. They are keeping me nulled but had to take them off for a tinker to work on me. He's almost done.

Where are you?

I don't know. I've been hurt. Shot. Hit in the chest and head. They tinkered my chest right away, but I had to rest before they tackled my head. They put me on an IV. They're about to sedate me.

I could hear her exhaustion and pain. Slender to the point of illness, Cass burned up enormous amounts of calories when she used her dreamer talent. Healing would also demand calories. They'd have given her the IV to hydrate and feed her.

I can't hold on long.

We're coming to get you. Touray has a brain-jockey. He's in a coma.

A recoil, a moment of silence.

He was infected when I checked him out, wasn't he?

Probably. Price thinks he had you shot.

Shit.

I could feel her self-recrimination through the link between us. Then . . .

I can't hold on. It's too much. Cass's mental voice had weakened and grown faint.

I'll find you.

I put every ounce of confidence I could scrape up into the words.

I know.

Her withdrawal was sudden and lacked any finesse. She yanked away, and it was like a hand grenade exploded in my head.

Chapter 4

Riley

I WOKE SHIVERING, with the familiar and disgusting feeling of worms wriggling through my body from head to toe. Healing magic.

My stomach lurched, and I tried to twist onto my side for when I spewed up my guts, but someone—several someones—held me pinned to the ground. My heart thundered in my chest. I felt like one of those cartoon characters that gets hit with a giant sledgehammer and squashes into a pancake.

Their voices washed together and sounded far away. I couldn't tell who was even there. Finally, I forced myself to lie still. It was the fastest way to get back on my feet and get back to the problems at hand.

I gritted my teeth as the wormy sensation continued. Abruptly, the worms turned into frenzied eels. At the same time, the air was yanked from my now-functioning lungs. All the voices fell eerily silent. My stomach thrust up into my throat again, and this time I couldn't swallow it back down. I managed to twist my head sideways before spewing, my lip curling in disgust at the sour acid taste.

Something I could only describe as a giant spatula lifted and turned me onto my side, holding me wedged there. That could only mean Price.

I coughed and tried to breathe, finding the air so syrupy thick I couldn't get much. My coughs deepened, tearing at my throat and lungs. I heard myself wheeze, and then suddenly the air flowed easily. I sucked in deep, gasping breaths.

A warm hand stroked over my head.

"Riley?"

Price spoke beside my ear, his voice strained.

"Come on, baby. Open your eyes for me. What the hell did you think you were doing? You told me you'd be careful, you wouldn't take unnecessary chances. Do you have a fucking death wish?"

That was *so* was unfair.

I struggled to speak but couldn't get anything out.

"We need to warm her up," Maya said, sounding unusually urgent. She was usually the definition of calm. "She's hypothermic. I've handled the frostbite and I'm keeping her organs functional, but Riley won't be able to maintain herself until we raise her core temperature."

I didn't feel cold. In fact, I didn't really feel much of anything but the worms. *Oof.* Now that I thought about it, that couldn't be good.

Maya was keeping me alive artificially. No wonder Price was pissed. Not my fault, though. Well, a little bit, since I hadn't had a chance to go see what mom wanted and she'd gotten desperate.

Vernon had a brain-jockey.

That thought ricocheted through my brain like a ping-pong ball in a cyclone. When had it happened? Before he and mom were married? Before she was killed? After?

And deeper than that, down where the betrayed kid in me lived, had he been in control of himself when he'd done all those things to me? Or had someone else orchestrated it all?

My mind went tumbling over the what-ifs and the potential this-leads-to-that ramifications. I was so occupied that I didn't pay much attention to the sudden argument that sounded overhead.

It couldn't have been long, however, until I started to shiver, my teeth chattering as my body shook. The sharp bite of pins and needles over my entire body had me gritting my teeth. Warmth seeped into me until, gradually, I began to relax into it and the shivering became small tremors that faded altogether, along with the wormy feeling.

"Riley? Baby? Come on, wake up."

I opened my eyes to find Price staring down at me. His eyes were white. Not good. He was still figuring out how to use his power, and white eyes meant the throttle on his magic was wide open. His face was drawn, deep lines bracketing his mouth and creasing his brow. I tried to reach up to touch his cheek, and discovered I couldn't move.

Taking stock of myself, I realized I was wrapped like a burrito in some kind of electric blanket, only the heat pouring out of it was a lot higher than what it should have been. I felt like I was inside a toasty oven.

"I'm okay," I croaked, even though I had no real idea if that was true, but I planned for it to be.

"No, you're not," he ground out.

I braced myself, waiting for him to rail at me for nearly dying again, for not being more careful, not taking care of myself. He didn't say any of that. Instead he straightened, rubbing a hand across his mouth as he stared at me.

"There's food coming," Maya said, moving into view. Her normally smiling face was somber.

She didn't say anything else.

I scowled, fear twisting my stomach. Price wasn't berating me, and she wasn't giving me the rundown on my injuries. Was I dying?

"What aren't you telling me?" I could barely squeeze the words out. I'd taken a lot of risks in my life and come close to dying more times than I'd like to admit, but it had never felt certain. Not like this.

Maya scraped her lip with her teeth and glanced past Price. He followed her worried gaze and gave a little shake of his head.

"They can't hear. You can speak freely."

She nodded and focused back on me. Her somber expression didn't fade.

"Physically, you're well, though your body has suffered a shock and will need time to fully absorb and integrate the healing. It will take a day or so if you take it easy, eat, and keep yourself hydrated. But that will mean nothing if you don't have a care with your talent. You've repeatedly pulled too much power through yourself in the last few months, and it's destroying you."

The relief that washed through me at her initial words crashed into a brick wall. "Destroying me? You just said I'm fine."

She shook her head. "I said you're physically well . . . for now, anyhow. But you have a physical self and a—"

She waved her hands, at loss for an appropriate word. Unable to find one, she shifted tack. "There is a part of you that allows you to channel magic. Call it your spectral- or astral-self. It's anchored in your body and separate from your spirit. It can be damaged, sometimes irreparably, when someone overuses their talent. Like you have."

"I don't understand."

"You essentially have two bodies that overlay one another. The physical one I can heal. The other I can't. No one can. You've been damaging yours. It needs time without you using your talent to heal."

"And if I do keep using it?" My stomach had twisted into a tight knot. I couldn't afford to not use my talent right now.

Maya gave a little shrug. "It will tear. Your body can't handle channeling magic without it. You'll burn yourself up."

"How long would I have before that happened?"

I stared at Maya, ignoring Price's muttered curse. He launched to his feet and stalked away, the air pulling so tight that all the hair on my body prickled uncomfortably. Maya rubbed a hand down her arm as she gave a little shiver.

"I can't say."

"But are we talking seconds here? Minutes? Hours?"

She'd begun to look aggravated. "I don't know. It doesn't matter. The point is, you should stop using your power until your astral membrane heals up. Before it's too late," she added pointedly.

"How long would that take?"

"Weeks, probably. Maybe more."

I didn't have weeks. Not if I wanted to find Cass and stop the senator.

I started wriggling free of my electric blanket burrito, missing the heat of it as soon as I freed myself. I pretended I didn't feel shaky and dizzy as I staggered to my feet with Maya's help. I took a deep breath, glancing first at Price who stood off to the side, arms crossed as he stared down at the floor. His eyes remained pearly white.

I had no idea how to soothe him. He probably didn't know what was going on with the senator and the martial law yet, but when he did, he'd realize I didn't have a choice about taking risks. I wasn't going to run away or hole up for a few weeks until I got better. It would be too late by then, and I had too many people

I cared about in danger. So did he. So did everybody.

I looked away to take in the rest of the room.

Taylor stood just beyond Maya, one hand firm on Erickson's shoulder. He knelt at the foot of where I'd been lying down, the bottom of the electric blanket clutched in his hands. She wore that mask of cool indifference she'd cultivated over the years, but her eyes were turbulent with emotion.

Erickson watched me but remained frozen in place. The navy blanket looked worse for wear, with charred stripes tracing across it where the wires had heated too hot. The smell of burned wire insulation and fabric drifted through the air, and I wrinkled my nose. It appeared Erickson had used his talent to help warm me up.

I nodded thanks, my gaze moving past to where Dalton stood behind Taylor, facing the other direction where the Seedy Seven stood, each pressed up against the far wall. The flattening of their clothes told me that Price was using the air to hold them in place and no doubt keep them from hearing anything we said.

I grimaced at Taylor who darted a look at Price and back to me. He'd anchored her down, too.

"Price. You have to relax. Let everybody go." I waited for him to respond, but he neither looked at me nor spoke. I sighed and staggered over to the chair my mother had yanked me out of and sank into it. The eyes of the Seedy Seven followed me. If nothing else, I had their attention.

"Price. Please."

Abruptly the air in the room loosened. I hadn't realized how tautly pulled it had been until it eased and I could draw an easy breath. Erickson slumped down to his hands and knees. Taylor rushed to me, leaning on the table to bend close, one hand closing on my forearm.

"What happened to you?"

Her voice shook, and I couldn't tell if it was anger or fear or both. Probably both.

"Mom dragged me into the spirit realm," I said in a low voice. "She had something to tell me." I hesitated, then gave an inward shrug. I had no intention of keeping the information secret, but I wasn't sure I wanted to share with the rest of the room, except maybe Price and Arnow.

I frowned, turning to look for her. She wasn't there.

"She went to get Price and then Maya sent her for food," Taylor said when I asked. "What did your mom tell you?"

"That we can't trust Vernon. No—" I said, catching her arm when she made a scoffing sound.

"He's got a brain-jockey," I said, my voice dropping into a whisper. "She's sure of it. She said that Mel corroborated, now that she's . . ." I was going to say dead, but Mel was Taylor's mom and her death was still raw for all of us. "Now that she's out of his reach."

Taylor's body went rigid, and her eyes narrowed to slits. I could see the wheels spinning in her mind.

Just then, Arnow arrived and set a giant silver tray on the table. It held a variety of food, including a pot of hot chocolate, a plate of eggs with a mound of bacon, a T-bone steak, a loaf of artisan bread, a jar of peanut butter and another of honey, a bottle of orange juice, and a package of Oreos dipped in white chocolate.

Hunger roared inside me. I barely got a thanks out before I started shoving food in my mouth. Maya poured out some hot chocolate for me. I gulped it, delighting in the sweet creaminess and the heat spreading from it.

"Are you going to tell us what the fuck just happened?" Lewis Fineman had resumed his seat at the far end of the table, his compatriots standing in a semicircle behind him.

"She's going to eat," Maya declared, and the look she shot them was glacial. "She needs the calories to recover."

"From what?" Vasquez demanded, hands on her hips. "What just happened?"

"Sit your ass down," Taylor said in a clipped voice. "She'll talk to you when she's good and ready."

Before any of the Seven decided to shoot her, or worse, I raised my hand to get their attention as I swallowed a mouthful of food.

"Please have a seat. I'll explain."

I shoveled more food into my face while they considered and then stiffly sank into their seats. I was going to have to talk fast if I was going to keep them on my side, and even then, I didn't have great odds.

Before I could begin, Price strode to the door and out without even a side-long glance at me. I stared after him. I wanted to chase after him and fix things, but I couldn't. We both knew it. The path we were on was going to take us to dangerous places. Maybe fatal places. But we didn't have a choice. Or maybe we didn't have a better choice. We were all going to have to put ourselves on the line if we had a snowball's chance in hell of saving Cass and Touray, getting rid of the senator, and saving the talented of Diamond City.

Taylor squeezed my shoulder in mute sympathy. She probably thought it was about me coming so close to dying again. Not that it mattered whether she understood. I did, and Price did, and so did the rock and the hard place grinding down on us.

I swallowed the now tasteless food and took a deep breath to ground myself. I couldn't lose it. I'd known this was going to be a tough row to hoe before my mother pulled me into the spirit realm and exposed how fragile I'd become. Learning that hadn't changed anything.

I put some steel in my spine and straightened, lifting my chin and squaring my shoulders. Taylor and Arnow stood just behind me, while Maya sat next to me. She took a scone from my heaping platter and buttered it. Dalton stood a few feet away, his back angled so that he mostly faced the Seven but could still keep Taylor in sight.

The corners of my mouth ghosted upward for a moment. He had the look of a hungry lion about to devour his lunch. Taylor was in for an interesting time with him. Not that she trusted him or ever would. Plus her relationship with her on-again-off-again fiancé, Josh, had ended badly. She'd been wrecked, and I had no idea if she was ready to move on or not, or if she still hoped they could work things out.

I touched the hollow at the base of my neck reflexively. Josh had changed drastically when he'd been kidnapped. Haunters had tortured his mind, even as someone else had tortured his body, feeding him Sparkle Dust to make him more compliant. SD was a magical drug that was instantly addictive and, over time and use, would turn people into literal wraiths. Touray had rescued him from the original kidnappers, but the damage had been done.

Josh wasn't the easy-going, kind man he'd been. He'd even tried to strangle me because I didn't kill him and put him out of his misery. The torture had woken his latent dreamer talent but had also crippled it, making him a haunter. None of us had seen him since the night he'd tried to strangle me. Maya had healed him and he'd disappeared. I couldn't regret it, not if it meant Taylor was safe from his newly developed savagery. At the same time, I couldn't help but feel sorry for him.

Not my monkey, not my circus, I told myself firmly, pulling myself back to the disaster at hand.

The funny thing was that the whole reason I'd opened myself up to the spirit realm originally was to grab up the Seedy Seven's traces so that I could get their undivided attention. And maybe a little respect. I had the former now. The latter . . . we'd see.

"As I said, we're going to get the Kensington artifacts."

Swearing, rolled eyes, table slaps, and shouted insults followed my announcement, followed by more demands to know what had happened to me.

Not fucking today. All my spoons were gone along with my fucks, and I was tired of dealing with these adolescent-brained killers.

I sucked in a breath, bracing myself against the hurt using my magic was going to give me, and gave a sharp tug on the seven traces. Every single one of Seven jumped liked they'd stuck a finger into an electrical socket. They'd be over the moon to know that my end had felt ten times as bad.

"What the fuck?" Wright demanded, rubbing a hand over his chest.

"You ready to shut up and listen now?" I gave another little tug and they each went a little pale, but they remained silent as they stared angrily at me.

"Thank you. I realize this is a long shot, and I'll be happy to entertain other ideas, but first let me lay it out for you. Gregg Touray has in his possession three of the artifacts as well as a vial of Kensington's blood, which I can trace to his workshop where I hope to find instructions on how to use the weapon."

"Can't use it without all five pieces," Fineman said.

"I know how to find those," I said faking lofty confidence.

In fact I *did* know how to find them, but knowing and doing were two radically different things. Doing was a whole lot of what-the-fuck dangerous on a good day, and as my short visit to the spirit realm proved, I was fresh out of good days. I had an idea how to make it a little less dangerous, but crashing at two hundred miles per hour rather than three hundred would still get a person dead.

I snorted inwardly. Apparently, I'd developed brain diarrhea. Hopefully, my ideas were worth more than liquid shit.

"People have been hunting those for more than a century. What makes you think you can find them now?" Fineman leaned forward on his folded arms, staring intently at me.

"I know where to look."

"And we're just supposed to believe you? You're certifiable if you think that bullshit is going to fly with us."

"I believe that Jackson Tyrell may have one or both of the remaining artifacts," I said. I didn't have any evidence. Just an instinct that said he'd been looking for the artifacts, too. He had the money and manpower to find them, if anybody did.

I cast a quick glance at Arnow. She'd been the one who'd planted the three known artifacts for Taylor's ex—an accountant—to find, knowing his connections would involve the Tyets. She'd been going after Touray and maybe Savannah— I'd never asked about the sting operation she'd had planned. Now I wished I had.

I lifted my brows at her, and she seemed to read my mind. She gave a quick headshake. She didn't know where the other two were.

"And if he doesn't?" Fineman's shrewd gaze drilled into me.

"Then Kensington's workshop will tell us where they are."

Flanders snorted. "And when it doesn't, we'll have wasted days." He looked at the other Seedy Seven. "We don't have time for games."

"Agreed," Matokai chimed in. "And we don't even know what the weapon does. Might be useless. Or broken. Or drained of whatever power it held."

"It's worth a try," I said.

"Is it?" Wright looked at his six compadres. "We need a plan that could actually work."

At least that meant that they didn't plan to pick up their toys and run for the hills. Like it or not, for this to work, I needed their help.

"You wanted to know what just happened to me just now. I took a little trip to the spirit realm."

That announcement earned me seven blank stares.

"You know, where dead people live," I clarified.

"You went to the land of the dead." Vasquez's upper lip curled into a sneer. "Do you think we're idiots?"

"It's not really a land, and my opinion of you hardly matters, but yes, I did." I continued quickly, before anybody else could interrupt. "I can follow dead trace, even Kensington's. Because I can travel into the spirit realm, I can go there and ask my great-whatever grandfather where the artifacts are hidden."

"You're serious," Matokai said finally.

"What do you mean, great-whatever grandfather?" Flanders pounced on that one.

I curled my fingers into a fist in my lap. "I'm a Kensington."

It felt so wrong to confess all of this. Any one of these secrets could get me killed, or worse. Taylor set a hand on my shoulder and squeezed. I wasn't alone.

"Holy shit," Erickson said.

"You're saying you can just go ask Kensington where he hid the artifacts?" Fineman asked. "Why haven't you done it before now?"

"That little visit to the spirit realm a few minutes ago nearly killed you. How are you going to survive to find Kensington and get the answers?" This from Wright. He sounded like the attorney he'd once been.

I pushed my tray back and leaned forward before anybody else could say anything, doing my best to give the impression of strength, even though something that resembled blind panic galloped through my veins. I had to pull off my end of things, and I didn't know if I'd be able to. Didn't matter. A lot of lives depended on me, and I didn't have a choice but to try. And succeed.

"I'll take care of my end of the deal," I said. "You just need to worry about taking care of yours."

"And just what do you think that is?" Fineman asked.

"Distract the senator. Keep him from taking over the city. Give me time to get the artifacts. And find me a powerful binder, maker, and dreamer."

According to legend, five powerful cardinal talents were necessary to make the weapon work. I'd do the tracer part, and I was counting on Touray coming out of his coma to be the traveller. I hoped Cass could be the dreamer, but I didn't know what shape she'd be in when we rescued her, so I needed to plan a replacement.

"I could take down a lot of the city's electrical network," Erickson offered. "Fuck up the Wi-Fi and cell towers. That could buy time. There would be a lot of confusion and difficulty communicating. Plus, it would shut down that PSA he's running on the TV and the call center line."

I didn't know if he was talking to me or the rest of the Seven. Didn't matter. It was an excellent idea.

"Do it," I said.

Erickson slanted a sharp look at me and then at the others. They nodded agreement. Well, at least we were on the same page as far as that went.

"We could start sniping them out," Blaine said, thoughtfully tapping her fingers on the table. "Guerrilla tactics."

"Bad idea. That would ramp things up," Arnow said. "The senator would call in backup. It'll be like cutting the heads of a hydra. We'll end up with exponentially more enemies and they'll be allowed to shoot at will."

"We can't just bet on the artifacts," Fineman said, surprising the hell out of me. He was actually considering my idea?

The others popped wide-eyed looks at him. He acknowledged them with a grimace. "She manages to find them, then it might give us the edge we need. In the meantime, we'll put together another game plan. No matter what happens, we need multiple prongs of attack. Guerrilla tactics could work, but not sniping. We could use dreamers to shift the soldiers' thoughts, maybe to rebel or go AWOL or something. But if we did that, we wouldn't have a lot of time to make a decisive strike before the senator retaliated." He shook his head, tapping his fist lightly on the table. "We can only go that route if we've got other approaches. Or if it's part of using the artifacts."

He said the last like the words tasted like shit but was clearly pragmatic enough to consider the Hail Mary option. I could respect him for that.

"A better bet is taking down the senator," Blaine argued. "We could get a brain-jockey into him; we can control his behavior. That would solve everything. Hell, that could give us control of the city so we could shut down the competition."

"People would notice," Flanders said. "They'd be looking for it."

"Not if we made him sick at the same time. Or hit him on the head. Give a reason for his mind to shift. Reveal an ongoing addiction or illness. We can make it stick. After that . . . make him decide to back off and negotiate with us."

"That will only work if you give up a lot of your illegal activities," I said. "Turn over a lot of your assets. Prove you're going to go on the straight and narrow. Otherwise nobody would believe he'd go for a truce of any kind. If he could declare it a good solution because of all the lives saved, and that he'll be closely monitoring us, then it might fly. Question is, do you have a dreamer capable of creating a brain-jockey?"

Cass could do it, but she wasn't an option. She and Vernon couldn't be the only dreamers powerful enough to create a brain-jockey, as evidenced by my father having one in his head.

"Not a problem," Wright declared confidently.

Taylor spoke behind me. "How are you going to get close enough to him to get the jockey into his head? He's got FBI and Secret Service twenty-four seven, and he's probably surrounded by nulls and binders, plus other magical protections. You're not going to get a traveller through those."

"We'll have to make a traditional attack on him," Flanders said. "Send in an army and take everybody out."

"He'll be prepared for that," Arnow said. "Even if you break through, Secret Service will have escape routes ready. You won't get him that way."

"Secret Service?" Dalton echoed, startling me. "They don't protect senators."

Arnow shrugged. "President and him are buddies. Ever since the assassination attempt on the senator right before the *Rice Act* passed, the president has assigned him a Secret Service detail. Plus Rice is expected to be the party's candidate when the president's second term ends. Anyhow, like I said, you won't get Rice in a straight-on attack."

"We will if we know the routes," Flanders said.

"How are you going to do that?"

"You're in the FBI. Find out."

Arnow shook her head. "I don't have access."

"I can find the data," Erickson said.

She shook her head. "The servers with that sort of information are stored in a secure vault protected by binders and nulls and cut off from all the other systems. The only way to tap in is at the source."

"Who would have access to that information?" Fineman asked.

She considered. "His chief of staff. The agent in charge of his security. He'll probably have a bugout team who've trained just to get him out of there. They'd have to know."

"That brings us back to needing a dreamer," Vasquez said. "Or haunters. Or good old-fashioned persuasive torture, but that's time consuming."

"Can you get assigned to the senator's detail?" I asked Arnow.

"It's unlikely."

"But if you volunteered?"

She shook her head. "He wouldn't trust me. I spent too much time in Savannah's organization. Plus, I've been running an off-the books operation."

"Do they know about that?"

She shrugged. "Maybe. Maybe not."

"Then it's worth a shot. You have no magical talent. I'm sure that's in your personnel file. That will certainly count in your favor. Your time with Savannah makes you a Tyet expert. And you could sweeten the pot by bringing him a gift to prove yourself."

"Gift?"

"A prisoner," I said. "Someone high up in Tyet. Or someone with a powerful ability."

"Like who?" This from Fineman.

I looked at him. "One of you. Unless you've got someone else who could fit the bill."

"What about Jackson Tyrell?" Blaine asked. "He's well known for criticizing the senator. Use him."

"Tyrell's a beloved philanthropist. Senator Rice would be destroyed in the media if he took in Tyrell," Fineman countered. "As far as we know, he has no magical talent, so the senator couldn't hold him on that basis, either."

He glanced at me as if to ask if I knew differently. I shook my head, then eyed Dalton. I'd never seen any evidence that Tyrell had a talent, but Dalton had worked for Vernon. Of anybody in the room, he'd likely know. He gave a shrug.

Then I had an idea. A wonderful, *awful* idea. I couldn't help the little smile that took over my mouth.

"I know just the person. He's a dreamer. Works for Tyrell. Goes by the name Vernon Brussard."

"Why him?" That from Vasquez who looked like she'd like to drive an icepick through my brain. Some people had resting bitch face; she had perpetual serial killer face.

"He works for Jackson Tyrell, who as you've pointed out is the senator's biggest critic. He also tried to kill me and he put the brain-jockey in Touray."

Fineman fastened on the last and immediately took the suggestion to nightmare territory. "So turning him over to the senator could get this Brussard close enough to put a jockey in the senator's head . . ."

He exchanged looks with the others and then turned to me. "Can you bring him on board?"

"He can't be trusted." Especially since he had his own brain-jockey. "Plus, like I said, he tried to kill me."

I pushed my hair behind my ear. I noticed my hand shook and balled it into a fist before dropping it into my lap. Did I tell them about Vernon's brain-jockey? How much did it matter? If he agreed to do this, then presumably the jockey would, too. It was a huge risk. We had no idea who was pulling Vernon's strings or what he wanted. All we knew for sure was that he played a long game.

"He will cooperate if properly inspired," Flanders said, and the others nodded with all the confidence of criminals who'd built their careers by "inspiring" people to do things. Savannah had given them a dose of the same when she took the hostages. It had angered them, but they also took it as business as usual.

"What sort of inspiration?" Taylor asked. "As far as we can tell, there's not a damned thing he cares about." The look she gave me said she, too, was concerned about his brain-jockey.

Blaine smiled as if to a small child.

Come into my parlor said the spider to the fly. . . .

"Everybody's got an Achilles' heel."

"But you've only got a day or so to find it."

Taylor's gaze flicked to Dalton and away. He might be able to help, but none of us could trust him that far. He had a long history with Vernon, and his loyalties were questionable at best. Did he know about the jockey?

"We're very good at what we do," Blaine replied with a smug look.

"Can you guarantee it?" Taylor asked. "We can't build plans on hopes and maybes."

Blaine's cheeks sucked in, eyes narrowing to slits. She looked at Erickson. "Deep dive. Now."

He started tapping on his ever-present laptop. "Last name again?"

"Brussard. Vernon Brussard."

While he did his thing, I ate. I still felt shaky, and my bones were ice. I was still trying to wrap my brain around Vernon having a brain-jockey and what that meant. The jockey had been in Vernon's head long enough to tamper with Mel's brain. I wish I'd been able to ask if she could remember how long he might have been messing with her. Of course, just because Vernon had the jockey didn't mean he hadn't been messing with her—with me—before that.

I rubbed my forehead. I wanted to believe my dad wasn't responsible for fucking around in my head, but it didn't really matter at this point. I had to deal with the Vernon that I knew, which was the brain-jockey version. And that meant talking directly to the jockey.

I couldn't help but wonder—did Vernon even know someone had messed with him? It wasn't a foregone conclusion. My father had certainly hidden his tracks well with me. I wouldn't be surprised if Vernon had deliberately made Touray aware, just to torture him.

I held in a sigh. This business was such a convoluted mess. Vernon's jockey controlled Vernon, but Vernon might or might not be aware that he was controlled. In the meantime, the jockey had either made or permitted Vernon to mess with Mel, me, Touray, and who knew who else?

"His real name isn't Vernon Brussard," Erickson announced after a minute or two.

"Nope," I said.

He glanced up at me. "You know? What's his real name?"

I was tempted to tell him to find it himself as sort of a test of his skills, but we didn't need to be wasting time. "Sam Hollis."

Erickson frowned. "Isn't your name Hollis?"

"Yep."

"He's a relative?"

"Our father." I swirled a finger to indicate me and Taylor.

All seven of them stared.

"Why the hell didn't you say so?" demanded Wright.

"What did you find?" Taylor asked Erickson, ignoring the question.

"Works for Jackson Tyrell. Has money. Connected to at least twenty corporations and banks. Bank accounts all over the world. No family, donates money to the Red Cross regularly, home residence listed in Miami, though . . ." Erickson drifted off a moment, tapping and reading. "He doesn't spend much time there. Looks like he moves around a lot. Records go back twelve years."

To when he'd disappeared.

"What about David Hollis? Just the relevant stuff."

Erickson continued to tap away. Red sparks flew from his hands and swirled around the laptop. He rested his fingers on the sides of the monitor and closed his eyes. They jerked back and forth beneath his eyelids.

"Born and raised in Diamond City. Parents died when he was sixteen. Only child. Worked in the mines, then joined the Bigan Tyet. That was taken over by Quorly, then Connab."

"All defunct. The man is a regular Typhoid Mary," Matokai said.

"Wait," Erickson said, a frown creasing his brow. He shook his head. "Somebody's doctored the records. Nothing is agreeing, except that he's male. The rest keeps changing. Birthday, family, racial heritage, employers, addresses . . . Can't tell what's true or not. I'll keep digging."

Shit. I sighed. Just when I thought I might learn something interesting.

"Can I talk to you a minute?"

I looked up at Taylor in surprise, then nodded.

"We'll be right back," I said, carefully standing, making sure I had my balance before following Taylor out. She surprised me by motioning for Dalton to join us. Foreboding clenched in my stomach. Wherever this was going, it wasn't going to be good.

Chapter 5

Taylor

ONCE THE DOOR closed behind them, Taylor took an inventory of her sister. Riley was way too thin, and bruises circled her eyes. Her normally pale skin held a blue tinge, and she kept her arms crossed like she was either cold or trying not to let anybody know how bad she was shaking. Taylor figured it was probably both. One way or another, Riley needed rest. She'd argue, but she wouldn't be any good to anybody if she didn't.

Her mouth tightened. She came from a family of powerful talents, and yet she'd gotten nothing. Nothing to help shoulder this immense burden Riley had taken on. They all had taken on, she reminded herself. And she had skills, just not the ones Riley needed.

Until now. She meant to do her part in this venture.

"I want to be the one to talk to Vernon."

Dalton made a low sound in his throat, and Riley stared.

"Come again?"

"Somebody has to go talk to Vernon. It has to be me."

"Why?"

"We don't have time to mess around. You and I are the only two we *know* he'll see without question. You can't risk going. Tyrell wants you too bad. He'd never let you leave." Without a talent, Taylor just wasn't that interesting. For once, that worked in her favor. "Anyway, you're in no shape to go. You need food and rest if you want to pull this whole thing off."

Riley looked like she wanted to argue, but the fact were the facts.

"It's not a good idea," Dalton said suddenly.

Both women looked at him.

"Who asked you?" Taylor couldn't keep the bite from her voice. The man set her teeth on edge. He always seemed to be hanging around, a constant shadow. Or stalker. She'd have objected more loudly except that when he was following her around, he wasn't after Riley. Besides, keep your friends close, your enemies closer.

"Your father won't hurt you, but Tyrell can't be trusted," he declared. "You can't take the risk."

She couldn't help rolling her eyes. "Hear that, Riley? Vernon won't hurt me. Until he does. In other news, Tyrell's untrustworthy."

Dalton made an irritated sound, and the corners of Taylor's mouth kicked up.

"Tyrell could try to hold on to you," Riley said. "Use you as a hostage against us."

Taylor shrugged. She'd already thought about it, but in the end, it was a necessary risk. She said so.

"What about Vernon's brain-jockey?"

The silent shadow that was Dalton jerked in shock. Or fake shock. "What brain-jockey?"

Taylor ignored the question. "What about him? I'm betting he's using Vernon to spy on Tyrell. If I threaten to expose him, he'll cooperate and make Vernon come with us."

"Or he'll cut his losses and kill Vernon. Or more likely, you."

"*What brain-jockey?*" Dalton's voice had risen slightly, cutting through the air like a whip-crack.

"He has one," Taylor said.

"Since when? How do you know?"

Her lip curled. "Your concern is touching. My father is lucky to have someone care about him so much. Don't you think, Riley?"

"Just because I don't like hearing he has a brain-jockey doesn't mean I'm his spy," Dalton snapped. "How do you know he has a jockey?"

"Our moms," Riley said.

His silver gaze drilled into her. "How do they know?"

Riley's expression turned frosty at the challenge in his voice. "Not that I have to explain anything to you, but Mel's been having memories. Now that she's dead, Vernon's mental manipulations are wearing off."

"Christ." He turned and walked a few steps away.

Riley focused back on Taylor. "Say you do go. What if the jockey refuses to cooperate? What if he attacks you instead? What will you do?"

Taylor took a breath and blew it out slowly, trying not to feel hurt or annoyed. She always wondered if Riley's concern was based on the real danger or the fact that Taylor had no talent to use as a weapon. Riley would kick her ass if she even suggested it, but Taylor still had her doubts. She always felt she had to prove herself.

"Then that option is out and you'll have to go to Plan B. None of us get to play it safe. This is worth the risk. We might be able to get to the senator before he really digs in. Every moment he's in power he becomes harder to kick out. I don't know why you're arguing. Somebody has to go, and I'm the best choice."

Riley sighed. "I know you're right. I just don't like it."

"I don't either," Dalton declared, returning to the conversation.

"Nobody asked you," Taylor said.

"He's got a brain-jockey. You can't trust that Vernon won't hurt you."

Taylor snorted. "He's *had* a jockey. For years. You've been swearing up and down he won't hurt us—now suddenly you change your mind? As far as you're concerned, he's the same man he's always been."

He scowled. Taylor glared back. She hated his eye-mods. She couldn't tell anything about what he was thinking or feeling. It made her want to needle him, make him prove he was human with human feelings.

"You aren't that stupid," he said, lip curling. "He's become a complete unknown. Whoever the jockey is, you don't know his motivation or his goals. You have no idea what he may do once he knows you've discovered him. He's been content to exist within the bounds of Vernon's character, but once you out him, the jockey will no longer feel compelled to do so. He'll have no reason to."

"I've got news for you, Dalton," Taylor said, putting her hands on her hips. "Vernon's always been a complete unknown. The fact that he has a jockey doesn't really make any difference, except that now we know we're talking to someone else and can negotiate accordingly."

His jaw flexed. Before he could speak again, Riley interrupted.

"When do you want to leave?"

"You're really going to encourage her in this idiocy?" Dalton glowered at Riley.

"For a guy who's hardly spoken twenty words since I met him, you sure have a lot to say, suddenly," Riley said.

"You've hardly been interested in my opinions."

"And I'm not interested now," she snapped.

She looked back at Taylor. "I'm assuming you pulled Dalton out with us in order to take him with you."

"He knows Tyrell's place and having him with me might smooth the way inside."

Riley nodded and raised her brows at Dalton. "Are you going to have Taylor's back? If not, tell us now. I'll send Jamie or Leo." She frowned. "Maybe I should, anyway."

"I'll go," Dalton said quickly. He looked back at Taylor. "But you're not taking any stupid chances."

"I'll do what I have to do, and you'll keep your mouth shut if I have to slap duct tape over it."

He bent closer. "Try it."

"I'll make sure to keep it handy," she returned, not backing down.

"This is fun and all, but if you two are just going to argue, I should go back in. Be careful," Riley said pulling Taylor into a hug.

Taylor hugged her back. "Always am."

"Keep me updated. Regular check-ins, okay?"

"Will do."

"Tyrell might not want to let you or Vernon go," Riley warned, stepping back. "Be prepared to go head-to-head on that. You might check if Savannah's got anything useful in her magical arsenal. You'll be heading into walls of nulls and binders, but you might find something that will give you an edge."

Taylor nodded. "I already planned to have a look. Good luck with the seven dwarves in there. Try not to kill any of them. And Riley, try to take it easy. You're in bad shape."

Riley's grin was weak. "No rest for the wicked."

She'd lost weight, and Taylor could see her tremble with exhaustion. "I'm serious. You can't keep pushing it. You'll kill yourself. And don't tell me you'll rest when you're dead. You almost got to try that out, a few minutes ago. It's not funny."

Riley heaved a sigh. "I'll do everything I can to stay healthy and whole," she promised.

"That's not real reassuring."

"Best I can do under the circumstances."

Taylor's throat tightened. "Your best sucks."

Riley gave a muffled laugh. "Get out of here. And don't take any unnecessary chances."

"She won't," Dalton growled.

"A little advice, Dalton," Riley said with a sideways look. "Don't push Taylor into a corner. Sometimes she thinks winning is more important than surviving."

Taylor snorted. "You should talk, Miss Pot."

Riley grinned. "I never said it didn't apply to me. It's in the Hollis genes. Better go. And don't forget to call." She gave a little wave and headed back to the room.

"Hey, Riley." Taylor waited for her sister to turn around.

"You should have Erickson start pushing on social media. Say that the senator's troops should be helping with search and rescue and putting out fires. Splash it everywhere that he'd rather focus on hunting the talented rather than helping those in desperate need. Post pictures of the bomb sites and the chaos. If Senator Rice has to put more soldiers on emergency operations, there will be fewer to get in your way."

Riley cracked a grin. "Good idea." She waved and disappeared into the meeting room.

Taylor turned to Dalton. "I've got to get a few things, then I want to see what I can find in Savannah's arsenal." She hesitated. "Don't hurry too much. Riley needs time to rest and recover. A few extra hours won't hurt our mission but might do a lot for her."

She turned to walk away, but Dalton stepped in front of her.

"You need to trust me." The words came out with dark intensity.

He was serious. Taylor gave a dry laugh.

"Yeah sure. When cows grow wings and fuck butterflies."

Dalton caught her arm before she could walk away. "Why not?"

"Seriously?" She pulled out of his grip. "First, you worked, and still may work, for my father, who has a record of attacking my family. He nearly killed

Riley. Second, even if you *think* you've quit working for my father, he's a dreamer. You wouldn't know if he was using you. And third, I can't imagine a single logical reason for you to have shifted your loyalty to us. It makes a lot more sense that you're keeping an eye on us for Vernon."

His jaw hardened with her words, the muscles flexing. Taylor thought he'd bluster and argue, so his next words startled her.

"The bit about the dreamer is fair, and if it makes you happy, I'll let Cass dig around in my head. Hell, I'll *pay* her to do it. As for why I quit Vernon . . ."

He looked away, his nostrils flaring. "You don't want to know."

"Try me. I would love to hear a good, believable reason."

He stared at the floor a moment, then captured her gaze again with his silver mod eyes. "The reason is you."

Taylor blinked. "Us?" she repeated.

"No, *you*." He poked a finger just below her clavicle.

She knocked his hand aside. "Very funny. I don't have time for jokes, or whatever that was supposed to be."

She started away, and he blocked her.

"It wasn't a joke," he snapped.

"Right. Little ole me made big bad you walk away from a man you practically worship. I totally believe that. Oh, and while we're talking, got a bridge you want to sell me? Maybe some oceanfront property in Montana? Or maybe the Panama Canal?"

Taylor started to step around him again, but he grabbed her wrist.

"How do I prove it?"

Something in the way he asked cut through her anger and resentment. She gave him a wary look. He couldn't really be serious.

It surprised her that part of her wanted to believe him, wanted to be the kind of woman who inspired that kind of change in a man like Dalton. He reminded her of the seasoned soldiers she'd worked beside in Afghanistan. He didn't back down and he didn't give up and he had a protective streak that matched his ruthless streak. She'd come to admire him, albeit grudgingly.

But she'd been stupid with men before. After her on-again off-again relationship with Josh had ended, she'd sworn off men for the foreseeable future. Josh had shredded her heart by breaking their engagement—which she knew now was because the FBI had involved him in an investigation and he'd wanted to protect her. She'd turned into a complete basket case. Looking back, it was humiliating how emotional she'd been. As if that wasn't bad enough, after he'd been rescued, he'd walked away without a word, like she didn't matter. She wondered if she'd ever mattered.

She wasn't going to let herself be so stupid again. Not for any man.

"Fuck if I know," she said after he began to look impatient. *Look, ma. He's like a real boy!* She quashed her childish response and focused on him. "I've been played too many times. My experience says that men lie. They leave and they don't look back and they don't care about the wreckage they leave behind."

His jaw jutted. "Not all men."

"Could have fooled me."

"What about Leo and Jamie? Or Price? He earned your trust."

The truth was Price had earned Riley's trust, and that was good enough for Taylor. Her sister had a better track record than Taylor when it came to judging men. Anyway, comparing Dalton to Price was like comparing a cougar to a bear. Both might be deadly, but that didn't make them anything like the same.

"Price never worked for my sociopathic father, and my brothers wouldn't know how to betray me. They'd die before that."

"You now that your father's actions might not be his fault. He's got a brain-jockey. Has had for years, if your mom is right. He might never have had a choice in what he did."

His words thrust a sword right into the heart of her turmoil. She didn't want to have hope. Didn't want to relive the devastation of losing her father when it turned out he had left on his own free will, had chosen to change his name and vanish. She most definitely didn't want to hear Dalton defend him.

Taylor twisted out his grip, putting a couple feet of air between them.

"You work as a lawyer in your spare time?" she asked, pushing acid into her voice. She needed more than physical space; she needed emotional space. "One thing that I can tell you for sure is that defending Vernon definitely isn't the way to make me trust you. Now if you're through, and even if you're not, we're burning daylight. I'm going to fetch my gear and head to the arsenal. Meet me there or not; it's up to you."

With that, she strode away, all too aware of the cloud of anger radiating from him as his robot gaze following her.

Taylor made it around the corner and up a set of stairs before she staggered against the wall. *No, no, no! Not fucking now!* Her legs melted, and she slid down the wall to the floor. Ringing filled her ears, and sparkling black dust full of lightening swirled through her brain.

Chapter 6

Riley

I RETURNED TO THE meeting, keeping my expression neutral. Taylor could handle herself. My problem was that I didn't like sending anybody into danger, but that wasn't a choice I got to make.

I gave Arnow a little nod to indicate things were all right, and then returned to my seat at the table.

"Good news," I said, before the Seedy Seven could pounce on me. "My sister has gone to talk to Brussard."

"We didn't agree to that," Vasquez said.

"Your agreement wasn't necessary."

If looks could kill and all that, I'd be roasting on a spit. Too fucking bad. I looked at Erickson. "If you find anything that could be useful, call her."

He mumbled an affirmative and went back to working on his computer.

My gaze gathered in the rest of Savannah's lieutenants. "Your job is to stall the senator's troops. Disrupt them anyway you can, but don't make the senator call in reinforcements."

I looked at Arnow. "You need to figure out access to the senator. You'll have to be ready for when Taylor has Vernon. I don't know how much time that gives you."

"I'll need to go to headquarters."

"You should also find out everything you can about where he is, who's guarding him, and anything else that might be useful. That means taking Erickson with you and breaking into that computer. Can you do it?"

She gave a nod. "Consider it done."

"That only leaves one last thing before we get to work," I said.

"Oh?" Fineman leaned back, folding his arms. I couldn't read his expression.

"If anybody's been paying attention, they know that there's been a little war here at Savannah's place. Since the senator's not stupid, he'll be sending troops to check it out and sweep us up in his net. It would be just the sort of triumph that would make a juicy news story. He's not going to pass up that opportunity. Win or lose, the footage would work for him. Either he proves what a great job he's doing or he justifies bringing in more troops."

"You want us to evacuate?" Matokai asked in surprise.

"Not at all," I said. "I want us to shelter here. We'll just have to convince everybody that we've left."

"We're listening," Blaine said, tapping her fingers on the table, her brows creasing with curiosity.

I didn't know if any of them had noticed, but they'd begun to talk to me like I was at least an equal. Progress.

"There's a warren of tunnels and hidey-holes under the property. Savannah was well prepared for a siege. She had water piped in straight from the river and off-the-grid turbines for electricity. She's got a store of food and other supplies. The quarters might be tight, but doable for at least a week or so.

"I figure if we withdraw down there and then stage an attack and destroy this place, no one will think to look for us underground. If we add the bodies of the dead from our fight with Touray, it will look like we died in the blast."

My stomach churned at the idea of using the dead as props to fool the senator's soldiers, but I didn't see that we had a choice.

"It's workable," Fineman said with a quick glance at his compatriots to see if they agreed.

Wright and Matokai nodded thoughtfully. Even Vasquez looked grudgingly amenable.

"We could set up turn-away spells to keep anybody from looking too deep," Flanders mused in his low, growling voice.

Fineman shook his head. "Better to create a chaos zone around the property, like all the broken magic from the attack went haywire. If anybody noticed the turn-away spells, they'd know something was up."

"Then let's get going," I said. "Do it ASAP. I can count on you to make all the arrangements?"

Vasquez sneered. "We'll get our part done. You just do yours."

Which meant grabbing Vernon, retrieving the Kensington artifacts from Touray's vault, and finding the last couple along with the workshop. Somehow the workload seemed to tilt heavily in my direction.

The seven of them exchanged a quick look. They'd have a contingency plan to save their asses hatched just as soon as they could get a little privacy. I didn't care as long as they didn't bug out and leave us hanging in the wind.

"Good luck," I said as I stood.

Arnow looked at me. "You realize how ridiculous it is to trust your father or his jockey to help us, don't you? You need to guarantee Brussard's coopera-tion," she said. "Otherwise he's just as likely to betray us."

I nodded. "I know." I looked past her. "Laura and Lewis, a word?"

Blaine and Fineman exchanged a startled glance and then joined us. I explained the problem of guaranteeing cooperation. "Do you have ideas?"

I was certain they did. This wasn't exactly an unusual problem for the likes of them.

"You're talking a stick, rather than a carrot, correct?" Fineman asked.

"He's unpredictable. A stick will work better than a carrot for him," I said. Of course, the stick only worked if the jockey didn't just cut his losses and kill him.

"We've got several options, but the simplest and most effective choice is to use a capsule with a neurotoxin. Once released, the toxin kills in under a minute."

"How is the release triggered?" Arnow asked.

Blaine fielded the question. "It will passively trigger should he try to use nulls or binders to protect himself, or if he should try to escape—he'll have to stay within approximately thirty feet of whoever serves as his handler. It would also trigger if a tinker attempted to withdraw the capsule without the correct spell key. The handler would also have a physical trigger, which would continue to work should Brussard somehow manage to null out the magical controls."

I was both impressed and repulsed, not to mention a little bit confused. "He'll have to walk through nulls and binders to get anywhere close to the senator. Won't those also trigger the poison's release?"

Fineman nodded. "We use a bio-gel to seal in the poison. It will break down without its preserving spell. Anyone with the spell key can recharge it once beyond the null or binder influence."

"How long can the gel last before the spell has to be recharged?"

"A half hour, give or take. The person's physiology can speed it up or slow it down."

I glanced at Arnow. "What do you think? You're the one whose life is going to be on the line."

"I'll make it work."

"Your tinker will also be able to provide extra motivation, as Savannah's son has recently demonstrated," Blaine said, her lip curling at the memory of the torture he'd inflicted. "If you can find a tinker willing to cause harm, that is."

Most tinkers, like doctors, had refused to do harm. I thought of Tiny, a younger version of Touray. He ran a crew on the Downtown shelf in one of the poorer and more rundown areas of the city. I hadn't seen him use his tinkering ability as a weapon, but I was pretty sure he wouldn't have an issue with it. Not if it meant protecting his people, and with the sweeps and camps, taking down the senator would definitely come under the heading of protection.

"I've got someone," I said.

"Good," said Fineman. "I'll send you several of the capsules along with instructions for placing and activating them," he told Arnow.

"Get it to me as soon as you can."

He nodded. "Of course."

He and Blaine headed for the door.

"Don't forget about finding a dreamer, a maker, and a binder," I said. "A traveller, too, if we can't wake Touray," I added, though the words left a bad taste in my mouth.

They nodded and departed without another word

I gave a sigh as the door shut. I looked at Arnow and Maya, who'd stayed in the background.

"Let's get to work."

Chapter 7

Riley

I CONSIDERED PLANS as I went to look for Price and update him. When I got back to Touray's sick room, it was empty. They'd already left for my place. Good. I'd follow with Maya.

I bumped into her as I stepped out into the hallway. She frowned, the closest I'd ever seen her get to angry.

"You will die if you go back to the spirit realm before your astral-self can heal."

I sighed. "I know. I'll figure something out."

Her frown deepened as she tilted her head. "I don't think you do know. I want to be very clear: you *will* die. Not might or could. It will absolutely happen."

"I get it." Not that it changed what I had to do. "We'd better go. Do you have a coat?"

We located Maya's winter wrappings in a giant mudroom on the east end of the house where the staff stashed their things upon arrival. I rifled through some of the lockers until I found a puffy yellow jacket. Orange fleece gloves and a black beanie completed my Halloween-themed ensemble.

Hoping it didn't have lice, I pulled the hat on and turned to locate Maya. She'd also dressed, pulling her snow pants up and tucking her dress in around her waist. She donned a hat and gloves and wrapped a burgundy wool scarf around her neck. I found a scarf for me and followed suit.

The sky hung low and gray, and the smell of smoke filled my lungs, the latter left over from Savannah's bombs. It didn't take long to track down a car. A small fleet had been parked haphazardly on the lawns. Most still had keys in them. I found a four-wheel-drive SUV. It started easily despite the cold. Hallelujah. I drove slowly over the snowy ground to the driveway and then out the gate.

Beyond the estate walls, there weren't as many signs of the recent battle with Touray's people as I'd have thought. Snow had disguised the blood, spent cartridges, and undoubtedly a few bodies, beneath a pristine layer of white.

I didn't bother heading for the tunnel leading down into Midtown. Since it was a main thoroughfare, it was a pretty good bet that the senator had set up a checkpoint there and probably at the subway entrances, too. Instead I headed for one of my family's secret passages.

Before Vernon had disappeared—when he was still my dad and his name was David—he and Mel had built a hidden rail system that ran between various safe houses and my stepmother's house. There were also several access locations on each shelf of the city. It had always seemed like a good idea, though thinking about it now, I realized how strange it really was to have our own private rail system hidden beneath the city. It suggested that even back then, my father must have had significant enemies, not to mention the enormous resources to have accomplished the task.

I wound through the streets, heading away from the Rim and the heart of the city.

"Where are we going?"

"To my place." I glanced at Maya. "Almost nobody knows where it is. It's probably one of the safest places in the city. Do you have family?"

"A daughter and two grandchildren. They live in Glenwood Springs."

"Good. They'll be safe there."

"Shouldn't we be going in the other direction?"

"It's likely the senator has checkpoints on the subway and the tunnel. I don't want to risk getting caught up in his net. Anyway, this will be faster."

It didn't surprise me that the roads had been cleared. Up on the Rim, people were too rich to put up with the inconvenience of snowy roads.

I wound through the wide, tree-lined avenues, keeping a sharp eye out for soldiers. We didn't see any, but that didn't surprise me either. The people who lived on the Rim no doubt contributed a lot of money to the senator, and the man seemed smart enough not to bite the hands that feed.

That wouldn't last. Most of those hands were talented, not to mention many of their owners were neck-deep in a Tyet. Sooner or later the senator would have to confront them or lose his credibility with his base.

I pulled into the deserted parking lot of a very exclusive club. "We've got to walk from here."

"Walk? How far?"

"About a mile and a half."

I parked in the back of the lot and hopped out. Maya followed suit, huddling deep into coat.

"I am not built for the cold," she said morosely.

I chuckled and headed off between a couple of buildings. This area was dotted with designer clothing boutiques, body mod centers, fitness spas, bookstores, coffee shops, and whatever else the uber wealthy were into.

The access tunnel to my family's rail system was located behind a fake utilities access door at the Kingelle auditorium.

The place looked like a ruined Grecian palace. Tall white columns in various stages of decay marched around the perimeter, thrusting up out of a snaking channel of water, the columns interspersed with fountains shaped like mythological monsters. A garden maze of wildly flowering plants circled the inside of the perimeter, and within that was the towering auditorium made of gold-veined marble.

A magical dome of warm air kept the snow off, the flowers blooming, and the water flowing throughout the winter.

I circled the exterior of the fountain channel until I reach the rear of the auditorium. A clump of arborvitae disguised the entrance to the utility tunnels running beneath the auditorium. Behind it, still hidden by the arborvitae, was a vertical pipe sealed with a steel cap that had been bolted into place.

I slid my fingers around the bottom edge until I found a set of three indents. Anybody else would have assumed they were flaws in the access pipe's cement casing. I pressed the tips of my fingers into them. A silent hum shivered through my hand and up my arm. After a moment, the heavy cap popped up a few inches. I swiveled it aside. Inside, rungs led down into darkness.

I swallowed, sweat springing up all over me. I refused to say that I was claustrophobic, but I responded to small, tight, dark places the way a mouse might respond to a lion. I clamped down on the fear. Since I didn't have a lot of choice, I had to suck it up.

I motioned for Maya to go first, since I'd have to close the pipe after we went through.

The opening was barely big enough for her to squeeze through. I followed, not giving myself time to panic, though my stomach twisted into a corkscrew and I regretted everything I'd eaten.

Once inside, I reached up to pull the lid closed. Stygian darkness wrapped us as the cap snicked into place. I counted five with each inhale and again with each exhale, trying to keep myself calm.

I pressed my palm against the wall between the first and second rungs. Light illuminated the darkness, a chain of glowing witchlights running down the ladder and lighting up a tunnel below.

I lowered myself carefully, my legs and arms protesting the slight workout. Tremors fluttered through my body. I clenched my teeth and kept going.

"You okay?" I asked Maya when I reached the bottom.

"I don't care for small spaces, especially when they are underground," she replied, a trickle of sweat running down her cheek.

I gave her a thin smile of sympathy. "Me either. It's going to get worse. Can you handle it?"

"Do I have a choice?"

"You can go back to Savannah's."

She shook her head, her shoulders squaring. "I need to look after Gregg. And Cass, when you find her."

I appreciated that she said *when*, not *if*.

"I'll get us out as fast as I can."

The tunnel was narrow, and I had to turn sideways to slip past her. I made myself push my fear to the back of my mind as I led the way to where the tunnel widened a few feet before dead-ending into a little cul-de-sac with a sudden drop-off about fifteen feet from the far wall. The air smelled of minerals and damp.

I went to the edge of the drop-off and reached above my head on the right side. The rock was rough and lumpy, with a lot of little divots. I felt around until I found the one I wanted and pressed my forefinger into it, counting to ten before letting go, and then pressing in for another five count.

A panel of square buttons appeared midway up the wall on the left. I ran my finger around the outer edge, and blue rings illuminated each of the forty buttons. None had any letters or numbers to indicate what they might do.

"This could take a little while, depending," I said to Maya as I tapped out my code. My voice sounded loud in the small space, echoing from the deep hole in front of us.

"Depending on what?"

"How far away our ride is. Give me a second—"

Another panel floated into the air, appearing like a hologram in one of the futuristic science fiction movies. It showed a three-dimensional map of our rail tunnels, with a half-dozen green and one red blip corresponding to magical rail-cars. The red one was located at my home, the rest scattered around at other stations or sitting hidden in-between.

I located the closest one and sent a summons. I didn't have to tell the one at my house to move. Once I set the destination on ours, it would take care of clearing the docking area.

"It should be here in a few minutes."

"It?"

"A personal subway car. It goes very fast, but this high up on the caldera, there are a lot of mine tunnels and other underground spaces to avoid, so the route is twisty and goes out east a bit and has some fairly sheer drops. I hope you like a good roller coaster ride."

Maya paled a little but gave a firm nod. "I'll be fine."

"You will," I said reassuringly. "It's very safe."

"Famous last words."

I grinned. "I won't tell anyone if you barf, as long as you don't say anything if I do."

Her wide smile lit her round face. "Deal."

A swirl of air pushing up from the bottom of the shaft warned of the arrival of the car. It glided silently up the shaft.

The aluminum exterior gleamed in the witchlight. Shaped like a sleek cigar, the controls at each end allowed it to run in either direction. It contained a line of eight red leather bucket seats and no doors. A bar ran just above the top of the window openings to make getting in easier. At either end were matte-black pilot consoles with a series of levers mounted on the sides. They curved in a semicircle, each facing a swivel seat that matched the passenger seats. Honey-brown wood paneling lined the interior walls.

"This is unexpected," Maya said, marveling. "I can't believe you've got your own subway."

"It's mostly for emergencies," I said. It had been my father's idea after my mom's murder. Or could it have been the brain-jockey's? How long had Vernon been infected with it? The jockey had to know about the subway and the family's safehouses. My stomach twisted. That meant they weren't safe. Luckily, my house had been built after my father disappeared, but even though we'd locked him out of the system, he could still sabotage it or use it to find us.

Hopefully, the system safeguards would have warned us if he had.

"You're going to have to hoist yourself in race-car style," I said, motioning to the bar above the windows.

"It takes a little practice," I said, helping Maya as she grabbed the bar and lifted her feet through, sitting on the edge of the window before scooching off to land on a narrow space between the seat and wall. She settled into a seat.

"The arm there drops down." I pointed to the nearest armrest that was pushed up into the vertical position. "It'll give you something to hold on to when we get going. Buckle in."

I left her to get situated and went to the forward pilot seat and hoisted myself through, settling in and fastening my seatbelt.

"Keep anything you care about inside the car," I warned over my shoulder.

I touched the console to wake it. I hated driving these things. Taylor loved it and always wanted to use the manual controls. I preferred the autopilot.

The console lit, and I set the course by touching one of destination buttons on the left side. In the middle was the speed control that included a slide bar and a number of presets. There was an emergency stop as well as a communication display to talk to other cars if needed.

"Hold on," I told Maya. "Here we go."

I touched the departure preset. Immediately, the exterior lights shut off and the car's interior lights kicked on. My stomach lurched as we dropped into the shaft. I shuddered as the walls closed in.

We descended about twenty feet, jolting as we hit the bottom. Headlights came on and illuminated the tunnel ahead. Not that I could see far. The tunnel dipped and angled away. The car rolled forward, and I curled my fingers around the arms of my seat, bracing for the sudden acceleration I knew was coming.

Maya shrieked as the car suddenly launched. We hit the dip going about fifty, and my stomach dropped. After that, we sped up, going downhill and then around a hairpin turn. We zigzagged upward before tilting downward in a near vertical drop that seemed to go on forever. The car leveled out and shot around a curve to the right and went straight, hooked back around at high speed and then climbed up, flattened out, and came to an abrupt halt. Around us, lights came on, illuminating a small platform inside a rock room.

I sat a moment, heart pounding. Sweat trickled down my neck and between my breasts. It felt like the walls were shrinking inward. I closed my eye and drew a couple of steadying breaths, then shut down the console and swung out through the window.

Maya still sat in her seat, both hands clutching the armrests. She gazed at me with wide eyes, her face tinged gray.

"You okay?"

"Wondering if I should stand on my head to get my stomach back where it belongs," she said with a weak smile.

"It's a thought. Do you need a hand to get out?"

"Might."

She pushed up the arm rest and stood, grabbing the two vertical hand bars on either side of the window. Her hands shook. She took a breath and awkwardly lifted herself up.

"Have you considered putting in a door?" She asked, grabbing my proffered hand and pulling herself out of the window.

"I don't know why my parents didn't put them in."

"I'm not made for this sort of thing. Next time I'll walk." She gave a little shiver as she looked around at the small stone chamber. "Can we go somewhere less confining?"

"Follow me."

I walked the seven steps to the wall, knelt down, feeling along the bottom until I found the locking divot. As soon as I pressed it, a passage opened onto a steep flight of stone steps leading upward. Price's shoulders would have rubbed the walls, and he'd have had to duck so as not to whack his head. At the top was a locked door.

I went first, grabbing the rail and hurrying up, keeping focused on the wall above. An invisible noose closed around my throat. I fumbled to unlock the door. I pushed and the wall pivoted. I staggered through the opening into my basement.

Carved into the bedrock, the space was all of ten feet by ten feet. The only furniture was a set of shelves piled with odds and ends. A thick coat of dust covered everything, except the walkway where it had been churned and scuffed away.

I turned to give Maya a hand up the last few steps.

"Almost there," I told her as I locked the door. "One last set of stairs and we're home sweet home."

"I hope you've got something strong to drink in there."

I grimaced. "Can't promise. I'm not that good about keeping things stocked."

"Let's get the hell out of here and find out."

Once again, I went up first. I pushed the door open and stepped into my kitchen. It was big enough to make a cook happy, though I barely had enough dishes and cookware to fill a cupboard. I might have a couple jars of peanut butter and jelly in the pantry, along with some ancient boxes of mac and cheese, ramen, and probably dust bunnies. I had some cans of soda and probably a half-dozen science experiments growing in the fridge. It had been quite awhile since I'd actually eaten anything here, much less cooked. I lived on protein bars and food from Patti's diner.

I did, however, have coffee and sugar. No cream.

Someone had put a pot on, and the glorious scent of fresh ground coffee filled the air. My knees went weak at the smell.

A massive circular fireplace separated the kitchen from the dining space, the chimney rising up through the second-floor loft. A wrought-iron spiral staircase led up to my bedroom and my workspace. I didn't have a lot of furniture. Mostly, I had a lot of giant cushions and a few mosaic-topped tables sitting on top of a bunch of colorful throw rugs. Beyond a sliding wood door under the stairs was a sunken bathroom with a natural hot tub fed by a hot spring, a toilet, and a shower big enough for an orgy. Sadly, I'd yet to introduce Price to it or the hot tub.

I wanted to grab coffee, but the voices in the living room drew me inside.

Price, Patti, Leo, and Jamie stood talking, while Touray lay on a makeshift bed on the floor. Standing beside him was an IV pole.

"Hello," I said, when nobody noticed our arrival. "How's Touray?"

All four of them spun around. "Riley!"

Patti grabbed me in a hug, before passing me to Jamie, Leo, and finally Price, who gripped me tightly, holding me when I leaned away. He studied me, brows furrowed, jaw tight.

I put a hand on his chest, looking at him anxiously. "Are we okay?"

He gave a bitter laugh. "Define okay."

"On the right side of the dirt?"

He grimaced. "Funny."

"But true."

"Promise me something," he said, tightening his grip. "Don't take risks you don't have at least some chance of surviving."

His sapphire gaze skewered me. His request wasn't unreasonable. Still, I hesitated. When I made promises, I kept them. I wanted to be sure I could keep this one.

He gave a little growl. "What's there to think about, Riley? All I want you to do is not to do anything you know for sure is suicidal. That shouldn't be hard."

"You know Maya said that using my talent could kill me. And I'm going to have to use it if we're going to find all the Kensington artifacts and use them."

He nodded, the muscles in his flexing. "Doesn't have to kill you. Maya only said *could*. So make sure it doesn't. Get creative. I want *that*, Riley." He looked over my head, gathering in the others, before his glittering gaze dropped back to me. "We *all* want that."

"It's got my vote," Leo said.

"Me, too," Jamie said.

"Just say yes," Patti said impatiently. "We'll all sleep better. *If* we get a chance to sleep, that is."

I wanted to object. I didn't want to be hobbled, not with so much at stake. But they weren't exactly asking for the moon. Or even a small mountain. All they were asking was for me not to take chances without at least a sliver of a chance that I'd survive.

"Okay," I said and instantly found myself crushed against Price's chest.

"Thank you," he breathed against my ear, his relief palpable.

His gratitude made me want to throw up. The two people Price loved the most, me and Gregg, and we were slipping away like smoke through his fingers. I should be able to offer more, to support him the way he supported me. He was my rock and wasn't backing away, even knowing what kind of pain and loss was coming at him like an avalanche. Unstoppable, unavoidable, deadly.

I had to do better. I had to find a way to get through this without killing myself. No matter what Maya said, there had to be a way to fix my astral-self. I just had to find it.

Before it was too late.

Chapter 8

Taylor

THE BLINDING dizziness that overwhelmed Taylor was swiftly followed by a gut punch of craving. She clenched her body against it, sucking in deep breaths to calm her racing heart.

After she'd been exposed to Sparkle Dust, Riley had managed to null out a lot of it, which wasn't supposed to be possible, but her sister didn't know the meaning of the word *impossible*, especially when it came to the people she loved.

Since then, Taylor had been having minor dizziness and craving. She'd shrugged those off, counting herself lucky that the aftereffects weren't worse, and anyway, it wasn't anything she couldn't handle.

Except that in the last few days, the spells had grown stronger and more frequent, not to mention debilitating. All because of stress, worry, and lack of sleep, she was sure. At least they tended to pass quickly. Already the dizziness had begun to settle.

Grimacing, Taylor pushed herself upright. Her head still swam, but her vision had begun to clear. It was like looking through a kaleidoscope of blinking shadows and blurry floaters, but that wouldn't last much longer.

Staggering like a newborn colt, she started off, sliding her hand along the wall for balance. Her body quivered with little earthquakes that slowly subsided. It took another minute for her gait to grow fluid as she regained control of herself.

Hopefully, she wouldn't get another attack until after she'd turned Vernon over to Arnow. The last thing she needed was Dalton questioning her competence.

Once she reached the suite of rooms she'd co-opted for herself, Taylor collected the few items she wanted. She was already wearing black military pants and a black turtleneck. She pulled on her bulletproof vest and attached her holster to her belt, checking to make sure her .45 auto was loaded and chambered. She tucked several magazines into the side pockets of her pants. Next she fastened a combat knife to her belt and strapped two flat knives to her forearms, pulling her shirt down over them. She strapped another combat knife to her right calf beneath her pants. Finally she shoved a .380 into the top of her left boot.

She was already carrying her multitool and lockpick case and wore a survival bracelet that contained a wire saw, a small knife, a flint, and the twelve feet of ripcord that made up the bracelet. She made sure she had her cell phone and grabbed her jacket. Her hat, gloves, and scarf were tucked inside its pockets, along with a pair of sunglasses.

All of her preparations took less than ten minutes, and she was out the door again.

SAVANNAH'S STORAGE vault was located under the formal garden, its entrance located behind a nondescript door at the back of a musty storage closet. A spiral flight of iron stairs led down a good forty feet, depositing Taylor into a rectangular room. The floor was carpeted, and the room held an assortment of chairs and sofas, all facing an imposing desk carved of mahogany and leafed in gold.

Fine art covered the walls, and a Greek statue of Artemis holding a bow with a man dead at her feet stood in the corner. Behind the desk was the door to the vault. Previously, a curtain of magic had disguised it, along with a giant Jackson Pollock painting. The vault door was made of steel and titanium, a good two feet thick, with twenty locking bars—four on top and bottom, six on either side. They pushed into steel-clad tubes in the basalt walls.

Shutting off the magic security had been easy enough, and then Jamie and Leo had made short work of the door. They were both extraordinary artists when it came to creating things with their metal magic, but they were like kids with fireworks when they got to use their talent for destruction and mayhem.

Taylor grinned. Some men never quite grew up, and thank goodness for that. Jamie and Leo as responsible adults would likely signal the apocalypse.

Her brothers had replaced the locking mechanism with a puzzle key. It involved dozens of linking and overlapping shapes that had to be manipulated around a circular wall board. Once in the proper pattern, the spoked wheel could be turned to retract the locking bars that Jamie and Leo had restored.

Taylor started in on the puzzle. She'd finally remembered the last tricky bit when Dalton arrived, padding quietly across the floor to stop a few feet behind her.

She spun the wheel and yanked. The heavy door drifted open a few inches. Taylor braced her feet and dragged harder, waving away Dalton's help. The door swung ponderously outward.

Automatic lights lit one by one along the outer circumference of the circular ceiling, spiraling along a snail-shell pattern to the massive center chandelier made of thousands of shimmering crystals.

Layers of concentric wood shelves on sliding rails lined the round walls, each packed full of magical paraphernalia. A giant card catalog stood in the middle of the room attached to a long table holding a half-dozen computers. A plush navy carpet swathed the floor. Library carts were lined up in a rack just to the right of the door. Dozens of canvas bags hung on hooks beside them.

Taylor had done a quick tour of the vault when they'd first opened it but hadn't paid much attention to the breadth of inventory.

She headed to the computers first. The card catalog was a redundant system, available in case of a power or magic outage. Normally, the computers required a password, but Erickson had already stripped those.

"Looking for anything in particular?"

"The usual," Taylor replied. "Nulls, memory foggers, paralyzers . . . that sort of thing. We have no idea what kind of reception we're going to get when we ask to talk to Vernon. Not that we'll get a chance to use them," she added.

Tyrell would be well guarded, as would Vernon. Still, they'd be using magic inside the compound, which meant that there might be opportunities to use a spell. It would make her feel better to have some kind of magical arsenal just in case.

Both of them tapped away at a keyboard. Beside each computer was a pad of paper and a cup of pens. Taylor wrote down a list of codes referencing shelf locations. She didn't have a clue how the shelves were actually organized. Certainly not the Dewey Decimal system. Hopefully, it would become obvious when they started looking.

The database search took longer than she liked. The entries contained precious few descriptions, and a whole lot of notations that said *developmental, random side effects, inconsistent, unstable, erratic,* or *use precautions.*

"Don't want to try any of those," she muttered.

"At least you have that much sense," Dalton said, glancing at her screen.

Taylor resisted the urge to slug him. "You don't like the way I do things, feel free to go bother someone else."

"Just calling it like I see it."

"You need glasses."

"I need a drink."

"You aren't the only one." Taylor slid a sideways look at him. "You going to be able to get us through Tyrell's security?"

His silver gaze met hers. "I imagine we won't have any trouble, once your father knows it's you who's come calling."

She snorted. "If you're counting on fatherly love, you'd better have a backup plan. My father couldn't give a shit about me. Besides, the jockey's the one in control."

Saying it out loud made her wonder. Had she ever known the real man? Had anything he'd said or done been of his own free will? Or had it always been the brain-jockey?

The sudden burn of tears caught Taylor of guard. What the fuck was wrong with her? But in a weird way, it felt like she was stuck mourning her father's loss all over again. Her mind skipped to Josh. After losing her father, and until Josh, she hadn't let herself get attached to any man. But Josh had been relentless in his interest—kind, generous, and honest.

Until he wasn't. Worst part was, she let him fool her twice. First when he dumped her, apparently to protect her from the mess he'd gotten into with the artifacts. Then he'd started calling, and she'd been all too happy to come running back, eager to make him see that they belonged together.

Her lip curled in disgust at herself. She'd turned into a needy beggar, hoping for a few crumbs off his table. Her jaw tightened. She hated remembering.

After he'd been kidnapped, Josh had become someone else. He'd been tortured physically and mentally, and he'd been dosed on Sparkle Dust. Unlike Taylor, he hadn't had someone like Riley there to null the effects. Maya had done her best to heal him, but nothing could entirely break the grip of Sparkle Dust. Not that she had any idea how he was doing. He'd walked away, and she hadn't seen or heard from him since.

Fool me twice. . . .

Taylor's mouth pulled into a thin, tight line. She *knew* she couldn't trust Vernon. If she did, she'd only have herself to blame when he betrayed her. Again. Jockey or no jockey, he was a slippery bastard. She'd sooner trust Dalton or Touray than him, and she wouldn't trust them to tell her the weather.

"Your father will see you," Dalton said with a certainty that spoke of either inside knowledge or unwavering faith in her father. Either way, it underscored the fact that she couldn't trust Dalton. He belonged to Vernon heart and soul, no matter what he said to the contrary.

"We'd better grab what we can and get going," she said.

Without waiting for Dalton, she grabbed a canvas bag and headed toward the nearest set of shelves. The codes were straightforward, with the first numbers corresponding to the shelving track. The outer circle was one, the middle two, and the inner was three. Then each shelving unit had a number, and each shelf had a number.

The shelves slid aside with the slightest push, so moving a half dozen at a time was easy enough. Taylor started in what appeared to be the bomb section. It included wasp, smoke, stink, flour, flash, sleep, and blinding bombs, among many others. Chewing her lip, she considered. The perimeter of Jackson Tyrell's place would be bound down and nulled, but likely, once inside, magic would work. Of course, they'd be searched and anything overtly tactical would be confiscated. She couldn't plan on using any of this stuff there, but potentially they'd be making a quick getaway from Tyrell's compound, which would mean eluding pursuers. Might be nice if they could stash a few caches of heavy firepower along the exfil route. The weapons would also be useful if they ran into any of the senator's soldiers.

She decided to collect several wasp bombs and two each of the stink, flash, sleep, and binding bombs. The flour bomb tempted her. When tossed in the air in a confined space and ignited, flour became a bomb. This would have its own ignition source, but there were no markings to indicate strength. In fact, all the bombs shared that flaw. She grabbed a couple and tucked her finds into her bag, and moved on.

Taylor made a face as she grabbed several trace nulls. She'd have thought Savannah would have had information on them, like how long they'd keep anyone from seeing her trace. She hated having to blindly trust them. All the same she grabbed a handful and another of magic nulls. Always nice when you could null out a spell. She then located some targeted sleep charms, see-in-the-dark charms, and what amounted to magical tasers in the shape of fingerless leather gloves with thin metal plates sewed into the palms. She tried on several until she found a couple that fit.

Taylor crossed the room to where Dalton squatted in front of a unit, pawing through a wood box.

"What are those?"

"Curses."

"What kind?"

"Not sure. They aren't individually labeled." He checked the list on the outside of the box. "Lice, itchy rashes, flea infestation, incessant coughing, sudden baldness . . ." He shoved the box back without taking anything and stood. "Mostly annoying distractions. Not very useful for us."

He looked at the next box. "Ah. This is what I wanted."

"What?"

"Kill line." He pulled out a thick roll of thin wire. "Anybody who touches it or crosses it will drop dead. Or that seems to be what the description said."

"What else did you find?"

He straightened to his feet. "Lights, heal-alls, mind protections, linked communications amulets, warming charms. A couple other things. You?"

Taylor went over her take and then held up a hand to show the gloves. "If you want a pair of these, they're over there." She pointed.

He strode across the room and found a pair, and then joined her. She had laid out her findings and was tucking some of them away in her pockets. He followed suit, and she pushed hers toward him and took some of his.

"I doubt I'll remember to use this stuff," she said. "Since I don't have magic, I tend not to rely on it much."

He went still and eyed her. "Has it ever occurred to you that your father messed with you as well as Riley?"

Taylor snorted. "I assume he did. Probably messed with my memories, same as her."

"He also made her unable to see his trace, and boobytrapped her talent."

"Yeah? What's your point?"

"Don't you find it strange that you, the daughter of two powerful talents, with siblings who are all magical, would be the only one who came out a neuter?"

"Luck of the draw," Taylor said. "Genetic lottery."

"Maybe."

He sounded unconvinced. Taylor hated the flare of hope that burst into flame in her chest.

"Even if he could, why would he?"

He shrugged. "Why did he do it to Riley? You should have Cass look at you, anyway."

Her stomach tightened so hard it hurt. She'd wanted a talent her entire life. Dreamed of it. She'd hidden her envy from her family, though she didn't doubt that, as a reader, her mother had known. Not wanting anybody's pity, Taylor had pretended she was perfectly happy with herself, her abilities, and her life. And most of the time, that was true. She'd learned she didn't *need* a talent, but oh, how she longed for one, if only not to be the odd man out in her family.

Could her father have blocked her talent? But she couldn't imagine any reason why he would. Anyway, why would he block her and not Riley? It just made no sense.

She gave a quiet sigh shook herself. The suggestion was ridiculous, and she had things to do.

When she didn't speak, he pushed harder. "Are you going to have Cass look?"

"There's no good reason. If my father could have suppressed my talent, he would have done the same to Riley."

"You don't know that."

She didn't answer. It was pointless. Instead, she headed for the door of the vault.

"If he did block your talent, it might not have been his choice," Dalton said, following. "It could have been his brain-jockey's doing."

She turned to shut the door and reset the lock. "Ask me if I care."

His eerie gaze fixed on her, a furrow appearing between his dark brows. "He could be as much a victim as your sister or Gregg Touray. He's been enslaved for years, watching as the brain-jockey makes him do horrible things to his family. It has to have been torture. You and Riley should be wanting to break him free, same as you're trying to do for Touray. He needs your help."

The hint of condemnation in his voice made Taylor's hackles rise. What the hell did he know?

"He doesn't need me; he's got you, who clearly has a hard-on for him. As eagerly as you're defending him, I'm finding it tough to believe you *aren't* still on his payroll."

Taylor watched in fascination as dark-red color seeped into Dalton's cheeks. His eyes narrowed, his jaw thrust out.

"I'm getting fucking tired of you bitching about how you can't trust me."

"Poor baby."

His mouth twisted. "You've got a seriously shitty attitude, you know that?"

"Just calling it like I see it," she said, echoing his earlier comment.

"What the hell do you want from me?"

"How about you just don't stab me in the back? If that's not too much trouble."

He leaned forward, bending so that his nose almost touched hers. "I'm not going away, no matter how bitchy you get."

"Be still my heart," Taylor drawled, stepping back and pretending to fan herself.

She totally ignored the way her heart sped up. She couldn't allow herself to feel drawn to him. *Cat's out of that bag*, she derided herself. Whatever. He was handsome as sin and had a bad-boy vibe that made her thighs ache. It was perfectly reasonable to admire the scenery and even daydream about getting him naked. That didn't mean she had to let her hormones run away with her.

He glared at her, and then his gaze dropped to her mouth, clinging there with predatory intensity. Butterflies fluttered in her belly.

Dalton's lips moved in a silent "fuck me," and he reached out and dragged her to him, his arms like iron bars around her. He dipped his head to kiss her, going slow as if giving her time to protest. Taylor couldn't make herself say a word. She couldn't breathe. Anticipation roared through her like a wildfire. Her tongue flicked out to moisten her lips and he made a guttural sound low in his throat.

His lips were a millimeter away from hers when her phone rang and shattered the moment. Taylor jolted out of her hormone-induced idiocy and shoved away from him. His arms dropped, and she backed away. Turning aside, she dug her phone out of her pocket. Heat flushed her cheeks.

She'd almost *kissed* him. She'd just got finished telling him how much she didn't trust him, and suddenly she wanted to kiss him? He was right. She did need to get her head examined.

Her phone rang again, and she thumbed the screen. She didn't recognize the number. Taking a breath to settle her pounding heart, she answered.

"Hello?"

Silence. Then, "Taylor?"

For a moment she couldn't answer. What were the odds that the man she'd been thinking about just a few minutes ago would call her now? And save her from kissing another mistake.

"Josh?" Icicles dripped from the word.

Another hesitation. "Yeah. It's me."

Her mouth tightened. "How did you get this number?"

"I've got my ways."

She waited for more, but he remained silent. "If this is a social call, I've got other things to do." Her words were clipped. Impatient.

He exhaled. "I need Riley's help."

She snorted. "You tried to kill her. She's not exactly your biggest fan."

"That's why I need you. You can talk to her for me. She'll listen to you."

That's why I need you.

Asshole. It took all her willpower not to throw the phone against the wall.

"I'm doing fine, thanks for asking. Course my fiancé/boyfriend got kidnapped and tortured and tried to kill my sister and then disappeared off the face of the earth without a word to me. That kind of blew chunks. But what's really weird is he suddenly calls me up on a phone he shouldn't have the number to and wants a favor. Like we're friends. Like I give a shit about him."

Josh didn't speak for a long moment. Taylor waited, wishing she could just hang up, her fingers tapping restlessly on her thigh .

"I'm sorry," Josh said at last.

What had she expected? Or more importantly, wanted? Whichever, his response wasn't it. "That's pathetic."

"Dammit, Taylor. What do you want from me? Yeah, I'm an ass. You should just be glad I'm the fuck out of your life."

"Maybe I should be, but turns out I actually loved you and was worried about what happened to you," she shot back.

"You need to let this go," he said, frustration sharpening his voice. "Let *us* go."

Anger boiled up, melting her icy control. "You can go fuck yourself. Consider this me letting go."

With that, Taylor terminated the call and flipped off the ringer. She shook with a storm of emotions. Fury, hurt, humiliation, and . . . relief. That surprised her, but she was grateful. Maybe her heart wasn't so much hurt as her pride. She decided the latter was preferable and she was just going to go with it.

She sucked in a breath and reached for calm. She would not give Josh free rent in her head, and she sure wasn't going to waste any more time or emotion on him.

"Are you okay?" Dalton asked from behind her, his voice gentle.

Taylor closed her eyes. Now the fucker pitied her. Wasn't that just peachy? A minute ago he wanted to kiss her, now she was a charity case. Why did the men in her life have to be such assholes?

"Totally terrific. Let's go." She headed for the stairs.

"That was your ex?"

"Duh. Now feel free to shut up as it's none of your damned business."

"How did he get your number?"

"Fuck if I know," Taylor tossed over her shoulder as she hurried up the steps.

He followed right on her heels. "If he has your number, then he can track you."

"And do what? Find me and tell me to my face he's dumping me? Let him. It'll give me a chance to kick him in the balls."

She topped the stairs and went into the store room. Dalton grabbed her arm and pulled her to face him, his expression a mixture of sympathy and irritation.

"Think about it, Taylor. He found your number. For a phone you got through Touray, who knows a thing or two about staying well under the radar. That's not beginner-level shit. How did he do it? Why? Is he working for someone? You said he tried to kill Riley, and now he wants to talk to her. Maybe he's hunting her and thinks he can get you to lead him to her."

Taylor hated that he made sense. Hated that she hadn't thought it through herself. She couldn't afford to let her emotions get the best of her. She'd seen too many soldiers lose their lives because they made emotional decisions. Not her. She wouldn't be the weak link that cost lives.

Inside, she folded in on herself, locking her feelings away.

"You're right," she said. "Maybe I should arrange to meet him. Find out what he's up to."

He scowled. "I didn't say that."

She shrugged. She was on solid ground here. If Josh was working for another player in this game they were playing, it was too dangerous not to get more intel. "It's a good idea, anyhow. I don't want to dump my cell phone. Someone might need me and not get the new number soon enough. Better to control the meet and find out what his game is. Neutralize the threat. If we meet him close by, we can easily do it on the way to Tyrell's and not waste much time."

"Sounds like you're looking for a reason to see him. Maybe you're hoping you can salvage your relationship."

His impassive voice pissed her off. After all, ten minutes ago he'd had her in a clinch and was about to kiss her. Now he acted like he couldn't care less if she still had a thing for Josh.

"Wouldn't be any business of yours if I was. But even if I were that stupid, doesn't change the fact that dealing with this head-on is the smart way to go. Now let me go before I rip your arm out of its socket and beat you with it."

His nostrils flared and his hands tightened, then he let go, but he didn't step away. Instead he leaned closer, his upper lip curled.

"It's my business because my job is to have your back and keep you safe. He. Is. Not. Safe." His finger prodded her just below her collarbone. "And why you'd want to be with the kind of bastard who'd turn his back on you is about as asinine as using spaghetti to rappel down a cliff."

"Your *job*? As in, the one Vernon sent you to do?"

His expression went livid. "I'm fucking sick of your suspicion. For the last time, I'm not working for your goddamned father!"

His voice rose, and for the first time ever, she was seeing him lose his shit. Good. He'd needled her enough. Now he could see what it was like.

"Well now that you've yelled about it, I can see that it must be true. I am now totally convinced."

He dragged his fingers through his hair, pulling several long strands free of his ponytail. "You're fucking impossible."

"Better than being stupid."

"Seems to me you've got a pretty good handle on both."

"Well then, having established that you are a giant asshole, and I'm a stupid bitch, shall we get to work? Yes? Good. Get the hell out of my way."

Chapter 9

Riley

"CLAY TOLD US what happened," Patti said, using Price's actual first name.

I never had. Maybe I ought to. Using his last name was a little impersonal, but he'd always been Price to me. I pulled away from the man in question to look at everyone.

"Are you okay?" Patti looked me up and down. "You look like shit."

"Feel like it. Going underground didn't help." I shrugged, trying to appear nonchalant. "Nothing a gallon or two of coffee wouldn't fix."

"You need sleep," Maya said, having checked on Touray. She gave me a narrow look. "You need rest to recover."

"Can't. I've got things to do."

She put her hands on her hips. "You can take some time to rest."

"That's true. You can," Patti said. "I've still got to go get Ben and bring back some more groceries. You can rest till I get back. The boys here can work on making shelters for people."

"*More* groceries?" I echoed, fixing on what clearly was most important.

"We stocked you up last time we were here," Leo said. "Remember? Right before you guys went to rescue the hostages?"

I perked up. "Does that mean there's cream?"

Leo rolled his eyes. "You are so predictable. But yes. There's cream."

"I'll get you coffee," Patti said. "Before you start drooling. Or climbing walls."

"There's a reason you're my best friend," I said, yawning.

"It doesn't take much to impress you, does it?"

"I'd do anything for coffee."

"I'll remember that." Price's voice rumbled above my head.

"TMI," Leo said.

"Oh, please," Jamie said. "You're the king of TMI." He looked at me before Leo could retort. "You get a plan going with the Seedy Seven?"

I took the cup Patti handed me, sipping and closing my eyes as the taste of hot nirvana slid down my throat.

"Did she just orgasm?" Leo asked. "Why can't coffee get *my* rocks off?"

"See? TMI king. And to answer your question, a light breeze would make you cream your jeans," Jamie said. "Coffee would probably kill you."

"Says the guy who blows a load just pulling his dick out to piss," Leo said, flipping Jamie the bird.

I snorted, laughing despite myself. Leo grinned and winked at me, and Jamie winged a pillow at his head.

"You only wish you can make a woman scream like I can."

"You make them scream, all right, in frustration and fear. Me, now, I make them come so hard they lose their minds," Leo said smugly.

"You walked right into that one," Patti told Jamie. "Now shut up so we can hear what Riley has to say. We're burning daylight."

Jamie shot a dirty look at Leo, but obeyed, muttering something under his breath.

The tightness in my chest eased at their familiar teasing. They had a knack for picking just the right time for their silly antics so that the weight of inevitable doom lightened slightly. It gave me hope.

"What was that, Jamie?" I couldn't help egging him on.

Patti shook her head in disgust.

"I said too bad there's no condom big enough to suffocate his ass."

"You're right. My dick's too big for a condom. Even king-sized."

"That's because you think you've *got* a dick, but the truth is you *are* a dick."

"Shut up," Patti told Leo before he could respond, pointing a finger at him.

At five foot nothing, wearing purple Doc Martens, black skinny jeans, a flannel shirt, and dramatic cat-eye makeup, Patti didn't look like she could stand up to a brisk wind. Looks were deceiving. She didn't take crap from anybody. As a minor binder, she didn't have a lot of power, but she knew how to leverage it. She also had several black belts in various martial arts, and she'd knocked both Leo and Jamie on their asses on more than one occasion.

Leo opened his mouth and then wisely shut it, stepping back with his hands up. "Whatever you say."

Patti swung around to malevolently eye Jamie. "You going to behave? Or should I hogtie you and stick your ass to the wall?" As a binder, she could easily do the latter.

"I'm behaving," he said sulkily. "But he started it."

"And I'm finishing it."

He drew a breath, clearly tempted to do something stupid, and then thought the better of it, folding his arms across his chest as he leaned back against the wall.

Patti swung back around to me. "How about you tell us what's going on?"

I sank down on a cushion and leaned back against the hearth surrounding the giant circular fireplace. My place was heated by magic, but I wished for the woodsy comfort of a crackling fire. Price sat down on the hearth beside me, one hand gently rubbing the back of my neck. I leaned into his touch.

Patti sat across from us, and Maya went to the kitchen. I could hear her rattling dishes and figured she was getting coffee for everyone. I wished her luck finding enough cups. I wasn't set up for company.

"When I tried to get the Seedy Sevens' attention by messing with their trace, mom pulled me into the spirit realm," I began, pulling my knees up to my chest and resting my cup on top of one. I told them what she'd said. When I got to the part about Vernon messing with Mel's head, Jamie and Leo both went deadly still. Price's hand moved to my shoulder, squeezing in gentle support. I hadn't really processed the fact that Mel had been one of my father's victims, too. It shouldn't have surprised me, but it did. How could I keep being blindsided by my father's duplicity? He was a living, breathing lie.

"This guy is a fucking disease," Leo said, launching to his feet, his entire body clenched with anger. "How did we not see it? We should have helped her! God-fucking-dammit!"

Jamie seethed quietly, staring at his clenched hands. "I'm going to kill that asshole. My mom, my sister . . ." His mouth twisted. "The fucker needs his throat ripped out."

"How do you know he hasn't tampered with both of you, too? Or Taylor?" the ever-practical Patti asked then.

Leo paled. "Fuck. It's like a disease. Are brain-jockeys fucking contagious?"

"We might have been," Jamie said, and now it was his turn to jump up, and he began to pace into the kitchen and back. He stopped, hands on his hips, his knuckles turning white as he dug his fingers hard into his flesh. "We need Cass back. Until we get cleared, we're too dangerous to you. Everything we hear or see could be available to Vernon and his brain-jockey."

"Only if you contacted him with information. It's not like you have a brain-jockey and he can see what you see and hear what you hear," Price said.

Leo darted him a glance. "You can't know that."

"Why would he need or want to put one inside you? You're just Mel's sons. He definitely might have messed with your head, but a brain-jockey? I don't think so. As for Taylor, I highly doubt it. Anyway, for Vernon's jockey to control him *and* you *and* my brother would be nearly impossible."

Leo gave a little nod, accepting the logic. "All the same, you shouldn't trust us. Who knows how we're programmed?"

"Fuck that," I said stoutly. "I'm not going to play that game. I may have doubted your sanity a time or two, but I have never and will never doubt your loyalty and love for me."

"This is the kind of crap that gives the talented a bad name and makes people support the senator," Maya said from the kitchen. "It's a pitiful shame."

"Agree. Things have to change. Not the way the senator wants, but they do need to change," Patti said. "It's way past time for good people to be in charge of Diamond City."

Leo scrubbed his hands over his face. "How did Vernon even end up with a jockey? Aren't dreamers naturally able to block something like that?"

I shrugged. "Apparently not."

Maya chose that moment to carry in the coffee on a cutting board she used as a tray. Leo went to help her serve. One of the "cups" she found was a small canning jar. I vaguely remembered a client had given me some jelly in it a year or two ago.

"Does this brain-jockey thing mean your father messed in your head because someone else made him do it?" Patti asked.

"Maybe," I said. "Maybe not."

"So we don't know if Vernon needs our help or needs us to kick his ass," Jamie said slowly. "We don't know what he's actually responsible for and what his puppet master is. This is fucked up."

I hadn't really considered the possibility that my father might need saving. The idea hit me like a punch to the gut. I just figured he'd got what he deserved with the brain-jockey. To think he might not be responsible for what he'd done to me . . .

The thought left me teetering on the edge of a canyon. I had no idea how to feel about that. Could I let go of my hate? Should I?

"How long has this been going on? I mean, what if the jockey made him murder your mother?" Leo asked somberly. "Touray put a hit out on Cass because of his jockey. Couldn't Vernon's have made him kill his own wife?"

His question hung in the air like a poisonous cloud. None of us spoke. I jumped when Price abruptly jerked to his feet and stalked out the front door. A sudden howl of wind erupted around the house, and a shiver went down my spine. It sounded like desperate souls.

Through the window behind where Patti and Leo sat, the world went white as the wind picked up the snow from the ground and blew it into a blizzard. We all exchanged puzzled looks, with everybody settling their questioning gazes on me.

"I have no idea what's wrong." But I was going to find out. I stood, biting back a groan as my stiff muscles protested.

"Maybe you should give him a minute," Patti said, eyeing the blur of white whirling outside the windows.

"Probably, but he's more likely to spill what's going on if I can catch him before he gets his shit together and transforms into Mister Tall, Dark, and Stoic."

I started across the floor but had only made it a couple steps before the door swung back open and Price stepped back inside. His eyes had gone milky white with only a hint of blue. Snow crusted his clothing and hair.

Shit.

He glared at me. "I knew you'd be following. Not everything is your problem. Sit your ass back down. You need rest."

"What's going on? What happened?"

"Didn't you hear me? Sit down. It's fine. I'm fine."

I flicked a glance out the window at the wall of white. "Yeah. I can see that.

How about you try again?"

He looked up and let out a string of curses before looking back at me. "Let. It. Go."

I didn't know what to do. Something was obviously wrong, and he was walling me out. If he were my sister or Patti or one of my brothers, I'd be relentless until he talked so I could help fix the problem. On the other hand, we were a couple. Did that mean I should give him space? Isn't that a thing that couples did?

I'd never had a relationship before, so what I knew about being a good girlfriend could fit in an eyedropper.

I looked down at my feet, considering, and then swung away in silent surrender.

"I'm just going to go to the bathroom," I said, looping through the kitchen and into the oversized bathroom, shutting the door firmly behind me. I went and sat on the closed toilet, wrapping my arms around my waist and squeezing my eyes shut.

You're doing what he wants, I told myself. *It's the right thing. You're being an adult. So it hurts to be shut out. Lots of things hurt. Suck it up. Nobody likes a whiner, least of all you.*

I knew I was being too sensitive, probably because of being so tired and the rawness of having the scab of my hate for Vernon peeled back and the old wounds exposed.

After a minute or two, I gathered myself, opened my eyes, and stood, flushing the toilet and running water in the sink so nobody would know I'd been freaking out. I didn't need anybody's pity, or Jamie's and Leo's teasing. They'd be all over me like flies on carrion.

I took a deep breath, squared my shoulders, and slid open the door.

Price waited just outside like an ominous statue, his eyes still playing the Casper not-so-friendly-ghost game.

I took a half step back, my cheeks flushing hot. "I didn't know there was a line. I'll get out of your way."

I went to squeeze past him, but he grabbed my arm and hauled me back inside the bathroom, sliding the door shut and dragging me over to the exterior French doors that led out into a courtyard. He pulled open a door. A wedge of frozen air pushed away the mounded snow, clearing a small space for us to stand. He pushed me out and shut the door. A bubble of still air surrounded us and kept away the worst of the cold.

Price dropped my arm and ran both hands through his dark hair. Long strands fell down over his forehead. He'd managed to shave earlier, but already dark shadows highlighted his chiseled features and crooked nose.

"Why can't you just let it go?" he demanded finally, hands on his hips as he glared at me.

I scowled. "I'm no longer asking. I'm respecting your privacy. I'm not going to pretend to be happy about it, but I'm backing off. I'm not the one out here making a stink."

"Because I know you're lying."

"I. Am. Not. Lying!" My voice rose as anger flooded me. I jerked out of his grip. "What else do you want from me? A notarized contract that I will not shove my stupid nose in your stupid business?"

He dragged his hands through his hair again, and abruptly spun away, his back rigid as he crossed his arms tight over his chest and stared out into the white gloom. The wind had grown more frenzied, a window into his increasingly turbulent feelings. I wondered how far the storm raged. Did it whip through the whole city or was it localized to just the Burrows? Or maybe the entire state had just succumbed to a giant wind event.

"We . . . *I* . . . could kill him."

It sounded like the words were made of glass shards, slicing Price's throat and tongue as he pushed them out.

I frowned, completely blindsided. "The senator? Won't work. It'll just bring more soldiers down on us."

"Not the senator. My brother. Gregg."

He turned back around. My mouth had fallen open, and I just blinked at him.

"I don't think I heard you right. Did you say *kill* your brother?"

He gave a harsh bark of laughter. "I know. It's ridiculous. But it could work. Gregg even tried to kill himself. But you said it yourself. Mel was freed of the brain control after she died. If Gregg died and we brought him back, it could break the brain-jockey's hold."

"Vernon's hold," I corrected, relief swamping me. For a second there I'd wondered if Jamie wasn't right and brain-jockeys were contagious. But Price hadn't been threatening his brother, after all. He was thinking of Touray to save him. The ultimate being cruel to be kind.

Once I started considering the idea, I realized it could work. "I wonder how long he'd have to stay dead?"

"Hell if I know." He shook his head and once again shoved his hands through his hair. "It's a crazy idea. There's nothing saying we could resuscitate him, or if he'd take permanent damage."

"Maya would be able to fix the last thing. It's bringing him back that could be tricky." I bit my lower lip. "Unless—"

I looked up from beneath my brows.

Price's expression was a mix of anger, fear, and resignation. "What?"

"It might be that I could hold on to him. Hold his trace so he couldn't cross into the spirit realm. Or maybe I could even push him back into his body."

His mouth thinned, and he sucked in a calming breath. I didn't think it worked. The vein in his neck throbbed like a drum. His teeth scraped across his lip, leaving behind white dents. His arms hung at his sides, his hands opening and closing with agitation.

"Okay. Presuppose that you could do that. Are you forgetting what happened earlier? What Maya said about you needing to rest and let your astral-self heal?" His voice had that patient cadence psychiatrists used with people having a mental break.

"No, but I have to try." The words came out before I even thought about them.

"You don't. That's why I didn't want to tell you. I could lose both you and Gregg in one fell swoop. He can wait until we find Cass."

I shook my head. "What if we don't get her in time?" *Or at all.* I batted that thought away as soon as I thought it. "Every day that goes by, your brother's body weakens. Plus what if he can't keep himself in the coma? You know he'd want to be here, fighting this fight with us. I hate to say it, but having his help could make a difference."

Price shook his head. "I won't risk you. I won't lose you both." He cupped my face in his hands, bending forward to lean his forehead against mine. "I can't risk it."

"What if I can do it without hurting myself?"

"How? You can't."

"But if I could? Would you let me try?"

He didn't answer for a long moment. "Only if you promised to back out the instant you started to feel things go south. I don't want you hurt any more than you are."

"I promise," I said.

He considered me, eyes narrowed. "Can I trust you?"

"I'll test how well I can hold onto his trace before we even get started. And I'm not going to do it alone. Remember how you guys helped me after we got out of the FBI building? You fed me power so I could erase our trace? I want to do that. Between you, Jamie, Leo, and Patti, I should have plenty power to work with. I'll just have to channel it, and hopefully that won't cause damage."

The words spilled out in a rush. I'd been considering the idea as a way to do all I needed to do to find the artifacts and the workshop. This would be a way to test out whether it would work, and how much damage I could avoid.

"I guess that could work," he said with a tiny tinge of hope.

"Let's go talk to Maya."

I grabbed his hand and flung open the door before he could change his mind. He tugged me back around.

"I'm sorry."

"Sorry?"

"For being a dick."

I smiled wryly. "You weren't exactly wrong about me. Not exactly right, either. I really was trying to give you space and not poke in where I wasn't wanted."

He gave me a pained look, tugging me close and holding me against him. "I always want you. I don't want to have secrets. I just want you to be safe. I love you."

His words melted me into a puddle of warm goo.

"I can't believe you're actually mine. That you put up with my crap."

"I don't exactly come crap-free," he said with a little smile.

"True. But you have a hell of an ass." I let my hands drift down to cover said ass and squeezed. "That totally compensates."

He laughed and his arms tightened around me. "You're perfect. I can't imagine my life without you."

"You don't have to. Your stuck with me forever. And Leo. And Jamie. And Taylor. And Patti. Probably Arnow and even maybe Dalton." I made a little face as I mentioned the last one. "You'll never be alone again."

"We may have to build ourselves a secret lair," he said, nuzzling my neck and nipping at my earlobe. "I like your family, but there are things I want to do with you that they don't need to know about."

A flush crept over my body. "Do tell."

"I don't want to tell. I like show." He took a breath and straightened, pushing me back. "Let's go get all the shit done so I can finally have you to myself for awhile. Remember you promised me two entire weeks without any interruptions. I'm holding you to it."

"Sounds like heaven."

He leered. The white mist obscuring his eyes had become just a light film, though the wind continued to whirl around us. Maybe once he got it started, it ran on its own for awhile.

"Uh-uh. I plan to be way too dirty for heaven. Dirty and, oh, so very wicked."

He said the last again my lips as he showed me just what he meant. By the time he lifted his head, I'd decided I'd sell my soul for more.

But first, we had to take down the devil.

Chapter 10

Taylor

"SO I WAS RIGHT. He was close by." Taylor couldn't help the smugness tingeing her tone.

Josh had returned her text almost immediately, agreeing to meet at a nearby memorial dedicated to the firefighter heroes of the 1949 Hercules Fire. It had swept across the mountains, driven by powerful winds. Added to steep canyons full of too-dry fuel, and the fire had swept through half of Colorado, wiping out towns and whole forests before a group of barely trained firefighters with magical talents had waded in to stop it. They'd succeeded, but it had cost them their lives.

"What are you going to do if he's got a small army waiting to kidnap you?" Dalton asked.

"Probably put a bullet in his skull."

She couldn't really imagine hurting Josh, even if he was threatening her. Then again, he'd tried to kill Riley. He wasn't the man she'd known, and she couldn't let old feelings get in the way of current reality.

They grabbed a compact little SUV from Savannah's fleet. She'd kept dozens, from Maseratis to vans to giant box trucks. The keys were already inside all the cars so that it was easy to get out of the three-story car barn.

Taylor had elected to drive, faintly surprised that Dalton showed no signs of manly chagrin at being relegated to the passenger seat.

The memorial lay on the south-central side of the Rim, in a long, rectangular park with a round reflecting pool surrounded by statues of the lost firefighters in bronze standing against a backdrop of titanium flames colored bright orange, red, blue, and green.

Both the memorial and the surrounding mountains and trees reflected in the pool, the ripples from the weather lending the reflected flames lifelike movement. In much of the winter, the water was allowed to freeze to create an ice rink.

Taylor pulled into an open parking space on the street, pleased to see that the memorial park was nearly deserted. A few people wandered around the pool, with two joggers making laps on the surrounding sidewalk and four skaters playing hockey on the ice. Only one coffee cart had come out and had set up at the far end of the park. Other than that, she didn't see any signs of lurking goons.

That didn't mean they weren't there, and if they were, they were professsionals or had the magical means to hide themselves.

Taylor scrunched her nose, wishing—not for the first time—for a small dash of Riley's talent. Enough to see trace, anyhow. *Which wouldn't help if their enemies had nulled their trace.*

She shook away the thought. Talent was no replacement for skill. She'd learned that lesson many times over. Besides, most useful magic she could buy. If you could rent talent, you didn't need to have it.

She pushed open her door and joined Dalton on the sidewalk. He scanned the area, his tinker-mod eyes flickering through various colors. Silver was his default, then orange, blue, red, yellow, and green. Taylor still had no good idea what he could see. Orange seemed to be infrared. She supposed that he probably had binocular and microscopic vision settings, too, and maybe night vision. He'd never been willing to say, though.

"See anything?"

"No."

"He said he'd be near the flames."

Taylor started walking on an oblique line in that direction, her boots crunching in the snow. Dalton stalked along beside her, head swiveling back and forth. He carried his gun close against his thigh, continuously studying the vicinity ahead and behind them.

Taylor finally caught sight of Josh standing near the Perpetual Buzz coffee cart. He held a cup, the steam curling off it.

She studied him as she approached. He looked the same but completely different. Gone was the genial man whose muscular body was smoothed by good living. In his place was a hollow-eyed stranger, face gaunt, body lean and hard. His blond hair had grown out, no longer stylishly cut and carefully moussed. Instead it was windblown and shaggy. Except for after a night of energetic sex, she'd never seen him with a hair out of place.

He wore jeans and a dark-green peacoat with black gloves. His skin was tanned with a rosy flush from the cold. Taylor couldn't remember ever seeing him in jeans. He always wore suits and ties with everything ironed and crisp. She found his lack of polish oddly compelling. Sexy even.

She really needed her head examined.

Josh waited for them to join him, casting a wary glance at Dalton, his gaze flicking to the other man's gun before returning to Taylor.

His gaze ran over her from head to toe. "You look good."

Her brows rose. "Not a good sign if you're going to start with a lie."

His brows furrowed. "I'm not lying."

"Then you may want to get your eyes checked. Why don't you get to why we're here?"

"Want a coffee?" He gestured at the coffee cart.

Taylor sighed. She'd kill for a triple espresso, but now wasn't the time. "Just tell me what you want."

He drew back slightly at her brusqueness. "I told you, I need Riley's help."

"Uh-huh, and you couldn't tell me why on the phone, and so now I'm here and don't have much time, so get to your point."

Taylor almost had to smile at Josh's confusion. She'd never showed him this side of herself. With him, she'd let down her defenses and let all her sharp edges soften. That, and much as she despised herself for this, she hadn't wanted to scare him off by being too independent or too outspoken. Unfeminine. He'd known the Taylor she'd wanted to be, but she was gone, and the old Taylor had returned. For good. She'd never let her guard down like that again.

Josh glanced at Dalton and back at Taylor. "Can we talk in private?"

"No," Dalton said, shooting Josh an icy look.

Josh stiffened, turning to face Dalton more squarely, his jaw thrusting out, his head lowering slightly like a bull about to charge. "I didn't ask you. I asked Taylor."

"And I answered. I'm her bodyguard at the moment, and she's not going anywhere without me."

"I wouldn't hurt her."

"You tried to kill Riley," Taylor reminded him.

He faced her again, the hand not holding his coffee bunching into a fist, his mouth pulling tight. "I'd just spent days being tortured and given Sparkle Dust. I hardly knew what I was doing. Cut me some slack."

"You said you *wanted* to kill her. You told her you knew what you were doing, even after she rescued you, and even after you sucked her into your FBI shit with those artifacts. Seems to me you've had all the slack you're going to get."

His mouth twisted and he looked away. His chest bellowed as he sucked in a couple breaths, and then he looked at her again.

"People are missing. *Friends* are missing. I need help finding them."

"What friends?"

He shook his head. "You don't know them."

She used to know all his friends. "You couldn't have told me this on the phone?"

He shook his head. "I think they've been taken. Kidnapped."

"Are they talented?" Dalton asked.

"Yeah."

"The senator's sweeps probably picked them up."

Joel shook his head, scowling. "They disappeared before he rolled into town. I need to know if they're dead or alive and, if alive, where they are."

"That's what all this cloak-and-dagger shit is about?" Taylor shook her head. "I don't buy it. You could have told me all this on the phone. What do you really want with my sister? "

"I just need her to do the trace. If I'd told you on the phone, you'd have just blown me off. I couldn't allow that. My friends are in serious trouble, and if I don't find them soon, they won't survive."

"And you thought, hey, Riley's a sucker. She'll help me after I tried to kill her. Is that it? Fuck off. It's too bad your friends are in trouble, but you're going to have pull on your big-boy pants and deal with it yourself. Riley's not available, and even if she was, I wouldn't let you get within a mile of her. Come on, Dalton. Let's go."

"Taylor, wait. Listen to me." Josh reached for her.

Dalton knocked his hand out of the way. "Hands to yourself, Junior," he growled.

The two men made an interesting contrast. Dalton, with his long black hair, high cheekbones, powerful chest, and quiet menace contrasted sharply with Josh's disheveled appearance.

He'd changed from an athletic sort of antelope or gazelle into a predator. Not a lean confident panther like Dalton but more a lone wolf, battle-scarred and wary, with that feral watchfulness that spoke of cautious deliberation and patient hunting. He might retreat, but he'd come back out of the shadows to attack again and again.

Both men were dangerous, in their own way. But Josh—he had a wildness to him, like he was walking on the edge and at any moment he could explode and send shrapnel flying everywhere.

"Just listen a minute, Taylor," Josh said, stepping toward her. Dalton shoved him back.

"Get lost. You heard her. She's done with you."

Josh bristled and stepped in close, standing nose-to-nose with Dalton.

"Back off, asshole. I don't know what rock you crawled out from under, but you can go straight back. You aren't Taylor's type."

Dalton sneered, his voice dropping into a deadly purr. "What is her type? A guy who tries to murder her sister? Who abandons her when the shit hits the fan?" His mouth curled into a crocodile smile. "Maybe I'm not her type, but I've got her back, and she doesn't want you."

He punctuated his last words with sharp stabs of his index finger into Josh's chest.

The man really had a bad poking habit. One day someone was going to break his fingers for him. Taylor watched the exchange, irritated that they acted like she was some kind of trophy they could fight over.

"Why don't the two of you just whip your dicks out and measure? It'll save time." She turned on her heel and headed back toward the car.

"Wait! Taylor!" Josh's voice rose with his urgency.

Footsteps crunched in the snow behind her, and both men overtook her.

"Cut the attitude, Taylor." Josh stopped in front of her, blocking her path. Dalton stood facing him, his shoulder slightly ahead of hers. "Riley helps innocent people all the time, no matter what the circumstances. Don't take your feelings for me out on innocent people."

She reined in her rising fury. "Riley is unavailable. You'll have to find another tracer. Now get out of my way."

Red flags burned in Josh's cheeks, and his blue eyes turned hard. "I don't fucking believe you. These are people's *lives,* and what's Riley doing that so important she can't be bothered to take a little time out of her day to help?"

Volcanic rage flooded Taylor. She was so pissed she could hardly see. So fucking furious she could almost feel the smoke rising from her as flames swept through her.

She took a step back, wrapping her arms across her chest in an effort to not rip Josh's throat out. Her gaze fixed on his chest.

"What is Riley doing that's so important?" she repeated in a flat, controlled voice. "Because of Riley searching for you, the strength of her talent became public knowledge and all the Tyet lords started hunting her. She was targeted by our bastard father—who turns out is still alive. He sent henchmen after her, but before they could kidnap her, she was captured by a nasty SD dealer who exposed her to SD. She escaped, but only after significant physical damage, and then was nearly kidnapped yet again. Did I mention she nearly died again?"

Taylor heard Dalton's low growl when she mentioned her father's "henchmen." The truth hurt, apparently.

She lifted her chin to look at Josh. He looked dumbstruck and had gone pale. His mouth opened, but she flung up her hand to stop him.

"But wait! There's more!" she continued in the cadence of a late-night infomercial. "The FBI got in on the action, and Riley's boyfriend got taken in. Never would have even happened if you hadn't got things rolling, shining a light on Riley. So we had to go in and rescue him, but in the course of things, my mother was killed and so was Riley. Thankfully her boyfriend managed to resuscitate her."

Josh's face continued to pale, his eyes widening. He swallowed, his Adam's apple bobbing.

Taylor gave him a death's-head smile. "But wait! That's right. You guessed it, there's still more. Over and over Riley has sacrificed herself to save you and every other innocent who happened along. Currently, my selfish, self-centered bitch of a sister can't be bothered with finding your friends because if she uses her magic in the slightest, it could kill her. It already almost did once today. You might be thinking, of course that will stop her from trying to save the city from Senator Rice's attack on the talented, but surprise, surprise, you'd be dead wrong about her. Again. Which means the rest of us are working our asses off to make it so she doesn't have to die."

By the time she got to the end, tears burned in Taylor's eyes and her voice had gone raspy and thick. She swallowed, refusing to give in to the fears that had just come tumbling out of her. She was *not* going to let Riley sacrifice herself. That meant she was going to have to make the plan to influence the senator work so that Riley didn't have to find or use the Kensington artifacts. And that meant standing here was wasting time she didn't have.

"You didn't mention what happened to you," Dalton said with a glance at Josh to see if he was paying attention. "Riley wasn't the only one Percy infected with SD."

"What?" Josh exclaimed. "You were exposed to SD? Are you—how—?" He stuttered over the questions as he examined her face closely. "You don't have wraith signs."

"Good genes." Taylor shot Dalton an annoyed look. She hadn't wanted Josh to know. It wasn't any of his business.

"I had that dreamer help me. Did she work on you, too?"

"Nope."

He frowned. "Why aren't you in a frenzy? You should be rabid for the stuff."

"That's none of your business. You gave up the right to ask me questions when you walked off without a word."

"Dammit, Taylor," he said, his mouth twisting in frustration. "Look. I'm not the man I used to be. I'm a monster, just like the people who made me. The only thing I think about is killing them. Slowly. Cutting them to pieces, bit by bit, and making them scream until their vocal cords shred and they're drowning in their own blood. There's no room for anything else in my head besides revenge. It's all I am now."

"That's all you *want* to be, you mean," she said, rolling her eyes. "Doesn't really matter to me. You do you. Do me a favor though, lose my number. Speaking of which, how did you get it?"

"Your accountant. Anthea Sharp. Told her I needed to find you. I may have sounded a little desperate."

That made a ridiculous amount of sense. When she'd had to close up her flying business, Taylor had given Anthea her number. Unfortunately, Anthea had a romantic streak a mile wide and she'd always liked Josh.

"I'll be sure and talk with her about client privacy." She gave a dismissive wave and headed for the car.

"Wait. I'm sorry about Mel."

The corner of her mouth kicked up in an arsenic smile. "Yeah? Me, too."

"And the SD. You're okay?"

"Like I said, none of your business." She strode rapidly away. Seeing him, getting a chance to say her piece, actually had made her feel a little more whole. Not as much as killing him might have, but she'd just have to live with the missed opportunity. Her mouth twitched into a humorless smile.

Dalton overtook her after a few steps. She ignored him. Time to get back to work and focus on keeping Riley alive and safe. She'd suffered too much already. She deserved a happy life with Price and maybe a couple of kids.

She couldn't help the sharp bark of laughter. Riley with kids. That would be insane. And hilarious. And so worth seeing.

"What's so funny?"

"Nothing."

"Sounded like something."

"It's something I'm not interested in telling you about."

"Why not?"

Taylor sighed and then decided she didn't have any fucks left. She told him the truth. "I don't want to get confused about what we are."

Silence.

"What do you think we are?"

"Not friends. Cordial enemies, maybe. Temporary allies."

She could hear him grit his teeth.

"You're wrong."

"How do you figure? Friends talk, let each other into each other's lives, care about each other. Cordial enemies are friendly on the surface but don't trust each other. Same with temporary allies. We definitely aren't friends."

"I *am* in your life. I have been for weeks."

She laughed out loud. "Please. You've been located near my physical position, but that's not remotely being in my life. I know almost nothing about you, and you sure as hell don't know me."

He stepped in front of her, blocking her way. "You think I don't know you?"

"You think you do?"

"I know you're loyal to a fault, stubborn, determined, generous, brave, and strong. You'd run into a burning building to save a litter of kittens. You've got a mouth full of razors, and you don't apologize for it. You've got money, but you don't flaunt it. You don't trust much of anybody outside your family, and you have shit taste in men if that asshole back there is any indication. You've also been trying to hide it, but you're still feeling the effects of the SD exposure."

Taylor stared, not letting her surprise show on her face. "How did you know?"

"About the SD? I'm observant. And no, I don't think your sister or brothers have realized yet. Arnow, maybe."

He stepped a little closer. He was taller than she by a good half a foot. She lifted her chin, refusing to be intimidated by his looming size.

"You know what else I know?" His voice dipped low.

"Oh, please. Do tell. I'm desperate to find out."

A ghost of a smile flickered over his mouth and vanished. "See what I mean? Razors."

Taylor glanced at her watch. "Are you almost done?"

He captured her chin, his thick brows dipping like raven's wings over his inhuman eyes. She resisted the urge to pull away. She wasn't going to let him think he bothered her. Unfortunately, he did bother her. A lot like Touray had when he kissed her.

She clearly needed a lobotomy. That would cure her of her serial bad taste in men.

"I'm not done. I'm not going away. *We* have a job to do and I'll be at your back the entire way, and well after that. Get used to it. As for what else I know about you . . ." The corners of his mouth flickered up. "You deserve a hell of a lot better than you've been getting. From your shithead ex to your father."

"Thank you, Dr. Obvious. I think the whole world knows that."

He shook his head, his thumb brushing back and forth along her jaw. "One of these days, I'm going to make you realize I'm not your enemy."

She started to tug out of his grip, but he slid his hand around the back of her neck, holding her still. She could taste his breath on her lips. Coffee and something masculine and sensual. Taylor's chest tightened, and her stomach tumbled over itself.

"You want me," he told her.

"I have shit taste in men. I believe you already established that." Taylor kept herself stiff, even though her treacherous body had ideas about rubbing all over him.

He smiled. "You didn't deny it."

"You're hot. You know it. You've got a great ass and probably the abs of a god. I'm not blind, and I'm not dead. But wanting you and fucking you are two different things, and I'm not about to jump out of the frying pan into an incinerator."

His mouth flattened into an angry slash. "If I wanted a meaningless fuck, I could call any of a dozen women who'd be more than eager to take care of my needs. The problem is I want you. *Only* you. Body and mind and even your barbed-wire-wrapped heart. I'm all in. When we fuck—and you'd better believe it's *when*, not *if*—it's going to be because you want me as much as I want you. In *every way* I want you. And when I'm inside you, my body wrapped around you as you scream my name, you're not going to call what we do fucking."

He spit the last word out and then jerked her forward the last inch and kissed her.

Chapter 11

Taylor

TAYLOR HAD EXPECTED Dalton's kiss to be demanding and fierce, but he fooled her. Again.

His mouth moved softly over hers, asking, offering, gifting rather than taking. His hands gentled, with just his fingertips along her neck and lower back holding her in place. Like she was a hummingbird he didn't want to frighten or risk crushing.

She couldn't remember the last time she'd been kissed with such reverence. Or any reverence, as if she were beyond precious. Priceless.

Josh had been a good kisser and good in bed. He had made sure she had as good a time as he did. But he'd never touched her like this.

She'd lifted her hands to rest against his chest, to shove him away, but the lightness of his touch and the unexpected sensual tenderness held her prisoner. It didn't hurt that his lips ignited a storm of heat inside her. A tremor ran through her. Her lips parted.

He took immediate advantage. He nipped her lower lip, and then he licked the spot as if to soothe it. He continued his gentle exploration, letting her choose to offer him more, to open herself up, to give him the invitation he wanted. Finally, she leaned into him, going up on her toes to get closer.

Dalton caught his breath and clamped her against him, one hand splaying across her back, the other cupping the back of her head as heat exploded between them. He delved into her mouth, his kiss turning hungry with an edge of desperation, as if he feared her vanishing out of his arms. His desire washed over her, and Taylor felt wanted on a level she never had before. Like he wanted her more than water, more than food, more than air.

A potent headiness swept through her. She could hardly think. Hot and cold chills ran down to her toes, which curled in her boots. This had *never* happened with Josh.

The shock of that realization had her going rigidly stiff. Her eyes popped open.

Dalton drew his head back almost instantly. "What's the matter?"

Taylor opened her mouth and then snapped it shut. What was she going to say? He knocked her world sideways and her actual ex-fiancé never had? Dalton, of all people. A man she didn't trust, whom she didn't even like.

Her lips pinched together. Dalton scowled.

"You can't tell me you didn't feel what I did, Taylor."

"I don't know what you felt," she prevaricated, trying to get her heart to stop galloping at a hundred miles an hour.

He gave a tiny snort of laughter at that and brushed a loose strand of her hair behind her ear.

"No? Then let me tell you. Free fall. Flying across the stars. Dancing on a comet. Breathing fireworks."

Taylor blinked stupidly at him. "What the hell? Is that poetry?"

"It's what I feel," he said, clipping off the words sharply. "What you feel. Your body doesn't lie, Taylor. You don't lie. So don't act like you're indifferent. You may not want to want me, but you do."

She gave a shrug like it didn't matter, even though his words hit like fists. Especially the poetic ones. "Okay. You're a champion kisser. Doesn't change anything."

His mouth ghosted into a smile again. "It's a step in the right direction."

"It's not a step anywhere."

The smile widened, but his eyes narrowed. The silver seemed to shimmer. "You keep thinking that if you want, but you're wrong."

Taylor opened her mouth to tell him to fuck off or something equally brilliant. Before she could, a wall of wind and snow hit them. They both staggered. Dalton grabbed her coat, but the wind tore her free. She stumbled a couple of steps before she found her balance, but then the wind caught her like a sail, pushing her a dozen feet. She knocked into something hard, pain exploding in her shin, and then tumbled to the ground.

She landed on crusted snow that had previously melted and refrozen. The wind scoured it, picking up whatever it could and spinning it into the air.

The snow blinded her, and the wind cut through her clothing. It had already been in the single digits, but the windchill had dropped the temperature down into the minus range, probably down into the minus teens.

Taylor struggled to her feet, the wind hammering her. Her hair blew free around her face, her hat long gone, along with her scarf and the elastic holding her ponytail. The wind tore the air from her nose and mouth when she tried to breathe. She coughed and pulled her coat collar up over her nose to make it easier to breathe and prevent frostbite.

She had to find shelter. And Dalton. Where was he? Shit. She turned and the wind slammed her full in the chest. She leaned into it, trying to get her bearings. She could see nothing. Hear nothing but the scream of the wind. Her eyes ached from the whipping cold. She narrowed them to slits, turtling down into her coat collar as much as she could. She fumbled to find her hood, finally jerking it up and yanking the strings tight.

Where was Dalton? Where was *she?*

Her mind scrambled to picture where they'd been standing, trying to figure out how far she'd been pushed from that point, but it was futile. She had no idea what direction she'd come from. Her best bet was to start walking and hope she found some place to shelter before she turned into an ice sculpture. Hopefully, Dalton would do the same.

Trouble was, in a whiteout like this, without anything to guide her, she couldn't walk a straight line if she wanted to. She'd end up going in circles and freeze to death before she even got out of the park. Not that she had a choice.

She started walking. More like trudging, sliding her feet and establishing her weight before taking another step. She decided to turn her back to the wind and let it help her along, rather than try to fight its strength.

She'd gone maybe a dozen steps before she was caught from behind. She gave a little startled scream as Dalton pulled her around and snugged her against his chest. Relief at seeing him made her body slump for a moment. He bent close to her hooded ear, shouting through the wail of the wind.

"I'm going to pick you up!"

He didn't wait for an acknowledgement, but swung her up in a fireman's carry, holding onto her legs as her upper body hung down over his back. Taylor clung to him, trying to keep herself as still as possible as he set off.

She couldn't have said how long he walked or how far. It seemed forever. Finally, he set her down and leaned her against something. The SUV, she realized.

He pulled the door open—good thing she hadn't locked it—and thrust her inside, shoving her across the back seat and climbing in beside her. He pulled the door closed, and the sound of the wind dulled.

She hunched over, shivering, trying to take stock of herself. Being out of the blizzard was the nearest thing to a miracle she could imagine at the moment.

Dalton's clothing rustled as he pushed back his hood. He put a hand on her back. "Taylor? Are you okay?"

"Not particularly."

"Are you hurt?"

He pulled her upright and pushed her hood back, examining her face. "You're too cold."

"Duh."

"No, your core temp is too low. I can see it. Give me the keys."

Easier said than done. Taylor fumbled, but her hands were ice inside her gloves.

"In my front left pants pocket," she told him finally when it was clear she wasn't going to be able to get them herself.

He peeled off his left glove and pulled her toward him, lifting her coat and wiggling his fingers into her pocket. Once he had the keys, he pushed her back and climbed over the front seat. He started the car and turned the heater to high before climbing back into the backseat.

He looked into the cargo area and fumbled for a few moments, then pulled an emergency case onto his lap. Inside were chemical packages for warming hands and feet, thin emergency-blanket packs, water, flares, and a variety of other items. Some were magical in labeled containers, but Dalton went for the ordinary ones first.

He tore open several hand warmers and shook them before pulling off Taylor's gloves. He pressed one pack between her hands. The sudden warmth almost hurt. He unzipped her coat and pulled the straps on her vest free, then pressed another warmer against her chest before zipping her coat back up. Next he unlaced her boots and pushed warmers into them before shoving her feet back inside.

He laid a couple on the tops of her thighs and tucked one behind her neck, careful to put it outside the shirt so it wouldn't burn, then shook out one of the silver-and-orange SOL blankets and wrapped it around her and held it closed.

The heat from the packs permeated her slowly. Her feet and hands ached as the cold dissolved, and soon the hand pack was too hot to hold. She dropped it onto her lap, flexing her fingers beneath the blanket, which reflected the warmth of her body and the packs back to her, creating a continuous buildup of heat.

By now the car's heater had begun to warm the air and her face no longer felt like an ice mask. She glanced at Dalton. His eyes were a bloody red.

"You need to take care of yourself, too" she said. Snow still clung to his eyelashes and clothing. He had to be as cold as she was, but still he didn't move, his attention entirely locked on her.

She pushed down the blanket and grabbed the warmer she'd dropped in her lap. She yelped as the heat burned her fingers, dropping it again. He grabbed her hand and pulled it toward him, turning her fingers over to examine them for damage.

Taylor yanked her hand away. "Dalton, listen to me. You need to get yourself warmed up before you end up hypothermic."

"First you."

She rolled her eyes. "Don't be an idiot. It's not a contest, and I *have* warmed up."

Sliding on one of her gloves, Taylor picked up the warmer and unzipped his coat far enough to set it against his chest. Just as he'd done with her, she broke open more packs and mirrored where he'd set them on her. When she went to take off his boots, he pushed her away.

"I can do it."

He fumbled them off and thrust the warmers inside, then shoved his feet back in again, leaving the boots unlaced. Taylor shook out a second SOL blanket and tossed it over him, then scooted closer, overlapping the blankets and pulling them over their heads to create a small cocoon-tent.

Taylor had begun to shiver. The tremors started deep inside and moved outward in seismic waves. Her teeth chattered together so loud she didn't hear what Dalton said, but suddenly he pulled off his jacket and stripped off hers. He wrapped his arms around her, pulling her close against his body, then pulled the blankets back over them.

"It's fine," Taylor said, though her chattering teeth made the words sound silly. "I'm warming up. Shivering is a good sign." All the same, she couldn't help snuggling into the wall of his chest, noting he smelled of spice and wood.

"Doesn't mean I have to like sitting here helpless and just watching it," Dalton said.

"Man of action."

"Damned straight."

"Sometimes there's nothing you can do but sit and watch."

"Luckily not today."

His arms tightened, and he pressed his cheek against her head. He squirmed and shifted them around so they lay across the seat. His back leaned against the door, and Taylor nestled on top of him. One of the blankets had slipped, and he pulled it up over them.

"That's better," he said.

"I'm squishing you."

His chest jerked as he laughed. "If you say so."

She fell silent, closing her eyes as she rested her cheek against his chest. The shivers had begun to die, and she'd begun to feel more human than icicle.

"How did you find me?" she asked after a few minutes listening to Dalton's heart thump steadily under her ear.

"Thermal imaging. In the cold you stood out like a beacon."

His eye-mods. "Handy." She wanted to ask him more about what he could see, but he'd made it clear before that he didn't like talking about it. "Thanks for finding me."

"I'll always find you."

He said it nonchalantly, like he was saying the sun is yellow or grass is green. The very lack of emphasis stole Taylor's breath. It sounded like a law of nature, like gravity or the earth turning. *Of course it could be a threat*, she told herself, even though she knew it wasn't.

She needed firmer ground. She switched subjects. "What should we do? We can't stay here forever. We'll run out of gas."

"I can guide us out of here."

"How?"

He hesitated only a fraction of a second, but Taylor noticed it all the same.

"I have a kind of sonar vision. It combines light and sound. I can ping off objects and get a visual of the terrain. I won't get details, but I won't drive into a building, either."

"Handy," Taylor repeated, at a loss for a better reply. She wanted to ask questions. Imagine if she could use that kind of magical tech in her airplanes. But

Dalton would likely just play the deaf, dumb, and blind card, which would only piss her off. She didn't feel like having to be mad at the moment.

Once again, silence fell.

"What else do you want to know?" Dalton asked suddenly. He'd begun to rub his hand slowly over her back and shoulders.

"I've always wondered what it's like in zero gravity."

He snorted. "That's not what I meant. What do you want to know about me?"

She considered her answer, and then settled on, "I'm not in the mood for landmines at the moment. So nothing." Besides she couldn't believe anything he said, so there wasn't much point.

"Landmines?"

Taylor sighed and started to shift herself up and away from him. He gripped her elbows.

"Don't."

"We've got to get to work," she said. "I've warmed up enough. Haven't you?"

"You're dodging the subject. What landmines?"

"Jesus fuck, Dalton. We're getting along at the moment. Do you really want to open Pandora's Box again?"

"What landmines?"

Taylor made an impatient sound. "Fine. First landmine: I ask you a question. You give me an answer. I don't know if I can believe you. I start to think about why I can't believe you and I get pissed. Second landmine: I ask a question. You dodge it. I get pissed that you're hiding things, and then I start to wonder how your secrets are going to hurt me and my family. Third landmine: I ask a question. I actually believe your answer. Later, I find out you lied and I'm bashing my head against the wall for trusting you when I knew damned well I shouldn't. Which brings me back to option one, where I can't believe you."

She pulled free of his grip, pushing his legs out of the way so she could sit on the seat and lace up her boots. After, she re-fastened her vest and pulled her coat back on. All the while he glowered.

She combed her fingers through auburn hair, wishing she had another elastic. She settled for braiding it and tucking it into her turtleneck. Hopefully, that would keep it out of the way.

Finally, she turned to face Dalton again. "We need to get to Tyrell's."

He frowned. "Maybe we should wait. Go join your sister and brothers."

"Why?"

"The storm. It can't be natural. It's got to be magical, and that's not exactly your run of-the-mill talent. Price has to be responsible, which means he's either lost it or something's come up that's made him unleash his power. And if Price has lost it, what set him off? Only thing I can think of is something happening to Riley. He didn't lose it like this when his brother jumped out of that window. Either way, we should check in."

"That's what phones are for." Taylor started digging for hers.

Dalton's words struck her hard. The bottom fell out of her stomach. She stared at her phone clenched in her hand, her knuckles turning white. *Had* something happened to Riley? Wouldn't someone have called? Leo or Jamie? Or could this be something he intended to do? And if so, why?

She slid a finger across the screen to wake it up and hit the speed dial for Riley. Nothing. Not even a single ring or a voice-mail recording. Panic rolled through her. She dialed Jamie, then Leo, then Patti. Nothing.

"I can't get through." Her voice came out raw and thin. She sat hunched into herself as she considered what to do. Quickly, she typed in Dalton's number. Nothing. So cell service was down. Caused by the storm? Impossible to say. The senator could have shut down service to make it tougher for people to organize or hide. Erickson could have done the same.

The storm would definitely help slow the senator's plans and put him off balance. That left him vulnerable. Even after the storm, he'd have to scramble to get things back on course. He might not be quite so careful as usual. If anything, this storm made it more likely that their plan could succeed. Maybe Price meant to stir up the storm for just that purpose.

A grim smile pulled her mouth flat. From the beginning, their plan hinged on so many what-ifs and maybe-coulds that it had never stood much of a chance. Now the odds of success might have increased by a few points. She'd take them, and while she was at it, she was going to believe Riley and her brothers were just fine. It's not like she had much choice. She said so, adding, "Let's go to Tyrell's."

"What? No. We need to find out what's going on. Going into Tyrell's could be a disaster."

"How? The best thing is to keep following the plan. We need Vernon's help, and the only way to get that is to talk to him. What's the worst that could happen?"

Dalton glared at her through slitted eyes. "I can't decide if you have a death wish or are just trying to push my buttons."

"Neither. I'm a realist. It is what it is and yeah, I get I could end up FUBARed, but we've all got to play our parts and this is mine." Her brows furrowed. "I pegged you for a military background, so you should know this already. You go where you're called to serve. Period."

He sucked a frustrated breath between his teeth. "This isn't the military."

"Same principle."

He looked away, staring out the side window into the storm. Taylor couldn't tell if he could see anything.

"Pushing your buttons is just a bonus," she added after the silence stretched. "Not that I think I could."

His head whipped around. His angular face went colder than the howling wind outside. "You *still* think my concern for you is just an act?"

Taylor wanted to respond with a fast affirmative, but the truth was that she no longer knew for sure. He'd created a small crack of doubt in her certainty. "I think there's a ninety-nine percent chance you're still working for Vernon," she said finally.

Dalton made a sound and punched the back of the seat, then swore as he shook his hand. He twisted to look at her again, his expression lethal. But then something seemed to click in his brain, and he took on a thoughtful look.

"Nine-nine percent? Not a hundred? That means you're starting to consider I might be telling the truth." He gave a grim smile. "It's a start."

"If you say so, but you've got a long way to go to make me believe in you, and you're running out of runway fast. For all I know you've got a brain-jockey up in your brainpan, too. That's not a whole lot of comforting."

"I don't."

She blinked. "How would you know?"

"Because strong emotion disrupts the jockey's control of the mount."

"And you've been feeling strong emotion? How do you know they're strong enough?"

"Because you piss me off so bad I can't see, make me want you so much I can't breathe, and scare me so much my heart stops," he said, his nostrils flaring at the confession. "Since being around you, I've been a basket case."

She stared, her stomach fluttering. "Funny, you seem about as stoic as a statue."

"Perhaps you need to be more observant."

"Or you could start acting like a real boy," she shot back. "You've got the automaton thing down pat. Hell, for all I know, under your human disguise, you're actually a robot."

"Just at the moment, I wish to hell I was. I wouldn't feel like strangling you. And I wouldn't give a shit if your stupid bravery got you buried six feet under. It would be a hell of a relief."

Before she could respond, he climbed back into the front seat and settled behind the wheel. "Looks like the wind might be slowing," he said in an obvious change of subject. "Still can't see for shit, though."

Taylor couldn't tell any difference but trusted that he could.

He put the SUV in drive and pulled out. Taylor crawled into the front passenger seat. "You'll want to head south. According to Erickson, Tyrell owns a dozen properties in Diamond City, but recent evidence shows him in a place across the river on The Spoon." The area was a mile-wide and half-mile-deep jut that curved like a spoon along the edge of the caldera.

Dalton nodded. "I've been there. Getting over the river might be tricky with this wind. That and the windshield interferes with my sonar sight. It's going to be a slow trip. You can take a nap."

"I'm good."

"You still cold?"

"No. Thanks for the help."

He nodded and fell silent. Taylor watched the white outside the window a few minutes, then turned to study him. Every few seconds his eyes flickered between red, green, and orange.

"What do the different colors of your eyes correspond to?" she asked but didn't really expect an answer. He surprised her.

"Red is thermal and infrared, green is night vision, orange is the sonar vision."

"What else can you see with them?"

"Blue is kind of a doppler radar."

"Like the weather maps?"

"Something like that. I don't have much range on that. Gold is a kind of CAD mapping system. It turns what I've seen into a kind of three-dimensional map overlay. I can study topography maps and other maps, and all that combines with my experiences of a place and creates an informational overlay. I don't use that one, much, though it has come in handy."

Taylor could imagine. "Is that all?"

He nodded. "The tinker tied them into my talent in order to keep the spells charged, so they don't fail at an awkward moment."

She nodded, biting back her next question. Why had he gotten the mods? But she didn't want to have him brush her off. Nor was she all that sure she wanted him to share himself. The less she knew, the easier it was to keep him at arm's length.

Her mind flitted back to their kiss, and her lips throbbed with the memory. She bit them together and looked back out the window.

"I joined the Navy when I was sixteen," he said suddenly. "Your father helped me fake my birth certificate to say I was eighteen. I'd known him for maybe six months."

"How old are you now?"

He cast a quick glance at her, clearly not expecting that question. "Twenty-nine."

Taylor did the math in her head. Her father had disappeared about ten years ago, but Dalton had known him for at least thirteen. Since before he'd become Vernon Brussard.

"What did he tell you his name was?"

"Vernon. I've only ever known him as Vernon."

"He left us three years after you met him," she said, trying to figure out what it meant that her father was already calling himself by his new name well before he'd disappeared. Why? And how had he been able to keep that a secret?

"I didn't know about you. Any of you. I barely knew Vernon. He was someone who showed up and helped me when I was desperate. If not for him, I'd have died by the time I hit puberty."

"How?"

He didn't answer right away, easing around something she couldn't see. The SUV bounced over something—a pothole or maybe rutted ice. A good thing it came equipped with studded tires or they'd be slip-sliding all over hell's last acre.

"I'd been in foster homes since I was five. My mom died, and my father was a tweaker. He got arrested, and that was the last I saw of him. I got moved around a lot. I wasn't easy to deal with."

"Still aren't," Taylor muttered.

He chuckled. "So sayeth the kettle. Anyway, I ran away from the last foster home when I was twelve. Almost joined a gang, but I didn't like taking orders and I wasn't about to deal drugs."

"The not liking orders thing must have boded well for your military career."

"I didn't have much of a choice. It was either the Navy or jail. And the Navy would only take me if I could qualify for SEAL training." He gave a little laugh. "I could barely swim. The chances of me qualifying weren't great, but I was terrified of ending up in jail.

"But anyway, I managed to survive on the streets, though winters were tough. I spent time down in the Bottoms, working for room and board in some of the brothels and SD dens, running errands for low-level Tyet soldiers, and doing a few odd jobs here and there.

"Everything was pretty good for me until that one day."

Pretty good? Scraping for a living on the street? Working in brothels and Sparkle Dust dens? His foster life must've been hell if street life was good. She couldn't help but admire him for all he must have gone through and the strength it must have taken.

"What happened on that day?" she prompted when he seemed to turn inward and forget he was telling the story.

"Shit hit the fan. I'd been cleaning up at an SD den for a few months. Places are half flophouse, half drug den. Landlords deal the SD to addicts and then rent them out as prostitutes or sometimes as freakshows, depending on the stage of wraithing they're at. Probably were selling some to that asshole Percy to make more SD."

He practically spat Percy's name. "I should have killed him when I had the chance," Dalton said. "One day I *will* hunt him down."

"Not if I get to him first," Taylor said. Not wanting to think about Percy's attack anymore, she turned Dalton back to his story. "So the shit hit the fan. What happened?"

"I got sent on a run to collect a supply of SD. Joe hated making the trip. He had a bad hip and a couple of crap knees, and it's a lot of stairs into Downtown. I went to the address, which turned out to be a bowling alley. I found out later there was a high-end casino underneath, along with a very expensive brothel, plus a drug distribution hub.

"Everything went smoothly. I picked up my package and headed out. The place exploded before I got clear of the door. I got thrown fifteen feet or so and landed face first in a tree. Knocked me out. When I woke, I was inside someone's bad acid trip. I guess the explosion exposed a bunch of people to SD. Magic was flying everywhere. All these new powers and no idea how to use or control them. People were screaming and shouting, and the bowling alley was on fire. A lot of gunfire. Whoever had set the bomb was picking people off as they ran for safety. I couldn't see much. I'd hit my head and broke my nose. Everything was a blur. Found out later I had a concussion and I was bleeding in my head."

"And you lost your sight?"

A flash of a smile. "Not quite. I was about to get real unlucky. I'd broken an arm and some ribs. I hurt like hell, but I had to get out of the tree before I caught a stray bullet." He gave a humorless snort of laughter.

"Should've stayed in the tree. I managed to get down finally and had no idea where to go. Couldn't see for shit. Took me a second to decide that heading away from the fire was probably my best bet." He shook his head. "Didn't make it more than a few feet before I took a bullet. Here."

He tapped a spot right beside his right eye.

"Went straight through and on its way out, sent bone shards through my left eye, destroying it."

Taylor stared at the spot where he'd pointed, even though he had no scars to show what had happened. "What happened next? How does Vernon figure in?"

"I passed out. When I woke up, they were still fighting the fire, but the shooting and magic show had stopped. Someone was talking to me. Vernon. He was telling me I was going to be all right, but I had to stay conscious.

"Long story short, he'd got me to a tinker and later paid for my mods. Said they'd be more useful than regular eyes. He was a Tyet man and everything I wanted to be and so I didn't object. He told me his organization was responsible for the explosion and he felt responsible for me. Anyway, he got me work and sort of watched over me. Helped me get the fake birth certificate when I got stupid and ended up in court. He said I had to go the Navy route, and if I survived, he'd make sure I was taken care of."

"And you became a SEAL even though you couldn't swim?"

"I had five days between signing up and the test. I spent most of it in the water."

"What was the test like?"

"A bitch. I was up against all these jocks, and here I was a scrawny kid with no education, no home, nothing, and I was supposed to beat them for a spot. We had to swim three miles in the ocean, bike twenty, and then run another five. I was doing good. Made good time. Then I got to the end. It was in this little clearing. The finish line was about a hundred feet away, and between me and it was a bear of a master sergeant with a wooden staff. His entire goal was to keep me from getting to the finish. I wasn't getting in if I couldn't find a way to get around him.

"I saw red. I was so pissed that I'd gone through all that and here was this asshole with a stick who'd been sitting in a chair drinking lemonade all day. I decided I wasn't losing. Not to him."

"What did you do?" Taylor found herself hanging on his every word, hardly paying attention to where they were going. Dalton was driving less than five miles an hour, so they hadn't come far.

"I charged at him, screaming like a banshee. He got all set and ready. Had a smug look like he knew exactly what I was going to do. I crouched like I was going to jump and when he committed to intercepting me, I dropped and punched him in the balls." A grin spread over Dalton's face. "He dropped like a fucking tree. I got up, stepped over him, and walked across the finish line."

He glanced at Taylor. "Nobody ever said I had to play fair."

"I guess not. Poor man. That had to hurt."

"Not as much as when one of the other guys jumped up like a ballet dancer and kicked him in the teeth. Knocked a bunch out and shattered his jaw. They took him to the hospital."

"How many made it through with you?"

"Twenty. Out of around a hundred and twenty recruits."

"And then after you got out, you went to work for my father," Taylor said, jumping ahead.

He shook his head. "With my background, I'm not suited for much besides Tyet work. Figured I could make a career out of it."

"You owe him a lot. He's your savior, your mentor." Implicit in her words was her doubt that he would repay Vernon with betrayal.

He was silent for a long minute. Abruptly, he stamped on the brakes. Thanks to the studded tires they didn't slide.

He turned to look at her. "Remember that day on the mountain? The day we broke your sister's boyfriend out of FBI detention. You told me to go back to your dad and I did. And then I came back. Do you know what I said to him?"

"Goodbye and thanks for the fish?"

Dalton gave her a confused look.

"It's from a book. What did you say?"

"I told him I was going to go take care of his daughters, and if he was the man I thought he was, he'd want me to keep them safe, no matter who came after them, including him. I told him not to expect favors. Thing is, Taylor, what you learn in the military, but especially in the teams, is that you choose your family, and that family has to mean more than anything else, including your own life. The men I served with are my brothers, and there's not a damned thing I wouldn't suffer for them, nothing I wouldn't do for them. They'd do the same for me.

"Your father has been important to me, and I owe him a lot. I've given him a lot. But he's not family. I might take a bullet for him, but he wouldn't take one for me. The minute I met you, I knew I was in trouble. I tried to fight it. I knew getting you to trust me would be next to impossible. But the trouble is that you and your insane family live by exactly the same code I learned in teams. By that day on the mountain, I knew I was going to fight like hell to be part of your family. To earn your trust and maybe more. I hope to God I can earn more from you.

"So let me answer the question you didn't ask: I'll sacrifice everything I am for you. You and your ridiculous family. Jamie and Leo, Riley and Clay, Arnow and Patti, Cass and maybe even Gregg Touray. Everyone you consider family is mine now, too. Whether they know it or not, whether they like it or not. "

Taylor's eyes widened with every fervent word. His sincerity was palpable. Fierce. It was hard not to believe him. Impossible, even.

"Wow."

He frowned. "What does that mean?"

"It's an expression of surprise."

"Is that all you're going to say?"

"I have to process."

He swore under his breath and faced the windshield, beginning their slow trek again.

A few seconds ticked past. Taylor's head whirled. For a man of few or almost no words, he'd said a lot. A question occurred to her.

"Why did you tell me all that? You've been about as tightlipped as a Russian spy up until now. Why did you suddenly develop diarrhea of the mouth?"

The last earned her pained look. "Because I need you to trust me. To believe me when I say that I have your back. You're about to go into a situation where your life is on the line. If you don't trust me, you'll take risks you don't need to. You'll keep secrets from me that could get you killed. Or worse.

"Your father is completely unpredictable, particularly now that we know he's got a brain-jockey, and Tyrell is a psychopath. A smart one. He's narcissistic, and he doesn't allow obstacles in his path. If you look like one, he'll mow you down without blinking an eye. He also won't hesitate to use you against Riley or anybody else he can. It would be a lot worse than anything Percy did you."

Wow. Again.

She felt his gaze flick to her as he waited for her to speak. He deserved more than a *wow*, even if she didn't know what she wanted to say. But there was one thing she did know. Had decided.

"I believe you."

Chapter 12

Riley

EVERYBODY STARED at us as we returned, worried gazes flicking to the window and back to Price.

"Everything okay?" Jamie asked.

It was Price's turn to roll his eyes. "Okay? Are you fucking serious? My brother's got a brain-jockey, he put hits out on his own friends, the woman I love is two steps away from death and spinning a full chamber for a game of Russian roulette, and we're about to go to war with the fucking government. At what point should I be *okay*?" He pointed out the window. "In case it isn't clear, that's exactly how I am."

I had my arm around his waist and gave him a little squeeze. He looked down at me and gave me a little wink. He was fucking with Jamie. With the truth, but still. I hid my smile as both Leo and Jamie shuffled uncomfortably.

"I'm fine," Price said, sitting down on the floor and snuggling me up against him. "Or rather, I will be."

Patti sat back down, folding her legs under her. "Let's just get on with this shit show. We're not getting any younger or smarter."

"Getting a whole lot dumber, if you ask me," Leo groused.

Once everybody was settled, I jumped right in.

"The second thing you need to know is that when I was coming out of the spirit realm, Cass contacted me."

That announcement caused a chorus of questions: *What did she say? Where is she? Is she okay?*

I explained that she'd been able to reach out because they'd taken nulls off to heal her, that she'd been shot several times, but I didn't know where she was, or who had her.

"But she is alive, and we *will* be finding her and getting her back."

I then recapped the discussion with the Seedy Seven and explained our plan.

"Taylor is going to talk to Vernon? Alone?" Jamie demanded in disbelief.

"Dalton is going with her."

"Like we can trust him. He works for Vernon. For all we know, he's got a brain-jockey, too."

"It's not likely," Price said. "The brain-jockey part. It's difficult to sustain even one, and I doubt Dalton is worth that kind of effort, especially if he answers to your father who is already under control."

"So she's basically on her own in a rattlesnake den," Leo said somberly.

"I think you're wrong about Dalton, but either way, she won't be alone for long," I said. "You and Jamie are going to join her as soon as you get done building shelters here."

"That could take days."

"Then do what you can in twenty-four hours. After that, we'll reassess."

Jamie scowled. "I don't like it. Once she's inside Tyrell's compound, we won't be able to get to her."

"You'll figure it out. You can at least use your talent to find out if she needs help and summon the calvary, if so. The good news is that by the time you go find her, we should know something from Arnow and Erickson. Which reminds me that we need to go back to Savannah's tonight." I looked up at Price. "We'll need you to keep the fires from the explosions we'll set from getting out of hand."

"Is it really necessary at this point?" Patti asked. "I mean, the storm is going to keep the senator pinned down. Even if it stopped right now, I'm betting there will be a fair bit of cleanup. Savannah's house will be low on the list of priorities."

"It's not stopping," Price said a little sheepishly. "I'm still feeding it." He looked at me. "I've got to bleed away some magic or I'll blow like a volcano. As my wind vortex expands, it's reaching out and sucking energy from the Gulf and from Canada and pulling warm and cold air masses to it. When they collide, we'll get a blizzard. A *big* one."

"How big?"

"Record-breaking, most likely."

"Can't you stop it?" Jamie broke in. "Push the masses away from each other?"

"I don't know. If I did, I could make things significantly worse."

"No," I said. "Better to leave it. The storm makes it more difficult for us, but everybody else will probably wait it out, including the senator. That gives us a little breathing room to find the artifacts, get Cass back, and wake Touray."

"We'd need help getting around," Jamie mused. "Though we can use the tunnel system. Wait. Wake Touray up?"

I nodded and explained. Up until now, Maya had kept quiet, sitting near Touray and keeping an eye on him. Now she rose to her feet with queenly dignity, her eyes fierce as she glared at me.

"I *will not* help you in this insanity. You'll die. I won't be able to help you, and I'm not going to be part of it."

"Just hear me out," I said. "It's not as much a risk as you think. Price, Leo, Jamie, and Patti will feed me magic. I should be able to do this without stressing myself at all."

"You have no idea how fragile you really are. The risk is too great." She shifted her accusing gaze to Price. "You could kill your own brother, all because you're too impatient for him to wake up on his own."

"That's not it," I said before Price could speak. I took his hand as outside the wind picked up again. Maya had struck a nerve. "We need Touray. We don't have a lot of time, and he knows more about the artifacts than probably anybody but Kensington. It's possible he knows enough to let us find the rest without me having to use my power. And even if not, he can gather manpower to help us against the senator. He may even have access to the senator that we don't know about.

"Maya, we have to try. Too many people's lives hang in the balance if we don't stop the senator now. Our window to do it is very small. We can't wait for Touray to wake up on his own, and even if we could, he'd still have a brain-jockey. We can't kill Vernon to free him, not if we want to use Vernon to influence the senator."

She continued to stare at me for a few seconds after I fell silent, and then she turned to stare down at Touray.

At least she hadn't said a flat *no*.

"If I help you do this, you'll have to test whether you really can use their power to keep you from hurting yourself worse before we do anything else. And you have to sleep. At least eight hours. Twelve is better."

"She'll sleep for twelve," Price promised. "I'll make sure of it."

"I'm perfectly capable of managing my own sleep, thank you very much."

"We can chain her down for you, if you think it will help," Jamie said to Price, totally ignoring me.

"Excuse me? I'm not a baby."

"Of course, not," Leo said. "We'd never chain up a baby to make sure it stayed in its bed and went to sleep."

"If you don't like shackles, we could make a cage," Jamie suggested helpfully.

"You're assholes. Go be useful. I'm apparently going upstairs to take a nap." I stood with excessive dignity and headed for the spiral stairs leading up to my room. Truth be told, I couldn't wait to lie down. "I'll expect a fabulously delicious meal when I wake up. With pie. And ice cream."

"Yes, ma'am," Jamie said with a little salute.

"You'll note that I am cooperating fully, so no sneaking shackles on to me while I'm asleep. Or making a cage. Or any other devious plan you've got in mind."

"We'd never do anything like that," Leo said with puppy-dog eyes.

"Just remember, every time you've played one of your practical jokes on me, I've gotten revenge. And every time I do, you regret ever having played a prank in the first place. I will get you back, and I will make the revenge ten times worse than the prank ever was."

With that, I swept up the stairs.

"Well, you've been warned," I heard Patti say cheerfully. "You won't get sympathy from me when she destroys you."

"*Destroy* is a little exaggerated, don't you think?" Jamie said.

"Actually, I thought it was understating it. I didn't want to scare you by saying she'd pulverize you or castrate you."

I could almost hear Jamie's and Leo's gulps and imagine them covering their precious jewels.

"Anyway, let's go start getting stuff done. We only have twelve hours," Patti said, and I could hear her walking across the floor, her Doc Martens thudding.

"Sixteen," Price corrected.

"You really think she'll sleep that long?" Leo asked doubtfully.

"No, but I'll find something to keep her in bed. We might make some noise, though. So I wouldn't be too prompt, if you don't want to hear it. Your sister can get loud."

"Please stop talking," Jamie said. "Never speak of having sex with my sister again or I'll wire your teeth shut."

I could hear Price's grin in his voice. "You do that and you'll find out what it really means to get smoke blown up your ass. You'll puff up like the blueberry girl from *Charlie and the Chocolate Factory*, only you'll be zooming off to space on a rocket of air."

"I really don't think I like you," Jamie said sourly. "You're just as bad as Riley."

"Probably not, but I do my best. Now if you don't mind, I'm going to go make sure she goes to sleep."

I hurried up the rest of the steps as Price mounted the stairs. I'd sat on my bed and begun untying my boots when he came in and shut the door. He looked around at the many candles sitting on niches in the rock walls, then at the king-size mattress sitting on a platform of wood and stone, then at the colorful pillows furnishing the rest of the room. I didn't have a mirror or a dresser. Inside my little curtained closet were a set of shelves and a small hanging space. I wasn't the clotheshorse that Taylor was.

"It's not much, but it's comfortable." I pulled off my boots and socks and tossed them aside. I stood and unbuttoned my pants and slid them off, then pulled off my shirt and bra.

"What are you doing?"

"Getting ready for bed. I like to sleep in the nude." I didn't really. I like an oversized sweatshirt and panties, but I was going for tempting and sexy, and a giant Broncos sweatshirt was neither.

I hooked my thumbs in the sides of my underwear and shimmied out of them, kicking them into the dirty clothes pile. I reached up in a full body stretch and pretended to yawn.

"You're killing me here, Riley." Price's voice had gone hoarse.

"I don't know what you mean," I said, crawling in between the sheets and turning to face him. "You all told me to go to bed. I'm just obeying orders."

He pulled his shirt off and kicked off his boots, peeling off his underwear and pants as he stalked over to the bed and climbed in beside me. He pulled the covers over us and hauled me into his arms, giving me a long kiss.

When he pulled away, I made a sound of protest. He laughed and rolled onto his back, pulling me snug against him, and pillowing my head on his chest.

"You need sleep, not exercise."

"I could lay very still and you could do all the work."

"No you couldn't."

"But it would feel so good," I said, licking his chest.

"Stop it. Go to sleep."

"If I don't, will you spank me? I like a good spanking."

"Riley," Price said, caught between laughter and a groan.

I sighed. "Fine, but you can't blame me for your blue balls." I reached down and cupped the anatomy in question, then slid my hand up over his very hard dick.

He grabbed my hand and pulled it away. "You're going to pay for that later."

"Promise?"

He rolled me away from him and wrapped himself around me, pinning my legs with one of his, and holding my hips tight when I tried to wriggle against his cock.

"Stop teasing," he growled against my ear before nipping at my earlobe. "Or I'm going to sleep on the floor."

Much as I was tempted to keep pushing him till I got my way, he was right. I was wiped out. Until I lay down, I hadn't realized how exhausted I really was. But then I'd been to hell and back—pretty literally—confronted a bunch of mobsters, got stuck underground with all the walls collapsing in on me, and then had to deal with Price's emotional crisis. Maybe I would sleep for the whole sixteen hours.

My last thought before I nodded off was to wonder how Taylor was doing and to hope she wasn't caught out in Price's storm.

Chapter 13

Taylor

THE TRIP ACROSS the Rim to Tyrell's lair took almost five hours. They were forced to circle around stalled cars and accidents and get out several times to clear snow.

By the time they got near their destination, dark had fallen and Taylor's stomach had begun to rumble. She'd also begun to squirm in her seat. She needed a bathroom and needed it soon. Peeing on the side of the road didn't appeal to her. She'd probably end up with frostbite in a very embarrassing place.

"We need to find a place to get some food and take a bio break," she said.

Dalton's brows furrowed. "Bio break?"

"Bathroom. If I don't find a toilet soon, I'm going to rupture something."

He lifted a brow at her. "Got ideas about where to stop? Most everything around here is private."

"I don't care if we break in to use a toilet. We just need to do it and soon."

"You might have mentioned it sooner."

"Noted. Now can you get a move-on?"

"I'll see what I can do."

"Oh goody," Taylor muttered, squeezing her legs together and bouncing in her seat.

It was only a few minutes later that he nosed the SUV up the slanted start of someone's driveway. The lights reflected off the wildly spinning blizzard-scape, making Taylor dizzy. She squeezed her eyes shut and shook her head before opening them again.

A few hundred feet later, the SUV stopped and Dalton put it in park but didn't shut off the motor. He put on his gloves and coat, pulling up his hood and tightening it around his face.

"Wait for me."

He got out and came around to Taylor's side. She'd followed suit with the gloves and coat, so that when he opened the door, she was ready. He held out a hand, and she took it, stepping out onto wet cement. The driveway was spelled to keep the snow melted. Thank goodness for small favors.

Dalton led the way, using his sonar vision, she supposed. She was aware of walls rising around them as they passed through some sort of gate into a more closed-in area. Here, snow piled up on either side of a broad sidewalk, blocking some of the wind. It whistled and howled, sounding like a bunch of jacked-up ghosts at a rave.

They reached a door, a service entrance, Taylor guessed. Not that it was any less magnificent than the rest of the architecture. Greek-style columns held up an ornately carved marble portico.

"Wait here," Dalton said loudly, bending close so that she'd hear.

With that, he vanished into thin air. A neat trick of his. He could jump through a wall. A few seconds later, he pulled open the double doors leading inside and motioned her into the tiled vestibule.

"There's nobody home. No heat signatures."

Taylor nodded and went past him, heading down one of the two outgoing hallways. She found a bathroom three doors down on the right, past a giant laundry room and a room that appeared to be a cleaning supply closet on steroids.

She made quick use of the bathroom, marveling at the level of bad taste the decorator had managed to cram into the place. The walls and ceiling were papered in a gold-lamé-and-red-velvet-patterned wallpaper. The white marble with streaks of gold and red glitter running through it matched the sinister-looking toilet. A gaudy gold chandelier crusted in crystals hung from the ceiling, and the fixtures and the mirror frames were all gold, and the towels appeared to be made from gold thread. What made the entire thing come together was the painting depicting the Last Supper hanging on the wall opposite the toilet. An ornate gold cross hung in the narrow spot just above the light switch.

Even the toilet paper was colored gold. It wasn't particularly soft, either.

Taylor finished her business, washed her hands quickly, and made her escape.

"Everything all right?" Dalton asked. He waited outside in the corridor, which was tiled in a lovely off-white travertine, with neutral antique-white walls with a series of woven South American art pieces running its length.

"Why do you ask?"

"You look like you saw a ghost."

"I'm fine. Why don't you use the bathroom. I'll wait."

He gave her a frowning look but went past. "Holy shit," he said, standing in the doorway. "Was the decorator blind? What the hell?"

"Hell might be right. Or heaven," Taylor said, smirking at his reaction. "If you figure which it belongs to, let me know."

He shut the door and emerged a few minutes later looking shellshocked. "Think they did that on purpose? Or did someone sneak in and vandalize them?"

"I think they paid a lot of money for it," Taylor replied.

"But the rest of the place is so normal."

"What we can see of it. I suggest not exploring."

"Roger that," he said with a slight shudder. "Come on. Let's see if they've got a kitchen."

He reached out and took her hand. They'd both removed their gloves and his hand was warm and strong. He started down the hall, and she didn't move, eyeing their clasped hands.

"What are you doing?"

He followed her gaze. "Holding your hand."

"Do you think I'm going to run away or something?"

"No."

"Then why?"

"I want to."

She hesitated and then gave an inward shrug. Whatever got his rocks off. She started walking with him, pretending that she wasn't enjoying his touch and was only enduring it for the sake of keeping the peace.

They continued down the corridor and came to small room with elevator doors on two walls. Taylor pressed the button on the left one and the doors slid open. They stepped inside and pushed the main level button. There were three floors above that and one below where they got on board.

Once on the main level, they located the kitchen near the back of the house. Floor-to-ceiling windows looked out on the blizzard.

Taylor wondered what had made Price stir up this storm. Had he done it on purpose or had he lost control? And why was it still raging? It had seemed to be calming earlier, but now the winds had picked up and the snow looked thicker with bigger flakes.

She pulled her phone out and checked for a signal. Still nothing. It pissed her off that even with magic, they still had to put up with regular technology for communication.

Dalton had stopped beside her, and she waited for him to tell her that everybody was all right, that she was worried for nothing. When he didn't speak, she looked up at him. His face had that indifferent expression he wore like a protective mask, but she was starting to be aware of his micro expressions. The miniscule narrowing of his eyes, the slight furrow between his brows, the almost invisible thinning of his lips, all of which added up to concern, or maybe anger. Or maybe gas, for all she knew.

"If you're all right, I'll see what there is to eat."

She nodded and he wandered into the kitchen, which was the size of tennis court, filled with high-end chef's appliances and every machine and gadget a cook could want.

As he checked the refrigerator and rifled through the pantry, she found a landline phone and picked it up, heart speeding up as she got a dial tone. She tapped in Riley's cell number. Nothing. She tried Leo and Jamie, then Patti, Price, and Arnow. The phones rang and rang without going to voice mail.

Taylor resisted the urge to throw the handset across the room and instead dropped it back into its cradle. It beeped to let her know it was happy, and she went to sit in one of the eight bar stools lined up on one side of the kitchen island.

Dalton had pulled out a number of things and stood staring down at them thoughtfully.

"Can you cook?" She could put together a gourmet dinner with saltine crackers, hot dogs, pickles, and a can of mushrooms.

He lifted his gaze to meet hers. "Do you want to eat fast and try to get to Tyrell's tonight? Or do you want to stay here until morning? I doubt anybody will come home."

"We don't have time to waste."

"If we go at dawn, we might catch everybody off guard."

"Does it matter? We're knocking on the door. It's not like they won't know we're coming."

He shrugged. "Maybe not. But it's already been a long day. Staying here would mean solid rest. We go to Tyrell's, even if he gives us a spare bedroom, there's no way we'll sleep. If we do, it'll be in shifts. Plus, he might decide not to talk to you until morning, anyway. Business hours or some other bullshit."

Her head tilted to the side. "You know him, don't you?"

"Enough. Your father is one of his closest aides."

"And you were one of his," Taylor murmured.

Dalton nodded. "That meant I was in the room with Tyrell a lot. He didn't pay much attention to me, no more than he did any other of his soldiers."

"He sounds like an arrogant asshole."

"He is. Very. So what do you think? Do you want to go tonight or stay? If we go, we eat sandwiches. If we stay, there are some steaks in the freezer."

"Why do you suppose the brain-jockey picked Vernon? And when do you suppose it happened?"

Dalton considered a moment before answering. "If I had to guess, I'd say the jockey picked Vernon either because the jockey made a connection between Vernon and Riley, or because he wanted someone close to Tyrell. The second one seems more logical."

"What was he like? My father, that is."

He blew out a sigh and shook his head with a sardonic smile. "Vernon holds everybody at arm's length. He talks and he laughs, but he keeps his cards close to his chest and doesn't let anybody know what he's thinking. He's moody. He doesn't explain what he's thinking, and if he does, chances are he's lying. Sort of a case of 'don't ask me any questions and I won't tell you any lies.'"

Dalton shrugged. "He's been like that since he found me. Whether the jockey came along before or after I met Vernon, he seems the same to me. I didn't notice any changes."

"You probably know him better than anyone. If anybody noticed, it would be you."

He gave her a sharp look. "You think I'm lying?"

She frowned. "No. Why would you say that?"

"It sounds like you think I ought to have. Or that I couldn't have missed it."

Taylor shook her head with a bitter laugh "Who am I to judge? I'm his daughter, and I never saw what he was. None of us did. He fooled us all."

"He fucked with Riley's and Mel's heads. He might have done the same with you and your brothers. He might not have *let* you see."

"He might not have let you see, either. Have you thought of that?"

Dalton's face pulled tight and cold. He had the look of a stone-cold killer. "I've thought about it."

"And?"

"And it makes me want to rip his throat out with my bare hands."

"You never thought about it before? That he might have messed with your head?"

A dry laugh. "I made a point of getting checked out regularly for the first few years I was working for him. Then I got stupid and trusted him. Now, will you answer my question? Stay here tonight or go beard the lion in his den?"

"I hate to say it, but I could use a nap," Taylor said grudgingly. "Maybe just a few hours."

"Steak, it is."

"Do you want some help? I'm a pretty good cook."

He shook his head "Go lay down on the couch. I'm not the best cook, but I won't kill you."

"Maybe there's wine," she said, returning to the living room beside the kitchen where a wet bar was set up.

"Anything stronger?"

"Like what? Scotch? Bourbon? Rum? Vodka? Other?"

"Any and all of the above."

Taylor scanned the bottles. It looked like the house owners were collectors of fine booze. She pulled down a bottle of Macallan scotch and poured it straight, adding a couple drops of water to each for the bloom. Returning to the kitchen, she passed one of the glasses to Dalton.

"Cooking helps me deal with stress," she said. "Can I help at least?"

"Keep the scotch coming. How's that?"

An hour later, Taylor was feeling full and semi-relaxed. Dalton had asked her questions about her flight business, about working for a merc outfit in

Afghanistan, about her family, about how she'd learned to cook, and a lot of other things. She'd managed to field her own questions now and again, asking about his military years, if he had any family left, and what sorts of things he did for Vernon.

He'd served six years anti-terrorist recon, going into places the US claimed it had never been. He'd been working for Vernon for seven. He thought he might have an aunt or uncle somewhere but had no real idea. As for what he did for Vernon . . .

"No doubt very much like what Clay did for his brother," he told her.

"How very specific of you."

"Do you really want to know? It's Tyet work. Little of it is pretty."

"But no one knows Tyrell is Tyet. He keeps that a secret, right? How does that work if Vernon is one of his top bosses?"

"Vernon runs things. He's the face. He makes sure either nobody remembers Tyrell, would rather die than betray him, or cannot even speak or think his name or remember what he looks like."

Taylor stared a moment, then shook her head. "I guess I shouldn't be surprised after what he did to Riley. No wonder people despise dreamers. They're fucking scary. I can't believe he never tampered with you."

Dalton's smile was cold. "He might have tried, but I've been completely loyal. He says that sooner or later, someone who's been tampered with will have a moment of brain dissonance and start subconsciously chipping away at some of the dreamer conditioning. Constantly renewing all the conditioning is time consuming and tiring. It's much better to have people who choose to be loyal."

"But you're not anymore. How does he feel about that?"

Dalton looked down at his glass and then took a slow drink. He set his glass down and met Taylor's gaze.

"I don't know that he knows."

Foreboding prickled through her. "Why not?"

"He may have mistakenly decided that I was joining you out of loyalty to him. That I would be watching you and reporting back to him. He may find it as difficult as you to believe that I have new priorities."

"But you do."

He held her gaze, robot eyes boring into hers. "I do."

"You do realize that telling me this could easily resurrect my doubts about you. I could easily decide that you really are watching and reporting."

"You could."

"Which could make your confession a clever ruse to make me think you're being honest while you're really still Vernon's hound."

He nodded and swirled the scotch in his glass. "What do you think?"

She studied him. In all truth, she had no idea. But after the events of the day, her gut said trust him.

She hoped it wasn't just indigestion.

"I don't *know* what's true, but I *choose* to believe you."

His eyes closed for a moment, then flicked open again. "Thank you."

"I'd better do the dishes." She stood and started collecting them.

"I'll help."

They had the kitchen cleaned in about ten minutes, and then set about finding a place to sleep. At the other end of the house they found two bedrooms linked together by a bathroom.

"I'm setting my alarm for five a.m.," Taylor told Dalton.

"I'll be ready when you are."

"Good night then." She hesitated in her side of the bathroom's doorway. The memory of their kiss flashed through her mind, and her body flared with heat. She quickly swung the door shut before he could notice.

What the hell was wrong with her? First she gets all hot and bothered when Touray kisses her, and then gets her panties in a wad when Dalton does it. Funny thing was that Josh hadn't stirred up any of her old feelings. In fact, they'd finally settled down in the grave where they belonged.

She rubbed her hands over her face. Jamie and Leo would tell her she needed to get laid. That this attraction for both men was just rebounding from Josh, hyper hormones, and too long a dry spell.

The old Riley would have told her to run like hell and not to be an idiot. The new Riley would probably tell her to follow her heart. But Taylor had a bad feeling her heart's navigation system was shot to hell and following it would only lead to disaster.

But it would be one hell of a ride.

Chapter 14

Taylor

TAYLOR SLEPT FITFULLY. She found herself tossing and turning. She'd have told herself it was because of being in a strange house or strange bed, but her time in a war zone had taught her to sleep when she could, wherever she could. Nor was it because of Dalton, though she found herself thinking about him whenever she woke. Her decision to believe him, to trust him, worried her. Was it really her own decision? Or the influence of Vernon, reaching out from afar?

She'd been keeping herself nulled. That had become standard practice for the family since Vernon's return. Luckily, since the nulls were directed specifically at dreamer magic, they allowed her to use other magic, like a heal-all, so he *shouldn't* have been able to influence her. But she couldn't be sure her nulls were still working, so he could have messed in her head to make her trust Dalton.

At the same time, she found herself wanting to trust him, and that worried her, too. To have made such a complete about-face in less than a day seemed insane, or at least suspect. She combed over the day's events, over their interactions. He'd opened up, and he seemed truthful.

And she *wanted* to believe him.

She pressed the heels of her hands against her eyes. She could *not* develop feelings for Dalton. He was the stereotypical bad-boy type, and nothing but trouble. But it would be funny to snuggle up to him in front of Leo and Jamie. They'd go ballistic.

And it wouldn't be so different from Riley getting together with Price. He'd been the enemy, too, and clearly he loved Riley and would do anything for her.

Dalton did not love Taylor. Was not in love with her. Could not love her. Why was she even thinking of him in terms of love? Riley was a bad influence.

The entire question was stupid, and clearly she needed a lobotomy.

At four a.m. she gave up trying to sleep and took a shower before dressing and returning to the kitchen where she found a stovetop espresso pot. She'd just started searching for coffee when Dalton sauntered in.

"I thought you said five?"

"Couldn't sleep." Her tone was sharper than she meant.

He frowned, propping a hip against the island folding his arms and watching her. "Something bothering you?"

She gave him a *no, duh*, look and continued her search, finally finding coffee beans and a grinder. She poured the beans in and turned on the grinder, using the noise to keep from having to talk. Not that she needed a reason. He seemed to have infinite patience and just waited like a stone lion, watching her as she filled the funnel of the pot, added water, and set it on the stove to heat.

Still not looking at Dalton, she pulled milk from the refrigerator and poured it into a small pot and put it on the stove, grabbing a wooden spoon to stir it with.

She expected Dalton to push, but he didn't. The asshole. Little did he know she could get just as irritated at him for not talking as she could for anything else he did or didn't do.

I am woman. Hear me roar. Then I will snap your neck like a cracker.

Taylor smirked at herself.

"Do you want breakfast?" she asked.

"I'd like to know what's bothering you."

"You are. Or maybe what we're about to do. Maybe I'm worried about my family. Cells still aren't working, and that storm is heavier, if it's anything at all." She jerked her head toward the windows.

"But there's something else," he said shrewdly as the espresso pot made sputtering sounds, indicating it was done.

"Stir the milk," Taylor ordered, handing him the wooden spoon as she went to rifle through the cupboards again.

She found two cups and some dark chocolate chips. She dropped chips into the bottom of each cup, and poured several ounces of espresso into each, stirring the chocolate to melt it.

The milk had started to bubble at the edges, and she took the pot and topped each cup. Setting the pot aside, she took her drink and went to stand in front of the window. The lights of the kitchen illuminated whipping snow outside. She watched it, still unsure why she was so unsettled.

Dalton came to stand beside her, sipping his drink. "This is good." He fell silent for a few moments. "What else is bothering you?"

Taylor made a face. "I don't know. I feel . . . off balance, somehow. Like there's something I forgot to do. Like that feeling you get when you wonder if you turned off the stove, except bigger. It's making me itchy."

"You have good instincts."

She shrugged. She wasn't so sure about that anymore. She wasn't so sure about anything anymore, for that matter.

She watched the swirling flakes, feeling a certain hypnotic pull as they spun between the darkness behind and the light from within.

Abruptly, they seemed to swarm toward, melting the glass and flying at her. She pitched forward in an endless fall. Her hands and feet went numb, and her body spasmed. Cold enveloped her. Bitter cold, like the thin air on the high mountains in the dead of winter.

The storm wrapped her in its smothering arms, spinning her and twisting her, sending her careening through the billions of whipping white flakes. Only now they turned colorful, like butterflies. They hardened, pelting her like rocks.

She struggled to get away, but there was nowhere to go. She balled herself up, but the pellets continued to strike, now penetrating her skin, burrowing through her with electric energy. She batted at them as they came at her and swatted some away, even as others drilled through her hands.

A buzzing sound started low and then increased in volume until it seemed to fill every corner of her, vibrating and whining, louder and higher, like a pressure cooker about to blow.

What was happening? An attack? The house's security? But that made no sense. Not now after they'd been in the house for hours.

Taylor still felt like she was falling, tumbling over and over through a psychedelic storm that seemed to be infinite.

"Taylor!"

She heard Dalton's voice from far away. A small sound, barely breaking through the incessant buzzing.

She listened, hoping to hear him again, to feel like she might get her bearings in this free fall into chaos.

The pellets drilling through her had turned to giant eels, lengthening and thinning and wriggling at her like brilliant-colored ribbons in the wind. One wrapped her neck. Then another. Another. And more and more. They squeezed, closing off her trachea and making it impossible to breathe.

She flailed, clawing at them, but though she could feel a thickening of their substance, she could not get a grip on them to pull them away. Her head spun and filled with a muffling fog that made it hard to think. Panic chewed at her, but she refused to let it overwhelm her. Instead, she kept fighting, focusing on the bands constricting her throat. She'd dragged at them again with clawed fingers, and for a moment it felt like she'd caught hold.

And then she could breathe. She gasped, drawing deep lungfuls as the fog faded. She found herself lying on the floor with Dalton straddling her stomach, his hands pinning her wrists, his hair hanging loose. He looked grim, his eyes shining silver.

"Taylor! Can you hear me? Talk to me. Are you okay?"

She blinked up at him, trying to figure out what had happened, and how she'd ended up on the floor.

"I . . ." The sound was soft, almost a whimper. Her body felt like it was short-circuiting. Her muscles twitched and jerked, and her tongue stuck to the roof of her mouth as if frozen in place.

"Shit."

He swung himself off her and picked her up like she weighed nothing. He held her tight as if he could make the twitching stop by applying pressure. It didn't help. He swore, turning in a circle as if uncertain what to do.

After a few seconds, he strode with her down the hallway, back to the bedroom where she'd spent the night. He laid her down on the bed, pulling off her boots and draping the covers over her. He stared down at her, rubbing his hands on his thighs.

He paced a few steps to the bottom of the bed and back.

"Tell me how to help you, Taylor. I know it was a magic attack. I used a null on you, and it stopped. I don't know what else I can do." He dug in his pocket and pulled out his phone. "Fucking hell! What the fuck good are phones if they don't work when the weather's bad? And how the hell does Clay deal with this all the time with Riley? She's a fucking disaster magnet."

He looked like he was about to throw his phone against the wall, but he shoved it back into his pocket instead and ran both fingers through his hair.

Taylor wanted to reassure him, and the truth was the twitches and jerks had begun to subside, though now it felt like she was about to get charley horses all over her body. She'd worked at gaining control of her tongue and finally bent it away from the roof of her mouth.

"Better," she whispered, though it sounded more like *bewher.*

He bent over her, one knee on the bed. "What did you say? Say it again."

"Better." This time it came out slower to *pedder*, but he got the gist.

"You're feeling better?"

She gave a jerky nod. "Attacked?" This time the word sounded pretty close to what it supposed to be. "How? Who?"

"I don't know. You're nulled against a dreamer, and I don't know what other talent can reach out like that. It could have been in the house somewhere, a booby trap, but then why didn't it snare me? And why would anybody booby-trap their kitchen and why didn't we trip it at dinner?"

She managed to get enough control of her arm to pull it up and rub away the itch on her nose.

"Thanks. Was strangling me."

"I know. I couldn't do anything to help. One second you're standing there, next thing you're keeling over and gasping like someone has a noose around your throat." He pulled the fabric of her turtleneck aside. The shift of the fabric against her wounds stung like a harsh sunburn. "You gouged the fuck out of yourself. I'd better get something to clean you up. Stay put."

As if she could go anywhere. She dragged her hands up to her neck to feel for herself. She finally fumbled her fingers under the fabric and yelped as she prodded the furrows.

He rummaged in the bathroom, and returned with some hydrogen peroxide, a couple of hand towels, and a box of Band-Aids. He tossed the latter aside as he looked at her neck again.

"Those aren't going to do a lot of good. I need to find some gauze."

He disappeared out the door. Taylor lay there first trying to relax, and then alternately trying to stretch out the burgeoning charley horses that seemed to be knotting up everywhere. She stiffened one leg, twisted to the left and then to the right and drew up her knee, then lifted her arms and neck, trying to stretch her back.

She was still shifting awkwardly when Dalton returned.

"What are you doing?"

"Charley horses," Taylor said and then gave a gasp and little whine as several clenched tight.

"Where?"

"Everywhere," she said, her body turning rigid. She could hardly move, and more knots popped up all over her body.

Dalton dropped his collected items onto a chair and whipped back the covers. He turned her over and began massaging her with long strokes, up and down her legs, arms, and back, up her neck and down again. Her clothing made it difficult for him to dig in the way he needed, and after a minute of not having much effect, he flipped her back over, yanked her shirt over her head, then unzipped her pants and pulled them off.

He resumed stroking, finding knots and rubbing circles, pressing to get the muscles to ease. One by one, he found them until, at last, Taylor lay panting, tears leaking from her eyes, her body feeling battered.

Dalton continued to massage her, his touch growing lighter, and soothing.

She managed to roll onto her back. He'd turned her several times in the course of helping her.

"I'm okay, now. Thanks."

She knuckled the tears away, annoyed that she'd cried, but then, tears tended to be a body's response to pain, so there shouldn't be any shame in them.

She'd seen many, many, *many* brave men and women cry when she'd been overseas. They'd cried for loss, for exhaustion, for pain, for the things they had to do, for missing home.

She'd never think of even one of them as weak, and neither was she.

"If one pops again, say so. Don't try to tough it out," he told her before drawing up the covers, leaving her upper chest exposed.

"Hold still. Those scratches are ugly. Let's get them cleaned up."

"What about a heal-all?"

He shook his head. "I'd have to take the null off you and open the door back up to whoever attacked you. This way is safer."

He helped her lift up her head and slid a towel beneath her neck to absorb the excess hydrogen peroxide, then popped the cap and poured it over her. It bubbled in the wounds and ran cold down her neck. She shivered.

Dalton dabbed at the scratches with a towel, and then reached for a roll of gauze, scissors, and tape he'd found. He bandaged her up with deft hands. When he was through, he sat back, frowning down at her like she was a difficult puzzle.

She started to sit up.

"What are you doing?"

"Getting dressed so we can get out of here."

He shook his head. "You need to rest."

"We don't have time."

"This storm is giving us a little, but more importantly, your hands are shaking. You're suffering from shock. If you keep going, you're going to collapse. Your body needs time to settle back into itself."

He stood. "Sugar will help. I'll be back soon."

While he was gone, Taylor grabbed her shirt and pulled it on. What did it say about her that she was annoyed he didn't seem at all turned on by her being mostly naked and him running his hands all over her?

"You're batshit crazy, is what it says," she muttered.

She got her clothes back on and crawled back under the covers when she started to shiver. Dalton returned a short time later, carrying a silver tray loaded with a variety of foods. Taylor squirmed upright, putting pillows behind her as Dalton set the tray on the bed. She made a face.

"That looks revolting."

He'd loaded the tray with a bottle of maraschino cherries, grape jelly, dried apricots, a jar of sprinkles, a bar of baking chocolate, marshmallows, maple syrup, a couple of candy canes, and an assortment of hard candies.

"You need sugar and you need it quickly. Trust me. You're going to crash hard in a little bit. How much sugar you get down will mean the difference between a tolerable hangover and you wishing you were dead. Here, try the chocolate."

He held out the baking chocolate. She eyed it and then him.

"What?"

"You're serious? You want me to eat that?"

He blew out an exasperated breath. "Yes. I told you—"

"That I need sugar. Baking chocolate doesn't have any. It's unsweetened."

He scowled, staring down at the bar. "Chocolate without sugar? Why?"

"Sometimes you need extra chocolate flavor but not extra sugar for a recipe."

"Oh. That's . . . stupid." He tossed the bar aside and grabbed the jelly and a spoon. "This is a good option. It goes down quickly and is loaded with sugar."

Taylor shook her head and grabbed the apricots, putting a couple in her mouth. "No thanks. Not eating jelly directly from the jar, especially grape." She gave a shudder. "Talk about disgusting. Didn't they have anything like cookies or ice cream? How old are the candy canes, anyway? Christmas was months ago."

"They don't go bad. Promise to eat something while I'm gone, and I'll go look in the freezer for something better."

She gave an exaggerated sigh and picked up the marshmallows and the container of apricots. "You can take the rest. I'm not touching those."

Dalton set the tray on the dresser within arm's reach and left again. Taylor ate the apricots and switched to the marshmallows, making a face as she ate the first fluffy white lump. The only good marshmallow was charred and sitting between two graham crackers on top of melting chocolate.

She popped it into her mouth and chewed, finally swallowed it down. She contemplated another but, instead, set the bag aside.

Five minutes later, Dalton returned. He scowled. "You promised to keep eating while I was gone."

"Actually, I didn't. I did try, but—" She gave a little shrug. "There's only so much disgusting you can shove in your mouth before you've just got to say no."

He growled and then shrugged. "You'll be pissed at yourself when you wake up and you're too wiped out to move. Plus, you'll probably sleep for at least four hours the way you're going."

That struck home, and Taylor sat up taller. They didn't have that kind of time. "What did you bring me?"

He held out a steaming cup. It contained coffee, plus a healthy dose of sugar. Taylor took it, drinking it about halfway before she stopped. "It's lukewarm."

"So you can drink it fast. Which you're doing."

She drank again. "What else did you bring me?"

He produced a roll of frozen cookie dough.

Taylor pounced in it. He'd already cut one end open.

"What's that for?" she asked, eyeing the spoon he proffered.

"To eat it with."

"It's frozen." She took a bite, closing her eyes as the sweetness hit her taste-buds.

"This is so good," she said. She held out the log of dough. "Want some?"

He eyed her, then reached out and pinched the glob off the end and put it in his mouth.

She'd eaten barely a quarter of the dough when a wall of exhaustion slammed into her. Her hands went limp, and the dough dropped to her lap. She looked at Dalton, her eyelids almost too heavy to open.

"Tired now."

"You were due. Let's hope we got enough into you."

He helped ease her down and pulled the covers up before sitting down in the chair opposite to the bed.

"What're you doing?" Taylor asked, her voice starting to slur.

"Watching you. Making sure you don't get attacked again." He combed his fingers through his hair. She liked it loose. It was sexy. She liked a man with long hair. She barely refrained from saying so.

"But you're tired, too," she said instead.

"I'll be fine."

"At least lay down." She patted the bed. Or kind of tapped her fingers.

"I don't want to fall asleep."

"Jamie and Leo say I snore and they can't sleep in the same room. You should be safe enough."

"I've slept fine in a war zone. Snoring isn't going to help a whole lot," he said with a half grin.

"What if I want the company?"

That wiped away his smile. "Do you?"

"Just as long as you don't expect me to be energetic." She yawned. "Now come here and be a giant teddy bear for me."

He looked bemused but took off his boots and lay on the bed beside her, though he remained on top of the covers. She gave a little gurgle of laughter that quickly faded. "You don't want to get into bed with me."

"I don't want to be trapped under the blankets if something happens," he corrected.

"Mmhm," was her only reply as she snuggled up to him, tossing her arm over his chest and pillowing her head on his shoulder. He wouldn't let anything happen to her. Odd how much she'd begun to trust that.

TAYLOR HAD WOKEN up with a hangover more than a few times in her life, but she'd never felt as bad as waking up after the magic attack.

Her eyes opened, and her lids seemed to stick to the surface of her eyes and scrape across them as she blinked. Something had died in her mouth, but not before somebody poured acid down her throat. Her head felt like a dozen drunk dwarves were dancing around inside, banging hammers against her brain while screaming death-metal songs.

She groaned and buried her face into her pillow. Only it wasn't a pillow, it was Dalton's arm. She lay on her side, with him spooned up behind her, his right arm under her head, his left curved around her waist.

"How do you feel?" he asked in a whisper.

She groaned again, and the slight sound made the dwarves pound her brain harder and faster.

"Need aspirin. Ibuprofen. Tylenol. A bullet to the head. Anything to help with this headache."

He smoothed her hair back out of her face, his touch gentle. "Give it a few minutes. It should subside a little, and then we'll get you in the shower and feed you. By then, you'll feel a lot better."

"You're showering with me?"

He tensed, and then heaved a sigh. "If I didn't know better, I'd say you were flirting with me."

"That would be ridiculous," she said, wishing the dwarves in her head would take a chill pill already.

"Ridiculous," he repeated dryly.

She wondered if he realized the lady was protesting too much and in fact Taylor *had* been flirting, tantalized by the idea of getting to see the scenery under his shirt. How would his long hair look cascading down over his pecs? Inquiring minds seriously wanted to know.

"How's your head? Better yet?" he asked.

"Not so much."

"Okay, let's try this." He pushed her away a little and rubbed her neck, his thumbs stroking up into her hair.

"Oh, fuck, that feels good," she moaned. "Please never stop."

"That could get awkward."

"Fuck awkward. Your fingers are magic. You missed your calling as a masseuse."

After a couple of minutes, Taylor had to admit that the pain had receded considerably and found herself alone in the shower while Dalton returned to the kitchen to fix breakfast. Or lunch. How long had she been asleep?

She'd turned the water on as hot as she could stand, and practically parboiled herself in the process. But when she stepped out, she felt mostly human again, though her neck looked like she'd lost a fight with a barbed-wire fence.

She found an unused toothbrush and some toothpaste and brushed her teeth before getting dressed, deciding not to bandage her neck again. She also found a hairdryer and took a few minutes to dry her hair so it didn't freeze solid when she went outside.

By the time she had herself put back together and returned to the kitchen, Dalton had scrambled some eggs, fried bacon, and made a stack of pancakes.

"Nice," she said, sliding into a seat and reaching for her fork. She'd meant to make a comment about him making enough to feed an entire football team, but all of a sudden she was ravenous. She dove into her meal like a lion taking down a wildebeest. The only time she paused was to sip on her coffee.

Dalton watched her in amusement, finishing his own breakfast, which was humiliatingly smaller than hers. It was still morning, but much later than she'd wanted. Almost eleven.

After finishing, she cleared their dishes, stacking them in the sink for the maid service, whenever they showed up.

"I can't figure out if the house owners got caught out in the weather, if they're snowbirds and have gone south for the winter, or if they are on vacation or maybe bugged out when the senator implemented martial law."

"Too much fresh food for them to have gone away for the season. If they were just elsewhere in town, the servants would still be here. Vacation is more likely. Otherwise, the place would be a mess. They'd have gone through the house like a whirlwind to take their valuables."

"At least they are out of range of the senator and his goons."

"Lucky them. Are you ready? We should go."

She poured coffee into the travel mug she'd found and followed. He held her hand outside to the car. The wind roared, and she could barely see a foot in front of her. The storm had definitely grown worse. What the hell was going on?

Dalton opened the door for her before going around and climbing in behind the wheel, starting the SUV to heat it up. Taylor took a moment to check her cell again.

"Still no signal." She'd been checking after ten or fifteen minutes since she'd climbed out of bed.

"You still want to proceed as planned?"

She nodded. "That's what Riley is expecting. If we don't do it, we could screw things up."

He nodded in a resigned way and put the vehicle in gear.

"You've got maybe an hour or two to figure out how you're going to convince Tyrell not to hold you hostage and get your dad's brain-jockey on board with the plan."

"I will," she said, with far more confidence than she felt. Which was to say, any confidence at all. She'd been thinking about her approach since she'd volunteered for this job, and she still didn't have a good plan.

"Maybe you should tell them that you brought me in as a prisoner."

He shook his head. "Vernon won't buy it."

"Okay, maybe you brought me in to protect me."

"Won't stop Tyrell from holding you hostage to get your sister's cooperation."

Taylor chewed her lower lip. She wished Vernon wasn't such a wild card. He'd already been one before they found out he had a brain-jockey, and now he was a total mystery. She assumed the jockey was spying on Tyrell, so it had to be a competitor or enemy. Of course, Tyrell could have had it done, but why? If he wanted Vernon's loyalty, he'd only have to instill that. Not much point in wasting a brain-jockey if he knew Vernon couldn't be anything but totally faithful.

If it was someone spying on Tyrell, it would give her leverage. The jockey wouldn't want Tyrell learning what he was up to. If he did find out, Tyrell would kill Vernon, which meant the brain-jockey would lose close-up access to Tyrell, probably permanently. Tyrell wouldn't fall for a scheme like it again.

She pondered this out loud to get Dalton's take. "If the jockey cooperates,

Vernon should be able to help us get away from Tyrell, should Tyrell try to lock us down."

"It's a good thought. The hard part is going to be getting Vernon alone without surveillance. Electronic or magical."

Taylor nodded agreement. "Maybe I could whisper in Vernon's ear while you distracted Tyrell. Or slip a note in his pocket. I could even write something on my arm and push up my sleeve so he can read it, and then pull the sleeve down again."

"What kind of message? It couldn't be long. He'd have to read it in a matter of seconds."

She considered for a few minutes. Then it came to her. "Not a note. A picture. A spider. Brain-jockeys are also called spiders."

He nodded slowly. "Could work, but how would he know you wanted to talk to him?"

"I'd hope it would be obvious by the fact that I hadn't announced it to Tyrell."

"Better to be sure."

He had a point. "I could write the word *talk* next to it."

"Or *negotiate*. But if Tyrell saw that, he might put it together. It's a big risk."

His hands flexed on the steering wheel and tightened, like he was trying to keep from punching the dash.

"This whole plan is a huge risk from start to finish. But unless one of us comes up with a better idea, I don't see a choice."

He gave a little shake of his head. "I don't either."

Less than an hour later as they pulled up in front of Tyrell's compound, neither had come up with anything else.

"I should write it on me now. I don't know if I'll have privacy to do it later, plus I may need to flash it right away."

Luckily, there were several pens in the console, along with a number of other handy supplies. Taylor found a black felt pen and pushed up her sleeve.

"I think you're going to have to draw it," she said, twisting her arm to look at where she wanted the message to go. "I want it to be readable with my arm extended, but close to the crook of my elbow."

She stretched her arm out toward him and laid it on the console and handed him the pen.

"I'm not exactly an artist."

"Do it like this." She pulled a notebook out of the eyeglasses slot beneath the navigation system and tore out a page. She drew a body shaped like a figure eight with an oval bottom, and then gave it eight legs. "Might be a good idea to color in the body."

He took back the pen and held her arm, his reddish skin dark against her ghostly white. He gave her a long look and then bent to make the drawing. Beneath it, he wrote *negotiate*, then blew lightly on the ink to dry it.

When he let go, Taylor nodded. "Good job."

His jaw tightened, and he looked out the front windshield and then back at her.

"Anything happens, if we get separated, I will come for you."

"I know."

"Do you?" He shook his head and touched the drawing with the tip of his finger, before looking back at her. "I won't let anything happen to you."

She put her hand over his. "You aren't responsible if something happens to me. Not your monkeys, not your circus."

His hand turned over and wrapped hers, his fingers tightening to the point of pain. "If something happens to you—"

He broke off, his mouth snapping shut, his jaw knotting. "If something happens to you, it will be over my dead body. I mean that."

"No. There's far more at stake than me. Our priority has to be getting Vernon to agree to go with Arnow to the senator and take him down. It's the only way to stop this netting up of talents and putting them in camps. People are going to go to jail for nothing more than what they are. Some could get killed for it. We can't let that happen."

He stiffened, his chin jutting, his eyes narrowing. "*That* is your priority. *You* are mine."

"But—"

He let go of her hand and reached for the door handle. "Suck it up, Taylor, and get used to it. I'm not going to get in your way, but I *am* going to make sure you get out of here alive and whole, or die trying."

Chapter 15

Riley

PRICE HAD SAID sixteen hours, and I almost made it. I woke up just ten minutes short. He held me against him.

"Did you sleep?" I asked with a yawn.

"Off and on. How do you feel?"

"Better," I said grudgingly. I hated telling him he was right. It would only encourage him.

"That must've hurt. Did you break something admitting that?" His chuckle rumbled through his chest.

I poked him in the side. "Just because you're right once, doesn't mean you'll ever be right again."

"Says the sore loser."

I stuck my tongue out at him and then sat up. He groaned as the covers fell away. He snaked out his arm to pull me toward him.

"Come here."

I resisted, pushing away his arm. "Uh-uh. There's a price for gloating. Anyway, we've got things to do."

He tightened his grip, pulling me over to splay on top of him. His hips bucked up against mine, his morning wood rubbing against me in just the right spot. I moaned. He smiled smugly.

"Come on, pay the Price for gloating," he said, punning on his name.

"*You're* the one who has to pay."

"I'm good with that. I like to be timely on my debts, so I'll just get started."

He rolled me onto my back and nuzzled my neck in a most delightful way. My legs fell open, and he ground his hips against mine. Sweet heat washed through me, an ache for him blooming in my belly.

"I like your revenge," he murmured, nibbling down my neck to my shoulder, and down between my breasts. I did my best not to react. He took it as a challenge.

He lifted himself up on his hands and knees and nibbled around the outsides of my breasts, holding himself over me so that his lips were all that touched me. I bit my lips and clenched my hands on the sheets, staring up at the ceiling.

Price slowly spiraled in on my left breast until his lips closed on just my nipple. He rolled it between his lips, and I took a sharp breath, my hips shifting. Then he flicked the sensitive bud with his tongue, shooting a zing! of electricity ricocheting through my body. He repeated the treatment on the right side, going back and forth with slow deliberation.

I wanted more, wanted him to suck down and fill me at the same time. But I refused to cave. He stepped up his assault, scraping his teeth lightly over each nipple, and that earned him a gasp. I arced my back up toward him, offering myself.

He pulled back. "Did that hurt? It sounded like it hurt. Maybe I should stop." He sat back on his haunches between my knees, looking down at me, his gaze running down over me and back up. "Do you want me to stop?"

I wanted more than anything to say no, to not let him win, but I didn't have a lot of willpower when it came to Price. I shook my head, and I ran my fingertips up the outsides of his thighs, stopping on his hips.

"Say it, Riley." He brushed his knuckles against a nipple. "I want to hear you ask."

"You're an asshole."

He smiled wickedly. "I know. But you still have to say it."

I debated only a moment. I ached with a hollowness and incompleteness, that only he could fill, and my body was on fire. I licked my dry lips.

"Please."

He smiled, slow and smug. "Please what?"

"Please get your ass to work and make me feel good."

"You're so romantic," he said, bending down over me again. He spread my legs wider and pinned me, bringing me to the edge of pleasure and then backing off. Over and over until I was panting and writhing and swearing at him. I wasn't keeping my voice all that quiet, either. I had a feeling Price wanted to drive me past control. To know that he could send me over the edge. To prove it.

And that's what he proceeded to do. By the time he slid inside me, I was making incoherent noises between begging him to fuck me. I exploded the moment he drove deep into me. He held himself still, sucking my breasts as my orgasm rolled through me. Before it quite ended, he began slow strokes, triggering an avalanche of little orgasms that did nothing to assuage the ache that had begun to build again when he started moving.

In between kissing me, and licking and biting my breasts, he murmured praises in my ears, encouraging me, telling me how good I made him feel, telling me how much he loved me and how much he loved being inside me.

Before I could come again, he withdrew and pulled me over onto my knees. He entered me again, one arm wrapping my waist to steady me, his other hand tugging on my nipples. I felt the slow shattering beginning and let out a whining moan. He moved the hand down to massage my clit, continuing his steady assault.

Once again I exploded, my arms and legs shaking with the force of it. I cried out loudly. It wasn't until then he dropped both of his hands to my hips, gripping hard and speeding his thrusts. My orgasm didn't seem to end, and suddenly he was there with me. He let out a loud groan, calling out my name as he thrust deep, holding me tight against him as he came.

When the last quake had subsided, he relaxed, releasing me. I melted facedown onto the bed. He lay down half on top of me, stroking soothing hands over me as he pressed kisses onto my shoulders and along the back of my neck.

"I love you," he said.

I turned my head to look at him. His earlier light tone had gone, and now I heard the stark fear. That what we were about to do would kill me and he'd lose me forever.

I rolled onto my side, cupping my hand around his face. "I love you. I'm not done loving you. I plan to be alive on this planet until I'm old and wrinkled. Don't give up on me."

He lifted his hand to grasp mine. "You're the best thing that's ever happened to me. I wish we'd found each other sooner."

That's when I realized that making love to me had been his way of saying goodbye. Just in case. Because this would probably be the last little bit of time we had together before we headed into war with the senator.

That gutted me.

I wanted to reassure him, but what could I possibly say? I was going to take risks, and the odds were against me.

Then again, the odds had been against me before, and I'd dodged certain death several times in the last couple months. No reason I couldn't do it again.

Wash, rinse, and repeat.

"Two weeks, just you and me, as soon as this is over, right?"

He blinked at the sudden change of subject, and then one corner of his mouth kicked up. "Two weeks."

"Somewhere warm. Like a tropical island. I'm tired of snow."

"You've got it."

"And no phones."

"Sounds like heaven."

The instant he said it, reality intruded and his smile faded. At the moment, heaven didn't sound so great.

I nodded and sat up. "All right. The faster we get this done, the faster we get to our vacation. Let's do this."

I cleaned up and got dressed. Outside, the wind howled. The storm had worsened as Price had predicted. At least it would have the senator's troops pinned down, not doing any damage, and buying us time. It would also save us from going back to Savannah's and destroying the mansion.

Only Touray and Maya remained downstairs, the latter curled up asleep under a blanket on a bed of cushions. I let her sleep and went into the kitchen and put coffee on. I found cold cuts, sliced cheeses, vegetables, and fruit in the refrigerator. I'd made a couple of roast beef and cheddar sandwiches by the time Price joined me. He'd showered, and his hair was wet.

I handed him a plate and pointed him toward the refrigerator. He tossed me a bottle of orange juice and snagged one for himself. We sat down at the little bistro table in the corner.

"I think I have an idea," I said after eating my sandwich. I toyed with a couple cherry tomatoes, pushing them around my plate with a stick of celery.

"That sounds ominous."

"It could be. Or it could be good."

"Well, at least it's intriguing. Care to share with the rest of the class?" He drank from his orange juice, watching me as he did, eyes serious.

"I've been thinking about my astral-self."

He set the juice bottle down, turning it in his fingers. "That makes two of us."

"Maya said it couldn't be fixed, but I got to thinking about after we broke you out of the FBI. On the way out, you guys fed me power, and I was able to erase our trace. So I was going to ask you all to do it again, this time so that I could help Touray. I thought that using yours might protect my astral-self."

I paused, and Priced nodded for me to go on, his expression wary.

"But then I thought maybe I can fix myself while I'm doing all of this. Right before that rescue when you cascaded, I was able to leave myself and go inside you, and I think I connected with your astral-self. If I did, it means I can touch it. I can manipulate it. I can maybe even fix it. I'm not sure exactly how I'd manage it, but I think it's possible with your help. Yours, Leo's, Jamie's, and Patti's."

I glanced back down to where I gripped the edge of the table.

"Only thing is, the attempt could backfire and kill me. It could also kill me before I had the chance to try, since I'd have to go into the same space I did when you cascaded, and that sucks a lot of energy, and I'm guessing it will put serious stress on me."

Price didn't say anything, and after a minute, when I couldn't stand the silence anymore, I looked up at him. He had his elbows on his knees and was watching me somberly.

"What do you want from me?"

Thud. Right to the center of the problem, no sugarcoating or easing up on it. I could have dodged, pretended he was talking about how I needed him to help me, but we'd both know I was just delaying the inevitable.

I gave a helpless little shrug. "I don't know."

"Permission?" He shook his head. "That's not you. You're more of the ask forgiveness after, type. So, what do you want to hear from me?"

I ran my tongue over the edges of my teeth as I thought about it. "I guess . . . I guess I want you to know—all of you: Jamie, Leo, Patti, Taylor, Cass, Arnow, and even Dalton and your brother—that I am fighting as hard as I can to stay alive, to stay here with you. That I'm not interested in suicide, that I don't have a death wish."

"Nobody thinks that."

I smiled. "If not a death wish, then very little regard for my own safety."

His smile was fleeting. "I'll give you that one."

"The thing is, even if I don't try and I survive helping your brother, I still have to trace Kensington back to his workshop. Then I'll have to help to make the weapon work. Either one of which is sure to kill me. You asked me not to take any risks I knew I couldn't survive. I don't know which will kill me, but I'm positive that one will. Unless I fix myself."

He didn't move as he absorbed my words, then scrubbed both hands over his face, running his fingers through his hair and knotting his hands behind his neck.

"It's the best hope you have of staying alive."

I nodded.

"Then you have to try." His voice had gone thick, and his hands fell into his lap.

Within the next hour or so, I'd either be dead or back to healthy. Within the next hour, Price's heart would either get ripped out of his chest or we'd have the hope of a future.

Good times.

WE MADE MORE sandwiches and cut into a cheesecake I found in the refrigerator while sorting out a plan for making this work.

A half hour later, the door opened and a gust of icy wind blew through. I heard boots stamping. Jamie laughed at something Leo said.

"You're late," I said as I went to see them.

Snow fell everywhere as they stripped off their coats, gloves, hats, and boots and they dusted off their pants.

"Shit's ugly out there," Leo said. He set aside the ski goggles he'd been wearing. "Must be a foot or more of new snow."

"Probably two," Patti said. "Which explains why we're late," she said to me, her gaze sweeping over me. "Please tell me you got some sleep."

I nodded, giving her a wry smile. "We've been eating. Are you hungry?"

"We got burgers just a couple hours ago," Patti said.

"I could eat," Leo said.

"Me, too," Jamie said.

Patti and I exchanged a long-suffering look, and I retreated into the kitchen. She joined me.

Price looked at me. "Do you want me to bring them up to speed? Or do you want to do it?"

"Up to speed about what?" Patti demanded, hands on her hips, glaring at me like she'd caught me sneaking out by myself.

"I had an idea," I said.

She shook her head. "Oh, hell. You getting ideas is always terrifying. What idea?"

"To try to heal myself." I looked at Price. "Do explain. I'll make some more sandwiches and pour coffee."

"Explain what?" Leo and Jamie stood in the broad opening of the kitchen.

"Riley's had an *idea*," Patti said dryly.

They both shot me suspicious looks. "What kind of idea?"

"Supposedly for her to heal herself," Patti said.

"Supposedly?" I echoed. "It *is*."

"If you're telling us the whole truth and not just select pieces," Leo said, tucking his hands under his armpits. "You like to leave out important parts."

"This time she's not," Price said, giving me a measuring look.

I gave a faint shake of my head. I hadn't lied or held anything back.

"Let's go in the other room. We'll get the fire going and you can warm up while I explain."

As they shuffled out, Patti looked over her shoulder at me. "Try not to accidentally poison us. You're not exactly known for your cooking."

I made a face. "It's sandwiches. I'm not exactly cooking."

"But you're very talented at fucking up food," Patti said, then sailed out before I could get the last word.

I worked slowly so that Price would have the chance to fully explain before I joined the scrum. I loaded everything on several plates that didn't match and brought them out. I offered Maya one first and then set the rest on the hearth.

A fire crackled in the fireplace, filling my house with the scent of woodsmoke. I breathed it in. I loved that smell. It reminded me of weekends when we were kids and a storm raged outside like it was now. We'd play games near the fire, or Taylor and I would watch as Jamie and Leo had contests over who could make something the fastest, using their metal talents to construct life-sized animals, intricate jewelry, boat replicas, and anything else we could think of.

"And you really think this could work?" Leo asked as he came to claim a sandwich. "Maya? What about you?"

She said nothing for a long moment. "I don't know. I've never heard of it being done. But then, I haven't heard of what you did to save Clay from cascading, either."

"It's my best shot," I said, standing so that the fire could heat my backside. "There's only one little problem."

"*Here* it is," Patti said, pointing an accusing finger at me. "You said you weren't hiding anything."

"I'm not. Hence me standing here with my lips moving trying to tell you."

"Okay, fine. What's the one little problem?"

"When Riley saved me, she went into cardiac arrest," Price said before I could. "I had to give her CPR. We're hoping that Maya will be able to heal any physical issues that derive from trying this."

"And that's a *little* problem," Jamie said.

"Little enough, considering Maya is here and an extraordinary tinker," I said. "Anyhow, it's this or just hope my astral-self doesn't disintegrate while I'm helping Gregg or tracking down the artifacts."

"Hope's a bitch," Leo muttered.

"And then you die," Patti finished. "Okay, I'm convinced. I'm in."

"Me, too," Jamie said.

"And me," added Leo.

I looked at Maya, who gave a little nod, her normally smiling face pinched with worry.

"Then it's a go. Finish eating and we'll get started."

Chapter 16

Riley

ONCE EVERYBODY had eaten their fill and we'd cleared the dishes, I went to sit between Price's outstretched legs. Leo and Jamie sat on either side, each touching Price.

"Where do you want me?" Patti asked. "In your lap?"

"Sit facing me so I can hold your hand."

When everybody was settled, I went over the plan one last time.

"Jamie and Leo, you're going to start. Feed Price energy. Price is going to braid together the energy from all three of you, and feed it to me. Hopefully, that will make it easier for me to pull on what I need."

I didn't bother telling them to stop if they started risking themselves. All three would totally agree, knowing full well they'd drain themselves to the last drop if that's what it took.

"Once I'm drawing on that power, it's Patti's turn at bat." I looked at her. "You've got the tricky one, and I have no idea if it will actually work. But I'm going to wrap my trace around my hand and grab yours. As soon as I do, I want you to put everything you've got into binding me to the here and now. That way, even if I come loose from my body, I'll have an anchor to keep me from getting sucked into the spirit realm."

"Does it even work that way?" Patti asked.

"Hell if I know, but this is the best plan we could come up with to keep my spirit pinned here. With any luck, even if I'm pulled from my body, I'll still be able to keep trying to repair my astral-self and then jump back into my corpse. Just don't get guilty and take the blame if it doesn't work. It won't be your fault. It won't be anybody's fault."

I glanced at my brothers to make sure they got the message, too. I couldn't see Price, but he'd blame himself no matter what I said. He had his hands around my waist, and I put mine over his and squeezed.

I turned my attention to Maya, who'd come to sit next to Patti, facing me.

"That's where you come in. Keep my body functioning so I've got somewhere to come back to."

She nodded.

I took a breath and blew it out. "All right then. Any questions?"

"Don't fuck up," Jamie said.

"Amen to that," Leo said.

"I love you. Do not leave me here on this earth alone with these animals," Patti said, her voice thick. She leaned forward and gave me a hard hug.

As she sat back, a drip of ice cold touched my neck and didn't melt.

I twisted around to look at Price. He'd put a tab on my neck, the same way he had when he'd hired me way back when. "Seriously?"

His somber eyes were misted over with white. He shrugged. "Seems prudent."

The first time he tabbed me hadn't been very long ago—a few months maybe— but it felt like years. Then when I told him to go away and leave me alone so I could sort out my feelings, he'd tabbed me again to tell me he'd wait for me. Thank God for that.

"Asshole." I said it softly, like an endearment, and then turned back around.

Tabs were magic's version of tracking chips. Putting one on me now was purely symbolic. It wouldn't survive the power surge I'd be getting. It was just Price's way of telling me he loved me and he'd follow me anywhere, whether heaven or hell. Figuratively, if not actually, though I wouldn't put it past him to try to find a way.

"Start any time."

I reached out toward Patti, palm down. She held her hand over mine. When I had my trace, I'd turn my hand over and she'd grab it. After that, everything was up to me.

As I waited for Price to feed power into me, I hardened my concentration. Last time I'd done anything like this, I'd gone into my trace so I could travel out of a prison. Then I'd gone down into my trace, cut through it, and made my way to Price's.

Each time, I had to sink down through a particularly dangerous spot. It was where my soul, what I supposed was my astral-self, lived inside me and attached to my trace. What made it dangerous was the fact that going into it was a religious experience. Both times I found myself lost in the joy and bliss of the place, if you could call it a place. It felt like becoming living sunshine, like becoming the entire world. The closest thing to heaven I'd ever experienced.

I couldn't afford to lose myself. I didn't have that kind of time. By the time I got it together, my astral-self could have shredded apart. I had to ignore the experience and immediately get to work. I had to triage myself and repair the worst problems, at least enough to stabilize myself and buy a little time to make full repairs.

If that was even possible.

No. I'd *make* it possible.

Power flowed into me from everywhere Price touched me.

I dropped into trace sight. Mine was easiest to spot. It didn't have the glowing jewel tones of everybody else's trace. Mine looked faded and graying, like the color had leached out.

If I didn't know I was in trouble already, that would have made it clear.

I clenched my teeth and reached into the spirit realm to grab it. The cold sank into my bones instantly, and my hand went numb. My body jerked and spasmed.

Fear exploded inside me. I had much less time than I thought.

I pulled my trace and hand out of the spirit realm and turned it over. I saw, but was too numb to feel, Patti's hand close over mine. I felt the binding take hold.

Hallelujah. That part of the plan was working. So far. I had no idea if it would keep me on this side of the spirit realm barrier, but at least it was a chance.

"Make sure Patti doesn't run out of juice," I croaked. "It's working."

I dropped down inside myself, going deeper and deeper until the pull of it took over, drawing me inside.

One thing I hadn't mentioned to the others was I couldn't really see the space. It was really just a blur and still was. But now, instead of feeling incandescent with wonder and delight, I felt only a mild surge. The pulse of it was weak and uncertain, without any rhythm.

Before, I'd been overwhelmed with glorious feeling. Now, the feeling was exponentially reduced, like being alone in a still lake at night, with only a flicker of movement around me to indicate that any life existed. Only in this case, that flicker was the embers of bliss and joy against ominous stillness.

As I took stock of where I was, I felt my heart stuttering far away and my lungs hardening and shriveling up. What did I do now? I'd hoped when I got to this point, that I'd know. That instinct would guide me.

I pushed my awareness outward, trying to get a sense of what I was working with. I began to visualize it against my mind's eye. It looked like cobwebs in a cave no one had ever entered. Strands hung loose or knotted in clumps. It seemed like the cobwebs should have formed a lacy cloth, but as if that cloth had rotted and fallen apart in places, leaving a moldering, tattered mess. Worse, the lace had a pattern to it. Lots of changing patterns, like a fancy tablecloth.

What would happen if I fixed things but didn't get those patterns right?

Nothing good if I didn't perform some triage and start getting to work on repairing myself, which I still didn't know how to do. But I'd figure it out, because my other choice was death, and I wasn't at all down for that.

As I considered the wreck of myself, I wished I'd taken up knitting or crocheting or weaving or, hell, even sailing.

A spasm ran through my body, and the energy of my astral-self stuttered and a section crumpled in on itself. Slices of pain knifed through me, and the entire mess of me rippled on an invisible wind. I could feel it splitting, like a threadbare sheet finally giving way. The power they were feeding me to fix myself was simultaneously ripping me apart. Ironic that. I needed power to fix what power destroyed and kept destroying.

I was out of time. My death had begun. Or rather, it had crested a mountain and was running full tilt toward the bottom where I'd smash to smithereens.

I drew on the magic from Price and my brothers, pulling it into me. Fire seared through me. Not my body, but my astral-self. My soul.

Pushing outward again, I brushed up against the hanging tatters. I shuddered. The feeling was intrusive and sent chills of wrongness and violation racing through me.

It was as if I'd stirred my fingers through my brain or poked at my heart, only much worse than either of those could be. I shouldn't be here. I shouldn't be touching this part of myself.

Ripples of faltering quivers juddered through the tangle of myself, and soon the entire thing shook erratically. I couldn't feel my body, but I had a sense of crumbling weakness and faltering.

I lost hold of the power from Price. It poured into me like a rain of fire, further adding to the damage. I pulled back up out of my core to regain some control.

Pain slammed into me. My physical body convulsed in a violent seizure. I couldn't breathe, and my heart pounded like a jackhammer. A grip on my ankle and worms wriggling through me. Maya had begun her work.

I caught hold of the energy from Price and dove back into myself. I immediately pushed out against the tatters, ignoring my nearly unbearable response.

I had to weave myself back together. Previously, when I tried to help Price, I'd forged a knife of energy to cut through my trace and push out to him. Now I had to make a needle and thread.

I gathered the energy filling me and focused. My attention zeroed down to extruding power into a long hard point. The first time I tried, I managed to stretch it out and thin it down, but as soon as I tried to sharpen the top into a point, the whole thing melted.

I gathered myself again, feeling the strain of trying to hold the hold the power in shape, even as the part of me capable of holding power was disintegrating before my eyes. With each snapped thread, I drew closer to dying. Maybe I was already dead and all that was keeping me here were Maya and Patti.

I honed the tip of the power, thinning and hardening it with mental taps and shaving the point like a pencil. More than once, the energy softened and started to lose shape. I kept at it, refusing to give up. Refusing to fail.

Again and again, I exerted my will over the magic and, at last, I had a stubby point that remained, even when I moved my attention away from it. It attached to me with a thick cord of energy. I'd been holding the flow in check. As it filled me, it stretched and pushed against my astral web, speeding the damage.

Even so, that pressure helped by lifting and stretching out the web, allowing me to see more of its shape and the gaping holes within it.

My first attempt at stitching together one of the holes was pitiful. My manipulation of the needle was clumsy. I stabbed through a piece of my web, and the pain overwhelmed me. Everything contracted inward, and if I'd had a mouth, I would have screamed.

I lost track of everything. I didn't know for how long. When I came back to myself, I fought despair. Everything I'd managed to do so far, I'd lost. The needle had vanished. My hold on the power had vanished. I was exhausted.

All the same, I couldn't give up.

I retreated to gather the power and built the needle again. It seemed to take forever, and holding the power was growing increasingly more difficult. As my astral web inflated again, it hardly seemed possible that I could begin to fix it. It was now more holes than anything else, and huge swaths of it curled up like fists of bramble or hung like the rotten sails of a ghost ship.

I decided to start small, though everything in me screamed to stop the worst first. But I needed to figure out how to do that, and that meant starting where I could more easily maneuver the needle and Frankenstein myself back together.

I started with a smaller tear. I took great care to weave the needle in and out between threads and not stab through. I essentially laced the two pieces together and moved to the next small hole. This one couldn't be pulled together. I had to recreate a section. Or at least a patch.

I turned the needle around one of the remaining threads and drew the line of energy to the other side and looped it around to anchor it. Back and forth I went, weaving a checkerboard net to fill the hole.

I moved to a slightly larger hole and repeated the experience, though this time I had to tie more knots in the cross-hatching threads, then weave through diagonally to strengthen the new fabric.

Just those few repairs made it almost impossible to continue. Pushing the needle out had become an exercise in torture. Like dragging myself across hot coals.

I had so very far to go.

I tackled a big hole next. I needed to, if I hoped to keep myself alive and strong enough to finish.

I didn't go for finesse. I zigzagged and stitched in and out and across and down and around. It was a mess. But as I filled in the gap, the dried, crispy, black edges of my astral web took on light and energy, softening into something alive. From it, I felt an echo of the joy and bliss that I'd felt so long ago.

When I finished that patch, I still felt like I'd been put through a meat grinder, but I could still keep going.

I moved on to another big patch, and then another. My repairs were exactly what you might expect a demented spider to weave while in the middle of having a stroke. But I didn't need them to be pretty. I needed them to be fixed.

And they worked. As I completed them, I felt a slow leeching inward of strength. Galvanized, I kept going.

When I came to a spot where I was going to have to run my needle through part of the web and not around it, I hesitated and then braced myself. This was so going to hurt.

I stabbed through the silky membrane. I'd been wrong. It didn't hurt. I could have handled that. This was so much more. So much worse.

I felt like I was stuck on the edge of dying: swimming in a vat of acid, buried in red-hot coals, gnawed apart by swarms of piranhas, torn apart in every direction, flayed layer by layer to the bone, to the marrow, until there should have been nothing left.

And then it was gone.

A moment of infinite pain, and out the other side. I rested, collecting myself, the echoes of the moment reverberating through me.

When I could function again, I had to re-form my needle yet again, but this time I didn't have to retreat to connect to the power and shaping the magic took no time at all.

I finished closing that spot and systematically finished the rest, deciding that if I had to stab through again, I'd leave it to the last.

Luckily, I didn't have to. By the time I finished, the feeling of utter bliss and incandescence had intensified to what I remembered. I allowed myself to bask in the feeling for a few minutes before retreating out into reality.

When I opened my eyes, I found myself slumped awkwardly over one of Price's thighs, my head resting on Leo's extended leg, with Patti and Maya still holding to me.

"Riley?"

Leo noticed I was back first. He pulled his hand from Price's shoulder and dropped from his seat on the hearth, grabbing me before my head could *thunk* onto the floor.

"Riley? Are you okay?" He sounded ragged. He'd gone pale and a little gray, his eyes bloodshot and his normally chiseled features looking gaunt.

"I'm okay." I promptly broke into a wracking cough, turning on my side.

The flow of energy from Price broke, and he pulled me up against his chest, rubbing my back.

"Here's some water," Jamie said.

I took the cup gladly and sipped as soon as I could manage. The wet seeped into my desert-dry throat, and the coughing subsided. I panted against Price a moment, then pushed away to look at everyone.

"You did it," Maya said in wonder, eyes white. "You repaired your astralself. How?"

"I think it might be a tracer ability," I said. "The web is the source of your trace, which let me *see* it, so I used magic to weave it back together."

She nodded. "It appears strong."

"It feels it."

I looked around at my brothers, Patti, and Price. They all looked similarly gaunt and gray, eyes bloodshot.

"How bad was it?" I asked.

"Not bad," Jamie lied with a dismissive shrug. "All in a day's work. I could eat though."

"Sugar," Maya said and disappeared into the kitchen.

She brought back a bag of dried cranberries. Jamie made a face at them but took a handful and passed them to Leo as Maya returned to the kitchen.

The bag was almost empty when she came back with a big bag of marshmallows and a box of chocolate bars. Someone had planned for s'mores.

"If we're going to eat those, we might as well do it right," Leo said and went to rummage in the kitchen, returning with a box of graham crackers and several roasting forks. He stabbed marshmallows onto two.

In the course of building my place, he and Jamie had made a little roasting box to the side of the main fire just for this purpose. Now he held them inside, and in no time they were golden crisp. He pulled them out and put them on the graham crackers and chocolate Jamie had readied for him.

I got the first one, which I passed to Patti. She protested, and I grabbed her hand and set the gooey sandwich on it.

"I feel so much better than any of you look. I can wait."

She took it and so did the others. I took over roasting duty while Leo scarfed his down.

"For the record," I said, "fixing myself was rough, but by the time I was done, I felt like I was back to normal. No pain from drawing on power, and I felt whole. *Feel* whole."

"Thank God," Price muttered. Marshmallow clung to the corners of his mouth, and crumbs littered his chest and lap.

I grinned at him, and he slowly smiled back, as if he was finally allowing himself to believe I really was okay.

After we finished the s'mores, we moved on to real food. Like all of them, I felt like I couldn't eat enough to fill the gaping void in my stomach.

They opted to make pizza and adjourned to the kitchen. Luckily, all of them had cooking skills and didn't require my help, which was good since I was the dictionary definition of kitchen disaster.

"What about Ben?" I asked with a frown, reminded of Patti's business partner. His talent was cooking, and his food was amazing. "You were supposed to bring him and his family here to be safe."

She made a face and shook her head. "He refused. Said not to worry. Because telling me that will totally make me stop. Stupid men."

"Hey, now, I resent that," Jamie said.

"And? Did you think you'd hidden your stupidity? Remember I *know* you. I've *seen* your dumb in action. Do you want me to remind you? I can give you a list, but it might take a couple of days to get through it all."

Jamie opened his mouth to say something, thought the better of it, and closed it again.

"Now you're showing evidence of having a brain," Patti said, then handed him a couple cans of black olives. "Be useful now, and chop these up."

"We've got this," Leo said, turning to look at me, Maya, and Price. "Why don't you all rest or something."

"First tell me what happened on this side of things," I said, munching on some potato chips. "I'm pretty sure I died or came close."

"You did." Price tipped up the beer he'd taken from the fridge and guzzled down half of it. He set it down and lifted me out of my chair before sitting down and pulling me onto his lap. He wrapped one arm around my waist and picked his beer back up with the other hand.

"So, what happened?" I asked, putting an arm around Price's neck and crossing my fingers that the chair could hold us both. If binding my trace had worked, we could maybe try the same thing with Touray.

"Wasn't long into it before you started having seizures," Patti said in a matter-of-fact way, but the way she attacked the onions rather than chopping showed that she was feeling a lot more than she was willing to let on.

"Maya started doing her thing—" Price began.

"I wanted to be inside you and ready," Maya said, having sat in my other bistro chair. Her eyes were back to normal. She drank a glass of orange juice.

Patti nodded. "Wasn't more than a few minutes after that something hit my binding like a freight train. Holding it took about everything I had. Leo ended up coming over and giving me a little of his juice when things started really looking dicey. After awhile, the pressure suddenly left."

"I was keeping your heart and lungs going," Maya said. "Then you took over again. I kept monitoring you, but you kept getting stronger." Her brows furrowed. "Until near the end. You suddenly seized again, and it felt like your heart was going to explode."

"When I stabbed through myself the second time," I said. "It hurt a little."

"Stabbed through yourself?" Jamie and Price chorused.

I explained what had happened and how I'd been able to repair my astral-self.

"So, like I said, I feel back to normal. Strong," I said.

"Good for you," Patti said. "But don't fucking do it again." She jabbed the knife she held in my direction.

"Or you'll kill me? Because that's what I was trying to stop."

Price's arm tightened on me, not appreciating my joke.

"No, but you'd never get another good meal at the diner again."

I made a face. That was a real threat. I ate most of my meals there, and Ben, Patti's business partner, was the best cook on the planet. But if Patti didn't like you or wanted revenge, your food would come out impossible to eat. Maybe it would be burned, but more often it would be covered in ghost pepper sauce and burn your tongue off in just one bite, or covered in a mound of salt, or maybe it would be dried so hard you'd crack a tooth on it. She could get creative, and Ben was smart enough to do whatever she wanted.

"At least this means that between the two of us, we should be able to keep Touray's spirit from crossing over when we kill him," I said.

Another thought occurred to me. If I could get ahold of the senator's trace, could I just pull his spirit out of his body? I'd forced a poltergeist to cross over when I'd gone after the hostages. The ghost had been helping Savannah's psychopath son, and in the end, I'd gotten rid of him by shoving him into the spirit realm where he belonged.

"I don't like that look," Jamie said.

I tucked my idea away for later and looked at him. He was leaning back against the counter, arms folded as he stared at me. Patti and Leo had also stopped what they were doing to look at me.

"What?"

"You've got that 'idea' look again. The one that always means you're about to do something dangerously stupid," he said.

"Don't you mean stupidly dangerous?"

"That too. What's going on in that twisted little brain of yours?"

"I was just thinking—"

"I hate it when she starts thinking," Leo said.

"You should talk," Patti said. "Not that I disagree, by any means, but the two of you are just as bad as she is."

"Not even close," Jamie protested. "How many times have we almost died compared to Riley?"

"That's a good question. Care to answer? I'm betting you've had a lot more close calls than you've ever let on."

Jamie's only response was a shrug and a little smile.

"Exactly what I thought." Patti looked at me. "Let's hear this idea of yours."

"I was just thinking, what if I could pull the senator's spirit right out of him? Pull it up like a weed?"

Before anybody could answer, another idea struck me. I sat up straight, my eyes popping wide.

"What if I could pull him out and put somebody else inside? Somebody could wear him like a senator suit."

Chapter 17

Taylor

TAYLOR HAD TO admit she was a little bit terrified. She and Dalton were about to be at Jackson Tyrell's mercy. She had a feeling he didn't have a lot of mercy going for him.

On top of that, Dalton's declaration that he'd get her out safely or die trying made her feel . . . she wasn't entirely sure how it made her feel. On the one hand, a little warm and fuzzy a man would do that for her, refuse to leave her behind. Of course, back in Afghanistan, even for private companies like hers, that was the standard. Nobody left behind. In the teams, Dalton had been steeped in that brotherhood, so it might not be particularly personal.

Still, it *felt* personal.

And it obligated her. She'd expected to go into Tyrell's with the expectation that all sacrifices might be necessary to complete her mission. She hadn't thought about Dalton in that equation. She'd figured he'd cover his own ass, and he had Vernon in his corner. But if he was going to put himself on the line for her—*really* put himself on the line—then shouldn't she be willing to do the same?

And if she did, would that mean screwing up the mission?

The thought knotted up her stomach, and deep down she knew she couldn't let that happen. Their tiny little group of crusaders was the only thing standing between internment camps and the city's talented, many of whom were elderly or children. Not to mention ordinary working people.

Diamond City definitely needed to change and reform, but the senator's solution wasn't the right one. Not by a long shot.

Once again, Dalton came around the SUV and held her hand as he guided her through the blizzard. She couldn't tell anything about where they were. The snow was more than a foot deep, drifting deeper where the wind piled it up.

They stopped at a gate. Dalton kept hold of her as he slogged down along the iron scrollwork to a guardhouse built into the towering brick wall. He pounded on the door with his gloved fist. Snow and wind muffled the sound. He beat on it again, and it opened, floodlights flaring all around.

The man inside held an AK up to his shoulder, the red laser sight hitting Dalton on the chest. He let go of Taylor's hand and stepped in front of her, raising his hands in the air as he did. She pulled out her .45 and stepped back and to the side, taking aim at the guard. The wind and snow disguised her form.

"Who are you? What do you want?" The guard had to shout to be heard.

"I'm here to see Vernon Brussard."

"In this fucking weather? He expecting you?"

Dalton shook his head. "No. Call him. Tell him Dalton's here. With his daughter. He'll want to see us."

The guard scowled and eased sideways to look past Dalton. "Where?"

"Right here. Lower your weapon." Taylor stepped into sight, holding her gun just behind her thigh.

The guard flicked a glance at her. "Get your hands where I can see them."

When she hesitated, another voice came out of the snow to their left. A woman, this time.

"Hands! Now!"

The female guard moved close, and her laser sight popped on, hitting Taylor high center mass.

Taylor lifted her arms, her gun pointing upward.

"Drop it," the woman ordered.

"I'd rather not lose it in the snow," Taylor said. "Mind if I just hand it to you?"

That was met with hostile silence, and then, "Grip first! Careful now, I don't mind shooting you."

At this range, nobody could miss a shot, even if they wanted to.

Taylor left her finger inside the trigger guard and let go of the grip. Dangling the gun off her forefinger, she held it out. The guard inside the shack stepped up to take it, careful not to block his partner's line of sight. He tossed the .45 inside and stepped back, gun still firmly fixed on Dalton, and motioned for them to enter.

Taylor went first. Inside was bigger than it looked, extending farther along the wall than they could see. The room they stood in contained a fireplace that appeared to run on gas or magic, a bunch of monitors and computer equipment, several racks of weapons and protective gear, and a round wood table with four chairs and a deck of cards with some poker chips.

Through the doorway leading deeper in, Taylor could see a kitchen and beyond that, a bunkhouse.

The female guard pulled off her balaclava, goggles, and headset, and tossed them on a table.

"Who are they?" she asked her partner as she lifted her gun again. "What do they want?"

"I'm Dalton Enoli. This is Taylor Hollis. We're here to see Vernon Brussard. She's his daughter."

Dalton kept the explanation minimal. At the mention of his full name, the male guard lowered the nose of his gun slightly. "Enoli? Let's see."

Taylor realized that the snow had turned both her and Dalton into abominable snowpeople. They'd both wrapped scarves around their faces and wore balaclavas underneath, and the snow clung thickly to them.

"I'm going to remove my scarf and hat," Dalton said, waiting for the guard to nod the okay before slowly unwinding his scarf. He dropped it to the floor, then peeled off the balaclava along with his hat.

Both guards drew back a bit in surprise, then the man relaxed and lowered his weapon. The female guard did not.

"Well, damned if you aren't the bastard himself," the man said. "Thought you was long gone." He glanced at Taylor. "And you're really the daughter?"

"May I?" she asked, motioning toward her head with her still-upheld hands. "Yeah, sure."

She stripped off protective gear, and as soon as the male guard saw her, he started nodding.

"Sure, I see it now." He shook his head. "Didn't know he had a kid. Did you?" He looked at his partner.

"Nope. Don't care. Get on the horn. See what the house wants to do about these two."

The male stepped back and grabbed a phone off its base and punched in a code. He kept a watchful eye on Dalton and Taylor the entire time, holding his rifle by the pistol grip.

Someone picked up. He conveyed Taylor's and Dalton's names and that they were there to see Vernon.

"Right," he said, and then hung up. He motioned toward the table. "Sit. This could take awhile."

"This?" Taylor asked.

"Finding out what they want us to do with you," the female guard said. "Now sit."

Taylor took a chair in the corner with Dalton to her left. The male guard pulled a chair back and sat, resting his rifle across his knees. The woman took off her coat and shook it out before hanging it up. She picked up Taylor's and Dalton's discarded clothing and tossed them on the table.

She was tall and well built, with broad shoulders and a lean runner's body. Her hair was shaved on the side and a few inches long on top. What was left was bleached white with blue tips. She had a dozen piercings in each ear, a couple in her eyebrows, one in her nose, and one in her chin. Tattoos circled low on her neck, peeking out of her shirt, but Taylor couldn't make them out.

The man had a similar physique, but a little bulkier, with full lips, a broad nose, and a wide face. He was shaved entirely bald, his walnut skin smooth. He had tiny gold rings in both ears, and a close-cropped goatee.

Both guards studied them curiously but didn't speak. The wind howled outside, and inside the silence reigned. It didn't bother Taylor. She took the time to look around and realized that everything inside ran on electricity or gas. The wall and the guardhouse was a dead zone for magic. Made sense. Tyrell would have reinforced the wall with blinders and nulls to prevent magic attacks.

There were ways around that. She doubted it would stop a traveller, since they used dreamspace to travel, and that couldn't be walled out. Same with Riley, who could go through the spirit realm. Inside the manor, though, Tyrell could and would put in protections that did keep them out.

But then again, what did she know? Maybe he had the money and enough highly talented people to create a bubble around the entire estate to keep intruders from traveling in or out.

The phone rang after about ten minutes or so, and the woman went to answer it.

"Marston," she said by way of a greeting, which Taylor understood to be the woman's name.

The person on the other end spoke briefly, and then Marston hung up without another word. She looked at her partner.

"They want them up at the house. Sending an escort. We've got to pat them down."

The man nodded as if that's what he'd been expecting.

"You first," Marston said, pointing at Taylor.

She rose and came around to the front of the table. Marston did a thorough pat down, stripping away all of Taylor's weaponry and assorted belongings, tossing them into a canvas bag she'd taken from a supply cupboard. Next was Dalton, who suffered the search with stoic calm, his belongings going into a second bag. After that, they were told to sit again.

Around twenty minutes later, a door opened into the kitchen area, a draft of icy air sweeping through the shotgun-style guardhouse. Marston went to greet the newcomers, while her partner eased to his feet, keeping his weapon ready as he faced them.

Marston returned, waving at Taylor and Dalton to get up. "Get your coats on."

After they'd dressed and put on their head gear, their two guards motioned them into the kitchen where four people covered in snow waited. They all wore motorcycle-style helmets with goggles, heavy jackets, and boots in gray-and-white camouflage patterns, and each carried AKs.

Two led the way out, followed by Taylor and then Dalton, with the last two bringing up the rear, carrying the canvas bags along with their weapons.

The storm hit them like a freight train, the noise drowning out all other sound, the wind buffeting them. Taylor stumbled over something hidden by the snow, and Dalton steadied her.

The walk seemed endless but probably wasn't more than a quarter to a half mile at most. The path that their guards had broken to come get them had already drifted over as if they'd never even passed through.

Though she exercised every day and was in good shape, Taylor still felt the burn in her legs and lungs as they finally slogged under some kind of exterior shelter. The hard thrust of the wind cut off, and the snowfall almost stopped. They entered a cleared walkway, about five feet wide with waist-deep snow on either side.

After a hundred feet or so, they came to what appeared to be some kind of courtyard, though it was difficult to say. The dull, gray light of the day and the blizzard made it hard to make out anything more than a few feet away.

They arrived at a nondescript door, and one of their lead guards pounded on the painted steel. It opened almost immediately.

Stepping through, Taylor and Dalton found themselves in what appeared to be an industrial garage, with shiny gray concrete floors, all kinds of equipment including snowmobiles, four-wheelers, snowshoes and skis, banks of lockers, racks of weaponry, some tables, a kitchenette with a mammoth coffeemaker, a dozen bunk beds in one corner, a little cubicle made of shelves and toolboxes, and on one wall, a door with the words *Bathroom* and *Showers* stenciled on it in yellow paint.

"This way," one of the guards said, and though the voice was muffled, Taylor thought it was probably a woman.

They went through a wide passage that emptied into a long room similar to the one at Savannah's where servants could keep their things, take breaks, and eat meals. The two guards leading the way stopped within, motioning with their guns for Dalton and Taylor to halt.

A short man with thinning brown hair, a round face, wire-rimmed glasses, and a tailored gray suit approached. His glance took in the two of them before flicking to the guards

"You can go."

"What do you want to do with their belongings?" The one Taylor thought was a woman motioned at the canvas bags held by the two who'd followed them in.

The gray-suited man pursed his lips and then extended a hand to take them.

"Put your coats and things over there." He motioned to a walk-in closet/locker room area. "There are hooks and shelves, as well as an assortment of house shoes. Please remove your boots. No need to tromp snow through the house."

Taylor grimaced beneath her scarf but did as told. She didn't like the idea of getting separated from her boots. If she had to escape outside, the soft leather moccasin slippers would hardly protect her feet.

After hanging up her coat and scarf and laying her gloves and balaclava on a wire shelf to dry, she selected a pair of slippers from the basket labeled *women's 8* and put them on. They were lined with sheepskin and felt warm.

Dalton followed suit, but when he followed her out, he surreptitiously slipped something into her hand. A ring, and likely a null. She lifted her brows at him, and he gave an almost imperceptible shrug. Where he'd hidden it didn't matter. Enough that he managed to get it inside.

She couldn't wear it—the guards had taken all her jewelry. Instead she tucked it into her pants pocket. Better if she could get it into her bra or underwear or even swallow it, but not while Tyrell's possum-faced little minion was watching. He'd kept an eagle eye on them from the doorway the entire time and would no doubt report anything they said to Tyrell or Vernon or both.

"Follow me," he said when they were finished, and strode off into the main area of the house.

Like Savannah's manor, this one had dozens of rooms. Unlike Savannah's, Tyrell had decorated his in a sleek modern style, using a lot of glass, wood, leather, and steel. The wall art was mostly black-and-white photographs or abstracts, which was echoed by the sculptures scattered about. The furniture looked uncomfortable with a lot of corners and edges, in direct contrast to the flowing lines of much of the art.

There were no signs of flowers or other greenery, no pillows or cushions, no flowing drapes. There was nothing soft at all, which gave the entire place a feel of dreary sterility.

As they went through, Taylor couldn't help noticing that Dalton fit well here, with his inevitable black clothing, which was always simply cut and never wrinkled. He rarely had a hair out of place. He didn't wear jewelry. He never slumped or really leaned, always carrying himself like he was on military parade.

Did he ever cut loose? Get drunk? Get silly?

Taylor tried to recall if she'd ever heard him laugh. A chuckle maybe, but nothing that might suggest he'd lose so much control as to actually break out into real laughter.

He was always serious and sober. She wrinkled her nose, trying to picture him relaxing, maybe by a pool drinking a margarita. But the very idea of him in a swimsuit broke her imagination. It would probably be made of steel and Kevlar with guns strapped to it.

Or maybe he lost control in bed.

She smiled to herself. It would be satisfying to break through that rigid self-control, not that she'd take him to bed. Though kissing him had been spectacular.

She frowned, trying to remember. Had his composure cracked then? In the car it had. He'd punched the seat. And said she pissed him off so much he couldn't see straight, made him want her so bad he couldn't breathe, and scared him so much it made his heart stop. That since he'd been around her, he'd been a basket case.

What the hell should she do with *that*? What did she *want* to do with it? With him? She'd started to trust him, against her better judgement. When he'd opened up to her in the car, he'd seemed genuine. Honest.

All of which didn't matter one bit at the moment, and she should focus on Tyrell and Vernon and stop worrying about her love life. Her brain hit the brakes hard. No, *not* love. Sex life, maybe. Fantasy life, maybe. But most *definitely not* love.

She shouldn't even put love and Dalton in the same sentence. In the same paragraph. Hell, she shouldn't put them together at all, because she sure as hell wasn't going to fall in love with him, any more than he was going to fall in love with her. Opposites attract, was all. He was interesting. And pretty. But definitely not love material. Maybe not even *like* material.

She mentally kicked herself. *Shut the fuck up, Taylor. Stop thinking about him. This isn't the time or the place.*

They arrived outside a set of wood doors. Their escort knocked and, without waiting for an answer, opened up the doors and ushered Dalton and Taylor inside.

Taylor had an impression of gray walls, a black-and-white rug, and more of the steel and glass furniture. The only color came from a giant abstract painting on the far wall. Its churning, swirling strokes in greens, blues, grays, and purples, reminded Taylor of a looming summer storm.

Her attention quickly centered on the ebony desk in front of the painting, behind which sat Jackson Tyrell.

Upon first glance, Tyrell appeared to be the dictionary definition of unremarkable. She knew better than to underestimate him. He undoubtedly cultivated this air of average ordinariness, with his soft, jowly round face, thin gray hair combed over the top of his head, the shoulders of a linebacker, and instead of a six-pack, he had wine-barrel abs.

He sat back in his chair, scrutinizing them as they entered. As they approached the desk, he gave Dalton a little nod.

"Dalton. Good to see you again."

"You as well, Mr. Tyrell," Dalton responded in the voice of a junior officer addressing his superior. "This is Taylor Hollis, Vernon's daughter. She'd like to see him."

Tyrell's brows rose as he turned his attention to Taylor. "I had the impression neither of his daughters wished to see him."

"I don't," Taylor said. "But I need to." She spoke coolly.

Despite his harmless appearance, Tyrell had shrewd eyes and a ruthless air about him.

"Need? That's a strong word, Miss Hollis. Why is it you *need* to speak to your father when you so clearly hate him?"

She cocked her head. "I don't suppose that's any of your business, Mr. Tyrell. None at all."

He considered her a moment. "Vernon works for me."

"That doesn't entitle you to know his personal business."

He smiled a crocodile smile, leaning forward to put his elbows on his desk, his hands touching at the fingertips like a fat spider on a mirror. "You're quite wrong about that, Miss Hollis. You can tell me and possibly speak with your father. Or not. The choice is entirely yours."

"What makes you think you're entitled to know *my* private business?" Cool, quiet, even-toned. No hint of the fury kindling in her chest.

His hands spread wide as he smiled. "Why, this is my house, Miss Hollis. Everything inside my house is my business. Anything that might get in the way of Vernon doing his job, is my business. If he has a cavity, I know. If he has a sniffle, I know. If he has a visit from a daughter who despises him, and who is involved with both Gregg Touray's and Savannah Morrell's Tyets, well then, I'm going to know why. And I'm going to know now."

His voice hardened on the last word.

"So, when you said I could tell you and speak to my father or not, you lied."

He smiled. "Actually, I said that you could tell me and speak to your father. The 'or not' simply refers to not having the option to speak to your father. Either way, you will tell me why you're here, and you will tell me the truth."

She could feel Dalton tensing, feel the anger running into him like a black hole drawing the light.

"I suppose you plan to use a dreamer on me. Or some sort of truth spell?"

"You would suppose correctly."

Taylor sat down in one of the black-and-steel chairs facing the desk and crossed her legs. "Bring it on."

The one thing she'd learned from her father, the one thing she'd practiced her whole life, was how to lie so that even a dreamer would be convinced. After all, she was just a mundane human. As for spells . . . the same method applied. Truth was in the eye of the beholder. All she had to do was believe the lie, and it became the truth.

She was very good at it. Better than Riley, even. She'd had to be to fool her mother, who could read emotions and had been a walking lie detector. Once Jamie, Leo, and Riley had figured out she could trick Mel, Taylor had become their designated representative. She couldn't always make it work, but that only made her more believable. Sometimes she lied when she knew they'd be caught red-handed. Catching Taylor in some lies made her mom think her reading radar worked every time.

Convincing a spell of the truth was cake compared to tricking a dreamer who knew you.

Taylor didn't know if she could lie convincingly to Vernon. He'd taught her how to do it in the first place, and he had the ability to rifle through her mind. Lying to dreamers only worked because they didn't think they had to dig deeper than the surface to get the real truth. They never imagined someone could hold belief in a lie so strongly it read as true.

But then, she didn't really need to hide from Vernon.

She waited for Tyrell's response. He studied her, clearly wondering what she was up to.

"We're burning daylight," she said as the moments stretched. "If you're going to interrogate me, I'd appreciate it if you lit a fire under your ass."

"Very well." He opened a drawer and took out an omega-style silver necklace. "Put this on." He held it out, hooked on one finger.

Taylor stood and took it, realizing it wasn't silver but was actually platinum. As she turned away, she surreptitiously dipped a finger into her watchpocket and touched the ring null to deactivate it. She returned to her seat and fastened the necklace under her hair. The cool metal rested just above her clavicle.

"When you get what you want, I'll just keep this as a token of your regret for your treatment of me," she told Tyrell. "Now what?"

"Harold, if you will." Tyrell motioned to the man who'd escorted them and who had since faded into the background.

Harold lifted her hair to the side and set his fingers on the necklace's clasp. "Speak lies and die."

A shimmer of blue rose up from the necklace. It shrank, tightening around her neck, but didn't squeeze.

"Not a very poetic spell," she said as Harold retreated again.

"Gets the point across, though," Tyrell said. "I prefer to be direct. Saves time and trouble. Now, Miss Hollis. Tell me why you want to see your father."

She cocked her head. "I thought these only worked with yes-or-no questions."

Tyrell nodded. "Your basic Walmart-level versions do. You're wearing a much higher quality piece. Now I recommend you answer the question. The necklace tends to get impatient, and you don't really want to die quite yet, do you?"

As she'd put on the necklace, it had occurred to Taylor that she didn't really need to hide her mission from Tyrell. He had just as much reason to want the senator out of the picture. He might even decide to help with that part of the plan. She just wouldn't let him in on the plan to find the artifacts.

"We're hoping he will help us neutralize the senator."

Tyrell's gaze sharpened, and he leaned forward. "How?"

"The plan is to use him as bait to get close to the senator, cast a null to kill the senator's personal protections, and then have Vernon do a little dreamwork. We then have the senator get the bright idea to set up a meeting with the major Tyets, and together they'll arrive at some sort of agreement. He'll have some sort of come-to-Jesus moment to make him believe this is the best choice for all involved."

"How would Vernon be bait?"

"We'd have an FBI agent take him in as a prisoner and make a big deal about how big a Tyet player he is. The senator will want to see him, if only for the photo op he'd get out of it."

"And you'll turn the senator into a puppet? Controlled by your father?"

Taylor shrugged. "I don't like it, but beggars can't be choosers. We had a dreamer, but she's disappeared and he's the strongest dreamer we know besides her."

"And how will you sell Vernon as a major player in the Tyet world?"

"Rig reports. We've got a guy who's a wizard with electronics. The senator's already suspicious. It shouldn't be too hard. Plus Gregg Touray will back us."

They hadn't actually thought of any of that before, but creating an electronic record would bolster Vernon's reputation and Arnow's credibility when she brought him in. Hopefully, Erickson could put something like that together. As for Touray, well she was certain he'd support their efforts. He would throw everything he had at stopping the senator, no matter the cost. So there was no lie there.

But did Tyrell know about Touray's condition?

Apparently not.

Tyrell sat back, studying her. "I'm surprised you aren't going after the Kensington artifacts."

"We thought about it. But even if we could find all five, we'd still need five powerful cardinal talents. We had three until our dreamer went missing, but that still would have left two to find, plus the artifacts. Fool's errand to go after them."

All of which was totally true.

"And if I could provide your missing pieces and fill out the necessary talents?"

Taylor's brows rose. *That* she hadn't expected.

"I don't know."

"I thought you said beggars can't be choosers."

"They shouldn't be suicidally stupid, either," Taylor said. "Play stupid games, get stupid prizes. The chances of you ending up with the weapon would likely dump us out of the frying pan right into the fire. I'm not sure which one of you is worse. You're corrupt to the core, and he's an anti-magic fanatic with an army at his back. Either way, the people of the city are fucked six ways from Sunday."

"I wouldn't lock up people for their magical abilities."

"Maybe, but you'd kill people, exploit the hell out of them, increase Sparkle Dust production, and then there's those experiments you had going on in the Marchont building before it was destroyed. All those Frankensteined bodies."

Taylor shuddered at the memory of the twisted, tormented bodies. She and Dalton had been looking for who'd been responsible but had hit wall after wall. The only thing they knew for sure was that Jackson Tyrell owned the Marchont building, he'd rented it to the FBI, and the experiments—at least Taylor assumed they were experiments—had taken place there. Nobody would ever have known if they hadn't gone in to rescue Price.

Accusing Tyrell was a shot in the dark. It wasn't a lie, but it wasn't necessarily the truth. It was both at the same time, so the spell didn't know if it should start strangling her or not.

"Sacrifices have to be made for science," Tyrell said. "But I was only a silent partner in that project. Savannah had charge of it. She had a tinker who was willing to ... Frankenstein ... different talents together in an effort to transplant talents to another person. Give them two. Sadly, success was limited."

Taylor's mouth thinned and she clenched her teeth, swallowing the bile that rose on her tongue at the casual way he dismissed the victims.

"Charming," she said, acid dripping from the word. "And you wonder why we wouldn't want to give you any sort of leverage over us or this town."

"It's possible you could end up with the Kensington weapon in the end."

"I'm betting you'd make sure we didn't, and anyway, this other plan is more likely to work. I just need to talk to Vernon."

"What makes you think he'll agree? What makes you think I'll allow him to participate in your little party? Or that I'll let you speak to him at all? I could just wait until you're so desperate you'll beg me to let you help with the artifacts. Or I could use you to pressure your sister into helping me. Word is Touray has three of the artifacts. She could easily get them for me."

"That only leaves the last two," Taylor said, watching him closely. "Do you have those?"

He gave a bland little smile but didn't answer.

"I've answered your questions. I want to see my father now."

"Why is Dalton here with you?"

She rolled her eyes. "To help me get in to see Vernon."

Tyrell flicked a glance to Dalton and back to Taylor. "Why would he help you, I wonder. What's his part in your plan?"

"You're looking at it. Well, actually, he was supposed to get me all the way to Vernon, but the big ape has gone into statue mode. Fat lot of good he is."

Tyrell's smile widened slightly but didn't reach his eyes. "Tell me, Miss Hollis. Can I still trust Dalton?"

She snorted. "Fuck if I know. Did you trust him before? I certainly don't."

Her first real lie. She concentrated on pulling her earlier doubts about him into the forefront of her mind, replaying the scene in Savanna's magic vault, letting herself remember the frustration, anger, and complete distrust.

The truth necklace remained inert around her neck.

"Maybe you need to be asking Dalton these questions," Taylor said. "As far as I know, he's just as much Vernon's dog as he was when he started tagging along after us."

Truth. He'd said he'd quit Vernon entirely when he'd joined them, and she'd decided to believe him. That meant he hadn't been Vernon's dog back then or now. Not that she wanted Tyrell to know that. Better if he saw Dalton as an ally, a loyal tool. Or maybe a big-ass royal tool.

Silently, she snickered to herself.

"Where is your sister?"

"In the city."

"Can you be more specific?"

"I probably could."

"Then I suggest you do so, if you want to see Vernon."

Taylor snorted. "Like I could see him if I answered your questions? I call bullshit."

"I'm still asking those questions. There's no bullshit."

"And pigs fly and fuck butterflies and make little piglet-caterpillars that turn into flying bacon bits. Sorry, but I don't believe you and I'm done answering."

She turned slightly in her chair, crossing her legs and primly resting her folded hands on her knee.

"I'm afraid that I decide when the questioning is over."

She nodded sagely. "Ask anything you want. I, however, will not be offering any more answers."

To her surprise, Tyrell chuckled. "You've got a temper to match your hair, don't you? Quite a firecracker."

"Wow, that wasn't condescending at all," she said. "Next you'll be patting me on the head and sending me back to bed so the Grinch can keep stealing Whoville's Christmas."

He chuckled again and shook his head, pushing back in his chair. "Very well, Miss Hollis. I will allow you to see your father."

"See? Or speak to?"

"Very good," he said approvingly. "I do like you. I can see Vernon in you."

"Did you know him before he was Vernon?" Taylor asked suddenly. "When he was still Sam?"

His brows rose, obviously startled at her question. "I did."

"For how long?"

"More than thirty years, now."

It was her turn to be surprised. That was before Riley was born. In fact, it was before her parents had even married.

"That long?" She wanted to ask if he'd noticed a change in Vernon's behavior over the years but didn't want to let on about the brain-jockey. If Tyrell didn't already know, he might decide to kill Vernon to get rid of the spy. At the very least he wouldn't let Vernon come take down the senator.

"Does that surprise you?"

"Yes. No. I don't know. I hadn't thought much about his life before I was born, before my sister was born." The confused beginning of her answer had caused the necklace to pulse and contract slightly. She had to remember to be careful.

"Vernon has worked for me for many years. He's been an invaluable member of my organization."

"The illegal one that you keep such a secret."

"I have very diverse interests, and he's proven himself invaluable to *all* of them."

"You sure he's not just fucking around with you? I mean, if he'd do it to family, why wouldn't he do it to you?"

Tyrell gave her one of those looks she used to get from male bosses who would tell her the equivalent of not to worry her pretty little head about it.

"I appreciate your concern," he said, "but rest assured, your father knows better than to step out of line. I'd venture to say he's one of my most trusted employees."

Taylor just barely resisted rolling her eyes. "Please. Stop gushing. Your faint praise is underwhelming. You run a criminal organization. Him being your most trusted criminal doesn't mean you trust him at all. It just says you trust all the rest less."

He smiled. "I'll say it again, Miss Hollis. I like you. You've got a formidable mind. If you should ever want a job, come to me. You could go far."

"Thanks, but I don't like the company you keep," she said, her upper lip curling. "Can we get back to the point of my visit?"

"I like a challenge, Miss Hollis. I think you *will* come work for me before too long. I have some terrific incentives. As for seeing your father—"

He looked past her to the silent Harold standing ready by the door. "Harold, fetch Vernon, please. Tell him I want to see him immediately in my private dining room. Also, tell the chef I shall have guests for lunch and to serve us there."

Taylor didn't bother to protest. It wasn't a battle she needed to fight. Not now.

When Harold had gone on his errand, she touched her fingers to the truth necklace. "Are you going to take this off now?"

He shook his head. "I think not. I rather enjoy your candor."

"You can shove my candor up your ass," she said with a plastic smile. "Why are you letting me see Vernon?"

Tyrell ignored her rudeness and focused on her question.

"It would benefit me to have the senator out of the way and shut down this martial-law business." He smoothed a hand over his tie. "The artifacts can wait a bit."

"So, you'll wait to come after Riley until we boot the senator out?"

"If I said yes, would you believe me?"

"I would if you put one of these on." She touched the necklace.

He shook his head. "Those are expensive. Wouldn't want to waste one just to reassure you. You'll have to live and learn."

She shifted topic. "I take it you plan to stay for my conversation with my father."

"I could watch on camera, but it's rather pointless if you know I'm watching. At any rate, my chef is quite stellar, and I'm sure you both are hungry."

She was. She was also sick to her stomach at the idea of seeing her father. Would she be able to show him the spider on her arm without Tyrell seeing? This plan had to work and soon. If Riley risked tracing again, she'd not survive.

A lump lodged in Taylor's chest. She had to convince her father's jockey, and with Tyrell in the room, she couldn't talk openly to whoever that was. On top of that, she had to keep worrying about the truth spell.

Tyrell stood and buttoned his coat, then came around to the front of his desk.

"Shall we?" He gestured toward the door.

Taylor stood and followed him, giving Dalton a quick glance. His face was expressionless, the look he turned on her distant and cool. She frowned. What was that about? She didn't have time to ponder.

Tyrell led them through several entertainment rooms, all decorated with elegant modern lines, which Taylor found cold. Like the man.

They passed through a broad open area, the overhead revealing a glass roof, with stairs winding upward to the various floors. A bank of elevators against the wall offered handicap access, not that very many of the kind of people who'd use these would be handicapped. Most would have all their ills tinkered away. But they also wouldn't want to have to climb stairs. Heaven forbid they actually had to work that hard.

The color scheme was once again monochromatic grays, with some wood elements, a lot of sculptures, paintings, photographs, a massive round firepit made from obsidian in the center, and a giant chandelier overhanging it all. The latter looked like a Chihuly piece. It was made of a silver-and-gray glass with filaments of silver woven through it, all lit up from within.

They went through an archway on the left and through several smaller entertainment rooms until they reached the private dining room. Or *a* private dining room, because Tyrell went through the French doors on the other side, crossed a corridor, and into a smaller dining room.

The table was made of glass with a base made of sculpted iron. The chairs were ebony wood with blue velvet seats and backs. The sideboards were black and glass, and the chandelier looked like something from an alien planet. A fireplace with a smoky glass front and black marble fronting finished it off. It all worked together to be dramatic and elegant.

"Please make yourselves comfortable. I'm going to freshen up. There's coffee on the sideboard."

He disappeared, leaving Dalton and Taylor alone. She knew better than to think they weren't being watched and recorded. She poured two cups of coffee and handed one to Dalton.

He took it without speaking, stalking around to the other side of the room to look at a series of black-and-white photographs on the opposite wall. Since they were studies of shadows on geometric architecture, she doubted his real interest. Given his rigid posture, he was clearly holding himself tightly, which meant he was on the verge of losing his shit, which meant he was pissed.

"What's wrong with you?" A reasonable question that anybody watching wouldn't translate into any sort of friendly exchange.

He didn't bother turning around. "You're a liar."

She blinked at the venom in his voice.

Realization dawned. Of course he wouldn't know she could lie with the necklace on. And she couldn't very well tell him now. Her brow furrowed. Unless she could. She lifted her chin.

"That's right I lied to you. What of it? Do you want me to repeat it for the cameras?" She gestured around the room. "You've got it."

She thought of Touray, of her father, infusing their truth into her words. "I don't trust you. I don't know why you would ever think I could. Know what else? You're a giant dick. Just like Price." She shook her head. "All of you Tyet guys are just the same. Always out for yourselves. Don't think I ever thought for a second I could trust you. No more than Riley can trust Price."

He stared at her, face like sculpted rock. A muscle twitched just below his right eye. Would he get it? He knew she liked Price. Would he understand that she could lie while wearing the necklace? If he didn't, then she was on her own and she'd have to start treating him like an enemy again.

It startled her how much she didn't want to do that.

"You're quite the bitch. No wonder your father abandoned you. I wouldn't have stuck around that mouth of yours either."

"Don't hold back on my account," she said. "I mean, if you want to hurt my feelings, you'll have to try harder than that. I got over my father a long time ago."

She thought she'd been pretty obvious, but he didn't seem to have received the message. Before she could try again, Tyrell returned.

"Vernon should join us in a few minutes." He'd changed out of his suit jacket and now wore a gray cashmere sweater over his shirt and tie. "Please, sit."

He waved them toward the table, taking a seat at the end nearest the fireplace. Taylor sat on his left, and Dalton sat beside her, leaving the seat to Tyrell's right for Vernon.

She started when she felt Dalton's hand on her thigh. He squeezed once and then was gone. She glanced at Tyrell, but he didn't appear to have noticed the gesture through the table's glass top.

The knot inside her stomach loosened. Dalton understood. She decided not to examine her relief too closely, and just chalk it up to not having to go this alone.

"I trust the rest of your family is well," Tyrell said, shaking out his napkin and motioning for a server hovering in the doorway to pour water and offer wine. "You have your sister and two brothers, correct? I'm sorry about the loss of your mother. I understand she died unexpectedly."

It took a moment for Taylor to find the breath to reply. She hadn't really had a chance to grieve her mother's death, and it was still a gaping wound.

"My family is fine," she said finally, not bothering to respond to his profession of sympathy. It was bullshit. A way to knock her off balance. "Do you have family? A wife? Children?"

He was a public figure, and she knew he was divorced and had three grown children from the first marriage, a couple more teenagers from the second, and was currently dating a model not much older than the second set of kids.

He smiled and sipped the glass of cabernet the server had poured him. Taylor nodded when asked if she'd like a glass.

"I have five children, all doing quite well. I am not currently married. You have never married, I believe. Nor do you have children, is that so?"

Like he didn't already know. He probably knew how many cavities she had and read the report on her last pap smear. Was he trying to demonstrate his depth of knowledge about her? If so, she wasn't even a little bit impressed.

"That's correct."

"A shame."

"Is it?"

"Children are a blessing everyone should experience."

"I'll keep that in mind," Taylor said dryly. "Here's hoping my uterus doesn't shrivel up in the meantime, though I could do without the inconvenience of a period and cramps. I could definitely do without the cramps."

He flushed slightly as she'd expected. Amazing how even the most ruthless men found the notion of a woman's period squirm-worthy. But then, they probably equated it with shoving a tampon up their dicks to stop themselves from peeing rivers of blood.

Such babies.

"Your mother worked for the FBI, I understand," he said, drilling down on her pain.

Revenge, maybe, for her period comment, or just continuing to push her off balance. He had, but she wasn't going to let him see it.

"She did."

"She was a reader?"

"She was."

"A good one, from what I've heard."

"I guess."

Taylor kept her answers to a minimum, letting him guide the conversation. Nothing he said at this point mattered anyway, and eventually her nearly monosyllabic answers would frustrate him into changing the subject or bore him of this one. Either way, she came out the winner.

"A rare talent, reading."

Taylor nodded.

"Interesting that with her talent and Vernon's that you ended up a neuter."

"Is it?" She made herself relax, keeping her expression bland.

"It must be frustrating to see your sister and brothers have such powerful talents and you have none."

"I never gave it much thought."

"That's because Taylor doesn't need any magical talent. She's magnificent without it."

Taylor went rigid as Vernon entered. He gave her a warm smile, reaching across the table to take Dalton's hand as the latter stood and stretched his out in greeting.

"Good to see you," Vernon said, his eyes creasing as he smiled.

Taylor stared at him, unsettled by a distinct sense of cognitive dissonance. On the one hand, she remembered her dad, smiling, teasing her, laughing as she, Riley, and her brothers got into a brawl, generally involving thrown food. But then there was Vernon, who had stolen Riley's memories, who'd rigged her brain to kill her if she tried to talk about her talent, who pushed her to be a loner, isolating her from the rest of the family and trying to destroy those bonds.

But Riley had been stronger than he thought, stronger than any of them thought, and she'd reached out to Price, her family, and friends, and she'd beaten Vernon.

He'd finished shaking hands with Dalton and now stood looking down at her, his smile wide. It made her want to puke, or better, to slug the look right off his face. She did neither, merely staring coolly at him.

His reddish-blond hair had grayed over the years, he had a few more wrinkles, especially around the eyes, and he was lightly tanned. He remained as trim as she remembered him being before he disappeared.

His smile never varied as he sat opposite to her and shook out his napkin, tucking into his lap. "I'm surprised to see you. The storm is rough. What brings you out in it?"

Taylor glanced at Tyrell. Hadn't he told Vernon already?

"Why don't we wait until after lunch is served," Tyrell said as servers pushed in several food carts and set everything out on the table.

Everything smelled delicious, from the rack of lamb, to the herbed chicken, both served with little pitchers of various sauces. Roasted vegetables, freshly baked bread, and several salads rounded out the meal.

After the servers loaded everybody's plates, they departed, closing the doors behind them. Tyrell activated a privacy shield that glistened like diamonds in the moonlight along the floor, walls, and ceiling.

"We can speak freely," Tyrell said, cutting into his lamb. "No one will overhear."

Taylor's stomach roiled with anxiety and anger, but she dug into her meal anyway. Working in a war zone had taught her not to pass up a meal. You never knew when you might get another.

"How are Riley and your brothers?" Vernon asked.

"As well as can be expected," Taylor replied sardonically, the cognitive dissonance growing into a surreal sense of having stepped into a Dali painting. "Though I'm curious. Would you rather that Riley was doing well, or that she was at death's door?"

A reasonable question, really, given he'd booby-trapped Riley's own brain to kill herself.

"As I explained previously, my alterations to your sister's mind were to protect her from my enemies."

"But not your boss." She flicked a glance at Tyrell.

Vernon followed her look. "Him, too."

That admission startled her. "And that didn't bother you?" she asked Tyrell.

"Your father wanted to be sure Riley grew up, even though he wasn't there. It was a smart approach."

She noticed that he didn't answer her question. Nor did his tone give any emotional clues away. She decided to let it go.

"And after she grew up?" she asked, turning back to Vernon. "What then?"

"I'd hoped to be able to remove the conditioning before it became dangerous."

"You hoped. How very generous of you."

He didn't seem cowed by the venom in her voice. "It was a calculated risk. And since it appears that she not only survived but she's thrived, it may have been a blessing in disguise. Would she be as capable as she is if I hadn't made certain alterations?"

Taylor stared. Was he for real? "You're patting yourself on the back? Are you fucking kidding me? She almost *died*, you asshole. And don't give me that 'what doesn't kill you makes you stronger' bullshit. Everything Riley is is no thanks to you."

He gave a gentle smile. "We'll have to agree to disagree. It's thanks to me that she had the skills, that you all had the skills that helped her survive after I left."

Taylor found herself clenching her steak knife as she simply stared at his audacity. No, not audacity. His psychopathic arrogance. He was congratulating himself for his despicable manipulations.

"That's like praising a rapist for teaching women to be wary of men. You're batshit crazy."

Even Dalton looked faintly gobsmacked. Tyrell only gave a faint shake of his head and a minuscule smile.

"Some lessons are hard, that's true," her father said. "That doesn't make them any less valuable."

Taylor clenched her jaw so tight she thought her teeth might turn to powder. She wasn't going to keep going down this road. It was like arguing with a fencepost. A violent, evil fencepost.

"Maybe you can make up for it now," she said, focusing on what she was here for.

"Oh? How is that?"

Taylor explained the plan. The brain-jockey had to be listening. At least, she hoped so. But even if he was, she wouldn't know if Vernon's agreement or refusal would come from the jockey. Having his agreement was crucial, or they might get into the middle of things and the jockey could decide to derail everything. At the same time, she couldn't show the spider drawing with Tyrell sitting right there.

She'd have to get Vernon in private. How she was going to do that, she had no idea.

"You said your enemies killed Riley's mom," she said suddenly as a weird ripple swept through her mind. For a second, she saw rainbow prisms flickering through the air, rolling like lights from a disco ball. She blinked, trying to clear her vision, trying to catch hold of the errant thought that had been dislodged by that ripple and now stuck in her brain like a splinter.

"Why would they do that? You also said her past caught up with her. Which was it?" And why hadn't any of them questioned that earlier? *Stupid question.*

"Elaine, Riley's mother, *was* a grifter. And certainly her past caught up with her. However, the man who had her killed for stealing from him was also *my* enemy, and he was killing two birds with one stone."

"How's that?"

"He wanted to teach me a lesson and make an object lesson of Riley's mother so that nobody else would cross him."

It made an ugly sense. "Did it work?"

"For me or others?"

Duh. "You."

"It did. I took the warning very seriously."

"So why did you marry *my* mom? Why have me? Your very existence in our lives threatens us. Oh wait, you're a selfish bastard, that's why, and all your 'protecting us' bullshit is exactly that."

"I loved your mother. And you," he said, his blue gaze sharpening with anger. Amazing how much he looked like Jamie, and he wasn't even blood related.

"Uh-huh."

"Do you think she would have married me if I didn't? She was a reader."

"And you're a very powerful dreamer. Chances are you fucked around in her head. In all our heads."

The moment's hesitation before he responded told her the truth. She'd already known about Mel but hadn't been sure about herself or her brothers.

"I did not adjust anybody's thinking except Riley."

"Sure. Whatever. It doesn't exactly matter, now. Are you going to help take out the senator?"

He sat back in his chair, fingers tapping on the glass in a slow beat. "It could work."

"Your boss here seems to be okay with it."

The two men exchanged a glance.

"You've been working toward this," Vernon said to Tyrell. "Funny how it just jumps into your lap."

"If it works," Tyrell agreed.

Taylor scowled. Dark currents ran under their exchange, and what had Tyrell been working toward? Whatever it was, she wanted no part of it.

"What are you two talking about?"

"Nothing you need to worry about," Tyrell said. "All you need to know is that Vernon will participate in your plan."

It was moments like this that she wished she had some sort of talent to kick his ass. She didn't doubt she could do it physically, but someone would drag her off of him before she managed to do much damage. After that, he'd likely have her killed, which wouldn't help anything.

She shoved her plate back and turned so that she faced Tyrell.

"You clearly are playing your own game, and that's fine, but understand this. If any of your machinations result in harm to my family or friends, I will personally make sure you regret it. Now, I understand that you think you're perfectly safe in your little castle with all your guards and magical protections, but dead or alive, I will come for you, and when it comes to my family, I'm not bothered with ethics or morals. I've got a spectacular imagination, and I don't mind gore."

He chuckled, entirely unimpressed. Not that she thought he would be. Didn't matter. He thought he had all the cards. She thought of Vernon's spider. The man was too arrogant to think his own pet hellhound might turn on him. She smiled, hoping that she'd be around when the truth came out. Hopefully, it would fuck up his world.

He noticed her shit-eating grin, and his faded, his eyes narrowed. He hadn't expected that reaction, and it clearly bothered him. Not because he was afraid, but because she wasn't.

She turned and looked at Vernon. "When can we get started?"

"Nothing's moving in this storm. We'll have to wait it out."

"We got here just fine."

"You may be stupid enough to risk your lives in this weather, but I'm not. The senator will be there when this blows over, as will your FBI friend. In the meantime, we can spend some time together. I'd like to catch up."

"Catch up? Are you serious?"

He leaned back and folded his hands in his lap. "Consider it the cost of doing business."

Her lip curled, and she replied before she actually thought about it. "I don't think so." A second later it occurred to her that it might be the perfect time to talk to the brain-jockey without Tyrell looking over her shoulder.

"It isn't a request."

She pretended to consider. "I can't imagine what we have to talk about. It's not like you've been interested in my life until now." Now that she'd protested so adamantly, she couldn't give in too easily or Tyrell would be suspicious.

"You're wrong. I'm very interested," her father said.

"I suppose I can come up with a thing or two to say to you."

He gave her a wry look. "I'm sure you can."

During all of this, Tyrell had remained quiet, watching them intently. Now he broke in.

"Perhaps you both need another drink. Something a little more substantial than wine."

He rose and went to a shelf along the wall. It slid upward to reveal a small bar within. Tyrell pulled the handle in front. A section of the wall, along with the interior rows of liquor, rolled out on drawer slides. A panel in front dropped down to reveal rows of different drink glasses. Tyrell selected four large shot glasses and set them on the narrow counter space. He sloshed in vodka and set the bottle aside, then handed out each of the glasses.

He lifted his in a toast. "To bringing the good senator to his knees." He tossed his drink back, and the other three followed suit, albeit more slowly.

Tyrell set his glass down, reached for the bottle, and poured a fresh round for everyone. He looked expectantly at Vernon, who lifted his glass in the air.

"To everybody getting what they want."

The second glass of vodka burned down Taylor's throat, and she was glad she'd eaten. Tyrell was already pouring another round, and she had a feeling that refusing wasn't an option.

"Dalton, how about you?" Tyrell said.

Dalton grasped the glass but didn't lift it. He contemplated it a moment, then raised it. "To survival." He drank.

Taylor could totally get behind that toast. Tyrell poured another round, and this time it was her turn.

"Here's to raising hell and kicking ass."

"Hallelujah," Dalton murmured, drinking.

Taylor finished her vodka and slammed the glass down on the table, bottom up. She glanced at Tyrell.

"What do you know about the senator? Vernon said you've been working toward this. I'm assuming a confrontation? Removing him from power? Short-circuiting his agenda?"

He gave her an appreciative smile that made her want to slap him. She did not want his approval. Mostly, she wanted to kick him in the balls and then drop him to the bottom of the caldera.

"I'll let your father fill you in on that, and anything else you need to know. Feel free to keep the truth necklace. The spell has worn off."

He gave Vernon a meaningful look that had nothing to do with the necklace, and then left, the privacy warding disappearing before he reached for the door.

Taylor watched him go, and then turned to her father. "What did he mean? Anything else I need to know?"

Vernon looked at her, but she wasn't sure he saw her. He looked far away.

"It means . . . endgame. Finally."

Chapter 18

Riley

"PULL HIM OUT like a weed?" Patti repeated.

"Who'd want to give up their own body to be Senator Rice?" Jamie asked, clearly doubting my sanity. "Couldn't just be some Joe Blow of the street. Would have to be someone smart and who wanted to take on politics and wasn't some sort of megalomaniac psychopath."

"Maybe there's someone who's getting old and wants to be young again," Leo suggested.

"Still would have to be sure they weren't just as bad as or even worse than the senator. They'd have all his power. It would be like putting a loaded gun in a toddler's hands," Jamie said.

"I say we should stick to the original plan," Patti said. "We don't need to overcomplicate this. It's already plenty complicated, and we're already going to have a tough time getting to the senator, changing his mind, and making that believable to the world."

"I agree." Price's chest rumbled beneath me.

He had his arm around my waist holding me snug in his lap while he used his other hand to eat and drink.

I sighed. "You're right. All of you."

"Wait. What? Did you say we're right? Did hell just freeze over?" Leo asked in mock surprise. "Can we get that in writing? I'd like a framed copy to put over my mantle."

"Me, too," Jamie said. "Maybe you could carve it in stone."

"Maybe you want it written in blood, too," I said.

"Good idea," Leo said brightly. "Let's do that."

"How about we talk about waking up Touray instead?"

That took the air out of the room. Everybody went silent, and then Patti spoke up first.

"How exactly?"

"I was thinking something along the lines of what you just did, only more. You could bind his trace, and I could hold on to it until his body registered dead, and then shove him back inside once Maya gets his body going again."

Patti just shook her head. "Easy, peasy, is that it?"

"No, just simple."

"Do you have any idea how to get him to go back into his body?" Jamie had turned a fork into liquid steel and now played at forming it into different artistic shapes.

"I'm hoping the fact that he will want to go will pretty much do the trick," I confessed. "I'll just be there to help him if he needs it."

"Dying severs the tie between body and spirit," Maya said. "It's entirely possible he won't be able to put himself back."

Price's arm tightened around me, his fingers digging into my side. I covered his hand with mine, lacing my fingers through his.

"We don't really have a choice. Not if we want to free him. Sure, Vernon could get himself dead and that ends the brain-jockey situation for Touray, but do we want to wait? What if killing Vernon somehow hurts Touray? We know if the victim dies, the brain-jockey's influence goes away, but we don't really know what happens if the brain-jockey dies. At least this way we stand a chance of controlling the outcome. I just wish Cass was here."

That's when I realized I could maybe get to her through the spirit realm, now that I had my strength back.

"One thing at a time," Price murmured, brushing the fingers of his other hand along my neck.

I half expected him to tab me, but he didn't. It didn't surprise me that he'd figured out where my head had gone. It annoyed me a little, but didn't surprise me.

I elbowed him. "Get out of my head."

"Can't. It's a jungle. I'm lost in there."

"Ha, ha. Very funny. Jackass."

His arm tightened around me again, and I could feel the shaking of his chest as he laughed quietly. It was nice to hear. Feel. Whatever. Now I just needed to get his brother back for him. I'd get Cass after that.

"When can we get started?" I asked, looking at Maya.

She shook her head. "I do not like the idea of this," she said. "I heal people, not kill them."

"Killing him *is* healing him in this case. And he's not going to stay dead," I said gently.

"You don't know that for certain." She knotted her hands together, her head bowed over them as she leaned against the kitchen counter.

I slid off Price's lap and went to stand in front of her, taking her hands in mine.

"If you don't think you can do this, it's okay. We can find somebody else."

But nobody we could trust as much. All the same, I didn't want to push Maya. She put her life and soul into healing people. Killing someone could break her. It's entirely possible that Savannah's son had started out fine, and her pushing him to mutilate and kill had twisted him so much he could never be normal or whole again.

Maya met my gaze, her dark eyes like molasses. She shook her head. "I won't leave him in the hands of someone else. I'll do it."

I nodded. "We won't let him get away from us. He's going to be okay."

She gave wry little smile. I knew she figured I was well intentioned but that I couldn't promise he'd be okay. And maybe she was right. Maybe I couldn't. But it wouldn't be for lack of trying.

I looked at Patti, Jamie, Price, and Leo. "How about you guys? Are you ready? Or do you need a little more time to rest?"

Jamie and Leo exchanged an embarrassed look and then grimaced.

"I wouldn't say no to a nap," Jamie said, clearly unhappy with having to say so. "We did a lot of work outside to create shelter for people, and then we helped you. I don't want to be the weak link when we take care of Touray."

Leo nodded. Patti pursed her lips thoughtfully, and then she nodded as well.

I itched to get started, especially since I felt better than I had in a long time. I suppressed a frustrated sigh. They knew the urgency of things, and if they said they needed to rest, then I should listen. "Okay, do you want an hour? Two? More?"

"How about an hour and then more food, and then we start?" asked Leo.

"Two hours, and then food," Maya said, overriding him. "It's better for all of you."

"I can't believe you're still thinking of food," Patti said to Leo. "Is there anything inside you besides stomach?"

He grinned and waggled his brows seductively. Or would have been seductive if he wasn't my brother.

"The ladies like me to keep up my strength."

"*Ladies* is an awfully generous term for the women you spend time with," I pointed out.

He looked wounded. "I'm offended."

"The truth is often offensive," I agreed. "And you," I said to Jamie who'd chortled through this exchange, "you aren't any better. Your dates"—I put air quotes around the second word—"all come from the local truck stop and get paid by the half hour."

"That's a true fact," Leo said, grinning broadly.

"Why do you think it's so funny when you're always his wingman at the truck stop?" Patti shook her head. "You two tomcats give venereal disease a bad name. You keep tinkers all over Diamond City in cars and diamonds. I can't wait until you run into a woman you want and can't have. You won't know how to handle it."

"Never happen," Leo declared, and Jamie nodded confidently.

"Famous last words." Patti rolled her eyes. "You guys are in for a hard lesson, I'm telling you."

"It definitely sucks."

That from Price. He shrugged at my questioning look, his smile looking pained.

He eyed my brothers. "Don't give ultimatums, by the way. You'll most definitely be kicking your own asses if you do."

They both nodded, respecting his experience, if not believing that any woman would ever give either one of them trouble. I could only hope I had front-row seats when it happened.

Before long, everybody had found themselves a place to lie down. Luckily I had a lot of cushions and pillows, and with the fire going, nobody was cold. I started to offer my bed up for grabs, but Price put a hand over my mouth before I could.

"If Maya doesn't want it, we do," he murmured in my ear. "I'm not sleeping on the floor so Leo or Jamie can be comfortable."

He had a point.

Maya refused, wishing to stay close to Touray. I raised my brows at Patti, but she made a shooing motion with her hand.

"See you in a couple hours, then," I said, heading for the stairs with Price on my heels.

"You aren't offering the bed to us?" Leo demanded, hands on his hips. "Some shitty hostess you are."

"I'm offended." Jamie shook his head in exaggerated disbelief. "After all we've done for you."

"What about what you've done *to* me?" I shot back. "Like the poison oak incident. Or that time with the yellowjackets. Or when you hot-wired the doorknobs to the house. And don't forget when you sealed me in the bathroom and then let loose all those cockroaches inside."

By this time both of them were laughing hysterically. I flipped them off and went upstairs.

"Cockroaches?"

"They bought hundreds of them. *Hundreds*," I repeated. "I'm sitting on the toilet and suddenly the bugs are all over me."

"How long did they leave you in there?"

"Not long. I wasn't supposed to be the target. Taylor was. Between the roaches and my claustrophobia, I went ballistic."

Even years later, the memory made me shudder. "I got revenge though."

"Much as I'd like to hear about it, I think I need that nap," Price said, yawning.

"It would probably give you nightmares, anyway," I said.

He turned on his side. "You're evil."

"Maybe, but only on days that end in Y."

He laughed and brushed my cheek with his finger. "Remind me not to get on your bad side."

"I have a bad side? I thought you liked all my sides."

His arms tightened. "I do."

"You're a masochist, then. Or nuts."

"What I am is lucky. Now shut up and go to sleep."

"Or?"

"I'll hide all your coffee."

"That's just cruel." But I obediently closed my eyes, listening to the steady in and out of his breathing, a little smile curving my lips. If anybody was lucky, it was me.

Chapter 19

Riley

"MAYBE WE SHOULD have tried this on empty stomachs," Leo said, having stuffed himself on the garlic bread and lasagna Patti had put into the oven before napping. She'd made it earlier in the day.

We'd cleaned the pan out and polished off a package of cookies.

Which meant it was time to work on Touray.

We gathered around his bed. It was funereal. Too weirdly like mourning around a corpse in a casket. I suppressed a shudder. Touray wasn't dead, and he wasn't going to be dead. Or at least not for long. Not if I could help it.

"Everybody know what to do?" I asked. Unlike the others, I'd eaten lightly. I knew myself well enough to know that when I got to this moment, I'd be feeling a whole lot of nauseous, which I totally was.

"If it looks like it won't work, get out," Price rasped. His hand clenched on mine. "I mean it. None of your lives are worth less than Gregg's."

Everybody nodded but Maya and me. She frowned, her thick brows nearly touching. I knew she was worrying about whether she should be taking part in this, whether she'd be able to save us all if we needed it, and whether Touray would even want us to try.

I wasn't sure about the last one. He'd gone to a lot of trouble to kill himself in order to save Price, the people in his organization, and maybe me, Taylor, Leo, and Jamie, too. Would he want us to risk ourselves to save him?

"Riley?" Price prompted when I didn't respond.

"I heard you."

"But you haven't agreed."

"I promised you I wouldn't do anything I didn't stand a chance of succeeding in. I can do this."

"But you'll back out if things turn and you can't?"

I chewed the inside of my cheek. "Okay."

He blew out a breath. "I'd feel better if you said that with actual conviction."

"I'm going to do this," I said. "That is my conviction. I'm not going to fail. Period, over and out."

"Riley . . ."

"Let's get this done." I looked at Maya. "You first. Tell me when you're ready."

Jamie stood beside her, one hand on her shoulder, prepared to offer her extra energy. She rested the fingertips of her right hand on his forehead. Her eyes went white, and she stared up at the stone-slab ceiling.

"Ready," she said after a half minute.

I looked at Patti, who nodded. We did the same things as before. I reached into the spirit realm and grabbed Touray's trace. I don't know what I expected, but it was the same as always, vibrant, bright-yellow edging the black. If all I saw was his trace, I'd think he was just fine.

I pulled out of the icy cold and flipped my hand over so Patti could bind down his trace, which she quickly did. I took my other hand and grabbed further up Touray's trace, wrapping it around my arm before pulling back out of the spirit realm again.

"Do it," I told Maya.

Even though I managed the two trace grabs with little effort, I accepted the burst of power from Price. He stood behind me, hands on my hips as he held me against his warm body.

I dropped into trace sight, letting the jewel-bright brilliance fill my vision. All of our traces were tangled up together and with all sorts of other peoples'. It covered us like silly string, sprawling across the floors and furniture. As I looked at Touray, I could see the flicker of yellow and black inside him.

I marveled at the strength of the pulsing glow filling him, evidence of a vivid, tumultuous will to live. A will that had driven him to commit suicide rather than be controlled by the brain-jockey. A will that currently kept him in a coma.

Then Maya killed him.

His trace lost some of its tension. Within him, the brilliant aura filling him dulled, color leaching slowly away.

I could feel its energy frantically grasping to stay anchored to his body. I tugged gently. It held, and then it gave with hardly any resistance. I swallowed hard, pulling Touray's nearly gray trace free of his now dead body.

How long did he have to stay dead for the jockey to leave? Was it anchored in the brain matter? Or in the trace? Maybe both?

Something jerked at his now entirely gray trace. It elongated, pulling taut against my grip and Patti's. It attenuated as the amorphous blob of light that had filled him suddenly started disappearing, as if sliding through the mail slot on somebody's door. A really old-fashioned door straight out of a sappy Christmas movie.

The pull on his astral essence grew stronger. It was going to snap. Soon.

I couldn't let that happen. I'd repaired myself but had no idea if I could do the same for anybody else.

Something had to give.

"Let him go," I said to Patti.

Price's fingers clenched, digging into me. "What?"

Patti didn't ask questions. Her release was instant.

"I'll be back." With that, I dove headfirst into the spirit realm, flying behind Touray like a kite.

Chapter 20

Taylor

TAYLOR PACED inside her guest suite. It contained a lavish bedroom, a sitting room, a bathroom big enough to throw a rave in, and a wall of windows that looked out on the storm outside.

Vernon had escorted her to the room and then left, saying he'd return, and to get some rest. Dalton had gone off with him. She sat on the edge of the bed wondering where the surveillance equipment was hidden and whether it was magical or actual tech. Maybe both. The room wasn't currently nulled, allowing for magical surveillance.

She tapped her fingers on her thighs, wondering where Dalton had gone with Vernon.

"Assholes," she muttered. "They go off and do whatever they want, and I'm stuck picking the underwear out of my butt until they feel like coming back."

She rose and paced a few times before stopping at the window. She stared out at the hypnotically swirling curtain of white.

Dumb. She whirled, putting her back to the view and squinching her eyes shut. Dalton had assumed last night's freak out had been an attack, but what if it had just been the storm? She'd been staring out into it. All the movement, like a strobe light on epileptics—could it have triggered a reaction? Maybe caused by her Sparkle Dust exposure.

She'd had an episode back at Savannah's. Could last night's event have just been a worse one? It made more sense than a targeted attack. She wasn't a danger to anyone. It didn't seem likely that someone would somehow search her out in the storm. In fact, the more she thought about it, the more ridiculous the idea became.

She stopped and looked at her splayed hands, tightening them into fists and splaying her fingers again. Tremors shook them, as they had off and on since she'd been exposed to Sparkle Dust. Not bad enough to lose her pilot's license—yet—but definitely worrisome.

She drew in a breath, counting four, holding it seven, releasing it for a count of eight. She repeated the exercise, trying to find calm. Instead, icy prickles spread over the soles of her feet and along the palms of her hands. She curled her toes and clenched her fingers, but the feeling didn't abate.

Stomping back and forth and slapping her hands against her thighs, she tried to force it away, but the prickles swirled around her wrists and ankles, up her limbs, swallowing her body bit by bit, until it felt like she was being jabbed by thousands of icy needles.

What the fuck? SD exposure couldn't be causing this, could it? It had to be something Tyrell was doing. Maybe the necklace? She fumbled at it, finding the clasp. It dropped to the floor, but the feeling didn't abate. She sat on the edge of the bed, wrapping her arms tightly around herself and bending down to rest her head on her knees. She focused on her breathing. She'd have to wait it out, whatever it was.

Colored light danced across her vision like spots from a disco ball. Her head whirled, and she tightened her muscles as she started to topple forward with dizziness.

Hands gripped her and then were snatched away like they'd been burned. "Fuck!"

Dalton. Where had he come from? Taylor scowled. She didn't need an audience for her meltdown. Once had been entirely enough.

"You feel like you've got a couple thousand watts running through you," he said, sounding royally pissed.

Like it was her fault. Her ire evaporated as spiky waves of ice followed by fire rippled through her skull, back and forth like waves sloshing in a bathtub holding a Labrador retriever on crack.

"Are you okay?" Dalton again, his voice sounding carefully calm.

"Obviously not," Taylor said through gritted teeth.

"Can you tell if you're in immediate danger?"

"Of what? Because this feels pretty fucking dangerous."

"Dying."

"Fuck all if I know."

"I'll get a null."

She didn't ask from where. She didn't care.

"What's going on?"

Shit. Vernon. The hole in the head she didn't need. Why was he here?

"She needs a null. Now."

"No she doesn't. She needs me."

"You need to leave. Now." The calm in Dalton's voice had shifted to anger.

"Get out of my way."

Taylor shuddered at the ruthless savagery in her father's voice. Before Dalton could respond, she heard a heavy thump.

"Tell me exactly what's happening," Vernon said, his voice low and in front of her like he'd kneeled down.

"Surveillance?"

"Taken care of. I don't want Tyrell seeing in here anymore than you do. Now tell me what's happening."

"What did you do to Dalton?" Taylor lifted her head, blinking to clear her vision, but now the colored spots smeared into streaks, like light trails on time-lapse photographs of highways.

"Nothing he won't recover from. Now what is happening?"

"None of your business."

She dropped her forehead back to her knees.

"It's damned well my business. The last thing I need is for you to go nuclear right now."

She tried to raise her head again and failed. "What the hell does that mean?"

Pain spiked through her eyes like icepicks, and she squeezed her eyes tightly shut, clenching her teeth against her moan. She'd be damned if she'd let Vernon see her pain.

"It means your talent has decided it's no longer willing to be bound."

Shock ricocheted through her. She had a talent? She'd imagined Vernon might have messed in her mind, but in her wildest dreams she never thought she had a talent, much less that he'd crippled her, just like he had Riley. Only he'd let

Riley have access to her talent. Somehow he'd shut Taylor's off. Made her believe she had none.

If she could have, Taylor would have ripped out his throat with her bare hands.

"What did you do to me?" she demanded, her voice hoarse.

"I made you safe, is what I did," Vernon said, and he clamped his hands on the sides of her head.

Instant defense mode. She twisted, kicking and throwing elbows and punches.

"Dammit, Taylor, sit still. If I don't help, your mind is going to rip itself apart. You've got a volcano about to erupt in your skull, and if I don't control the force, you'll end up a vegetable and the rest of us will probably end up in the morgue."

He put his hands on her head again, and she kicked out, hitting him in the leg.

"Like you care about me, asshole! You caused the problem, and now you expect me to believe you're going to help me?"

Even as she spoke, she felt panic rising. Something was definitely happening, and she couldn't control it. How could she help herself? How did she use a talent she'd never known she had?

"The hard way it is."

She heard the words, and then something exploded against the side of her head. The momentum of the blow knocked her sideways and she tipped off the bed. She didn't remember hitting the floor.

It could have been seconds or hours later when consciousness returned. A weight sat on her chest and held her arms prisoner, while hands clasped her head in a tight hold. Pain streaked through her mind as if a chisel jackhammered through her skull.

She couldn't see. She couldn't even tell if she opened her eyes. She could hardly feel her body beyond the ripping pain in her head.

Try not to fight me.

Vernon's words came into her mind. Instantly, Taylor struck at him.

"Get out! Get out of my head!" She shouted the words in her head as well as out loud.

She bucked and kicked, twisting to escape from the weight on her chest. She wrenched an arm free and swung, connecting with flesh. She hit the spot again, and then a sharp cold stab in her mind and she could no longer move.

Panic washed away the rage. It swelled, and she felt like a hummingbird trapped in a tiny box. She was no longer coherent, could no longer think logically.

Dammit, Taylor, you're making this harder. Get yourself together and calm the fuck down. I'm trying to help. I'm in your head. You can feel the truth. I am not lying.

He pushed the words into her like pins into a pin cushion, down where she couldn't ignore them. The words calmed her, though not because she took comfort in them. Rather they reminded her that fear tended to get people killed.

She wasn't going to fall prey to it. She'd flown helicopters and planes in a war zone.

She pulled from the icy reservoir of calm she held deep inside her, forcing away the terror.

You, of all people, should know that you can fool magic into believing lies are truth.

Not when I'm this deep, and not with your talent. It's impossible.

I don't believe you.

Well, you can believe this. Unlocking a half-blown binding is more dangerous for you now that I've had to paralyze you. If you can't stop fighting me, you're going to have permanent damage.

Despite her better judgement, Taylor couldn't help believing him. As he said, his words felt true, plus it wasn't like she had a choice. She was at his mercy, and this was a battle she couldn't win. She made herself relax, her heart rate slowing, her adrenaline subsiding. She concentrated on breathing slowly and evenly.

Good girl.

What are you doing? What did you do to me?

I sealed your power from you.

The sense of betrayal actually hurt, which was ridiculous. She knew what he was. Finding more proof of it shouldn't do more than make her angry. But this man was her father. She remembered him pushing her on the swings, the smell of his pipe tobacco as she snuggled with him on the couch and watched Christmas movies, the bubbling laughter as he waltzed her mother around the kitchen at breakfast. So many good memories.

Which could all be fake.

There were many good times. And they were real.

Inwardly, she snorted. *Right. Why are you back? What do you want? You're a self-serving prick. If you're helping, there has to be something in it for you.*

There is.

What?

I want to save your life.

Why? What's in it for you?

Let's just say I want you to succeed in your mission. Now be calm as you can. I'm going to release the rest of the bindings. Try to trust me. I'll bring you out of it.

Trust him. Right. She'd sooner trust a starving great white shark not to eat her if she were dropped bleeding right in front of it.

Coherence vanished again as something snapped free in her mind. Her head exploded with fireworks, then turned into an acid trip as memories became tangible and started happening all at once.

Another *snap.*

Her heart and lungs convulsed.

Snap.

Volcano.

Her mind spun, and she felt like she was plummeting from a great height.

Something squeezed her heart in a vise. It felt like fish hooks had pierced her mind and a giant was jerking on them. Magic flowed into her, a tide of shining stars and fiery lava.

Your talent is free. I'll help you deal with what I can, but follow your instincts. I'll let you have your body back now. That should help. Keep calm and focus. There's a real chance you could cascade.

Taylor wanted to ask if he knew what her talent was. It might help her deal with it, but she couldn't articulate the thought. She pictured her father reconnecting her to her body like someone plugging in an appliance. All of a sudden, sensation hit her and she convulsed, her entire body quivering and shaking.

She rolled onto her side and pulled her knees up, drawing in hard, panting breaths. Swirls of color squiggled and squirmed across her vision. *Good.* She could see again. Sort of.

She pushed herself up on her elbows and knees, resting her head on the floor.

The power flowing into her continued to build with nowhere to go. She had no idea how to stop it or how to let the pressure off.

She scrabbled inwardly, trying to grip the power. She felt like a toddler chasing fish in a pond. It slipped from her grip, and she tried to grab it again. It darted away again.

It pushed at her, drilling into her, through her. Electricity ran over her skin, and actual sparks spun away.

You need to pull back. Get yourself under control.

Duh.

What sort of talent was it? Her mother had been a reader, and Vernon was a dreamer, both very powerful. Riley was a tracer, and Leo and Jamie were metal talents—again, all very powerful. None were full-blood siblings, but surely she should fall somewhere in amongst those.

Not that talents were genetically linked; at least, no one had proven it. But strong talents often bred true in families.

She searched within for some kind of instinct to tell her what her talent was and what to do with it.

Nothing.

She straightened her arms so she was on her hands and knees. She blinked, trying to clear her disco vision. Gradually the swirling, streaking lights steadied and grew more distinct. She found herself looking at two bright-colored lines, one cobalt blue with shimmers of orange and yellow, and one scarlet ringed with black and blue.

Taylor blinked. Was that . . .? Could it be . . . trace? She was a tracer? But why did Vernon bind her powers and not Riley's?

She sat back on her heels, gazing around herself. Hovering in the air beside her was a complicated network of light, like the fine roots of a great tree. It was all scarlet, black, and blue, tangling together with pulsing life.

Taylor reached out to touch it. Her fingers met a soft surface. She scowled and pushed against it. Cold enveloped her fingers, and the resistance vanished. She stretched forward, stroked her fingers through the tangle. Movement flittered through it like wind through cobwebs.

A hoarse shout and loud swearing as the entire thing contracted and yanked away. Pain exploded in her arm as something struck it, then a different pain zinged through her mind.

"Do that again and I will drop you like a sack of cement." Vernon.

"What did I do?" But she knew. Jubilation bubbled up in her. She'd touched his trace. She'd *touched* his trace! That wasn't a minor talent by any means. Then the meaning in his words seeped through and anger roared. Who the hell was he to threaten her after he'd put her in this situation in the first place?

Without thinking about the how, she reached for his trace where it looped over her body. Her hand reached into the merciless cold of the trace dimension. Her fingers and bones ached almost instantly. How could Riley stand this? To launch herself fully into it? No wonder it had nearly killed her.

She gripped Vernon's supple trace and pulled back out. She folded it between her fingers and pinched like she was kinking a garden hose.

He gasped and dropped to his knees, face gray. Taylor wrapped her fist around the kink and squeezed with all her might.

Vernon drew a choking breath and flung his arms out, fingers flexed, his back arcing backward.

"Stop," he gasped, and she felt a burst of acid in her mind.

She squeezed harder, snarling. "Get out of my head or I swear to God I will rip your trace up like a weed." Instinct told her that she could. Longstanding fury, resentment, and hurt urged her to just do it.

Temptation sang to her. She took a breath and dismissed it. Their plan needed Vernon.

"Please. Stop," he begged and she felt something withdraw from her mind.

Her hand relaxed, but she didn't let go of his trace. She had questions. He was going to answer them.

Vernon fell forward onto his hands, panting heavily.

"Why did you bind my talent?" she demanded. "Why did you cripple me like that?"

"Because you were dangerous," he rasped. "Your talent emerged by the time you were just a few months old. You'd have killed people."

Okay, she didn't like it, but that was kind of reasonable. *If* he was telling the truth.

"Why didn't you tell me I had a talent? Why didn't you take the bindings off when I got older? Did mom know?"

She couldn't believe her mother would have kept the secret of her talent from her. Maybe as a child, maybe for safety, but not later.

"I didn't tell her. You'd been nursing and somehow she fainted. Did you do it? I don't know, but I decided not to risk it."

"That doesn't explain why you never told me. Why you left me bound.

Wait, I was going to erupt as some point, wasn't I? You left me totally unprepared to handle that. I might have killed someone when it happened. You really are a psychopath, aren't you?"

"I did what was necessary."

"For what?" There was almost a plaintive note in her voice that she hated hearing, worse, she hated that he heard it, too.

"For . . ." He paused.

"Don't bother," Taylor said. "If you have to think about it that hard, you'll be lying."

"You needed protection as much as Riley. More, even. You had a talent every Tyet, every hood on the street, would want to have at their fingertips. Riley can follow trace, and she can touch it, but she can't reach inside someone's body to get it, and she can't pull it out of them or break it. You can. You can easily kill with your talent."

"So can a lot of other talents," she scoffed. "Tinkers can cut arteries, detach brains, break bones—a zillion ways to kill."

"It's not the same. You don't have to touch the person. You only need to grab their trace."

"Dreamers don't have to touch someone to kill them."

"That's kind of true, but we can only work through the target's mind. We have to convince them to kill themselves, and that can take time. Even convincing the autonomic system to stop working takes time. You can do it nearly instantly, and what's more, take strength from it. You could wipe out an army and only feel drunk on the power those deaths gave you."

"Lucky me," Taylor muttered, shuddering inwardly.

"It's not an easy burden to bear, and one you'd have been forced to use."

"Oh no. You don't get to be the hero here. You didn't do me any great favors. You claim to have protected me, but all you really did was maim me. And Riley. You can say it was for our safety"—she put air quotes around the word—"but you don't do anything that doesn't serve you. Besides, if you really wanted us to be safe, you wouldn't have put a bomb in Riley's head or left me to face the dam breaking without any warnings, preparation, or help."

Vernon had gained his feet and now leaned back against the dresser, arms crossed, as he considered her. He was handsome still, Taylor thought grudgingly. Resentfully. She wished the last ten years had put him through a wood chipper. Apparently, Karma wasn't ready to take him on yet.

The skin between his brows furrowed. "I had planned to be around to help you both. Anyway, I can't tell you what you want to know."

"Can't? Or won't?"

He lifted his shoulder in clear dismissal. "The question now is whether you can make use of your talent or if it will control you. Will the tail wag you or you wag the tail?"

"That may be your question, but it sure as hell isn't mine."

Her glance moved passed him, and she saw Dalton sprawled on the floor on the other side of the bed.

"What did you do?"

Her heart thumped as she went to check the pulse at his neck. It beat strongly. She glared at Vernon.

"What's wrong with him?"

"I gave him a brain clap. He'll come around soon."

"What's a brain clap?"

"A mental slap, if you will. Right in the middle of his brain. It's like hitting someone over the head but from the inside and without the risk of concussion." His brows rose. "You seem awfully worried for someone who doesn't like him."

"Damned straight," she said. "Our plan needs him. Plus, I'm not the psychopath you are. I don't happen to like seeing people die, not even my enemies. Though I'd be willing to find out if I care about you dying. I'm betting on not."

"And how does Dalton fit into your plan?"

At that moment, Taylor realized two things. First, she had the privacy to talk to her father's brain-jockey. And two, that jockey now knew all about her newly discovered abilities. The latter sent a chill down her spine. The jockey now had an incentive to reach into her mind and control her.

Straightening to her feet, she considered her options. She had no way to keep herself safe, and as far as she knew, he hadn't tried anything in the last few minutes while she was totally vulnerable. That meant he was either spread too thin, she wasn't useful for his plan, or he didn't have the power. Not that it mattered. It was the perfect time to talk to him.

Pushing her sleeve up, she twisted her arm so he could see the spider.

"It's time we talked, whoever the fuck you are."

Chapter 21

Taylor

CONFUSION FLASHED through Vernon's eyes and then shifted to knowledge. His stance didn't change, nor did his expression or body language, but Taylor knew she was no longer talking to her father.

"So you know, do you?" the spider asked, and nothing about Vernon's voice indicated that he wasn't the one speaking. No change in tone or cadence or pronunciation. A shudder ran through her. The brain-jockey was completely integrated, and Vernon had no clue.

The part of her that had still been holding onto resentment against Touray for putting a hit on Cass dissolved. Seeing a brain-jockey in action destroyed any idea that Touray could have resisted the jockey's control.

Vernon crossed his ankles, folding his hands together. "To what do I owe the honor of your visit with me? I'm assuming it has something to do with your plans for the senator."

"We need Vernon, which means we need you to let him, or maybe make him, come do his thing. Question is, are you willing?"

He made a shrug face. "What do I get out of it?"

"I don't even know who the hell you are. I have no idea what you get out of it, except the senator stops being a problem for the talented of Diamond City. I'm assuming that's a plus for you."

"I'm not particularly concerned about the senator."

Suspicion made her scowl. "Why not?"

"He isn't in a position to touch me."

That caught her up short.

"Wait. Do you already control him?" It was the only way she could imagine not being afraid of the senator's hold on the city. Or maybe. . . . "Do you have something on him? Blackmail material?"

Her mind raced forward, thinking what hold the spider—as she was beginning to think of him or her—might have on the senator.

He burst her bubble. "I do not ride him, and the rest is not your business."

Vernon's smile gave her a shiver, because while it certainly was *his* smile, it also held something else, something not at all him, and even though she couldn't quite identify it, it hit her in the gut with a visceral sensation. It called up something she didn't expect. Anticipation. Or maybe eagerness for a challenge. Maybe both.

"What will it take for you to let Vernon help us?"

"Come work for me."

That set her back on her heels. "What?"

"I want you to work for me."

"I don't even know who you are, and I very much doubt I want anything to do with you."

"And yet you need me."

"I need Vernon," Taylor corrected. "And from what I can tell, you do too, if you want to keep up your surveillance of Tyrell and be able to use Vernon to do your bidding. He can do things you want without leaving your fingerprints all over it. That makes him a valuable asset. If you don't let him help us, I might just reveal your presence to Tyrell. Or kill Vernon. Or maybe both."

That smile again. Her father's and yet not. Maybe it was the eyes. "Very good. You are just as smart as I thought you would be. And your talent—that's a new one on me. Your father has depths that I have not yet plumbed. We could do a lot together."

"A lot of mayhem and destruction, I'm guessing," Taylor said sourly.

"It wouldn't be boring."

"That's just another way of describing the Chinese curse. *May you live in interesting times.* Not boring and interesting aren't exactly positives."

"They aren't necessarily negatives, either," Spider countered.

She folded her arms and cocked her head. "Okay. I'll bite. What exactly do you have in mind?"

"For you? Persuading people to make certain choices and perform certain acts."

She rolled her eyes. "How stunningly cryptic of you. But if I understand you correctly, you want me to be your thug. I'd be threatening people's lives—do this or else—is that about right?"

"A fair assessment, though there would be more to it than that. You've got loyalty and you're smart. It would be more of a partnership."

"And exactly why would I trust you?"

The conversation was surreal, and not really getting Taylor anywhere.

"You have no reason, not now. But soon there will come a time when we meet face-to-face, and I will ask you to think carefully when that time comes."

Taylor frown in confusion. "About?"

"You'll know. In the meantime, I want to tell you a story, by way of good faith."

Her gaze narrowed, and a chill ran down her spine. Foreboding thickened in her stomach.

"Fairy tales?"

"If you like. I'll keep it short. Once upon a time there was a man. Handsome, of course. He was involved in a Tyet. He'd been working his way up the ladder and was now in the Tyet lord's inner circle. He was sent out to kill a young woman who'd crossed a line, only when it came to the point, he couldn't do it. He'd taken a fancy to her. It wasn't long before he was in love.

"He returned to his Tyet lord and made a deal that would allow him to marry her and he'd make sure she didn't screw up again. Eventually, his boss agreed, but the man's failure to carry out his duties caused a hairline crack in their relationship. The lord wondered if he could really trust his favorite lieutenant.

"Time passed, and the lord grew annoyed as the man focused more on his wife and daughter and less on the organization. Clearly, his loyalties were divided. Too much so. This Tyet lord decided it was time to return the man to the fold. He sent an assassin to murder the wife. Later, he told the man he'd had it done and why, and if the man wanted his daughter to live, he'd buckle down and remember where he owed his allegiance.

"Determined to protect his young daughter, the man agreed, but swore vengeance, though it could take him years. Within a few months he'd taken out the assassin who'd killed his wife—the name of whom was a gift from the Tyet lord to appease him. He continued working for the Tyet lord, pretending loyalty while always seeking his revenge. Death wasn't enough. He wanted to destroy the lord."

"Vernon," Taylor said somberly as the missing pieces of what had happened to Riley's mother fell into place.

"Very good."

"And Jackson Tyrell is the one who had Elaine killed."

"Yes."

She rubbed a hand over her mouth. "It's an interesting story, but why tell it to me?"

"So that you can tell your sister that her father loved her. Loved you both, actually, but his determination to get revenge overwhelmed everything else."

"The murder was over twenty years ago. What's taking him so long?"

"To protect himself, Tyrell makes sure his employees know that if they turn on him, their families and friends will pay the price. In fact, if Tyrell should turn up dead, the dominos will begin to fall, and in order to be sure that the murderer pays the price, *everybody* in Tyrell's orbit will pay. And everyone in their families will pay. It's incentive for his employees to keep him alive. It's a way to guarantee loyalty."

"And we thought Savannah was bad," Taylor muttered. "I still don't get why you told me that. What do you care if my sister knows the truth or not? What difference does it make to you?"

The corners of his mouth quirked appreciatively. "I don't particularly care, but you do, and I wanted to give you something of value. So that when the time comes, you will hesitate to jump to conclusions."

"Conclusions about what?"

"You'll see. I suggest you may want to take Tyrell along with you to see the senator. They are not friends, and it may gain you some favor."

Taylor considered that intriguing bit of information. "Not friends. Does that mean they are enemies? Or just polite adversaries?"

"There's nothing polite about their relationship, and enemies is too mild a word to describe them."

He glanced at his watch. Or rather, the Spider glanced at Vernon's watch. Taylor gave a little shake of her head. This two-people-rolled-up-into-one thing made her head hurt.

"I have no intention of coming to work for you," she declared.

His brows rose. "Wouldn't it be more strategic to lie and tell me you might?"

She shrugged. "I'm not a good liar, and you're not worth the trouble to try."

"Aren't I? You need Vernon, and therefore you need me to let him accompany you. I could easily change his mind." His smile said he enjoyed the double entendre, that the change of mind would be literal, not figurative.

Taylor bristled. "Then I Tyrell about you, which means you give up having a valuable mole, especially one so close to Tyrell."

Spider studied her a moment, and then tipped his head. "Very well. But we will revisit the prospect of you working for me again. I suspect you'll be more amenable after."

"After what?"

"You attend to the senator, of course."

That wasn't what he meant at all, she was almost positive.

"Yeah, sure, whatever." Something occurred to her then. "Vernon said it was time for the endgame. And Tyrell said he'd explain what the deal with the senator was."

"Ah, yes. Well, I suppose your father can tell you that himself." He touched his fingers to his forehead in a salute. "I'll see you soon. Don't worry about further surveillance in here. As a token of my faith."

His hand dropped, and just like that, she found herself looking at just Vernon. How she knew for certain that Spider had retreated, she couldn't say, but she'd have bet her life on it.

Would he realize that he'd lost time? Or had Spider given him some kind of memory?

She looked down at Dalton who'd begun to stir. "About time," she said, flashing her father a contemptuous look.

"I told you he'd come around."

She hooked a hand under Dalton's shoulder and held her other hand out for him to grab. He groaned as she helped him ease up.

"Are you okay? Vernon said he hit you with a brain clap," she said by way of warning him they weren't alone.

"Feels like I got hit by a missile." He rubbed the side of his head with the palms of his hands as he leaned his elbows against his knees.

Deciding to let him recover, she focused back on Vernon, hoping to catch him off guard. "What did you mean before by *endgame*? And what's the deal with the senator and Tyrell?"

Vernon didn't miss a beat.

"Jackson and the senator have been skirmishing with each other for many years. Jackson supports a talented-inclusive society, and of course the senator wants a talent-free society. He wants to put us into reservation camps and make us second-class citizens. He wants to take away our voting rights, as well as any right to hold office at any level.

"He wants to make unlicensed magic use a crime. He wants to mandate that the talented serve six years in the military and serve on the front lines almost exclusively. He's been passing legislation and gaining allies for years. Riley's boyfriend got tangled in that legislation only a couple months ago. He was taken by the FBI and allowed no rights and was subjected to torture. Jackson wants to stop that nonsense."

"If Tyrell's on the other side of this argument, why'd he just happen to own the facility where the FBI took Price after they arrested him?" Taylor asked. "Where they were performing horrific experiments on the talented." She repressed her shudder at the memory. "Are you going to try to tell me he didn't know what was going on? I'm not buying it."

"Certainly he did, but he's not been looking to win the battles, he's angling to win the war. He's polished his image so that he can step into the void when the senator tumbles off his pedestal, as he's about to do. He'll be able to vouch for the natural causes that force the senator to take a step back."

"And if we want to leave him in place as a figurehead? Get him to reverse his positions?"

"In theory that's fine, but in practice that'll take too long. Jackson will be able to move more quickly and gain more ground for the talented with the senator out of the way."

Taylor wanted to point out that Vernon was out to exact revenge on Tyrell eventually, and if he did, that would leave the void open for some other fanatical asshole to step in. She couldn't say so without revealing Spider, and she didn't want to do that. Not yet, anyhow. She needed Spider's cooperation to make the plan work. Besides Spider would just monkey with Vernon's mind to make him forget.

She glanced at the whirling snow outside the window. It didn't look like it was going to let up any time soon. She doubted that Riley and the others would wait to implement the plan. In fact, while the senator was snowed in was the best time. He'd not be expecting an attack now.

She remembered what Spider had said about taking Tyrell along. Maybe they should. It might mean chopping off all the heads of the hydra all at once. And hoping they didn't grow back double.

"It occurred to me that your boss may want to come along," she said. "If this is his endgame, he might want to be there."

Vernon's brows rose. "You want to bring him along?"

Of course. Spider couldn't just make him agree. That would be too easy. Taylor was going to have to work for it.

She shrugged. "If he's that big an enemy of the senator's, then he'll make better bait than you for getting in to see the man. We could even say Tyrell has come calling, rather than saying he's a prisoner. I'm sure the senator will be curious and want to know why he's there."

Vernon nodded thoughtfully. "It does give another option. I'll suggest it to him."

"Soon. Like right now. We really can't wait for the storm to pass. Riley won't. She'll expect us to keep with the plan."

She said that for the benefit of Spider. She knew she couldn't trust him for the long term, but he'd make sure they could leave soon. He seemed to want this mission to succeed.

He has his own reasons, she reminded herself. *Don't underestimate him, and definitely don't take him for granted. He's not your friend and only a very temporary ally.*

"I'll get back to you. Stay here."

With that, he left.

"Like there aren't guards every five feet," Taylor muttered, then glanced down at Dalton who was clambering to his feet.

"You okay?"

"I'm fine."

She eyed him. His skin was verging on gray, and he staggered a little to the side, as if he was dizzy.

"Maybe you should sit down."

"What happened?"

"I talked to the brain-jockey. He's not going to interfere with us getting to the senator."

"And?"

"And what?"

"Was that all?"

She sighed. "No. You look like you're about to pass out. Sit down. I'll fill you in."

He glanced at the bed and chose a wingback chair. It was too low for him, and his knees stuck up awkwardly. Taylor sat on the edge of the bed facing him and went over all Spider had said. Except the part about working for him. Neither did she tell him what had gone down with Vernon. Dalton didn't seem to remember anything about her meltdown before Vernon had shown up. Probably Vernon had smudged that little memory away.

She couldn't complain. She wasn't ready to talk about having a talent. But then again, maybe he already knew and hadn't told her. Maybe that's why he'd kept hanging around.

She eyed him speculatively. He returned her look, gaze narrowing.

"What?"

She prevaricated. "Are you feeling okay? Mentally? No aftereffects?"

"I've got a headache that a couple hundred aspirins couldn't touch, but other than that, I'm fine."

He kept looking at her expectantly, like he knew she had a bomb to drop. She wasn't entirely sure why the hesitation. Disclosing her new talent took their relationship to a level of intimacy she wasn't sure she wanted. She should at least tell her family first, shouldn't she?

But what she should do didn't really matter at the moment. She and Dalton had to be able to rely on each other if they were both going to make it out of this alive. That meant confiding in him. That meant trusting his word. Was she ready to do that?

Chapter 22

Riley

TOURAY ENTERED the spirit realm with a flash of blinding white light. I had a moment where the urge to yell, "Don't go into the light!" nearly overwhelmed me, but I kept my mouth shut and tumbled in right after him with no fanfare whatsoever.

As usual, the vicious cold bit its sharp fangs into my flesh, sending piercing aches plunging deep within. I figured I had maybe a minute before I'd have to leave. I didn't want to damage myself so soon after healing myself up.

Touray's spirit remained amorphous, looking like a hank of yarn a cat had attacked. It was the complete opposite of the two women who came at me as if they'd been waiting. They probably had. My mother, and Mel.

Looking at them together, I was floored. They looked like sisters, or maybe mother and daughter. A good twenty-five or more years separated their actual ages—my mom remained the age she'd been when she died—but the similarities of build, features, and hair were significant.

Vernon had a type.

I started to hug Mel, the pain and joy at seeing her fighting in my chest. She held up a ghostly hand.

"Don't. It isn't a good idea here, and especially while you are attached to him." She gestured toward Touray. He bobbed at the end of his trace like a helium balloon. His colors had gone gray in my house, but now they'd returned, jewel-bright.

"What is happening?" my mom asked. She looked strained. I didn't think a ghost could look like that.

I caught them up in a few sentences that left out a whole lot, but then, time wasn't on our side.

"We've got to stop the senator, which means we have to get the brain-jockey out of Touray. And that's what we're doing now."

Neither asked for details, not that I gave them time.

"Is Kensington here? Can you find him? I need his help."

"It's possible. I have never seen or heard of him here. He may have let himself disintegrate or been restored to the world in some fashion."

"Reincarnation?"

"Or possession. A ghost. Things like that."

"Can you see what you find out? We need the artifacts, and he's the fastest way to find and understand them."

They both nodded, watching warily as Touray's blob of spirit settled over my shoulders like a cloak. I felt a simultaneous tugging and pushing at my spirit. As if he wanted in.

"I have to go. The cold is too much."

"You look better than before."

I nodded. "I am, but that will change if I don't get out of here. I'll be back." With that, I firmed my hold on Touray and dove back toward the living room.

And hit a brick wall.

I fell back, sensation radiating through me, like I'd hit an electric fence. Only with acid mixed in.

"The veil that separates our worlds is impassible for us," my mother offered. "I thought maybe with you . . ." She trailed off, the rest of the sentence obvious.

Shit. I had to get us both through and fast.

"You said ghosts get out. And spirits for rebirth. How?"

Both spirit women shrugged.

"Not even a single little clue?"

"To escape, it takes great determination and hunger."

"I bet." Well I was sure hungry to leave and to take Touray with me. I wasn't letting Price down by losing either of us.

I glanced at my shoulder where Touray's spirit form wrapped me. The same tugging-pushing feeling pinched at me.

That's when I got an idea. Probably a bad one, but it had possibility.

I tugged on Touray's trace, pulling him free of my shoulder so that he hovered in front of me. So far so good. Of course, that was the no-brainer easy part. Now for the up-shit-creek-without-a-paddle-rubber-ducky-or-hip-waders part.

"I'd appreciate your help," I told him, not knowing if he could hear me or if he was discombobulated by dying and had to get his shit together still. I imagined that was pretty much the norm, and eventually you put yourself back together and took on the appearance of your life and could communicate.

How does one stuff a spirit inside? Did I stuff him in my mouth or snort him up my nose?

If I snorted him, I would call him Snotman for the rest of his life.

Without any ideas, but well aware that I was out of time, I decided to go for swallowing him. I grabbed at him, trying to compress him as I brought him to my mouth.

I heard Mel and my mom make squeaking sounds of disbelief and concern, and then I pushed a Tyet lord in my mouth. And not in the good way, either.

It was like a kid grabbing fistfuls of cotton candy and loading as much of it as possible into their mouth before some sane parent could take it away. Which is to say, Touray sort of melted and flowed inside me. Not down my throat like I expected, but sort of spreading through me like heat from the sun. But fast. And super cold. All of a sudden, I wasn't just deep-freeze cold, I was liquid-ni-trogen cold.

I looked around me like I could actually see the veil. The truth was it existed everywhere and nowhere. Anywhere I was, I could make the hole. I did just that and pitched through again. This time I stuck in something thick and dense. Like cold molasses.

I reached out to grip the sides and push through, but there were no sides. I started kicking and making sweeping breaststroke motions to maybe swim through. That got me what felt like an inch or so, but no farther.

What the fuck? Anytime I'd passed through before, it was like going through a thin layer of permeable glass. Now, it had turned into a swimming pool of peanut butter.

Thinking quickly, I went another route. I couldn't push myself through, but maybe I could find something firm on the other side to anchor on and pull myself. I stretched ahead of myself, reaching.

No dice.

By this time, I was past the point of feeling anything. No pain, no cold, nothing. And I was sleepy. So sleepy.

At least using my magic wasn't killing me. Any silver lining in a disaster, right?

As I stretched, I noticed the other trace clinging to me. Price, Pattie, Leo, Jamie, Maya, Taylor, Dalton, and so many others. I was covered in trace lint.

I felt my entire body smile at the idea.

I grabbed them, winding my hands in as many as I could, and I pulled. At first I stuck fast, and then suddenly popped free, launching forward like I'd been shot out of a circus cannon.

I hit the floor of my house. My face hit a pillow, my shoulder and hip hitting the stone floor. I barely felt the explosions of pain that I knew had to have happened, but my nerves were frozen.

Hands grabbed me, pulled me upright.

"Riley?"

"She's frozen. Get her by the fire."

"Get her coffee."

I dug my heels in, refusing to be pushed.

"Touray first," I said, my mouth bending stiffly.

"No," Price said, starting to lift me up so he could carry me to the fire.

"Better. He's inside me."

"Come again?" Leo said.

"Inside you?" Patti.

"Is that safe?" Jamie.

"Not that I know of," I said. "But it got us out, so there is that."

Price put his arm around me, pulling him against his warmth as he guided me the few steps to Touray's bedside.

"Here."

Patti shoved a blanket over my shoulders. Price adjusted me so I could pull it snug, then tugged me back against him.

"Drink this."

Jamie shoved a cup of coffee in my hand. I sipped. It was cool enough to gulp, and warm enough to spread relief through me. It was creamy and sweet. I handed the cup back.

"Okay." I drew in a deep breath. "Time to see if we can bring him back. Definitely bring him back," I corrected, aware of Price going rigid, his arms tightening.

I should just duct tape my mouth shut out of principle.

"What do you need us to do?" Patti asked.

I looked at Maya, who knelt at the head of Touray's bed, hands clasping his face, her eyes shut.

"Cross your fingers," I said, and dropped into trace sight.

I had to get Touray out of me, and I didn't think sticking my fingers down my throat to vomit him up was going to work. I doubt I could talk him out. I didn't even know if he could hear me.

I was going to have to go inside myself again. At least this time I wouldn't be screwing around with my own trace.

"Don't worry. I know what I'm doing. Stay calm." Even though I meant to reassure everybody, I knew saying it would only freak them out. But I was about to lose track of my physical self and go rag-doll in Price's arms. That would freak them out even more.

I dove inside myself, letting go of my physical awareness. This time, instead of looking for the root of my own trace, I searched for Touray's distinctive colors.

I didn't know what to expect. I'd never really looked at my own inner trace before. The filaments whirled and coiled through me, constantly moving as if on an ocean current. Make that currents. They looked like the roots of a tree, like the ones on stylized jewelry showing the tree of life. I guess that image had its root—terrible pun, Riley—in the reality of trace. Did trees and plants have trace? Or were they a different kind of embodiment of it?

Not the time for idiotic philosophy, I chastised myself. Get Touray back in his body.

I kind of expected him to have spread out and made himself at home. Man-spreading his trace all through me, as it were.

But he'd pulled into a tight ball somewhere around my lungs. A bright streak rose up my esophagus and out my mouth.

Perfect.

I pushed my awareness out into the trace in my arms and lifted my hands to my lips. I could only see the spiraling corkscrews twisting and wreathing through my hands and fingers. I pinched those around Touray's trace and pulled, just like a magician pulling a length of handkerchiefs out of his mouth.

Touray pulled back for a second, then flowed out of me.

I had a really insane urge to go brush my teeth right about then. Maybe wash my mouth out with gasoline and bleach.

I was both surprised and pleased at how easy it was to remove him. Given how hard everything else had been lately, I thought for sure it would be yet another trip through the wood chipper.

"So far so good," I murmured. "Open his mouth."

I thought Maya would do it, but Leo got there first and pressed open Touray's mouth, holding it open.

I made myself go to the other side of the bed by Touray's head and pulled his trace down near his face.

"Do your stuff."

He just hung there, his color fading. So much for easy. Being inside me must have kept him alive-ish, but now his spirit was losing vitality. I held his trace still and pushed magic into him the way the others had lent me theirs. Instantly, he brightened. Okay, so he just needed a battery. Just call me the Energizer Bunny.

I waited for him to dive into himself, but he just kept hovering like a helium balloon. Maybe if I poked him with a knife, he'd pop and fall into his body. If only.

"Riley? What's happening?"

The ragged worry in Price's voice squeezed my chest.

"I'm working it out," I said by way of reassurance.

I didn't think it had the desired result. His hands tightened, and he made a low sound in his throat.

Time to punt. Again.

Pushing my hands into the trace realm, I grabbed hold of Touray and wadded him up in a ball, which was not as easy as it sounded. Imagine trying to grab a bunch of spaghetti floating free in water. Like that.

I ended up kind of twisting and wrapping until I kind of had him in a knot. Bits of him kept springing free.

"Can you make him take a deep breath?" I asked Maya, as I held the ball of Touray just above his slightly open mouth.

Abruptly, he sucked a deep breath like he'd been punched in the stomach. His mouth opened a little more, and I shoved him down, stuffing him inside and clamping my hands over his mouth to hold him inside. Most of him. Little tentacles and loops had escaped and groped around like they had somewhere to go.

A second later, more started coming out his nose like a pair of bizarre hemorrhoids. I pinched his nose and contemplated how I could cover his eyes if he tried escaping that way. I mean, what the fuck was he thinking? He was home. He should be kicking back in his recliner, turning the engine over, rolling around to get his stench everywhere. None of those metaphors remotely worked, but the point was, he shouldn't be acting like he was breaking out of San Quentin.

"He needs oxygen," Maya said.

"He can wait until he gets back inside himself where he belongs."

I leaned down near his ear, which really wasn't all that useful given he was in his own mouth, but whatever.

"I swear I will let you suffocate if you don't get yourself back in your body and wake the fuck up. *And* I'll tell the entire world you died of because your lover shoved a lightbulb up your ass and it broke and you hemorrhaged before anybody could save you. It'll be in all the papers. Gregg Touray died of a sex act gone terribly awry. That will be your forever legacy. Is that what you want?"

I heard a choked sound of laughter cut off from Leo and Jamie.

Nothing happened.

What else could I do?

I scrabbled in my mind for something to do.

"C'mon," I muttered. "You're too stubborn to go out like this."

Still nothing.

"Do it again, Maya. Make him take a deep breath."

I let go of his mouth and kept his nose pinched as he sucked in a sobbing breath, his chest expanding.

Before I could cover his mouth again, all the weedy tendrils vanished, sucked inside him. Holding my breath, I waited. All at once, his body shuddered and his eyes opened. He stared straight up, body rigid. Maya lifted her hands. He breathed on his own.

I chewed my lip. Just because he was back in his body didn't mean he was back to normal. He could be half brain dead for all we knew.

His gaze shifted suddenly, locking with mine. Within, I could see a depth of rage that iced the marrow of my bones. Gregg Touray was a dangerous man on the average day, but right now he looked demented and yet carefully controlled and laser focused. Like a velociraptor stalking its prey.

I shuddered, despite myself.

"Shove a lightbulb up my ass?"

Not what I'd expected him to say.

"It worked, apparently."

The corners of his mouth twitched in something that could have been a smile. Could have been indigestion.

"You killed me."

"Seemed like a good idea at the time." I hesitated. "Are you alone?"

Stupid question, really. It wasn't like he'd be able to say if Vernon was still there if Vernon didn't want him to. Or he might not even know he still had a brain-jockey. Only a dreamer could say for sure."

"He's gone."

Touray's certainty surprised me. My expression must have given me away.

"Once my body quit working and you pulled me out, he didn't have anything left to hold onto. I could feel him letting go."

He snarled the words, his lips thinning with his anger.

"Don't take this the wrong way, but I'd still like a second opinion."

He grimaced. "Me, too."

"Can you move?"

Maya's question made me look at her in surprise and then back at Touray.

He grimaced and sort of flopped his right arm up in the air, and it fell back down. "I'm feeling a little disconnected," he admitted.

"Is that normal?" Price asked, but none of us had an answer.

"It's not all that surprising," Maya said.

I was impressed by the way she confirmed complete uncertainty while still managing to convey reassurance.

"I could eat," Touray said. "Feel like I haven't eaten in weeks." He looked around at each of us and settled on me.

"Thank you. I owe you."

"Damned straight. And don't think I won't collect. I'm thinking my own snowmobile."

This time his smile was actually visible. "Not much of a price for my life."

This was getting awfully close to warm-and-fuzzy territory. That was just too bizarre from him.

"Yeah, well, I wasn't really doing it for you, was I?"

He looked past me to Price, lifting a hand. Price grabbed it.

"Nice to have you back. You flattened my Jeep." The roughness of his voice and the white of his knuckles betrayed the depth of his emotion.

"I'll replace it. Get you a snowmobile to match Riley's, too. How long have I been down?"

"Few days, give or take," Leo said as I scrunched my forehead. I had no idea how long it had actually been since we'd left Savannah's compound. A day and a half? Two? Three?

"That's all?"

"You expected longer?" Patti asked.

"I wasn't sure I'd ever come out of it. I wasn't going to let that bastard use me again." An expression of pained regret washed over his face. "I had Alexander Dimitriou, Liv Castillo, and Mark Kinsey killed. Took out hits. And Cass." He looked at Price and then me. "Tell me she's alive."

"She is," I said.

He slumped, closing his eyes with a long sigh of relief.

"But she's captive somewhere," Leo added.

Touray came alert again, eyes like icepicks. "Who has her? Where?"

"We're not sure," Price said. "We haven't been able to go look for her."

"What? Why?"

Something about our silence gave us away.

"What is it? What's going on? What happened with our attack on Savannah's place?" He hesitated, and his mouth tightened. "On you."

"It's a long story," Price said. "Let's sit you up and get some food in you."

"I should remove the catheter," Maya said.

Talk about TMI. I didn't need to be thinking about Touray's dick having a tube up inside it. Scratch that. I didn't need to be thinking about Touray's dick. Full stop.

"Let's go in the kitchen," I said to Patti, Leo, and Jamie. Price could help Maya.

I stood, having sat on the side of the bed at some point. I wobbled, and Patti put a strong arm around me.

"Steady."

Leo came around the other side of me and helped walk me into the kitchen.

"I'm not an invalid," I complained. "I can walk. I was just dizzy."

"You just visited the land of death," Leo said. "You don't know what you can or can't do."

"I'm just hungry."

"You just ate no more than an hour ago."

"But I used a lot of calories." I added a little whine to my voice so they could feel sorry for me. "Plus, I just got done healing up. So I deserve to eat again. Anyway, you're hungry, too. Admit it." Safe bet. He was *always* hungry.

"I swear you're really a hobbit," Jamie said from behind us. "As much as you like to eat, you'd think your kitchen would be stocked a little better."

Patti and Leo let go of me, and I sat at a kitchen chair.

"I've got all kinds of stuff," I protested.

"Only because we loaded you up," Patti pointed out. "Mostly because we didn't want to starve."

"And I appreciate it. Now will you feed me?" I asked. I rubbed my stomach and gave them the big eyes. "I'm wasting away."

"Why is it she'll ask for help when she doesn't need it, but won't when she really does?" Jamie asked the other two, and the three started to work.

"She's an idiot," Patti replied. "I've been tempted more than once to put her up for a Darwin award."

"Don't you have to actually die to win that?" asked Leo.

"They could make an exception. Her exploits have qualified her many times over, otherwise," Patti said tartly as she chopped bell peppers. "Are there any 'It's a Wonder She's Survived This Long' awards?"

"I'm sitting right here," I said.

"We know," Leo said without turning around from whatever he was doing. "Maybe there's an Idiot's Hall of Fame she could get into."

"If not, we could found one. Riley would set a high bar, but not every entrant has to be as wildly stupid as her." Jamie this time.

"Again, right here," I said.

"Hush. The adults are talking," Jamie said.

"You people suck. I thought you loved me."

"We do, but we're very clear on who and what you are."

"Which is?"

"A moron."

"Reckless."

"An adrenaline junky."

They all spoke at once and then fell into reminiscing about the times I'd committed abject stupidity, as Patti labeled it.

At some point about ten minutes into the cataloging of my escapades, I saw Price and Maya help Touray to the bathroom. He was about as graceful as Frankenstein, but at least he was upright and walking mostly under his own power.

When he came out, they brought him into the kitchen and sat him down at the table.

Patti brought him some toast and a banana. He eyed it like it was horse shit dipped in cockroaches.

"What the fuck is that?"

"It's called food. Part of the b.r.a.t. diet, for which you appear to be particularly qualified."

"Brat?"

"Bananas, rice, apples, toast. The diet of anybody recovering from the flu or norovirus or whatever stomach hell you're suffering. In your case, you haven't eaten in days. Your stomach probably doesn't even know what it's supposed to be doing. So you're going to start very slow."

She said this while pouring hot water over a teabag and setting that beside him.

"I want coffee. Black."

"And yet you're getting mint tea." Patti looked in his cup. "Kind of yellowish brown. You're welcome."

"She's correct," Maya said, pouring herself a cup of coffee and liberally adding cream and a sprinkle of cinnamon. "You need to ease into food or you'll end up sick as a dog."

"For how long?"

She shrugged. "Long enough. Depends on your stomach. Now, if you'll all excuse me, I could use a rest. Wake me when you need me again, or in twenty-four hours, whichever comes first."

Picking up her coffee, she retreated to the living room, casting me a wry look as she left. I had a feeling she knew that she'd be waking up sooner rather than later, since I had every intention of going after Cass as soon as I had refueled.

Touray blew out an annoyed sigh and picked up the banana, eyeing it malevolently. "I hate bananas. What are you making?"

"Meatloaf. Baked potatoes. Roasted vegetables. Garlic bread. Spaghetti and meatballs," Patti said, rifling in the refrigerator.

"All that?" I asked, and my stomach grumbled. Already the scents of garlic, onions, basil, and oregano had filled my kitchen.

"All that," Leo said. "I'm betting there aren't any leftovers, either."

"While it's cooking, you can get me up to speed," Touray said, setting the banana aside and frowning at his toast.

Price had pulled a chair up to the table and sat between me and his brother. He'd popped open a beer and guzzled half of it before setting the bottle down and reaching for my hand and holding it on his thigh.

I let him tell his brother what had happened, from making a deal with the Seedy Seven to rescuing the hostages, the senator's martial law, and our plans. Touray listened without asking any questions, either demonstrating formidable willpower or lack of imagination. I was going with the first.

"And now here we are." Price lifted his beer in a toast and drank.

Touray had finished his toast and now rubbed his hand over his jaw. It was thick with bristles. Give him another day or two, and he'd have a full beard going.

"This is a clusterfuck. Your sister is with Dalton and your father at Tyrell's?" he asked me. "Do you know how dangerous that is? She's alone in a pit of snakes with no way to protect herself."

I agreed, but I also had faith in Taylor. "You pays your money, you takes your chances."

"What the fuck is that supposed to mean?"

"It means Taylor's well aware of the risks, but she's smart and has skills. She's the best choice for this particular leg of the plan, and she'll get it done."

He stared at me, his dark eyes both hot as coals and cold as the depths of hell. "You must have hit your head on something really hard this morning. Your brain is full of crazy."

"Like a fox." I gave him a shit-eating grin. I wasn't going to be let him intimidate me or push me around. "You can either get on board and help, or you can shut up and stay out of the way. We've got a better chance with your help, but either way, we're going to do what has to be done."

He sat back, studying me, his gaze moving to Price, Patti, Jamie, and Leo, and back to me. "Your clowns, your circus. Is that it?"

"More like our city, our people, our problem to fix. Same as you. The senator thinks the talented are out for themselves and that everybody else resents us."

"You think he's wrong?" His brows rose, and his lip curled like he found me ridiculous.

"He's part right. But he's also wrong. Ordinary people *and* talented resent the Tyets and the way they use magic to push people around and take whatever they want. Some of us—ordinary *and* talented—want to look out for those who can't watch out for themselves. Some of us want to make sure everybody gets taken care of. Talented have certain advantages, but that doesn't make us better or more valuable. It just makes it easier for us to bully others, and it gives us more responsibility to police ourselves and lend a hand to whoever needs us."

"Pretty speech, but naïve, don't you think? People are naturally greedy and selfish. They look out for number one, and if that means knocking down their neighbor and climbing over their body to get up the mountain, that's what they'll do."

"You're wrong."

I didn't bother hiding my disgust at his cynicism. Yeah, there were people like that. But given the chance, most were kind and generous and tried to help others when they could. At least in my world.

"You've been hanging out with the wrong crowd, but that doesn't matter at this point. We're still going to take down the senator and protect the city. Only question is, what are you going to do?"

"Help you, of course. You're right. The only way to pry the senator out of here is to make him back down and soften his stance, and the only way to make that believable is with a dreamer."

"And you'll get the artifacts from your vault and give them to me? In case our plan doesn't work?"

"And I'll be the traveller you need to use them. But you'll still need a dreamer, a maker, and a binder."

"I don't suppose you've got any ideas?"

"Cass, of course, if we can get her back."

"We're getting her back," I said. "That's next on my list. I just don't know if she'll be in any shape to help us."

"Can you get through a null field?" Touray asked. "You said she was protected."

"I did okay getting out of that cage you put me in when we first met," I said, the tart edge of my voice telling him I hadn't forgiven him for that. "A binding field will be harder, but I'll do it."

Price's hand tightened on mine, but he didn't say anything. We both knew that I had the capability, but it was more than a little risky. But as I'd said about Taylor, you pays your money, you takes your chances. Getting Cass back was worth it. She was family, same as Patti, same as Touray.

"It should be me. I put the hit on her." Touray looked haunted, and the rage had returned to his eyes.

"Vernon did," I corrected. "He had control of you."

Touray's brows creased. "That doesn't make sense. He and I had a deal, and I was following through. Killing Cass, Dimitriou, Castillo, and Kinsey didn't serve him at all."

He shook his head, his blunt fingers drumming the table. "There's got to be another player. Maybe it's the same one who has control of him, although to keep a tight leash on us both would be practically impossible. Particularly overcoming a dreamer as strong as Vernon. I've never heard of anybody in Diamond City with that capability."

"Maybe they've kept under the radar," Price suggested.

"Possible," Touray said doubtfully. "But it would be hard to hide."

"For a dreamer of that caliber?" Leo asked, leaning back against the counter, the steel of his butcher knife turning liquid. He watched it as he idly pulled thin filaments from it, weaving them into a lace pattern. "I imagine a dreamer like that could brain check anybody who got near him. It would be tricky but not impossible to make sure they forgot him, or at least his talent."

"And if he set up decent security, he could keep a pretty tight lid on that information," Jamie added over his shoulder. "Or he's from out of town."

"Unlikely on that last," Price said. "The closer the proximity, the better the control of his victims. To manage Gregg and Vernon from a distance would take an incredible talent."

The meatloaf and potatoes were in the oven and smelled heavenly. Patti and Jamie were working on some kind of dessert. I contemplated rummaging for a snack. If Touray hadn't finally eaten his banana, I'd have stolen it.

"Could be a she," Patti pointed out. "Don't assume it's a man." She set an apple in front of me. "I'm only giving you this because I can barely hear over the sound of your stomach."

I snatched it up and took a giant bite. "Thanks," I said as I happily crunched the sweet fruit.

"So, basically this dreamer could be anybody," Price said.

"Yep," Leo replied with gallows cheer. "But don't worry. Good news is it doesn't really matter. Whoever it is has no reason to like the senator either and would be nuts to get in our way. My bet is if they found out what we were up to, they'd do what they could to help us out."

"The enemy of my enemy is my friend?" I asked.

"Something like that."

"Maybe, but I swear by all that's holy I'm going to kill the bastard slow when I find him," Touray said grimly. "The fucker is going to wish he'd killed me when he had the chance."

"First, we take down the senator," I said. "He's the more dangerous one right now."

"We hope," Touray said grimly. "We have no idea what this dreamer asshole's endgame is. For all we know, he's holding the senator's puppet strings."

I snorted. "If he is, we'll kill two birds with one stone, but I doubt you'll get that lucky."

Touray dragged his fingers through his hair. "How long until we eat?"

"Half hour or so," Patti replied.

"Then I'm going to take a shower."

I watched him walk toward the bathroom and then at Price, who had the expression of a man expecting a bomb to go off.

"That should give me enough time to fetch Cass."

Chapter 23

Gregg

GREGG LOCKED THE door on the bathroom, pausing just inside to draw a heavy breath. He'd needed to be alone. Needed to come to terms with . . . everything.

He'd ordered the deaths of three friends. The knowledge sickened him like nothing ever had before. He'd done shit things in his life, a lot of them, but he'd always protected his people: his employees, family, and friends. That protection was sacrosanct. And he'd not only failed, he was responsible.

He'd murdered them.

His stomach lurched, and he barely made it to the toilet before the banana and tea surged out of him. He retched again and again, tears running down his face.

He braced his hands on his knees breathing raggedly. The others blamed the jockey, but they were wrong. So very wrong. The proof was in the fact that he was standing here.

Strong emotions could free a trapped mind, and they had when he'd used his lust for Taylor to escape the jockey's hold long enough to jump out the window. But calling in the murders of his friends—of Cass, whom he loved like a sister—he'd not felt enough to even jar the jockey loose for even a second. He hadn't cared enough, selfish bastard that he was.

That wasn't all. He'd been careless and allowed himself to be invaded in the first place. He'd thought he was careful, but he hadn't been, and that was his fault, too.

He straightened and pulled off his shirt, balling it in his fists as he stared out at the blizzard, trying to trace back the likely infection point. When had it happened? The most likely time was when he was taken by Tyrell. After Cass had pulled out Tyrell's programming, she'd said she'd seen something odd and wanted to recheck him after his brain settled back into normal patterns.

It just didn't make sense, though. Tyrell didn't need a jockey. He'd already had Vernon manipulate his brain. And the jockey was unlikely to be Vernon. The man had given Gregg the clue to figuring out he'd been tampered with. Why would he do that if he'd already settled in as the brain-jockey?

Gregg could think of no other likely suspects. He was careful, keeping himself protected at all times. When had someone had the chance to get to him?

Unable to come up with an answer, he threw his shirt aside with frustrated violence and stripped off the rest of his clothes. The more he moved, the more he lost the feeling that his body was somehow foreign. He grew more graceful, his gestures less jerky.

He'd lost muscle. He could feel his weakness, but his mind was sharp, and except for his hunger, he felt good enough to travel, good enough to get back to work.

Except he'd killed his top three lieutenants.

The idea of returning to running his Tyet made his gorge rise again. He swallowed hard. His grandiose plans felt hollow. He hadn't been able to protect himself; he'd betrayed his most trusted friends.

Turning the shower to scalding, he stepped under the spray, facing it and bracing his arms against the wall as the water poured over him, opening his mouth to wash out the bitter taste of bile. Nothing could wash away the guilt.

He tipped his head forward so the water pounded the back of his neck. He felt . . . untethered. Without purpose. Wrong. Guilty. Uncertain. Like the ground rolled beneath him and he couldn't get his footing.

Experiencing such feelings was not normal for Gregg, and he didn't know what to do with them. As a rule, he didn't allow himself to feel. Emotions were liabilities. A sentimental man had weaknesses for enemies to exploit. Control was fundamental to running a Tyet. His only exception had been his brother, and Clay could handle himself.

Now, all of a sudden, Gregg felt stripped of all his armor, naked and exposed to the elements. He couldn't set aside or crush his feelings. They whirled inside him like sawblades with a power he couldn't overcome.

He needed to act. That was it. Get revenge for Dimitriou, Kinsey, and Castillo. And Cass.

He squinched his eyes closed, refusing to give in to the guilt and fear thrusting through his gut. He'd get her back safely. Then he'd let her take her own revenge on him. She would be merciless, as he deserved. She would make him pay for ordering the hits. Maybe that would stop the awful emotions churning in his soul.

A kind of calmness settled over him, and he took a breath. He had a plan. He had a goal.

And after?

He shied from the thought, even as his body seized, clenching like a fist. Breathing became an effort. *Why?*

A niggling voice answered: *You're not fit to lead. You're a liability.*

The uncertainty he'd managed to tether down tore free and gnawed at him again. How could he expect loyalty after what he'd done? Having the jockey gone wouldn't restore the faith and trust of his people.

At that moment, reality sank in.

He was *free*.

Profound relief slammed him. He sagged, falling to one knee. He'd jumped out that window with every intention of killing himself. When he hadn't succeeded, some primitive instinct inside him had grappled onto the void of unconsciousness to prevent him from waking and becoming a puppet again.

He owed Riley a debt he could never begin to repay. He owed her his life, his soul. Not just her; her entire insane family, including Patti. And Clay. She'd risked her own life for Gregg, and that had to have cost his brother more than Gregg could even imagine. He'd never been in love, never committed himself to another person the way Clay had to Riley. His brother would die for her; he'd suffer for her. He'd give up everything—including his soul—to keep her safe, whole, and happy.

Obviously, she'd do the same for him. Gregg wasn't stupid enough to think she'd helped him because she liked him. Hell, he'd been out to use her since he found out about her. Make her a prisoner—a comfortable one—and force her to work for him. Before he'd known how strong her talent was, he'd considered killing her to keep her from distracting Clay.

No, she'd risked herself for Clay and only Clay. She returned his complete and irrevocable commitment to her and wasn't willing to let him lose his only family. So much that she'd lay down her life to save Gregg.

He scrubbed his hands over his face, which was covered in stubble. Fuck, but Clay was damned lucky to have that intense, deep connection.

The thought caught him up short. *Wait.* Where the fuck had *that* come from? Clay was lucky? His entire world bound up in the well-being of another person? His happiness subject to whatever was going on her life? *That* was lucky? Since when?

Gregg had never wanted anything like that. In fact, he'd avoided entanglements like the plague. Romantic relationships were messy and inconvenient, and he never wanted to be led around by his dick. He liked fucking without strings attached. He made sure his dates had fun and walked away satisfied, and promptly forgot about them.

So why did Clay's relationship with Riley give him a twinge of envy? More than a twinge, if he was honest.

Refusing to think about it any longer, he scrubbed himself down and stepped out of the shower. He found some disposable razors in a drawer and scraped off as much of his sprouting beard as he could, then put back on the clothes he'd been wearing. Pajamas. He'd have to see if he could scrounge up something else. And shoes.

Blowing out a frustrated breath, he grabbed the door handle and exited the bathroom. Time to get back to living.

And revenge.

The sounds of laughter and teasing combined with the scents of cooking food lured him back to the kitchen. There was something off about it, though. A strain in the voices as if they were working too hard to keep things light.

He stopped in the doorway. His gaze swept the room and came to rest on Clay, who looked homicidal.

Where was Riley?

Gregg frowned, glancing through to the living room. Empty. Was she upstairs? But the look on his brother's face said she wasn't. His expression said she'd was doing something dangerous.

His frowned deepened into a scowl. He walked in, putting his hand on Clay's shoulder. His brother looked up at him with eyes skimmed over with white.

"Where'd she go?"

"To get Cass."

Fury burned through Gregg's veins. "Alone?"

Clay nodded, grooves bracketing his mouth. "It's a one-man show. She went through the spirit realm. She thinks she can bring Cass back through it."

"Why didn't you go with her? So she has backup?"

She was going into who knows what kind of situation, but she'd certainly be outnumbered and outgunned. It was as close to the definition of suicide mission as he'd ever heard.

"She didn't think she could carry two at the same time on the way back."

Greg swore and threw up his hands. "Why the fuck didn't she wait for me? I could travel to get Cass."

Clay shook his head. "Cass's captors have her nulled. Riley can still trace her, but you wouldn't be able to find her, and after what happened the last time she travelled with you, Riley didn't want to chance going into dreamspace."

That was a kick in the balls.

"So we sit here useless as tits on a boar?"

Clay nodded. Right then and there, Gregg's envy dried up. He never wanted to feel anything like the desolation etching his brother's face. It couldn't be worth it.

"Any whiskey around here? I need a drink."

"Way ahead of you," Jamie said, setting a bottle of single-malt scotch on the table, along with several juice glasses.

He poured a couple of fingers into each. Gregg picked up one as the others took theirs. Nobody fed him bullshit about his tender stomach. Leo lifted his glass.

"To Riley." He tossed his whiskey back.

The others echoed him and did the same. Gregg swallowed, appreciating the burn that ran down his throat and warmed his belly.

He didn't know how, but once she came back, he was going to make sure Riley didn't take any more dangerous risks. For Clay's sake. She needed to take herself out of the line of fire, or his brother was going to stroke out.

Gregg was not going to let that happen, even if he had to chain Riley down, wrap her in nulls, and nail her feet to the floor.

Chapter 24

Taylor

DALTON WATCHED Taylor through slitted eyes, like he was halfway to passing out but doggedly holding on to consciousness. His silver eyes interrogated her, demanding she tell him what she wasn't telling him.

It was as if he could read her like a book. That both annoyed and pleased her, the latter of which she also found highly irritating.

At what age did a woman finally grow out of being a sixteen-year-old girl waiting for her crush to notice her and hanging on to every look, every word, in case it gave a clue into the boy's inner workings? Because that anticipation and excitement curled in Taylor's stomach now, even while her brain told her not to be stupid, and the world was imploding, and her family was risking their lives. Told her why this wouldn't be a good time to distracted by contemplating Dalton's abs or wondering what his hair would feel like running between her fingers.

It was totally sane to wonder all that at a time like this. She rolled her eyes at herself so hard they nearly got stuck. Her hormones had rarely listened to her brain. They weren't going to start now.

She stood and paced, wishing for a drink. Dalton just watched her.

"What do you remember?" she asked finally. "About when you came into my room at first."

His eyebrows drew together, and his mouth twisted. "Nothing."

She sighed. "I was having a kind of an attack, a little like what happened back at the mansion last night. I heard you come in, and then Vernon showed up. You told him to leave and he knocked you out with a brain clap."

Dalton sat up, looking angry and worried. "What happened? Are you okay?"

She gave a little shrug. "Who the hell knows? Turns out I was in the middle of a something like a psychotic break related to the fact that he'd bound my talent when I was a kid. You were right all along."

His morphed into a mask of fury mixed with a healthy dose of disgust. "Fuck. I was hoping I wasn't."

She wrapped her hands around her elbows, holding her arms tight to her stomach.

"He said that I was too dangerous as a child and so he bound my power and made me forget about it. Something must've loosened the bindings. Exposure to SD, maybe, or maybe they just wore out. Anyhow, I'm guessing that's what hit me in the house. It's probably what's been causing my dizzy spells. Anyhow, after he knocked you cold, he helped me."

Suspicion furrowed his brow. "How?"

"I don't really know. I was fighting him pretty good, so he incapacitated me. I came to a little while later while he was finishing up."

Dalton took a moment to digest that. He sat with his elbows on his knees, watching her like she was a human puzzle.

"What happened after?"

"That's the interesting part. All of a sudden, I kind of went to this alternate place with a lot of glowing light lines. I grabbed on, and it turns out it was Vernon's trace. I guess I could have killed him."

Dalton cocked his head. "Use his trace to kill him?"

"Evidently." She sat on the bed opposite to him. "That's apparently my talent. To be able to kill someone by doing something to their trace."

He gave a little whistle. "That's a serious talent. I've never heard of that one."

"Vernon seemed to think it was rare. Anyhow, right about then I figured out that I could talk to his brain-jockey, so I showed him the spider on my arm."

"And?"

She recounted the conversation, including the stuff about her mother.

"Vernon's been looking for revenge on Tyrell all this time?"

"That's what Spider wants us to believe. You've been around him. What do you think?"

Dalton's expression turned thoughtful. "I've never seen him make any sort of move against Tyrell or even challenge him. I never doubted that he was completely loyal."

"But?"

"He's obviously good at keeping secrets. If it's true Tyrell killed your mother, and your father loved her as much as he says, then yeah, I can see him getting single-minded about revenge. Nothing else would matter."

Something in the way he said it caught Taylor's attention. "You sound like you know something about that."

"No," he said. "Not exactly." His gaze remained fixed on her. "But I can see where a man that in love might dedicate his existence to revenge if that love was taken from him. Price would get it. Maybe your brothers and Riley. I could see you following that road, too, if you want to know the truth. For someone you loved, of course."

The intensity of his gaze made it impossible to look away.

"You're probably right," she said, and her mouth curved in a slight smile. "And it looks like I have the means to do it, too. Angel of death." That she wore a smile as she said it didn't repulse her the way she felt it ought to.

"Think Tyrell will come along?" she asked, deciding to change the subject.

"To see his enemy get taken down? How could he pass it up?"

"Then why not say he wanted to get in on it at dinner?"

"He's a chess player. He doesn't make fast moves. He likes to think things through, and—" He broke off with a little grimace.

"And?"

"He's got ties. As big a move as this would be, he'd want to consult with others."

"What ties?"

"I don't know specifics. Other Tyets. Big ones. Deepwater. The kinds that run government and influence world economies."

Arnow had said something about those. She'd run across them when she'd started running an off-the-books team.

Taylor shook her head. "I really don't like this. The more we find out, the more complicated it is, the more people are involved. I have to wonder if this is going to even solve the problem or if Tyrell will cause something even worse. Diamond City needs to be free of Tyet politics, local and deepwater."

"Never happen. If anybody tells you different, they're lying."

"But why not?" she pushed. "Why can't we just get rid of the Tyets and take back the city? Then the government wouldn't have a reason to step in."

"The diamonds for one. SD is another."

"So we pay taxes. They get their cut, and with any luck, we'll wipe out SD and the recipe for how it's made, which takes drugs coming out of here off the table. That should be enough for them."

"Obviously not. Senator Rice is just one person of many in Washington eager to regulate magic and mitigate our supposed advantages. Their solutions are to handicap us or relegate us to second-class citizens. That, or enslave us to use us. With so many of us here, Diamond City is always going to be the battleground for that war."

"Goddammit," Taylor swore, rising to her feet. She stomped around the end of the bed and back. "I know you're right, but I keep thinking we can change it. We *have* to change it. We can't just accept that that has to be the way it is. What are you laughing about?"

"I'm not laughing. I'm smiling. If anybody can change things, it's you and your ridiculous family."

She bristled. "Ridiculous?"

He settled back in his chair. "Oh, please. Jamie and Leo? Their pictures are in the dictionary next to the word. Then there's Riley, Clay, and now his brother, Gregg. Stir in Patti, who might as well be your sister, and you've got an extraordinarily talented group of people with no idea of their own limits and willing to jump into a wood chipper at the slightest provocation. How many times as Riley come close to kicking the bucket, and those all in the last few months?

"Now *you're* getting in on that action. And Clay . . . look what happened to him. His brother's in a coma. All of that in the name of doing good. So yes, ridiculous. Ridiculously brave, ridiculously determined, ridiculously loving and compassionate, and ridiculously danger-prone."

Taylor glared a moment, and then shrugged. "I guess I can't argue that. What's it say about you that you decided to jump into our messes with both feet?"

"I'm clearly just as insane as all of you," he said easily.

"You sound heartbroken about it."

"I'm exactly where I want to be."

"I'm glad one of us is." She glared at the door. "I'm getting tired of waiting here. I just want to get going and get this whole thing over with and maybe have a chance to relax for five minutes."

"I love an optimist. What sort of thing do you plan to do for relaxation?"

She knew he was trying to distract her, to keep her from doing something stupid, like storming out in search of Vernon and Tyrell, even though there were likely guards standing watch outside.

"I don't know. Hot tub, maybe? A massage? Costa Rica?"

His brows lifted. "One of those things just doesn't belong. Why Costa Rica?"

"Always wanted to go. And Ireland. Machu Picchu. Azores. Lots of places, really. I've not been anywhere outside of Afghanistan and Iraq. Always wanted to see more of the world. Hike across Spain. Stuff like that."

"You planning to go alone?"

"For awhile, I thought I'd take Josh, but now, yeah, probably. "

"I'd go with you."

His eyelids had sunk low into that sleepy way some men do when they don't want to sound like they care and hide their eyes so people can't read their expressions. He didn't have to worry. With his eye-mods, he might as well have been a robot.

"If you asked," he added.

"I'll keep it in mind."

"You do that."

Curiosity pinched her. "What about you? What do you plan to do to relax?"

He shrugged. "Maybe a jaunt in a hot tub. Possibly a massage. Trip to Costa Rica."

"Sounds familiar."

"Does it?"

"You planning to follow me?"

"If you happened to be in the neighborhood at the same time, I couldn't help that, now could I?"

"Some people might call that stalking."

"I expect some people don't know a woman like you is perfectly capable of handling herself. And that's without your new talent."

Taylor appreciated the compliment more than she should have. Inwardly, she purred. She wondered if he knew how much she needed to hear that, or if he was just trying to suck up. He sounded sincere enough, but a sudden rush of doubt chilled her. She'd been so wrong about Josh. Could she trust herself to know if Dalton was telling the truth?

"Did I say something wrong?"

Oh that was annoying. She didn't want to be anybody's open book. "You just complimented me. What could be wrong?"

He sat forward again, gaze tightly locked on hers. "I don't know, but your expression did that thing where you go icy and shut down. I'd like to know why."

"Indigestion, maybe."

He blew out an irritated breath. "Just speak your mind, Taylor. You don't hold back with anybody else. Hell, you don't usually hold back from *me*."

"Fine. You said something wrong. Or not. I can't decide. That's the problem. Happy?"

He shook his head slightly. "If you think that clarified anything, it didn't."

She made a little frustrated sound and resisted the urge to hit something. "I don't know if I can trust myself to know if you're fucking with me or not. My recent track record sucks."

She walked across the room, needing distance between them. He rose and followed, stopping in front of her and waiting until she looked up at him.

"Taylor, I respect the hell out of you. I find you very capable. Do I want you running into trouble without backup? No. Do I think you might be getting in over your head? Probably, but you know I'm not the only one who thinks so. You do, too. Everybody does because this whole plan is one giant Hail Mary.

"I could tell you I find you gorgeous and funny and when you get irritated, you could strip the hide off a water buffalo and I think that's sexy as hell. You're honest, direct, protective, and something of a mother hen.

"But I won't say those things right now, because I'm pretty sure you'll tell me to fuck off. I've been real careful to stick with the truths that I think you'd be willing to hear from me, so when I tell you that you're more than capable of handling yourself without your talent, I'd appreciate it if you'd believe it. Particularly since you know as well as I do that it's true."

Taylor made an annoyed face. "You know, it's shit like that that makes it really hard to hate you."

"Thank God for small favors," he said dryly. "I guess that's steps in the right direction."

Taylor chewed the inside of her lip. The bastard was making her like him. Then again, it wasn't all that surprising. Her tension eased slightly. Dalton was her rebound. No wonder she was all hot and bothered. Here he was, a gorgeous bad-ass who'd showed her a little interest, and like every other woman after a bad breakup, she'd responded like a starving woman to a bucket of fried chicken.

She gave a little nod. It totally made sense, and knowing the truth made it a lot easier to set aside her feelings. If they weren't real, then she didn't need to waste time worrying about them.

"How long do we have to wait to find out if Tyrell is going to come with us?" she wondered aloud in a complete change of subject. She hopped up on the dresser.

Dalton frowned. "As long as he wants us to. What just happened?"

"What do you mean?"

"Are you really going to pretend you don't understand?"

That was the problem with him. He said what was on his mind and didn't beat around the bush. He went in for the kill, regardless of the potential embarrassment it might cause him or anybody else.

She sighed. What the hell? He wanted honesty? He could have it. No skin off her nose if he got a little butt-hurt. "Fine. You're my rebound guy. Whatever I'm feeling is temporary."

"I'm not your rebound," he said in a stony voice.

"Of course you are. You're the definition. I mean, I can't just fall out of love with Josh that fast. How shallow would I be if I did? I was ready to marry him."

He rubbed a hand over his mouth, his expression grim. "You aren't shallow. You weren't going to marry him. In fact, you were never in really in love with him, if you ask me. Not the deep, soul-wrenching, forever kind."

He closed the distance between them until his chest was only a couple of inches from hers. He looked down at her, his breath warm on her cheeks. Lifting a finger, he drew it down the side of her face, pushing a tendril of hair behind her ear.

Despite the gentle touch, his voice was harsh.

"It will *never* be a rebound between us. You don't like it, in fact you hate it, but you *want* me. You like me. And that idiot you were with was a joke. He wasn't worthy of you, and he'd never have lasted. If he'd been any kind of a man, he'd never have involved you and your sister in his shitshow with the FBI. He didn't even know you—the real you. I do. The fact is that like or not, you and I are supposed to be together, and the sooner you figure it out, the better. Until then, I'm not going anywhere. Just the same, I'll thank you not to use my name and 'rebound' in the same sentence."

Taylor eyed him. "You're awfully sure of yourself. What are you going to do when you find out you're wrong?"

His smile was slight but appreciative. "I'm not wrong. But just in case you think your bullcrap is going to work, know this: that right there, that mouth of yours, drives me up a fucking wall every time you start slicing and dicing with it, and it's gonna keep me coming back forever."

He dipped his head until his lips just brushed against her, light as a butterfly wing. His voice dropped to a low rasp.

"If we weren't currently in danger of getting interrupted at any moment, I'd let you prove just how indifferent you are to me. Just how much you don't want me. How long, do you think, after I started kissing you before you started moaning? Before you demanded more? Before you pushed me onto the bed and climbed on top and took what you wanted?

"That's what I want to see. I want you to take control. I want to watch your face the whole time, watch your passion and hunger take over as you take your pleasure. I'd give you every last little thing you ask for as many times as you wanted, except for one."

He moved nearer her ear. "I'm never going to agree to be a fling of any kind. I'm in it to win it."

Before Taylor could answer, not that she had one because her tongue was stuck to the roof of her mouth at the image he'd painted, someone knocked at the door.

It was time to go handle the senator. She'd think about Dalton after that. Oh who the hell was she kidding? He'd guaranteed that she wouldn't be able to get him out of her mind.

And she couldn't even manage to be mad about it.

Chapter 25

Riley

THE COLD CLOSED around me in a steel fist. I ignored it, along with my hurt feelings and irritation. Had to get over those.

I arrived in the spirit realm and found my mother waiting. I didn't see Mel.

Did they get along? My mother had loved my father. A lot. Would she like the woman he married so soon after she was murdered?

I caught myself up short. How did I *know* she'd loved my father? Nothing in my memories of her were necessarily true. They could all be implants. And even if they were true, that didn't mean I'd seen what was actually happening. I'd been just a little girl, after all.

She looked so much like me. Same hair, same curves, same eyes and mouth. Tears burned my eyes, and I longed to hug her. But even if I could have touched her, there was no time.

"Your friend survived?" she asked.

"Not exactly my friend, but yes."

"And the jockey?"

"Gone, we think. I'm on my way to get a dreamer friend. She was shot, and we think someone is holding her captive."

"We haven't found Kensington, yet."

She didn't sound all that hopeful that they would find him.

"I'd better go. It's cold." Talk about an awkward and stilted conversation. It was like talking to a stranger. I supposed that was more accurate than not. I barely knew her. Did she feel the stiffness between us and regret it?

"Good luck. Be careful."

"Thanks. Mom," I tacked on at the last minute.

I focused on Cass's trace. Her energy ran strongly through it, which meant whatever healing they'd done on her had helped. Good. Cass would need that to survive the spirit realm.

Following her trace was a matter of simply pulling myself along it, using it to guide me. I reached the point it exited the spirit realm.

And I hit a wall.

Damn it. I'd hoped I'd get out of the cold before I hit binders or nulls. I touched the wall. It felt like the seam where ice and water meet. That infinitesimal layer of the spirit realm between my hand and the wall prevented me from being able to tear it apart.

I ached from the cold. I was rapidly reaching the point of having to retreat or freeze to death. My stupidly stubborn gene kicked in. Hopefully not my fatal flaw, but I'd be damned if I left without Cass.

The simplest way to disable a null or a binder was to overwhelm it. Simple wasn't easy, though, because a lot depended on the way the nulls and binders were built and what sort of power you brought to the table. I'd learned to unwind them—out of sheer necessity, to be sure—but I had figured it out.

Now necessity had a gun to my head again.

I scrambled for an idea. One came to me, but how to do it?

I pushed at the wall again. I could vaguely see the power of it beyond the smoke-colored spirit-realm veil. How could I break through the spirit veil and access the wall?

I imagined ripping a hole in it like a rubber raft and the magic erupting. Or maybe popping a cork from a champagne bottle.

But I didn't know how to make a hole. I scrabbled for another idea, but I kept coming back to that one.

Time was running out. The painful ache of the cold had faded, and numbness had moved in. I'd cut through my own trace. I'd sewn myself up. Surely, I could figure out a way to poke a little hole in the spirit realm.

I pulled off my gloves. Focusing on my bare hands, I closed my eyes, concentrating on feeling for the texture of the spirit realm beneath my fingertips.

Not easy when your fingers are frozen. I knew it had to be there. Otherwise, I could have touched the wall. I pushed, reaching for the real world. For a moment, I felt a hint of warmth.

That was it.

I thrust into that space again, and this time I curved my fingers, concentrating on infusing my null power into each digit. I felt a thickening, a pulling as I scraped the skin of the spirit realm, but nothing happened.

I did it again, shoving with all my might, my fingers hooking hard. I felt a rucking up like of a thin rubber membrane. It pulled and stretched but didn't tear. All the same, I was encouraged. I dug harder, forcing all my nulling energy into my fingers. I just needed a tiny hole. A pinhole would do it.

I didn't feel the membrane tear. Instead, I found myself in the center of a nuclear explosion.

It felt like standing in the center of Krakatoa as it went off. The entire world shook and rumbled, and suddenly I was shooting forward on a violent burst of energy.

My entire world turned into a fiery kaleidoscope. Color strobed and battered at me. I bashed into something hard and lay stunned. At least the cold numbing my body delayed the pain.

Cold washed around me like salt waves on a reef, breaking and eddying. Spirits swarmed over and past me. Power pounded, thundering against my body in relentless waves. The pressure on my eyes and ears was immense. My heart stuttered, confused by the thuds hitting my chest like blows.

Jesus fuck—what had I done?

I curled into the fetal position, pressing my face into my knees and putting my arms over my head. I'd opened a doorway between the spirit realm and the living world. Which was the point, but I hadn't really thought it through.

I imagined that scene in *Ghostbusters* when the dickless politician shuts down the containment center and all the captured creatures explode out into the city to cause all kinds of chaos. Except I'd been sitting on top of the reactor when it blew, and this time *I* was the dickless wonder who shut the damned thing off, so I had no one to blame but myself.

Diamond City was already a frozen wonderland, but how far would the cold extend? To the Equator? Into Africa? Australia?

I became aware of a high-pitched sound. It was thin and sharp, like a wire pulled too tight and then plucked with a diamond nail. The sound razored through my bones, making me ache all over, especially my face, wrists, hands, and feet.

All my teeth felt loose, and I clenched my jaw. My eyes vibrated in their sockets, and I suddenly had the overwhelming urge to pee. The pelting continued, like I was the target of a paintball firing squad. Thank goodness for my coat and cold-weather clothing, otherwise the pain would have been significantly worse.

"Riley? Is that you?"

Cass's voice electrified me. She sounded confused and weak, but she was here. Or rather, I was *there*, with her.

I uncurled myself, flinching from the continuing hits. I pushed up on to my hands and knees. I shook, though whether it was from cold or from reaction, I didn't know.

My vision fuzzed and blurred. I blinked until it cleared and found myself looking down at a glossy cement floor. I lifted my head. I was in a small room. The walls were cinderblock painted pale yellow. A steel door with no handle blocked the only entrance. There were no windows.

I sat up on my heels and twisted around. I found a toilet, a sink, and a twin bed. Cass perched on the bed, propped in the corner, a blanket pulled up under her chin.

She looked dreadful. She'd always looked borderline anorexic, but now she looked like a Holocaust survivor. Her head had been shaved, increasing the effect. Her eyes were sunken and surrounded by purple circles. Her skin was the same color as her teeth, and her lips had a slightly blue tinge. A ragged red scar started on the right side of her forehead, streaking back a few inches.

"Riley?" she repeated, her brow furrowed.

I remembered then that I was wearing a balaclava. I pulled it off.

"It's me."

She closed her eyes and swallowed, then opened the again. "I didn't think you'd be able to get through."

"It was tricky." Understatement. I dropped into trace sight and once again, the chaos of color surrounded me. It didn't seem to be stabilizing any.

I pulled myself out again. "Are you okay?" My gaze went to the ugly scar on her head.

She reached up and touched her fingertips to it, wincing. "They healed me but didn't want to let me out from under the nulls for any longer than necessary, so they didn't quite finish. Assholes."

"Who are they?" I shook my head. "Never mind. We can talk about it later. Now we have to get you out of here."

"How?" She frowned again. "What's happening? You keep twitching, and I can feel . . ." She drifted off, turning her talent outward.

"Spirits," I said. "A lot of them. Escaping the spirit world. I kind of poked a hole in it so that the power would overwhelm the nulls and binders blocking you off, only—"

I broke off and spread my hands, offering a weak smile. "Pandora's Box. I'm not sure if we're going to be able to get out of here that way."

She sniffed like she had a cold, and scooted toward the edge of the bed. It was obvious the effort was exhausting.

"I'm willing to try. Anything to get out of this hole."

I'd begun noticing how low the ceiling was and how tiny the space was. I shuddered, fighting off my claustrophobia. You'd think I'd start getting used to it by now, given all the exposure "therapy" I'd had, particularly recently.

I focused on Cass's face, trying to ignore the fact that the walls and ceiling were falling inward on top of me. My gaze hooked on the scar again. Anger flared. Whoever had done this, whoever had taken control of Touray and hurt my friends, was going to pay. One way or another. At the very least, I'd make sure they couldn't do this to anybody else ever again.

"What do we do?" Cass asked.

"You aren't exactly dressed for this," I said, looking her up and down. She had on a thin cotton shift with a pair of socks beneath the blanket she clutched around herself. Given how skinny she was, no wonder she was cold.

I stripped off my coat and passed it to her. "Put this on. The balaclava, too."

After she got those on, I passed her my gloves and then eyed her legs. My coat hung down to mid-thigh on her, but there was still too much exposed. Maya could help any frostbite Cass developed, but if Cass's body was too weak to survive, Maya wouldn't be able to do anything.

Picking up the blanket Cass had dropped, I wrapped it around her waist and tied at her waist and ankles.

"I can't walk," she complained.

"You don't need to. You need to not freeze to death."

That left her feet. The socks she wore were nearly see-through. I bent and pulled off my boots and put them on her.

"What about you? You need those," she said, trying to pull away. "Don't be stupid."

"I'm not in danger of dying," I said. Lied, really. Because what the hell did I know? I'd been in the cold longer than I should have been and still could barely feel my fingers or toes, not to mention the rest of me. I had to be grateful for that, since the invisible bombardment continued to strike at me.

"What's happening to you?" Cass asked, eyes narrowing at me. "You've got red spots all over your face. Like you're getting the measles or something."

"Or something," I said. "We can talk about it later. Now we should get out of here. Your guards could be coming to check on you at any minute."

I dropped into the spirit realm and wound Cass's trace around my waist. Just in case. I was covered in trace from Leo, Jamie, Price, Touray, Maya, and Patti. I grabbed Price's and pulled back out.

"Ready?" I didn't wait for her answer. I wrapped her in a hug and pulled us both into the spirit realm.

Chaos buffeted us, knocking us around like a kite in a storm. Spirits grabbed at me, winding around me. I shimmied and knocked them off, concentrating on Price's trace.

I pulled myself along it as fast as I could. The cold ate into me, and I worried how Cass was faring.

The storm raging in the spirit realm tossed us, and one minute it felt like the current was behind us and the next, driving at us like a freight train. I kept hauling us along, my body growing colder and colder. Thank goodness I'd wrapped Cass's trace around me, as I was forced to let go of her in order to keep us on track.

I poured all the energy of my talent into getting us through. Spirits noticed me and clung to me like leeches. I felt them sucking on my power, feeding themselves.

What the fuck?

I couldn't risk trying to shake them off. I might also shake off Cass.

I finally reached the point where I could pull us back through into my house. Exhaustion and cold made me fumble. I gathered all my strength. Here the spirit barrier remained intact. I dragged us, feeling like I was trying to lift us out of a pit of mud.

Finally, the barrier gave. The spirits clinging to me peeled away, and I could actually feel *popping* as each let go. It happened rapid fire, like a lit brick of firecrackers. Each ached with a peculiar metaphysical bite, of spirit more than flesh. It wrapped me in an exploding layer of bubble wrap. A mottling of pain. Raindrops of acid pinging all over.

Next thing I knew, we landed on my kitchen floor. I banged my shoulder and head on a chair as I fell. I twisted, trying to land underneath Cass. She'd break like a dropped plate if she hit the slate floor instead of me.

I landed with a meaty thud.

Once again, I was too numb to feel much. I took stock of myself. Cass lay half on me and half on the floor.

"I think we're alone now," she mumbled.

"What?"

"You know, the song. From the 80s or whatever. 'We tumble to the ground and then you say: I think we're alone now.' We tumbled to the ground. Rather hard. What a stupid song."

I laughed. "You're such a nerd."

Just then, someone lifted Cass up and Price swooped in to grab me. I snuggled into his warmth.

"Are you okay? What happened? You look like you've been in a hail storm."

"She opened a hellmouth," Cass said.

"Excuse me?" That was Leo.

"*Buffy the Vampire Slayer*," I said. "Duh." I didn't watch much TV. Never had, but Patti made me watch with her on occasion.

"What the hell does that mean?" Jamie demanded.

"I did a thing," I said. "I'm hungry. Is dinner ready? Cass needs Maya."

Jamie dropped a necklace over my head. A heal-all. Instantly, a wormy feeling dug into me, spreading throughout my body. I made a face.

"Deal with it," Price growled, correctly interpreting my expression.

I stuck my tongue out.

"What happened?"

"Can we go sit by the fire? I'm cold."

Price made a frustrated sound but carried me to the hearth where he set me down. I scootched as close to the flames as I could. He sat beside me and snaked an arm around my waist like he was afraid I was going to end up in the fire. I leaned into him.

Patti handed me a cup of hot chocolate, and I sipped gratefully, doing my best to ignore the squirming worms burrowing deeper inside me. I wondered if that's what maggots felt like. 'Course maggots only liked dead things, so I'd never know. Thank goodness for small favors.

"What the hell happened? Is Cass okay?"

Touray stalked into the room wearing the pajamas he'd been wearing before, his hair combed back from his face and his feet bare. It was as jolting as seeing Santa Claus dressed like a stripper. I remembered when I'd first met him. He'd been in his element, confident—arrogant, really—and cocky as hell. He'd been totally in control, totally sure of himself and his place in the world.

I wondered if he'd change now. I was sure he never imagined he could be vulnerable to something like a brain-jockey. Or anything at all, really. He'd thought he was invincible. Now he'd learned the hard way that he wasn't; he couldn't travel or pay or talk or beat his way out of everything.

He wasn't always enough.

That had to sting. Hard lesson to learn. She knew that first hand.

"So far, we know that Riley opened a hellmouth and she's covered in a mess of bruises," Leo said dryly. "Maya is checking out Cass."

All of us looked over to where Cass lay on Touray's hospital bed. Maya, looking a little bit groggy, sat beside her. She held Cass's hand and rested the other on her forehead.

"Is she all right?"

Guilt wasn't something Touray wore well. His body tightened, and his mouth pulled into a hard line as he waited for Maya's answer.

"We'll see," she said absently, lost in her task.

"There's nothing permanently wrong, though." He made it a statement rather than a question, though clearly he wasn't sure.

When she didn't respond, Touray made a sound in his chest and started pacing. My living room was not made for pacing. He had to kick aside pillows and dodge around Patti, Jamie, and Leo, looking all the while like he wanted to pick a fight.

I explained what had happened. After I was finished, Leo whistled.

"A hellmouth, indeed."

"What sort of impact will that have? Demons? Vampires? Gods crawling out of the woodwork?" Jamie asked, shaken.

I rubbed my hand over my face. "I don't know. I don't know if it will close itself up or how tearing a hole in it will change anything in the living world."

"You had to do it," Patti said. "You couldn't leave Cass there."

I smiled at her but didn't answer. I wasn't so sure she was right. I'd been so focused on helping my friend that I'd lost sight of the bigger picture.

"Saving the city means saving the people you love," Price murmured in my ear as he tightened his arms around me. "You did the right thing."

"Did I, though?"

"Yes."

His certainty bolstered me a little, but my stomach and head still ached with trepidation. Only bad things could come of ripping a literal hole in the natural order.

"Why aren't the damned phones working?" Touray clenched a hand around his cell, looking like he was fighting the urge to throw it against the stone wall.

"Erickson said something about shutting them down, didn't he?" Leo asked.

"Could it have been the senator?" Patti asked.

"Maybe," Jamie said. "But he'd have to get telecom companies on board. Or use magic."

"But he doesn't like magic," I said. "That's his whole platform: magic is evil and anybody who performs it is sick or evil."

"You're so naïve, sometimes," Jamie said. "Just because *you're* not a hypocrite doesn't mean he's not. He's a politician. That's the definition. Lying, greedy, cheating, hypocrites."

"I'm not naïve."

Both of my brothers snorted. I wanted to argue the point farther when Cass popped up in my head again.

You guys want to keep it down? You're giving me a headache.

"Because a bullet didn't already do that," I responded.

"What?" Leo and Jamie said at the same time.

I waved a dismissive hand. "I'm talking to Cass. Are you okay?"

Well I've got a world-class tinker doing disgusting things under my skin. So I guess I'm rocking life.

"Life being the operative word."

So Touray had me shot? For real?

I couldn't tell if she was pissed or not.

"Sort of. He had a brain-jockey. It's gone now. We killed him and brought him back."

Several moments of silence passed. *Killed him? Touray? You know, this update thing would be a whole lot easier and faster if you just let me grab all your memories for the past . . . however long it's been.*

Normally, the idea would have made me cringe into a corner and scream no, but this was Cass and she'd been deep in my mind more than once. I trusted her.

"Do I have to worry about you having a brain-jockey, too?"

No. I set booby traps in my head for that kind of thing. None have triggered, so nobody even tried. Probably because they were waiting for me to heal up.

"In that hell hole?"

I didn't say they were smart. Are you going to let me look?

I heaved a sigh. "Fine, but no critiques."

That sounds ominous. Oh wait, what have you and Price been up to? I mean, I haven't got laid in awhile, but hetero sex doesn't do it for me.

I flushed. "Too bad for you then. Now get on with it."

It's going to hurt some.

I sighed. "It always does."

Won't be as intense as other times. Here we go.

All of a sudden I felt a *push* inside my head. I grimaced as an ice-cream headache curved around the underside of my skull, wrapping my brain. Wriggling little eels burrowed into my memories. I shuddered. It was worse than healing. I set my cup down and pressed my fists against my eyes.

"How long is this going to take?"

Stop being such a baby. And you realize that you can just talk to me mentally, right? I'm in your head.

"Let me have my delusions."

You're nothing if not delusional. Hold on now. Try to relax.

Ha. As if. I drew in a long deep breath and let it out slowly. My entire body went rigid as a sense of peeling back, like rolling back a sardine can lid, hit my head. The sensation repeated several more times, each time triggering tremors. My brain skipped backward with each peeling, to when Touray leaped out the window, to loading the hostages into Price's Jeep, to fighting Savannah's serial killer son, to Price leveling a stretch of forest.

The memories flicked past like flashes from a flip book. With them came smells and sounds. The salt of fear, the shriek of panic, the echo of death.

Okay, got it. It'll take me a few minutes to assimilate it all.

With that, she withdrew. Little barbs caught in my head, detonating with little acid explosions as they pulled free.

I swore as I twitched and jerked. Price massaged my shoulders, rubbing his thumbs up the back of my neck. I leaned back into his touch.

"Keep doing that. Just for the next hundred years or so."

"I take it Cass is up-to-date now?" Leo asked, one dark brow rising.

"Mmm," was all I could manage.

"Can we now get off the pot and go get the senator?" Patti asked. "While we have the possibility of surprise?"

I looked at Touray. "Can you travel?"

He glared at me, eyes glittering. "I'll damned well do what I have to do."

"Then we need to get Tiny, the artifacts from your vault, and find Taylor and then Arnow." Easy peasy.

He gave a sharp nod. "You all go find your sister, and I'll take care of the rest."

"Just take care of it," Patti repeated. "Talk about being the lone ranger. Or maybe you want to be a martyr. You don't even know who's in charge of your organization right now or if some intrepid soul will kill you on sight. You showing up all by your lonesome could be awfully inconvenient for some wannabe Tyet lord. And that's presupposing you're even up to travelling that much, not to mention carrying passengers."

"You're second-guessing me?"

Patti met his irritated incredulity with an unapologetic, "Totally."

His eyes narrowed, and he turned into his most ogre-like self. Which was pretty ogre-y, if you asked me. Or maybe he was more like the fee-fi-fo-fum giant. Or a troll. Either way, he was pissed as hell, and it was too damned bad for him that Patti was about to rip his balls off. You'd think he'd have developed a better sense of self-preservation by this time in his life.

"What the fuck do you know? You're a minor talent at best, not to mention a two-bit waitress in a dead-end job. *You* might not be able to handle your power, but I can damned well handle mine. If I couldn't, I'd say so."

Patti gave him a long look, and then she examined her nails as if they were the most important things in the world.

"Sure you would, oh great and powerful Oz," she drawled. "Because assholes like you with delusions of grandeur always admit their weaknesses and never do stupid, shitty things out of pride and arrogance.

"After all, stuff happens. Doesn't mean it's your fault. Friends don't get shot in the head, for instance, and your brother's girlfriend doesn't end up in a cage about to be abandoned by the guy who promised to protect her, and magically talented people don't end up getting stuffed into internment camps because your rival decided to motivate you by blowing up parts of the city."

Patti looked at him when she finished, her eyes wide. "Wow. Now that I think about it I'm *so sorry* I doubted you and didn't see how unbelievably capable you are. Thanks to your amazingly persuasive assurance of your competence, I do. How fabulous is that? After all, you are so fucking reasonable, how could anyone not buy your brand of bullshit? Maybe you should bottle and sell it. Really spread your kind of stink all over the world."

With that, she stood. "Now if you'll all excuse me, this two-bit waitress with a dead-end job and minor talent is going to go get our meal on the table. At least I can be useful in my limited way." She smiled at Touray. It promised he'd be regretting his insults, starting soon.

She disappeared into the kitchen.

I shook my head at him. "Man, you are stupid."

His nostrils flared, eyes flattening like a snake's. He really didn't like people challenging him, and he definitely didn't like being called stupid. Too damned bad. This kettle had no trouble calling the pot black. I knew a whole hell of a lot about being stupid.

I disentangled myself from Price and stood, facing off against Touray. Come to think of it, he reminded me more of an angry buffalo bull. Hardheaded, angry, and willing and able to trample anybody in his path.

"I don't know where you learned your leadership style. Maybe you read *The Art of Being an Asshole* and took it a little too much to heart, or maybe giant fucking asshole is your personal style, but you'd better get on fixing your attitude and quick. This isn't your personal little dictatorship where you make decrees and everybody jumps to do your bidding. We're family and we all get a say, and dirty looks and crappy insults aren't going to cut it. Welcome to the new world order."

His mouth twitched, and finally he grimaced. "I'm not used to people questioning my capabilities."

"Is that supposed to be an apology? An agreement that you'll play nice in the sandbox? Because if so, it sucked big time. I notice you don't have any trouble questioning anybody else, by the way. Seems to me turnabout ought to be fair play, or are you that thin-skinned you can't handle a little challenge in your life? Even if it is from a minorly talented, two-bit, dead-end waitress. Who, by the way, is so going to make you regret you ever decided to throw shade at her, and I am going to enjoy every second of it."

He growled. "I apologize for the insults. That was shitty of me."

I pointedly looked side to side, gaze sliding over my grinning brothers, and then back to Touray. "Who are you apologizing to?"

"He can shove his apology up his ass," Patti said from the doorway. She was wiping her hands on a dishtowel. "If you're hungry, come eat."

"I'm starving," Cass suddenly said, sitting up and swinging her legs over the side of the bed.

The livid scar on her head had disappeared, and the color had come back to her face. She even had a short cap of hair. Her gaze when to Touray.

"Hello, asshole. Word is you tried to kill me."

Chapter 26

Gregg

CASS'S WORDS PUNCHED a hole through Gregg's chest, and it was all he could do to stand upright.

"Can you all give us a minute?" he asked, his gaze locked with Cass's.

She looked skeletal, her skin tight on the bones of her face, eyes sunken and bruised. It wasn't just from getting shot and held captive. Her power burned her up from within, and she used it far more than she should, though suggesting that to her was generally met with a rude gesture and crude remarks.

She didn't like people telling her what to do, but then again, who did? Anyway, her sharp nature was one of the reasons he liked her. He always knew where he stood with her.

The others slipped into the kitchen. Gregg folded his arms over his chest, body braced as if against a hard wind.

"I put a hit out on you," he said, not allowing himself to look away from her condemnation. He deserved it and so much more. "And Dimitriou, Castillo, and Kinsey. You're the only one who survived."

His teeth soldered together as he stopped speaking, the muscles in his jaw knotting.

"And you think that's your fault."

"Don't you?"

She made a face. "I didn't exactly clue into it when I was fixing Vernon's handiwork in your head, did I? Here I was supposed to be making sure you were clear, and I missed it. If anybody's to blame, it's me."

He shook his head. "You did all you could. You told me you thought something was off and that you needed things to settle before you could know for sure. You did as much as you could in that moment."

She just gave him a disgusted look. "How about I believe that when you start believing you couldn't have stopped the jockey from controlling you?"

"But I could. I *did*. I jumped out a window. Strong emotions work. You know the drill." He thrust his hands wide. "Why didn't putting a hit out on you three bring up that emotion? How could I just murder my friends without putting up a goddamn fight? Anyway, I *let* the bastard into my head. I was careless." He spoke low, spitting the words like bullets, emotion battering at him.

"Okay then. My fault and your fault, and no fault of the asshole pulling your strings." She dusted her hands together and stood, swaying as she found her balance. "I'm glad that's settled. I'm hungry."

He strode forward, gripping her arms. "It wasn't *your* fault." He couldn't allow her to think it was.

"Nice thing about being a dreamer, I can make up my own damned mind," she said, shaking him off. "What makes you think you can tell me what to think?"

"It's the truth."

She rolled her eyes. "Since when do you care about the truth? You're a gangster. Pull up your panties and get over it."

He glowered. "Get over it? Cass, I put a fucking hit out on you. How the hell am I supposed to get over that? How are you? I'm supposed to have your back, and instead I stab you in it."

"Same way you get over everything else. You shrug and move on. Or, you want me to go in and fiddle around so you don't have to be all angsty hormonal teenager?" She wiggled her fingers at his head.

He made a guttural sound and stepped back, curling his fingers into fists in an effort not to strangle her. How could she just dismiss this like it didn't matter?

"You're going to give me a stroke."

"Look, Gregg. This whole *mea culpa* thing is a bad look on you. I'm too tired to act all butt-hurt so you can feel as bad as you want to, so you're just going to have to get over yourself. Now I'm going to go eat. Feel free to join us, if you can leave behind the crybaby bullshit."

She brushed past him and disappeared into the kitchen. Gregg couldn't help his thin smile. Cass didn't do tactful. He could always count on her to never pull punches, even if she was hitting below the belt.

And she was right about one thing: wallowing in guilt wasn't useful. If he wanted to atone for his sins, he needed to pull his shit together and get back to work.

THE FIRST ORDER of business was clothing. Gregg felt practically naked in the pajamas and with bare feet. He didn't like the feeling of vulnerability that came with it.

He travelled into his primary residence—located in Midtown along the edge of the city shelf and surrounded by trees, giving it the feeling of being in a mountain cabin. A very luxurious one.

Not wanting to run into anybody, he stepped into his bedroom. It didn't appear to have been touched since he'd left. He froze as he caught sight of the mirror where the brain-jockey had put him through his paces when taking control of his body and mind. His gorge rose and he swallowed, jaw jutting. No more of that bullshit. He had to put it behind him and focus on what to do now.

He dressed in dark jeans, a dove-gray silk tee shirt, and a black sweater with a zipper neck. He put on socks and laced on heavy boots, then armed himself.

He slid on a shoulder holster with a compact Glock .45, adding extra maga-zines to the storage pouch. He strapped another gun to his leg and pulled his denim down over it. He strapped wicked knives to his waist and grabbed a small collection of nulls and other spells, distributing them to his pants pockets.

Pausing a moment to consider, he went into the bathroom and brushed his teeth. The meal Patti had served had been revolting. At least for him. Everybody else enjoyed it thoroughly. He couldn't help a small smile of appreciation. It might have been petty, but she certainly made her point: don't bite the hand that feeds you. Literally. The others had found it hilarious and told stories of how she'd punished each of them with inedible food that they had no choice but to eat or face a repeat of her wrath.

And Cass called *him* a gangster. Gregg was starting to understand there was a lot more to Patti than he'd given her credit for.

The thought gave him pause.

She wasn't the only one. He'd ridiculed Riley for thinking she'd take over Savannah's organization, but damned if she hadn't done exactly that. She'd earned the unqualified support and respect of his brother, separate from Clay's love for her. Cass also respected her. Trusted her. Accepted her leadership. She'd never been willing to commit to him in the same way. Riley's brothers took her orders, and despite being complete buffoons, they were also smart and capable, and Gregg had to admit he'd welcome them into his organization and likely give them leadership roles. Same with Patti.

All of them followed Riley's orders and together they'd achieved a lot. That realization struck him like a frying pan to the head. For the first time in his life, it occurred to him that he might not be the best one to lead this charge to get the senator. Even as the others were going over the plans, he'd assumed he'd step in and take over.

He shook his head in unfamiliar self-disgust at his reflexive arrogance. Not only wasn't he going to swoop in and take over the operation, he wasn't going to have any greater say on the plan than anybody else.

Surprisingly, it didn't bother him as much as he thought it would. In fact, it felt . . . freeing. He didn't examine that too closely. He had a feeling he wouldn't like what he found.

He travelled from his bedroom to the vault to collect the Kensington artifacts, putting them in a canvas bag and setting them back on the shelf. He'd leave them within the safety of the vault until he fetched Tiny. Before that, he should look into what had been happening among his people.

Unfamiliar reluctance washed through him. He remonstrated with himself. Nobody would know about the brain-jockey, nor would they know his responsibility for killing Kinsey, Castillo, and Dimitriou. He just had to arrive, pick up the reins, and take charge.

For the first time in his life, he wasn't eager to do so. He scowled. Was that a residual effect of the jockey? He hadn't let Cass check him. Not in her condition. The jockey was gone. He knew that without a doubt. It was enough. Maybe the jockey had made alterations Gregg didn't recognize. This bizarre desire to avoid returning to his proverbial throne was completely out of character.

Still, he *felt* like himself.

Famous last words of people whom dreamers had tampered with. That was the point—making them feel like their thoughts were normal.

He fought the urge to knock his head against the wall. He didn't like this uncertainty, this feeling of having been castrated, his balls dropped in a drawer somewhere. He felt unmoored. Unsure of who he was or who he wanted to be.

Even more terrifying, what if his brain was just fine and he *was* thinking for himself? What was he supposed to do with these feelings? Hell, what he wanted most was to hunt down the jockey and then the anonymous assassins who'd killed his people.

A sudden avalanche of questions hit him. How had their families taken the news of their deaths? Did they even know? Who would have told them? That sort of thing was his responsibility.

A headache pulsed behind his eyes.

Liv Castillo had a sprawling family. The youngest of seven, she had nieces and nephews, cousins, aunts, uncles, and grandparents. Alexander Dimitriou had two kids. His husband was dead, and his brother looked after the children. Mark Kinsey had two stepdaughters and two more girls with his wife, Julia. They were all younger than ten. Too young to have their father ripped away.

He gave a harsh laugh that echoed through the vault. And when was a person old enough for that sort of hell?

Gregg drew a ragged breath. This wasn't a choice. He couldn't abandon what he'd built; he couldn't abandon his plans. Diamond City needed someone to drive out the vermin and protect the populace. The only way he could do that was at the head of a Tyet.

For the first time in his life, he wished there was another way.

Chapter 27

Taylor

SAVED BY THE KNOCK. Even so, Taylor's heart thumped in her chest as if she'd just run five miles uphill in a snowstorm. She backed away from Dalton and went to the door.

Vernon stood on the other side, his blue eyes—so much like hers—flicked from her to Dalton and back. Had he been listening on the other side? Did he know they were working together?

She supposed she'd find out soon enough, right when it would bite hardest. "What's the news?"

"Jackson has elected to join us. He's of the mind that he could reason with the good senator. Or at least his wife. Jackson and Mimi Rice have a history."

"The 'I hate your fucking guts' kind, or the 'I would do anything for you' kind?"

"Closer to the second than the first."

"He thinks he can get her to use her influence to get the senator to lay off Diamond City and the talented?"

"He didn't say."

"Did you ask?" Taylor eyed him as if she could tell if he was lying, which she couldn't. Especially not with a brain-jockey riding him. Anything that struck her as a hint of lying could be indigestion on the jockey's part.

"He didn't say," Vernon repeated. He looked past her to Dalton whose eyes had narrowed to slits.

"Got something on your mind?"

"Keep your fucking hands out of my head," the other man growled. "We had a deal."

"You were in the way, and I didn't have time to explain. I'm assuming you're getting us where we're going?"

"We'll need better transport. A four-by-four isn't enough. Snow plow would be better. We could shove stalled vehicles out of our way instead of going around."

Taylor blinked, astounded at the speed with which Dalton shifted from pissed to plotting. Had his anger even been real? Or did he just tuck it away in order to get on with the mission? Either was plausible. Given he'd been in the teams, chances were he'd learned to bury his feelings under a rock in order to get his job done.

"We've got some one-ton SUVs kitted out with continuous tread, snow blades, and flash heat. They should get us there."

"Some?" Taylor echoed. "You're not thinking of taking more than one vehicle, are you?"

"Jackson doesn't go anywhere without a protective detail."

"How nice for him, but he's going to see the senator without. For one, we may say he's a prisoner or at least unwilling to come. For two, we don't need to be calling attention to ourselves. The FBI is bound to have outfitted his compound with state-of-the-art and state-of-the-magic security. They've got to have cameras that do what Dalton's eyes can do, probably even better. They are going to see us coming if we come through the front door, and a goon squad isn't going to make them relax any. If we go in a back door, we're going to want stealth, not an army."

"It's not negotiable," Vernon said. "Jackson and I will ride in a separate car. You two will be accompanied by three guards, as will we. You'll agree because you have no choice."

"Whatever. Are we going now?" she asked.

Vernon checked his watch. "Half hour. Someone will come for you."

He departed. Taylor shut the door, pressing her hands on it like she needed to hold it shut.

"You okay?"

"Fine."

"Sure. I can totally tell."

She swung around, eager for a fight. "Then why did you ask?"

"Because I had a vague and stupid hope you'd talk to me about it."

"Sucks to be you then, doesn't it?"

Dalton gave that little smirky smile again, like he enjoyed her antagonism. What was he, a closet masochist?

"Do you ever talk to anyone? Your sister? Brothers? A friend?"

Taylor scowled, deciding to deliberately misunderstand him. "If you aren't deaf, and I didn't think you were but am now wondering, you'd know that I talk to a lot of people. In fact, I'm talking to you right now."

"My file indicated you had some good friends from the sandbox. Plus a few you were tight with in your teenage years. Do you talk to any of them?"

Her anger flared, and she stalked over to him, poking her finger into his chest to punctuate her words. "Fuck. Off. A file? Seriously? Do you know my shoe size, too? Where I buy my underwear? Kind of tampon I like? Just how in-depth did this file of yours go? And why haven't you mentioned it until now?"

He reached up to gently fold his hand around hers, holding it still against his chest. Taylor shivered and told herself it was pure anger. Nothing else.

"Your father told me some basics, but I wanted to know more. I put together a file on your entire family, plus Patti, Clay, and Touray, and I did background checks on all your employees. If you want to read them, you can. It's thorough because I'm thorough so I know more personal things about you than you undoubtedly want me to."

"Like what?"

He shook his head. "You can read it. I'm not going to piecemeal it out."

Taylor pulled away, needing some space. It wasn't that she was really surprised. If she'd bothered to think about it for more than a second, she'd have realized that of course he'd have files. Any good security agent would, and Vernon had supposedly sent him to look out for Riley, and then he'd made it his mission to look after all of them. Knowing habits, places she liked to go, and generally know her, was pretty standard.

Didn't mean she had to like it. She said so.

"To quote a very smart and smart-assed woman, sucks to be you. It's done, can't be undone, and I'd do it again. So feel free to rant all you want, but I'm not going to apologize."

Her brows rose. "Rant?"

"Rave, shout, yell, scream, nag. Whatever you want, really."

"Can I just skip to kicking you in your balls?"

He smiled a dare. "You can try."

"I just discovered I have the power to kill with my talent. Are you sure you want to antagonize me?" Taylor's ire had cooled as her humor rose.

"Haven't you heard? Only the good die young."

"Well you certainly aren't that."

"Not even a little bit."

"Doesn't mean I couldn't kill you."

"But that would leave you alone with your father and Tyrell. You won't do that."

"So I should wait until later?"

Dalton opened his mouth to say something, and in that moment, an avalanche of bone-chilling cold hit her. She flew sideways in the air, bouncing against the wall above the bed's ornate headboard and remaining there, pinned by an invisible fist.

Cold enveloped the room and seared her flesh, burrowing deep. Magic flooded into her along with adrenaline. It flowed so fast that it was like using a firehose to fill a pool. She reached for it, but it ripped from her grip. Probably for the best. She didn't know what she'd have done if she could have grabbed it. Streaks and blobs of colored light flowed past, stretching and twisting like she was having an acid dream.

Her heart jackhammered. She struggled uselessly against the pressure holding her, like a turtle on its back.

Abruptly, it vanished. She pitched forward onto the bed. The relentless cold continued to gnaw at her.

Taylor heard herself breathing raggedly. Dalton grabbed her and turned her onto her back.

"Taylor? What's happening to you? Are you okay? Talk to me." He snapped the words like a drill sergeant.

She couldn't have answered if she wanted to. Her entire being was focused on the torrent of power that now pounded inside of her, surging and sloshing like waves driven by a storm. Her skin stretched, and her tendons and sinews drew taut as the pressure built.

What the hell was happening? More importantly, what was she supposed to do now?

Riley would know. Or she'd figure it out. Riley *always* managed to figure something out. But then, her sister had had years to learn about her talent. Taylor had had minutes and now the final exam was here. If she failed, she didn't think she'd live to know about it.

She wasn't going to last another thirty seconds at this rate.

A blob of muddy-brown light separated from the torrent and drifted to her, sinking down to settle on her chest. She felt it wrapping her, and it suctioned up some of the overwhelming power, its color deepening into dark burgundy as it did. Her relief equaled her fear. The blob seemed to be saving her, but how long before it sucked her dry and killed her?

It would have to hurry if it wanted to get a full meal before the cold got her.

Taylor tried buck it off her, but it didn't move. She reached up to grab ahold of it and when she did, her hands closed on something dense, almost solid, and electric.

The blob sucked her hands inside and she felt something wrapping around them like staticky, sizzling wires. The jolts ran up her arms and made the rest of her twitch.

"Listen, child. There is little time. You've accidentally absorbed a great deal of power from the rift. I'll siphon off what I can, but it won't be enough."

Taylor heard the words but couldn't tell if they'd been said aloud or in her head. The latter sent a roar of panic through her, but she made herself focus.

"Who are you?" Icy frost plumed from her lips as she spoke.

"Kensington."

"Zachary Kensington?"

"Yes."

She choked out a laugh. "Right. The guy we need right exactly at the time we need him. I was born yesterday at the same time I fell off a turnip truck. Who are you really and what do you want?"

She had a sense of irritation and disgust from the invader. "I *am* Zachary Kensington."

Because repeating it with emphasis was totally believable. Taylor would have told him to fuck off, but since she was on nuclear overload and didn't have the time or focus to spare, she went with getting rid of him as quickly as possible.

"Okay, fine. I'll play. Talk fast. What do you want?"

"You must destroy the machine."

"What?"

"When I was alive, I created a machine that required five cardinal talents and myself to operate. After we used it, I broke it in six pieces and hid all but one. Someone has discovered them. The protective containers have been opened. You must find and destroy them."

She shook her head. "No. We've got three pieces of your weapon and have been looking for you to find out where the last two pieces are and to help us put it back together. It's the only way to save Diamond City. Wait, six pieces?"

"It is not a weapon. It should not be put back together. It was made for using only once, and then the situation was dire."

"It's dire now. The magically talented are getting locked up. Soldiers are overrunning Diamond City, taking people. We have no way to fight back, except with your weapon."

"It is not a weapon," he repeated. "It is a machine for memory."

"I don't understand." She'd begun to shiver, her teeth clicking together. She couldn't take the cold much longer, but she wasn't sure she could escape it. It felt like she'd been swallowed by the spirit realm.

"Back then, we did things. *I* did, with my talent. Selective culling. Murdering the worst to create changes in society." He paused. "There was a lot of rot in the apple. After, we made everyone forget how they'd been living. Made them happy to get along. It worked, but afterward, I dismantled the machine. Too powerful and too dangerous. No one should have that kind of power." He seemed to be struggling to make the words.

Taylor reeled. She couldn't be understanding him right. "Wait. What? You killed people and then used the weap—the machine," she corrected, "to make people forget what you'd done?" She realized she'd started believing he was really Zachary Kensington.

"Yes. And made them forget how things had been, how'd they'd been living. They had to be willing and ready to change to the new way of doing things. Of living without constant warring."

"That sounds perfect. We'll do that again. Tell me how."

The words came out in hiccupping stutters. She panted shallowly, lungs aching. It felt like she'd climbed up Pikes Peak in the middle of winter. Barely any oxygen and way too fucking cold. She hardly felt it when Dalton crawled up onto the bed and wrapped himself around her, pulling blankets around them both.

His warmth was like catching a fleeting glimpse of sky on a stormy day. He didn't seem to notice any of the chaos or Kensington's blob of energy. His arm passed right through as he wrapped it around her.

At first she didn't think Kensington would tell her. Finally, he spoke.

"Gather the pieces in one place with masters of their cardinal virtues. Put them together. Link them using the key. Cast a forgetting over the city.

"I warn you—the machine charges a high price. Death will follow for all those who take part. But for another's sacrifice, I would not have survived. You will not get so lucky. There are journals in my workshop. The key will lead you there. I must go."

"Wait! Why did you come to me? Why not my sister, Riley?"

She had a sense of him scowling. He radiated anger, irritation, and impatience. "Because you share my blood and my talent. I felt you come to your power years ago, and then nothing. I believed you dead. Then a short time ago, you erupted like a dormant volcano. When the walls between worlds was breached, I was pulled to you like a fish on a hook. I would have been drawn to you when the boxes were first breached, but somehow your power failed to summon me. When it finally did, I could not refuse its call."

Why not? She didn't ask. She could feel him fading, and she had more important questions. "Where are the rest of the pieces? How do we put them together?"

"They will know."

Who will know?

She didn't get a chance to ask. His light faded into fluttering of petals that drifted into nothingness. The cold ebbed slowly, and the whirling kaleidoscope lights faded. Taylor gasped, trying to get enough air inside of her. Dizziness made it hard to see clearly. Dalton rubbed his hands up and down her back. She lay on her side and he'd pulled her flat against him, one leg wrapping over hers.

"C'mon, warm up, Taylor. I can *see* how cold you are. You've got to warm up."

She broke out into hacking coughs as she managed to draw deeper breaths. Her lungs spasmed and squeezed, refusing to unclench. But even as she fought for air, her brain clung to Kensington's warning.

Death will follow for all those who take part.

That meant Riley. Touray. Herself, if Kensington told the truth, though how she fit into the equation mystified her. Plus whatever binder, dreamer, and maker they found to help. All would die.

"Taylor? What's happening? Taylor? Can you hear me? Jesus fucking Christ!"

As Dalton shouted the last words, he launched himself away from her.

Magic crackled inside and around her. Kensington had siphoned some off while they spoke, no doubt allowing her to have a coherent conversation and keeping her alive. She tried to twist to see Dalton but felt like she'd fallen into concrete.

"Taylor, you're overloading. If you don't discharge some magic, you'll go into cascade."

"Don't know how," she gasped, staring up at the ceiling as the world closed in on her.

"Can you feel me?" he asked.

He'd taken her hands and pressed them flat to his chest. His energy bubbled like hot silk under her palms.

"Yes."

"Feed it into me."

"How?" she asked weakly. Her body twitched, and she couldn't seem to get a breath.

"Feel the power move through you and push it through your palms into me. Concentrate. You can do it."

The power moved through her all right—like nuclear pinballs on speed. They rocketed through her, ricocheting and multiplying. Before long, she'd be so full of them they wouldn't be able to move anymore. Instinct told her that would be very bad. Probably fatal. She'd be barbecued from the inside out.

Visualizing the power in her mind was next to impossible. Her mind wouldn't focus. Then she realized she could actually see it, if she went into trace sight. She found herself dropping into it before she realized she'd done it. Instinct. It does a body good.

She looked down at herself and though it was difficult to get a good view while lying flat on her back, she could see the growing storm of power within. It whirled with tornadic fury, barely contained by her flesh.

She'd begun to feel physically bloated, her skin stretching taut, her insides squeezed. Something had to give and soon or she'd rupture wide open. Still relying on instinct, she reached out to the power, more than a little surprised when it seemed to draw in slightly as if listening for her command. Picturing herself reaching out to it, she took a gentle hold and half pushed, half pulled it into her chest, up and down her arms.

Her hands lit up like beacons. As she became dimly aware of Dalton speaking, his voice rising with urgency, she also felt her body twitching and jerking. He held her hands tight to her chest, telling her to try or do it or something like that. A rushing sound like storm wind blowing through an aspen forest filled her head, drowning him out.

Her hands burned. The pain grew and turned sharp and just as quickly became unbearable. Gritting her teeth, Taylor focused everything she had on pushing the power through her palms into Dalton.

The dam broke. Power flooded his body.

He screamed.

It was muffled as if he fought against making a sound, but it was enough. Taylor jerked away, but he refused to let her. Power continued to drain into him and as it did, the pressure within Taylor grew bearable. The rushing in her ears quieted, and she became aware of two things at once: her own panting and Dalton's hoarse gasps.

When he still wouldn't let her pull away, she curled her fingers under and knuckled him hard while at the same time pulling back and cutting the flow of energy. It was easier than she thought, the power answering to her will. She'd got rid of enough not to be in danger. As she thought about it, the power seemed to flow away. Maybe she was getting the hang of this.

Dalton sat back on his heels, his head hanging forward, his chest bellowing as he sought to catch his breath. He let go of her hands and his dropped to his sides. Taylor squirmed upright set a hand on his thigh.

"Did I hurt you? I'm so sorry. I didn't know what to do." The words vomited out in a mix of guilt and shock. "Are you hurt?"

He lifted his head. Before she knew what he was doing, he'd grabbed the thick bedspread and pulled it up around her.

"You're shivering."

Taylor snuggled into the bed spread. "Did I hurt you?"

"I'm fine. How do you feel? What happened?"

Her eyes narrowed. He'd screamed. Dalton would barely wince if he broke his leg and the bone stuck through his skin. Screaming meant he'd gone far past his limits and control. She couldn't imagine what kind of pain that had taken.

"Don't bullshit. I hurt you. I know I did. Is it bad? How can I help you?"

He lifted a hand and cupped her face, his mouth tight. "I. Am. Fine. Tell me what happened."

"You *screamed*," she insisted stubbornly.

He rubbed the back of his neck before. "Yes, I did. You hit me with a hell of a wallop, but it's done and I *am* fine. Nothing permanent."

Her brow furrowed. "I can't tell when you lie." She searched his eyes for a hint of deception, but the mods gave nothing away.

"I'm not lying."

She scraped her lip with her teeth, her frown deepening. "I can't tell," she said again.

Anger flickered across his expression. "I don't lie to you."

She considered. "I don't know that that's true. Riley lies when she wants to protect people," she observed, her body was starting to settle into mere tremors, but she felt numb. Even where she touched him and his heat leached into her, it felt like thick plastic separated them.

"I think you might lie to protect me." The way she'd lie to protect the people she loved. Like she wouldn't tell anybody about the artifacts or how to find the workshop.

His eyes closed, and he muttered something she couldn't hear, even as close as he was.

"What?"

"I said you're too damned smart for my own good. I probably would if it meant keeping you safe." He spoke as if barbed wire wrapped his throat. "Will you please tell me what happened?"

"Didn't you hear?"

"You were talking, I could tell, but you barely made any sound and nothing I could understand. It's like you were halfway in another world."

She sighed. "I don't exactly know what happened. It's like the spirit realm opened and it spilled into ours. I could see trace. A lot of it, whirling around and spinning so fast I couldn't see. And then Zachary Kensington plopped down on my chest."

Saying that out loud bemused her. Of all the gin joints in all the world . . . and he'd been drawn to her. Because her talent had called him. Because they were alike.

"Kensington? For real?"

"He said so. He could have been lying, but my gut says it was him."

"What did he want?"

He listened without a word, not that it took very long to tell.

"The artifacts are the backup plan, anyway," she said. "There's no reason to say anything at this point."

"And if the primary plan fails?"

She blew out a tired breath. "Everything I am tells me to keep it a secret and protect my family," she admitted.

"But?"

"I promised to help Riley." She shook her head. "We've been lied to most of our lives. It's been me, my brothers, Riley, and my mom against the world. I can't betray them. I'll have to tell the truth."

He nodded understanding. "How are you feeling now?"

"Cold as a witch's tit."

"You were in hypothermia," Dalton said. "It wouldn't have been long before your body started shutting down."

"It's still cold in here." She frowned. It wasn't a physical cold. At least, not for anybody else. It was left over from the spirit realm. Or maybe whatever door had opened up between the two realms remained ajar.

Dalton rolled away from her and off the bed. "I'll get the fire going."

Taylor maneuvered under the covers and curled up into a ball to help build heat within her cocoon. She heard Dalton messing with something in the sitting room, and then a small *whump* when the gas fire kicked on.

"That should heat the room pretty quick." He folded the bedspread in half and laid it doubled on top of her

Just then a fist pounded on the door and then it flung open, bouncing against the wall. Vernon came flying in like his ass was on fire. He stopped dead, looking first at Dalton and then Taylor rolled up in the blankets.

"What happened?"

"Good question," Dalton replied. "What the fuck *did* happen? One minute she's standing there, next she's in hypothermia and shivering so hard I thought she'd break bones. It was an attack, and with Tyrell's wards being what they are, nobody could get through from the outside. It had to be one of your people. You said everybody was loyal. You made *sure* of it. That means it was you, someone you gave access, or you're incompetent. Which is it?"

He'd gone into robot mode, sounding entirely logical and curious more than angry. If she didn't know better, and she *did*, Taylor insisted to herself, she'd think he was still working for Vernon or Tyrell or both.

"Wards are broken all over the place. Not nulled or drained but broken. Whatever hit, it was big." He studied Taylor. "I can send for a tinker."

"You can shove your head up your ass," she said, interrupting whatever Dalton might have said. "I don't want any of your people near me, much less have one of your tinkers messing around in my body."

"She's okay," Dalton said. "At least as far as the hypothermia goes. I got her under the blankets and the fire going. She's still low. Hot chocolate would help, along with high-calorie food."

Vernon stepped outside and said something to someone and then returned. "You have no idea what happened?" he asked Taylor.

"Hmmm," she said. "Let's see. Something magical happened to me that almost killed me. Do I know what or how? Gosh, maybe if someone hadn't walled me off from my talent for my whole life, I might have a frame of reference, but as it is, I'm a fucking babe in the woods and no, I don't have any idea what happened except I got seriously cold, seriously fast."

Dalton frowned, pretending confusion. "Wait, walled you off from your talent? What talent?"

Good man. If she didn't trust him, she wouldn't have told him about her new-found talent.

"Did you see anything?" Vernon asked, ignoring Dalton.

Streaks and balls of light. They were weird, though. Stretching and rippling. She shook her head. "It's hard to describe."

Vernon nodded. "The lights were likely you seeing trace, though I don't understand why or how, even."

Dalton's brow furrowed in well-acted confusion. "She's a tracer? Like Riley?"

"Something like that," Taylor said. "Vernon, here, bound it when I was a kid so that I couldn't use it. I didn't even know it existed."

"But . . . you do now?"

"Yep. Happened when your boss man hit you with a . . . what did he call it? A brain clap? Yeah, that was it."

He looked at Vernon. "You fucked in my head just to tell her she had a talent?" The clear question underneath asked why Vernon hadn't trusted Dalton with that information.

"You aren't my man, anymore," Vernon said. "You made that clear. Anyway, the bindings had worn through and had started to break. She was about to go insane and kill at least a few people on the way. I didn't have time for conversation."

Dalton nodded as if that made sense or maybe to suggest he was okay with the explanation. Whichever one it was, Vernon bought it.

"She's not quite a tracer. I'll let her tell you about it."

Taylor snorted. "As if."

She'd wriggled upright and scooted to the edge of the bed, dragging the blankets with her. She didn't want to look like a victim with Vernon around. She didn't him to think he could take advantage.

"How long before you're ready to go?" he asked.

"Her temperature is still too low to risk going outside," Dalton said, surveying her with red eyes. "She's just over ninety-five degrees. She should be at least a degree higher before risking the wind and the cold."

"She's not going out in it. She'll be in a Snowcat," Vernon replied.

Just then a guard stepped in the doorway. He wore a sidearm on his hip and carried an automatic rifle, which he currently had swung behind him where it hung from its strap. He carried a tray holding a carafe and several coffee cups along with a plate piled with danishes and donuts.

Vernon directed him to set the tray on a low table and then the guard withdrew. Taylor wondered if the guards went armed to the teeth all the time, or if it was because of what had happened.

Dalton poured a cup of hot chocolate and handed it to her. She sipped, grateful for the heat and creamy sweetness. She drank it as fast as she could without burning her tongue, or without burning her tongue *much*, and then held her cup out for more.

By the time she'd finished the second cup, two donuts, and a cherry danish, she felt a lot better, and also needed to pee. She left the two men rehashing their travel plans and went into the *en suite* to do her business.

Looking in the mirror, she discovered she looked like she'd suddenly developed anorexia, plus a case of vampirism. Her eyes were sunken and bruised-looking, her face pale as paper, and she guessed she'd lost at least fifteen pounds. How? Wrestling with the power? What else could it be?

She scrubbed her face with hot water and ran it over her hands and wrists. She grabbed a wax-paper-wrapped glass from the corner of the sink and drank a couple glasses of tepid water. Hopefully, getting to the FBI meetup wouldn't take as long as getting to Tyrell's, or she'd be needing several pitstops.

As she returned to the room, both men fell silent.

Dalton looked at Vernon. "Make sure to load her SUV up with food supplies. Coffee, water, sugary snacks, nuts, dried fruit. If she keeps dropping weight the way she is, she'll be a corpse before morning."

"Sure," Taylor said, going to stand in front of the fire. "Please do talk about me like I'm not here. I can't tell you how much I enjoy that. Oh, and while you're add it, why don't you discuss all the ways I'm incompetent and need to be carefully coddled so I don't break a nail. I'm just so dainty," she added in whispery, high-pitched baby voice.

This time her irritation with Dalton was real. He gave her an impatient look and promptly ignored her as he turned back to Vernon.

"What about Mr. Tyrell? Was he hurt in the attack? Will he still be coming along?"

"He wants to be there when the senator gets taken down."

One of Dalton's brows rose. "I wouldn't have thought he'd take the risk. Someone just blew through all his wards. He ought to be heading for a bunker."

"Things have come to a head. He wants to deal with the senator once and for all and agrees that this plan has a good chance of success. To hedge his bets, he's planning to bring along his Kensington artifacts."

Taylor's stomach twisted. "He what?"

Vernon nodded. "He's been hunting them down for awhile. Word is that Gregg Touray has the rest, and if changing the senator's mind doesn't work, we might be able to activate the weapon and use it to save the city from the good senator's plans."

Taylor didn't have time to react before a knock sounded on the door jamb.

"Everything's ready," a guard said and withdrew to wait.

"Are you recovered enough?" Vernon asked Taylor. "We can wait a few hours for you to rest."

Like he cared. "Absolutely."

He motioned for her to exit before him and fell in behind her, Dalton bringing up the rear.

Taylor paid little attention to where they went, her mind caught up in worrying about the artifacts and whether they'd have to use them, wondering whether Arnow and Erickson had figured out a way in to the senator, and wondering if everybody was already waiting for her, Dalton, and Vernon to show up. And when the fuck would cell service come back online?

Chapter 28

Riley

"WE JUST HAVE TO trace them," I said, shoving my dead cell back into my pocket. "The good old-fashioned way."

Price looked at me with one eyebrow raised. "You're not going to just dive through the spirit realm and go to her?"

I winced. "I'm not sure that's wise at the moment. Not after poking a hole in it."

"Wise and you aren't often used in the same sentence," Leo noted.

Price and Jamie nodded agreement. I stuck my tongue out at them.

"I get the job done, don't I?" Which was true. I had a good record for completing the jobs I was hired for, and for tracking down stolen kids on the side.

"I have no idea how," Jamie said. "A priest, a rabbi, and a Riley walk into a bar. Havoc ensues. Dead litter the ground. Bloody, broken, and bruised, she crawls out holding the lost ark in her hands. Or the grail. Crystal skull? Whatever she's looking for, she gets. It might be a little cracked and the world might be ending, but she succeeds." He shook his head. "I don't know why you don't play the lottery every day of your very charmed life."

"I wouldn't call it charmed," Price said, cutting through Jamie's levity, his face turning dark. "In fact, I'd say she's more of a disaster magnet. I don't know about you, but I'm tired of nearly losing her."

"That's true," Jamie said, having no funny comeback for that.

I appreciated him trying to keep the mood light, though. I could always count on him and Leo to laugh in the face of danger. Ragnarök. The apocalypse. Running out of the good beer. Penile dysfunction. Whatever.

Touray had left just minutes ago after forcing down the meal Patti had prepared. For the rest of us, it was delicious. For him, it was soaked in grease, both over and undercooked—which was quite a feat, overly spiced to the point of burning his tongue off at the root, and cold.

To his credit, he ate it without a word, and his wry look at Patti said he got the point.

"Is everybody ready?" I asked.

We'd all geared up for the cold, each of us carrying a variety of weapons, both magical and ordinary.

"As we'll ever be." Cass was bundled up in enough coats and long underwear to look like she'd put on a hundred pounds. Maya's healing and the food had done a lot for her, and she wasn't nearly as pale as before.

We had no idea how serious the bullet wound to her head had originally been, or whether it had affected her talent at all. Brains were funny things, and even if healed up by tinker, they might not work the way they had before.

On the positive side, Cass was herself, still in-your-face honest, still grouchy, still rude as hell. She also claimed to feel more than well enough to come with us.

"Have you been able to get any sense of Taylor?" Patti asked as we trooped to the door. "Is she okay?"

I shook my head. "She's heavily nulled."

That could mean she'd nulled herself, that she was with Tyrell and possibly imprisoned, that she'd gone to find Arnow, or a dozen other possibilities. The only way to find out was to track her down. And Dalton. I still didn't know if I should have trusted him with her. Not with him thinking Vernon was the bee's knees.

We trouped outside into the storm, and a bubble formed around us. I was wishing for snow shoes or even better, snowmobiles, but I didn't have any. *Gotta put those on the shopping list*, I told myself.

We'd elected to go the overland route, since we had no idea how our secret tunnels had faired with the explosions. The trip from Savannah's hadn't gone near any of those locations and had been safe enough, but now that we needed to go into Midtown and possibly Uptown, that was no longer the case.

I figured Price could keep the storm out of play as far as walking went, but I didn't know if he could do anything about the snow. At least eighteen new inches had fallen, but I was betting it was more like two to two-and-a-half feet. That meant the drifting was going to be a bitch. I hoped we'd be able to find some kind of transportation we could steal, like snowmobiles. Still, we were going to need three. Maya had stayed behind.

We clambered out of the Burrows and out onto one of the wide industrial streets running near my house. Price led the way, his shoulders set and his head down.

The still bubble around us became more of a wedge, pushing everything before it out if its way. I was awed that he was managing that sort of control.

His efforts made the ground far more walkable, though ruts remained in the compacted ice layering the road. Road clearing wasn't a priority out in the warehouse district, and there'd been a lot more important things to do since the explosions.

I still had no idea how many had died or been wounded. I didn't know how well the hospitals were handling the influx of patients, and I didn't even know if emergency workers had managed to put out the fires.

The storm could have helped or hindered their efforts, though I figured it was probably more of a hindrance, especially with visibility being gone. Fire-fighters would have a hard time finding each other and their equipment, not to mention figuring out where they needed to be. Add in deep snowdrifts, and it had to make for a real clusterfuck. The exhaustion of slogging through snow weighted down with their suits and tanks and equipment would strain everybody to their limits.

Hopefully, people weren't dying because of it, but I couldn't be all that sorry. The storm was also doing the same to the soldiers sweeping up the talented. Whether Price had intended it to or not, he'd bought us time to deal with the senator.

Going through the Downtown was harder. There were far more obstacles, and a lot of cars had been deserted in the gridlock. On some roads, they'd been knocked aside by magic and piled up on the sidewalks and against buildings like a metal salvage yard.

What I hadn't expected were the people who joined us. Some came out of cars, others out of buildings, some had been tromping their way through the storm. Covered in snow, shivering and sometimes limping, they pushed inside the bubble wedge.

Despite our hurry, Price slowed so that no one who joined us got left behind, broadening and lengthening the space to allow more room.

Few spoke. All were exhausted, shoulders bowed with the weight of it. Here and there, some left, while others wandered in.

Taylor's trace still didn't seem to be going anywhere. She'd never checked in, thanks to cell service going down. I knew she'd continue on her mission, but every passing moment made me itchy to make sure she was okay. At the same time, I didn't want to risk jumping through the spirit realm.

Wouldn't it be nice if I could separate my astral-self from my body and zip out to follow her trace? Or maybe I should get a magic mirror or an 8-Ball and let one of them do the work. Maybe, while I was dreaming, I could sprout wings and fly.

I sighed and kept walking, my brain nagging at me to *do* something. I chased ideas around and around but kept returning to the idea of following her trace with my astral-self.

I considered how I might go about it. It wouldn't be like removing Gregg from his body. I'd still be anchored to myself, which meant I wouldn't be risking getting sucked into the spirit realm and not being able to get back. The question was how would I separate my astral-self from my body? And if I managed it, how far would I be able to go without breaking the tether holding me to my body and this world? Would my body shut down without my astral-self inside?

I had an idea on how I might do it, *if* it could be done. I chewed my lower lip. Trying would be low risk. If I did manage to step out of my body, I could wait to see how it handled me being outside of it. If it looked like things were okay, I'd follow Taylor's trace. If not, I'd step back into myself and figure something else out.

No time like the present.

I slowed and drifted back toward the end of our caravan before sinking down into myself. Instead of dropping down into the heart of my trace, I stopped in what I decided must be my chest. Of course, it could have been my big toe, not that it really mattered. All around me my astral-self pulsed with a steady rhythm, like a heartbeat.

I settled myself, letting my awareness seep outward into my astral-self. When I'd stabbed it through, the pain had felt like someone ripping my spine out of my body. Touching it now felt buzzy. Softly electric, like swimming in carbonated water.

I mapped the edges of my spirit, getting acquainted with it, and fully inhabiting it. Now for the hard part. I braced myself for pain and gathered myself, drawing my astral-self inward. It coalesced around, well, me. And it didn't even hurt.

I didn't stop to ponder that particular little miracle and instead pushed out of my body. My flesh held me fast. All right then, I'd try another way. I bumbled against my insides until I found an opening. I wriggled through it and kept going through a maze of flesh and bone until suddenly I streamed out into the world.

I looked at myself. I stood like a statue. My trace emerged from my nose. Better than further south, I supposed. I waited a long minute as Patti and Leo noticed I wasn't moving. They started trying to figure out what was happening. The main thing was I was still breathing and my astral-self remained vibrant. That was all I needed to know.

I swooped down and coiled around Taylor's scarlet-and-gold trace. Hopefully, when I reached the point where it was nulled out as I figured it would probably be, I wouldn't lose it.

I flung myself along her trace, skimming along like a missile. The world passed in a blur. It wasn't long before I hit a null wall. I could feel Taylor's trace extending beyond. Was I going to let some nulls or binders stop me?

Not a snowball's chance in hell.

I rammed against the wall and poked astral fingers into it. It gave only slightly. I hooked my nails into it and dragged on it. All I needed was a tiny hole or one little frayed thread.

The walls were well constructed and well tended. They seemed to be at full strength and didn't offer any weak spots. I drew hard on my power and hit it again, and this time I created a kind of suction when I struck. A little bit of energy from the wall bent outward and I grabbed it.

I pulled, pinched, and twisted, using my talent to disrupt its orderly energy at the same time. Finally a piece broke loose. That was enough to let me create an actual hole by tearing through the carefully woven spells. I had no idea what would happen as a result, except that the disruption would expand and probably cause a chain reaction throughout the wall until a lot of energy was released. In other words, an explosion. Probably a big one.

Hopefully, neither Taylor nor I would get caught in it, but I'd reached the point where taking the risk was more important than not.

My awareness shot through the crumbling wall, clinging like a bloodhound to Taylor's nulled trace. It wound about, fading to almost nothing and then strengthening again. Eventually, I followed it back through the wall. Or what was left of it. As I passed through it again, I felt its energy crackling and seething, its massive power unravelling with no place to go.

It was going to be an ugly ending. Wild magic wasn't very predictable. It's why, when I went through or took down a null wall or binder wall, I spooled up the power. That alone was dangerous. Just letting it loose like this without tending to it took the danger to a whole new level.

I found the end of her trace when I ran into another null wall. This one didn't feel so thick or sturdy, but as I explored it, I realized it wasn't a wall at all. It was a container of some kind, and it was moving. A vehicle then, with Taylor inside.

I didn't attack the nulls, since I didn't want to kill my sister. Instead, I tried to figure out where she was, but with the storm, I couldn't make out any landmarks or street signs. Luckily, I didn't need to know. Leo and Jamie could figure it out.

I thrust myself back to where I'd left myself and the others, swirling back up my nose and taking up residence in my body again. It took a second for me to connect to my flesh and remember how to work it. I blinked and shook myself.

Patti, Cass, Leo, and Jamie circled me. Price stood back a ways, eyes white and staring upward. The other people who'd joined us stood in a cluster muttering and anxiously watching me.

I didn't wait for them to chastise me for taking risks. After all, everything had turned out fine.

"I found Taylor. She's on the move in some kind of vehicle."

I began to shiver. Being outside my body hadn't insulated me from the cold of touching trace. My hands were numb, and my arms ached all the way up to my neck. A streak of ice ran from my nose down into my stomach.

"Do you know where?" Leo asked.

I shook my head, grateful they weren't bombarding me with recriminations. "I couldn't tell. The trace was really hard to follow in the first place, and I couldn't get any landmarks."

"Then it's time for us to do our thing," Jamie said, nudging Leo with his elbow. "Bet I can find her faster."

"That's a bet I'm willing to make. What are the stakes?"

"How about I don't kill either one of you?" I said, crossing my arms. I did it to look menacing, but really I just wanted to pull my heat back into myself.

"That can be the bonus," Leo assured me.

"That can be the whole enchilada," Patti declared. "Get on with it, you idiots."

They might have looked abashed, but it was hard to tell with their balaclavas and goggles on. Then both looked around. Leo headed for a parking meter that had been bent sideways almost level with the ground. He pulled off a glove and squatted down to grab the shaft.

The steel turned liquid soft and burrowed down into its hole, driving below the sidewalk. Who knew where it went next. He'd tie into the metal infrastructure of the city and begin his search.

Jamie had grabbed a lamp post and was in the process of doing the same. I half expected to hear them trash talking each other, but either finding Taylor was important enough to keep them focused or Patti had cowed them.

Cass came and linked her arm through mine.

"You okay?"

"Why wouldn't I be?"

"Don't even start with me. Isn't one of us, including those idiots you call brothers, who don't know that whatever you just did took a lot out of you. You're shivering."

Patti grabbed my other arm so that I was wedged tightly between them both.

"Do we need to be worried?"

"Not about me. I'm a little cold, but otherwise fine."

Patti leaned forward so that she could see Cass. "Do you believe her?"

"She knows we'll kill her painfully if she lies to us about it, right?" Cass asked.

"You'd hope she might have figured it out. She's not a complete idiot."

"Then she's probably telling the truth . . . this time."

"I knew I should never let the two of you meet," I groaned.

"She's my sister from another mister," Cass said. "We were clearly separated at birth. Patti's got a bad attitude, no patience for dumbasses, and no filters. We could be twins. Plus, she prefers playing dirty to playing clean, and she protects her family like a honey badger. Just like me."

Cass stood on her toes, leaning into me and said in a loud stage whisper that practically echoed down the street, "That includes your gorgeous ass and those too-pretty-to-be-allowed brothers of yours, in case you didn't know. Though I will punish them if they don't stop trying to one-up each other."

Punishment by Cass would be at least as unfortunate an ordeal as punishment by Patti.

"Can I watch?" I asked.

"Center-row seat," she promised. She let go of me. "You'd better go and reassure Price. He's freaked out, even if he doesn't show it."

Patti let go as well and gave me a little push in his direction. "You may want to be more careful with him," she said. "He's a little on the fragile side."

I stopped in front of Price who didn't look at me.

"Hey."

"Hey," he replied, still without looking at me. Before I could figure out what to say next, he continued. "If you're thinking you have to apologize for something, you don't. You've got your stuff to do, and I'm wearing my big-boy pants."

"Cass and Patti think you're upset," I said warily, trying to gauge if he was lying to protect my feelings.

"I'm worried. I'm always going to be worried. I hope you don't expect me to be calm and relaxed when you're off doing dangerous things." He cracked a half smile.

"No, but your mouth is saying one thing and your eyes are saying something else. Like you can't look at me."

"I'm concentrating. It's hard to do when I'm both talking *and* looking at you."

"What are you concentrating on?"

His smile took on a malicious edge. "I dumped a bunch of snow on all the fire sites to make sure they are out, and now I'm making a snow maze."

Not at all what I expected to hear. "A what?"

"Tall walls of snow throughout the city. I'm putting openings in for people to pass through, but knocking them down will take time and effort, plus having to move the snow after will keep the soldiers and city personnel busy for a little while."

"Nice."

He shrugged. "It makes it easier for people to get to where they need to be. Plus, I'm barricading the soldiers up on the Rim."

"Buys us some time when the storm breaks."

"It's starting to move on. Can't tell how long it will take to clear out, but it's headed toward Kansas and Nebraska next, from what I can tell."

"I think I've got her!" Jamie hollered. "She's in some kind of snow vehicle. It's got treads and . . ." He trailed off, frowning. "There are two of them. Maybe it's not her."

"Where?" Price had redirected his attention to Jamie.

"Coming down Brenchman," Leo said. "In Uptown. Not much is moving in the city, and these are heading in the right direction. They're heavily nulled. Can't get a read on anything inside. It's probably her."

"I was about to say that," Jamie said. "Anyway, I found her first. I win. You owe me."

"A kick in the ass, maybe," Leo muttered.

"Can you guide us there?" I asked.

"No need," Price said. "I've got them."

"I wonder where they are going," Patti said. "We aren't going to catch up with them on foot."

"For now, they're headed toward Midtown," Jamie said.

"Doesn't change the fact that we're on foot and they're moving a whole lot faster than we are," Patti said. "We need to find transportation. Then if Price can clear the roads for us, we can intercept them."

"On it," Leo said, straightening up. "Clay, can you move us along so I can find something that will fit us all?"

Price nodded, and the bubble started moving. The cars lining the road had largely been tossed aside and weren't worth considering. We came to an intersection and turned right, away from where Taylor was.

"There's a parking garage on the next block," Price said before I could say anything.

It took only five minutes to get there. Leo went inside and before long, I heard the rumble of a vehicle starting up. A few minutes later a blocky-looking Mercedes SUV nosed out of the entrance. It only had seating for five, but neither Patti nor Cass took up a lot of room.

The three of us squeezed in the back with Jamie, while Price took the front passenger seat.

"You couldn't find something a little bit more roomy?" Cass wondered aloud as she shifted to sit on Jamie's lap.

"This was closest," Leo said. "Besides, don't you love the buttery leather and heated seats?"

"My seat is currently being heated by your brother," she said sourly. "Between my bony ass and his bony legs, it's not comfortable."

"I'm offended," Jamie said. Then frowned. "I think."

"It was meant as an insult," Cass assured him. "You might want to consider doing some squats to get a little meat on your chicken legs."

"I'll take it under advisement."

"I feel bad abandoning our passengers," Patti said, eyeing the people who'd taken refuge in our bubble.

"They'll be fine," Leo said. "They can shelter in the parking garage if they need to."

Everybody fell silent as Leo negotiated the roads, with Price clearing the way. We could only manage about twenty miles an hour, which made the time stretch interminably.

"We could play 'I Spy,'" Cass suggested.

"Sounds awful to me," I said.

"Well, we can't play charades. Truth or dare, maybe, but it would pretty much have to be all truths, since dares would probably be limited to eating boogers or kissing people."

"Pass," Leo and Jamie said together.

"Definitely not," I agreed. "There are things I really don't need to know about my brothers, and I'm not really excited about booger-eating. I gave that up a long time ago."

The last earned me a laugh from Cass.

After that, I nodded off, leaning my head against the window.

I woke awhile later when we stopped. Patti's head was on my shoulder, and Cass was asleep on Jamie.

"What's going on?" I asked, nudging Patti.

"They're close," Leo said. "How do we want to handle this?"

"They're inside vehicles that are well protected," Jamie said. "We need to get them out."

"Flat tire?" Patti suggested.

"They're running on treads. We might be able to lock one up," Jamie said.

"Could high-center one," Leo said. "Wouldn't have to worry about what spells they have to protect the treads. We'd want to push steel up through the road base. Chances are the vehicles are equipped to melt snow or ice if we tried using those."

"But they'd get out to check what it was either way, wouldn't they?" I asked. "That's all we'd need."

"We need them to open up both vehicles. If the people in the second vehicle wait to see what the problem is before getting out, we'll be stuck breaking in if they decide it's an attack."

"And high-centering would look natural? A hunk of steel sticking up through the road?"

"How about a giant pothole?" Patti suggested. "You could do that, couldn't you?"

"We could claw away the road, sure," Jamie said. "Hey, Clay. Can you cover up a hole so they don't see it?"

"Think so."

"Let's get to work."

Jamie and Leo got out, leaving us sitting in the middle of the road. Not like there was any traffic. They both approached the same light pole and set their bare hands on it.

"Let's hope they don't stick," Cass said.

"I don't know. It would be funny," Patti said.

"But messy," I said. "And they'd whine."

"Men are such wimps," Cass said.

"I'm sitting right here," Price said.

"Present company excepted," Cass said, patting his shoulder while rolling her eyes at Patti and me. She mouthed the words *big baby*.

I tried to hide my giggle.

We couldn't see anything happen, but after a few minutes, Jamie opened Price's door.

"We've got it ready. I don't know how good their visibility is. They might just drive into it without any need for you."

"Doesn't hurt to be sure," Price said. He leaned back against the seat and closed his eyes.

Several minutes ticked past.

"Okay. I've got it. There's a thin layer of air on top and snow is dropping down on it. They shouldn't see it."

"How far away?" I asked.

"Around the corner," Jamie said. "We should hear it when it happens."

I grabbed the door handle. "I want to watch."

We all came around the front of the car. Price shrank our bubble down so it was only about five by ten feet and led the way.

"What's the plan?" Patti asked.

"I'll know when they open up and I can see their trace," I said.

"What if they have nulls?" Patti asked.

"Jamie and I will build a cage at the outer edge of their range," Leo said blithely.

"I'm feeling a lot like a third wheel," Patti sniffed. "It's getting old."

"You'll get your chance later," Leo promised.

"I'd better. I'm tired of sitting on the sidelines while everybody else gets to have fun."

"If you want to call near-death experiences fun," I said.

"Better than sitting around on my ass like I'm a complete idiot."

"Nobody would ever call you an idiot. Actually, you'd be called the smart one and the rest of us would be the idiots," I said

"Maybe idiot's the wrong word. How about useless as a fart in a wet paper bag? Tits on a boar? A bag of dicks? Well, maybe a bag of dicks would be useful. Probably better than having a man attached most of the time."

"I think she's insulting us, Leo," Jamie said.

"If you only think so, you're dumber than I thought," Patti said.

"Ouch," Leo said. "Someone is bitter."

"Again, duh," Patti said, rolling her eyes. "Have you met me? Of course I'm bitter. It's the center support wall of my entire personality."

She leaned closer to me. "Tell the truth, somebody dropped them on their heads when they were little. Mashed their little brains up."

"It's very likely. They've been trying to hide it for years, but we've all seen the signs. We've just been trying to hide the truth so they don't have to know what cretins they really are, but it looks like the cat has torn open the bag."

"Better for them to know and learn to adjust," Patti said sagely.

"Unless you want me to make them forget again," Cass said over her shoulder. "But that would mean they'd just still keep doing stupid shit."

"*Et, tu?*" Jamie said to her. "I expect it from them, but you barely know us."

"I'm a very good judge of character."

"Says who?"

"Your sister, for one. Of course, doing stupid shit runs in the family, so it's not exactly tough to see."

Before Jamie could respond to that, I stepped in. "I don't suppose you could do something useful and tell us how long before they get here?"

"Five minutes maybe," Jamie replied.

I was aware of a building looming behind me. I assumed we were facing the street but couldn't see anything but solid white. None of us spoke as the minutes ticked past, hunching into our coats and waiting.

Jamie and Leo had pulled a puddle of steel from somewhere, ready to bind anybody who might need it.

We heard the rumble of engines and the crunch of their tracks over the snow. I clenched my fists in my pockets, my heart pounding. Taylor was inside one of those vehicles, but was she a prisoner? And if so, were we putting her life in danger?

The plan was sound, I told myself. Anyway, if she was a prisoner, this was the best time to break her free. If she wasn't, then we were just picking her up on the way to see the senator.

The sound of one of the vehicles hitting the pothole sounded loud despite the muffling snow. The engine roared, and metal squealed in a high-pitched sound. It sent an involuntary shiver down my spine, like fingernails on a chalk board. Whoever had revved the engine took their foot off the gas, and everything quieted, leaving only the low rumble of the two engines, along with a hint of the squeal in the background.

"They're opening up," Leo murmured.

I dropped into trace sight. The snow faded from sight, and instead I saw a sprawling panorama of trace, looping and tangling in every color imaginable. Running through it all were thousands of gray trace lines. I let those fade from my attention and looked for Taylor's distinctive scarlet and gold.

"Five people, two are Taylor and Dalton," I said. "I recognize his trace."

We heard voices, but no words, then loud swearing. More steps and the clank of metal on metal.

"Someone went to the second vehicle," I said. "Door's open," I said as more trace appeared. "Four more, it looks like."

"Got 'em," Leo said, seconds later. "Only there are five more from that second vehicle. You're off your game, little sister."

Or . . . "I can't see Vernon's trace, remember? He's probably the last one."

Leo nodded. "Good point. Shall we go see? Nobody's armed anymore, and nobody's going anywhere."

Price didn't answer, but began walking forward, extending the bubble around us and spreading it forward until we had a cleared space and could see the big snow machine that sat at a tilt, its front end sunk into a giant hole. Behind sat another. Standing just outside the rear vehicle were four people in full-on white camo, all wrapped in coils of steel. Inside sat Tyrell and Vernon, both also restrained.

Two more white-clad people knelt beside the hole, each within their own little cage. Dalton and Taylor stood beside the open doors, both wired up. As soon as Leo and Jamie saw them, their restraints melted away.

Taylor turned to take in the scene, and I ran over to her and threw my arms around her.

"You okay?" I asked, stepping back to look her over. "You look like you lost twenty pounds. What happened?"

Taylor gave a wry grin. "A lot. We need to talk. Vernon and Tyrell have agreed to be bait for the senator."

Before I could answer, Jamie and Leo each swept her up in a hug.

"At least they're useful idiots," Patti observed to Cass, as they came up to stand beside me.

"What do you want to do, Riley?" Jamie asked, having hugged Taylor and shaken hands with Dalton.

"Do you mind?" Tyrell called out. "It's damned cold, and we're not dressed for it."

I glanced at him and Vernon. They were in shirtsleeves, with no hats or gloves, their outer gear likely stashed inside the vehicle. They stood inside round cages about twelve feet in diameter.

I returned my attention to my companions. "Looks like we're ready to go hook up with Arnow and Touray."

"He's awake?" Taylor asked, then her eyes narrowed at me. "You were three-quarters dead last time I saw you. Wait, and is that Cass? What the fuck is going on?"

"Like you said, we need to talk," I said wryly. "But the upshot is, Touray is awake and free of his jockey, Cass is healed up, and so am I."

Taylor stared and then shook her head. "I'm a little afraid to ask how you managed that."

"I was very motivated."

She licked her lips and glanced around. "I need to talk to you. All three of you. Privately."

Foreboding curled in my stomach. "Are you okay?"

"Can we just talk?"

"Over here," Leo said, grabbing my elbow and towing me with him, while Taylor fell in behind and Jamie brought up the rear.

Tyrell hollered something again, but I didn't pay any attention. Probably not the smartest thing to do if I wanted his cooperation, but I wasn't in the mood to be nice, and anybody who was a friend of Vernon's was scum by definition.

Leo held me tightly. I tried to pull free, but he just held on tighter.

"What's your damage?" I complained

"I'm making sure we don't lose each other," he said as he shoved me around in front of him and around the corner of the building. We'd breached the bubble Price had made, and the wind and snow slammed into us. I staggered, and Leo braced me.

A second later he pushed me against the wall, huddling close as Jamie and Taylor came in to join us.

"Fuck, it's cold," Taylor said.

"So talk fast," I said.

A wind break of steel formed behind us, enclosing us in a half-circle, courtesy of Leo and Jamie.

"Thanks," Taylor said, shaking off the snow that clung to her coat and hat. "I want to say this quickly with no questions. Got that?"

She waited until we all nodded.

"I've been having episodes since I got dosed with Sparkle Dust. I thought it was just a reaction, and maybe it was in part."

I'd already drawn a breath to ask what she meant by episodes when she held up a hand.

"No questions, remember? I got hit with a big one when Dalton and I found shelter from the storm one night. It was bad. He saved my life, I'm pretty sure."

I opened my mouth and then snapped it shut and waited for more.

"After we saw Tyrell, we were put in a suite to wait until the storm played out, and I had another one. Next thing I know, Vernon is there and doing things in my head. He claimed if he didn't help me, my head would explode. He tells me that he bound my talent when I was a child because I was dangerous."

Her lip curled on the last word, then she continued. "Anyway, I can see trace. And I can touch it. More than that, I can break it, which apparently means I can kill people and I can do it from a distance. I'm not sure what else I can do."

I gaped, totally at a loss for words, all my questions popping like soap bubbles.

"Shit," Jamie said, drawing the word out.

"That motherfucking asshole," Leo snarled. "He's done nothing but attack this family. He needs to be dead."

"If we could get hold of the senator's trace, you could just kill him," Jamie said, staying focused for once.

I shook my head. "We talked about that. Killing him is a bad idea, unless there's no chance that magic could be blamed. It would have to be *very* obviously *not* magic related, and even then a lot of people won't believe it. Otherwise, more soldiers will show up. Maybe the entire army. Our best bet is still to change his mind. You talked to Vernon's brain-jockey?" I asked Taylor.

"I did. It's behind us, at least as far as letting Vernon do the mental adjustment to the senator."

"You think we can trust it?"

She shrugged. "These days, I don't trust anybody I don't know and most the ones I do, but it's not like we have much choice. For whatever it's worth, Vernon so far has been cooperative. Plus he convinced Tyrell to come along, and that was Spider's suggestion. So—"

She shrugged.

"Spider?" Leo asked.

"That's what I have been calling his brain-jockey. It's shorter than Puppetmaster From Hell."

"Okay. We're still following the plan," I said. I was getting itchy to get moving. To get this over with.

Each of them nodded.

"Touray is meeting us at the FBI building. He'll be bringing the artifacts and Tiny. Once we get there with Vernon and Tyrell, Arnow can let the senator know she has them."

"About the artifacts," Taylor said, and her face turned grim. "Tyrell brought his with him. He's got them in a leather sack. I've also learned some things about what the weapon does and how, but the rest of us should hear it, too. But we can wait until we meet up with Arnow and Touray. He'll need to hear it, too. And Tiny."

Her expression and the somberness of her voice raised the hair on my arms. Whatever she had to say, it wasn't good.

Just then my phone chirped. Everybody else's did the same. I dug out my cell. I had a bunch of texts and missed calls. Most from Taylor, some from Arnow, a few from old clients.

I pulled off a glove to text Arnow. She'd called but not texted and hadn't left a voice mail. I wasn't sure she was anywhere she could safely answer, so I typed out a simple *on our way* and hit *Send*.

"Ready?" I asked as the others checked their own phones.

"We might want to take Vernon's and Tyrell's phones from them," Taylor said as she pocketed hers.

"Good idea."

The curved steel wall surrounding us melted to the side and reformed as a fat post. We trudged back to where the others waited inside the bubble. Dalton stood near Price. Cass and Patti had climbed up inside the crippled vehicle out of the wind. Everybody else remained as we'd left them. Somebody had given

Tyrell and Vernon coats and hats.

"Everything all right?" Price asked as we returned.

"Are you going to free us now?" Tyrell demanded in a stony voice.

"Soon," I said and turned to Price. "Everything's good. I'll fill you in later."

He nodded, his white gaze traveling to my brothers and then to Taylor before returning to me. "Your cell come back on?"

I nodded. "I sent Arnow a text. We should take Vernon's and Tyrell's."

"Already done," Dalton said, his usual robotic expression firmly in place. His gaze moved to Taylor and stuck there.

"We should get going. I don't know where Arnow is going to want to meet, but it'll probably be in Downtown near FBI headquarters."

My phone chirped again, and I checked it.

"Speak of the devil." I held my phone up for Price to see.

Parking garage.

"What do you want to do with Tyrell's soldiers?

Stuff them in the broken vehicle? Leo and Jamie can seal it up long enough for us to get out of here and then they can find their own way home."

Price nodded, and I looked at Leo and Jamie who'd heard and were already releasing the soldiers one at a time and herding them toward the vehicle. Cass and Patti jumped out with Dalton's help and came to stand beside me.

"I'll get the sack of artifacts," Dalton said and went to fetch it.

"What's the word?" Patti asked.

I opened my mouth to reply and then considered. "I can't believe I'm actually going to say this, but Cass, would you be able to pick it up from my head and relay it to Price and Patti? Save the explanations?"

Like the rest of us, she'd rolled up her balaclava into a cap and pulled her goggles down around her neck. Her brows rose as if doubting she'd heard me correctly, and I shrugged.

"It's faster, anyhow."

"You asked for it."

That was my only warning, as she sent a seeking tendril into my mind. I didn't know if it was because she'd done it often enough before, or if I was just getting used to it, but it didn't feel as awful as in the past. It made me shudder out of the sheer invasiveness of it, but the pain was the kind you get when you bump your head. Nothing really to whine about.

It didn't take her long to scoop up the memory of my meeting with Taylor and the boys. I felt her withdraw with a sharp pulling sensation on the inside of my head, and then a kind of elastic bouncing back, like someone had popped my brain with a rubber band.

I could track her progress with Patti and Price by the way they winced and hunched up like annoyed cats, and then a grimace followed by a look of dawning awareness. Simultaneously, they shot a look at Taylor.

"Curiouser and curiouser," Cass murmured. "Your dad is quite the piece of work."

"That's one way of putting it," I replied. "I prefer psychopathic asshole, but you know, supposedly his shit behavior might not be his fault. It might be his brain-jockey's."

"At least you're coping with it," she said with dry humor. "Anyway, Taylor seems to be handling her magic. Getting a talent this late in the game could wig a lot of people out, maybe send them to the loony bin. Or could just go out of control and fry them like an egg."

"You're such a ray of sunshine," Patti said.

"Truth sucks, but at least it's real," Cass replied.

"Can't argue with that," Patti said. "And you're right. Taylor can handle it."

Even though part of me worried, I agreed. "She's too damned stubborn to let the power win. To let Vernon win," I added after a moment.

"You should talk," Cass said.

"Be nice if we could update Arnow on what's going on," I said. Even as I spoke, an idea wormed up through my gray matter. As ideas went, it was both brilliant and diabolical with a dash of funny. I looked at Cass. "Think you can reach out to Arnow and update her on everything?"

An evil grin stretched her mouth wide. "She'll be pissed. She doesn't like anybody invading her head. Kind of like someone else I know."

"Bonus for us then," said Patti.

"Give her everything since we left Savannah's," I said. "Pretty sure she'd rather know than not, even if she doesn't like how she's getting the report."

"You want to warn her?"

"No, but I will." I tapped out the message and hit *Send.*

Sending a cable coming in from above.

"Did you just send her a line from *Radar Love*?" Patti asked with a giggle as she read over my shoulder.

"It's apt, and if she doesn't know her obscure 70s rock songs, then that's her fault."

I nodded at Cass. "Do it."

"You don't want to wait until she replies?"

"Nope."

"And you call me evil." Cass went vaguely cross-eyed as she reached out to Arnow.

I looked at Patti. "Keep an eye on her. I'm going to help sort out our transportation."

Dalton had retrieved a leather knapsack. He tossed it onto the front passenger seat as Leo and Jamie loaded the six soldiers into the crippled snow machine and sealed it up.

"We took out the electrical system," Jamie said. "They can't communicate with anyone."

"What about their cells?"

Leo rolled his eyes. "Please. This isn't our first rodeo."

It was probably overkill anyway, since it wasn't like they could summon any real backup. Not in this snowstorm.

"How do you want to proceed?" Dalton asked, joining us.

"How many of us can fit into that?" I pointed at the remaining machine.

"Comfortably?"

"Comfort isn't the priority. It's clearly able to get through the storm and would give Price a rest," I said.

"Price doesn't need a rest," the man in question declared from behind me.

I ignored him. I could have explained that he didn't know what he needed, since we didn't know what he'd have to do later. Conserving energy was the smart move, and he was a smart man. But since he'd probably have fainted in shock if *I* made the argument, I didn't. I just looked expectantly at Dalton.

"It'll be assholes and elbows, but we can fit all of us in there."

"I say we do it," Taylor said. "We don't want to get separated."

Leo and Jamie nodded agreement.

"Then let's load up," I said.

Cass had finished her sending and stood leaning against Patti who had an arm around her.

"You okay?"

Cass gave a little nod. "Just cold, and a little hungry."

I dug a protein bar out of my pocket and handed it to her. I usually carry them everywhere, just in case.

She took it, making a little face at it before tearing it open.

We gathered at the second transport—a Snowcat, according to the logo on the fender— which was sort of like a giant heavy-duty van on four sets of treads. It had a pair of bucket seats in the front, a bench seat, and a small cargo area in the back with two fold-down seats that faced each other.

"I'll drive," Dalton said. "I can see through the storm."

"Clay can sit shotgun," Patti said, taking charge. "Riley, you sit on his lap. Tyrell and Vernon can sit in the rear cargo area. The rest of us can shove into the middle seat.

My phone chirped again, and I glanced at the screen. Arnow.

You're an asshole.

I grinned.

Yes, but now you're fully up to date. As a control freak, I know you appreciate that. What's your ETA?

No idea. Probably an hour or two, depending on the roads. Could be more. Any news on the senator?

Nothing. Erickson got the communications network running again but will be setting off rolling outages across the city. It'll make it look less like an attack that way, while still giving authorities something to do to keep them busy.

You two safe? Haven't triggered any alarms?

Turns out Erickson's as good as he thinks he is. Don't tell him I said that. He's tapping into the senator's and his staff's communications to see what they are chattering about. Might be useful.

Good. Sit tight. We'll be there as soon as we can.

You mean I can't take a minute to go snowboarding? What a terrible task master you are. I'm going away now.

Be safe.

I put my phone in my pocket and looked at Price. "How are you doing?"

His brows furrowed. "Have a headache. Could use some water and something to eat."

"But your power is staying well under control?"

"I'm not going to fry myself, if that's what you're asking. My sense of self-preservation is far better than yours."

"I'm pretty sure that's an insult."

"Truth hurts, doesn't it?"

"You say stuff like that, and yet you still want to get laid," I said, making a face at him.

He smirked. "If you don't want me, you just have to say no."

I heaved a heavy sigh. "As if. You're as addictive as Sparkle Dust."

"You complaining?"

"Not even a little bit."

He pulled me against him and planted a quick kiss on my lips. "Good."

From there, we all headed for our assigned seats.

"We are not your prisoners," Tyrell declared as Jamie released his restraints, then grabbed his arm and guided him to the Snowcat's steps. They folded down between the treads. "We are here because we want the same thing you do."

"You aren't prisoners," Jamie agreed. "We're just erring on the side of caution."

"So you take our phones and weapons?"

"You took ours," Taylor pointed out.

"It's protocol. And we didn't know what you wanted or what dangers you might present," Tyrell replied.

"Exactly," Jamie said. "Protocol. You'll have to be patient with the rest of us. Taylor has had a chance to know you and trust you, but the rest of us are a little nervous. After all, you've got enough money to pay for one of those satellites with laser guns that can burn a person to cinders in the blink of an eye."

Tyrell ground his teeth as Jamie threw his words back at him.

"You watch too many movies, Mister Lawrence. My understanding is that we're on our way to meet with Senator Rice and reorganize his thinking. We've volunteered to be bait. Surely that earns us a little trust."

"Yeah, but you know that story about the scorpion and the frog? You're both psychopaths, and who knows if you'll just decide to go with your natures and start killing people."

"I'm not a psychopath," Tyrell growled through gritted teeth.

"Oh, my bad. Sociopath. Is that one better? I'm not up with all the latest nutjob jargon," Jamie said.

"Careful, son. You've got me at a disadvantage now, but it won't last."

"Won't it?" Jamie smiled in an unfriendly way. "I guess I'll have to enjoy it as long as it does, won't I?"

"We should null them," Leo said. "Make sure they can't use their powers for evil and all that."

I didn't even know if Tyrell had a talent. If he did, it wasn't part of his public persona, but I wouldn't be surprised. The man knew how to keep secrets.

"Already done," Dalton said. "While you were talking," he explained when I looked at him. "The Snowcats are equipped with standard defensive and offensive supplies. I unloaded the other one into this one and put a nulling cuff on each of their wrists."

I flicked a glance at the Vernon and Tyrell.

"You can check them if you want," Dalton said in a carefully bland voice. His face was just as expressionless. "If you think I didn't do it right."

I wanted to trust him. I did. But a lot rode on this mission, not the least of which was the safety of the people I held most dear.

"Wait a second, Jamie," I said, before he could put Tyrell into the Snowcat.

I grabbed Tyrell's left wrist, wrapping my hand around his null beneath his long-sleeved shirt. Power resonated from it, and the construction of the null was solid and tight. I stepped back and did the same to Vernon.

"I agreed to help you. I don't need to be nulled," he said to me in a conversational tone.

"Given your shitty track record, I think we'll stick with what guarantees we can scrape up. Anyway, it's part of the disguise, right? You and your boss being our prisoners?"

"The FBI's prisoners," he corrected.

I shrugged. "Indulge me. Oh, wait. You have no choice. My bad."

I stepped away to let Leo and Jamie load them up. Despite Dalton's cool demeanor, I could feel him seething. He *wanted* to be trusted. That kind of want wasn't about doing his job for Vernon, unless my father was a whole lot more inspirational than he seemed.

Abruptly, he stepped in front of me as I went to climb up into the front passenger seat with Price.

"I want to talk to you. And her." He jerked his head at Cass. "Now."

His expression had become animated. And pissed. Really pissed. I hadn't seen robot-boy lose it before, and it made me unexpectedly reassured to know he *had* emotions.

"Can't it wait?"

"Not if you keep thinking I'm your enemy."

"What are you proposing?" I asked even though I could guess exactly what he wanted. His willingness—eagerness, even—made me wonder why he hadn't proposed this before. It's not like we'd ever thought he'd really broken ties with Vernon. Even if he *thought* he had, Vernon was a hell of a dreamer and could make Dalton believe anything while still using him as a spy.

"Cass can dig through my brain has hard and as long as she wants," he said.

"If your father has messed with my head, I want to know. If he hasn't and I'm telling you the truth, then I want you to know. Fair?"

"Fair."

I looked at Cass who'd heard her name and come to stand beside us. Price had hopped down from the Snowcat the second Dalton had approached me and now stood behind the other man, body coiled and ready.

"Are you up for this? If not, we can do it later." As in after we'd dealt with the senator.

"It has to be now," Dalton said, stepping toward me.

Price caught him by the shoulder before he could come any closer. Dalton stopped, but otherwise didn't acknowledge Price's grip.

"I can do it, but it'll have to be fast." Cass looked at him. "Fast hurts."

"Do it," Dalton ordered.

"How bad? Is he going to be able to drive?" I asked. "We don't need him incapacitated."

He gave a harsh bark of laughter. "Even if you can't trust me?"

"Even then," I said. "Just because I don't trust you doesn't mean you aren't useful."

"Thanks," he said acidly.

"Don't blame me," I said. "You're the one who showed up out of the blue and tried to kidnap me."

"And since then I've been completely loyal."

"So you say. Anyway, kidnapping isn't exactly something a person forgives all that fast."

"I'll be fine," Cass said. "*And* I wouldn't mind knowing if we can trust you to have our backs. Ready?"

She didn't give him a chance to respond. She grabbed his hand and he went stiff, like someone had jolted him with a taser. A moan escaped his lips, and he sank to his knees, settling down on his heels.

I felt sort of sorry for him. Taylor came over, her face taut with concern. I lifted my brows at her. I knew she was conflicted about him. She was drawn to him, and at the same time, she didn't like him. She'd also said she'd been turned on by Touray when he'd been kissing her. It had been a ploy to break his brain-jockey's hold enough to let Touray jump out the window. I'd seen Touray look at her, though. Like a wolf eyeing its supper. Kissing her might have been a ploy, but I doubted he was particularly disappointed in having had to do it.

Anything Taylor felt for Touray and Dalton could easily be chalked up to a rebound situation. All the same, she looked worried about Dalton. Really worried, like there was a connection there.

He'd saved her life, she'd said. That would create a bond. Plus they'd been alone together for a couple tense days. Had something happened between them?

She met my gaze and gave a little wince and then a tiny shrug. I gave a minute shake of my head, looked at Price and then Dalton and then back at her and returned her shrug. Price had turned out not to be the enemy I'd thought he was. Maybe Dalton wasn't either. Who was I to judge?

She gave a tiny smile of understanding.

Price moved over to stand behind me and pulled me back against him, holding me in the circle of his arms. I leaned into him. I hadn't really known him a whole lot longer than we'd known Dalton. I'd known who he was and reported kidnappings to him here an there, but once I spent time with him, I'd fallen fast and hard, and he for me. It was entirely possible Taylor and Dalton had done the same.

Another moan escaped Dalton, this one lasting longer. Taylor clenched her teeth and crossed her arms tightly, no doubt to keep from breaking the link between Cass and Dalton. Not that it would. Cass hadn't had to grab him at all, but contact speeded up the connection process. Breaking her hold on him wouldn't break the psychic grip she had on his mind. It *could* distract her, however, which could cause problems, maybe even fatal ones.

Taylor shifted, digging the toe of her boot into the snow where she stood. I knew how she felt. The need to move, to *do* something, when all you could do was wait sucked big time.

The minutes ticked past. I tried not to get antsy. Leo and Jamie had loaded Tyrell and Vernon into the Snowcat and come to stand with us, along with Patti. It felt somber, a little bit like standing around a hospital bed waiting to find out if the patient was going to wake or not.

None of us spoke, not even to lighten the tension. Leo and Jamie bracketed Taylor, offering her silent comfort. Even my clueless brothers had picked up on her concern.

"All right," Cass said after a few more minutes. "He's clear. I'm going to knock him out now. It'll make the withdrawal easier on him."

As soon as she spoke, Jamie and Leo moved to grab him. He slumped, and they laid him out flat, waiting for Cass to let go. When she did, Dalton's hand flopped down on the snow. Taylor hadn't moved. Her face was the definition of stricken. I wasn't sure she could move at that point.

"Vernon doesn't have a hold on him," Cass said, giving herself a little shake. "Dalton doesn't have any ulterior motives for working with us." She glanced at Taylor. "Maybe one. He's had a tough life."

"Definitely fits in with us, then," I said. "How long before he wakes up? Is he going to be okay to drive?"

"Probably a few more minutes," she said. "He's going to have a whale of a headache. Should use a heal-all on him. That will help. Have no idea if he'll be able to drive. Depends on him. Everybody's different, but I wasn't gentle, and I went through his brain like a thief ransacking a bank vault."

"Let's get him off the snow," Price said. He, Leo, and Jamie grabbed hold of the unconscious man and carried him to the Snowcat, hauling him up to lay across the bench seat.

"How about we start this thing up and get warm?" Patti said, then crawled over the massive console into the driver's seat.

The beast of a vehicle rumbled to life, a puff of diesel fumes sweeping through the cabin. Most vehicles still ran on fuel, at least in the winter. It was more reliable, since magic had to be refreshed, more so after storms and cold.

"Got any emergency food supplies in here?" I asked Tyrell, ignoring my father.

"In the forward floor compartment," he said.

Leo and Jamie grabbed the D-ring and lifted up the panel, exposing a whole collection of food, medical supplies, water, and who knew what else. The food wasn't particularly appetizing, being MREs, but they were filling enough, and there was a magically activated heating cube we could dip the pouches into for about ten seconds and have a hot meal.

The cabin was large enough for Cass to stand up straight. I perched on the console facing the rear, and Price sat in the passenger seat, while Leo and Jamie squatted on the floor. Taylor wedged herself in the floor space behind the driver's seat near Dalton's head.

Leo fished out a heal-all in the shape of a brass disk hung on a chain. He passed it to Jamie who hung it around the unconscious man's neck and activated it.

We slurped from the pouches and drank water, none of us speaking. Leo had found a box of candy bars that he passed around. The sugar hit my system with a jolt.

"I don't suppose they have a triple shot mocha down in there somewhere, do they?" I asked.

"Afraid not," Leo said. "But you can have this delicious pouch of not-at-all-natural lemon-mango-strawberry applesauce."

I made a face at the combination of flavors.

"You sneer, but the preservatives in just one pouch will guarantee you don't age a day in the next decade at least. Plus it's vegan."

"Let me pretend to think about it. Uh, no."

"Beggars can't be choosers," Leo pointed out.

"At this point, I'm not begging, and I don't know that I'll ever be hungry enough to risk it."

"Give it to me." Dalton's rasping request had us all looking at him

"You broke him," I told Cass. "He's clearly gone psychotic if he wants that bag of slop."

"Or he lacks any taste whatsoever," Patti offered. "At least in food," she added with a sidelong look at Taylor, who hadn't moved. She just sat there braced against the side of the vehicle, arms resting on her bent knees, watching Dalton with hooded eyes.

"Are you going to give me the damned thing or not?" Dalton winced. "Christ. Did you hit me with a sledgehammer?"

"More like a jackhammer," Cass said. "Sorry. You did ask me to do it."

He put his arm over his eyes like the light was too bright. "Did it work?"

"You're clean," Cass told him.

"Like I've been saying."

"And now we can believe you," she said.

"What about that mango-strawberry crap?" He lifted his arm high enough to peer out. "I'm hungry and parched."

"And desperate, apparently," Leo said, passing the pouch over.

Dalton opened it and sucked down the contents as he squeezed the pouch empty. "That hasn't improved since I was overseas. They can make drones that will tell you somebody's eye color, but they can't make decent-tasting MREs."

"So you want another?" Leo asked, heating up a pouch of Tuscan chicken and beans.

"At least," Dalton said, and he pushed himself upright, swinging his feet to the floor, leaning his elbows on his knees, and putting his head in his hands. "Got a bottle or two of ibuprofen?"

"Won't help," Cass said cheerfully. "Give the heal-all a chance. Shouldn't take too long."

He sat up straight, taking the open pouch from Leo and slumping back against the seat, tipping his head back to swallow its contents, and stopping to chew a couple of times. He didn't look at Taylor, and I wondered if he was angry with her for having to prove himself. Or maybe he just didn't want to see what she really thought of him. Or maybe I didn't have a clue what was going on and should let them figure it out. Probably that.

I gave a mental shrug. Her love life was her problem. Or rather, her domain. She wouldn't like me giving her my opinion, and romantic advice from me wasn't worth the toilet paper I wrote it on. What I didn't know about love would fill an ocean. I was barely figuring things out with Price. My best advice to her would be, don't fuck it up, now that we knew Dalton wasn't Vernon's puppet or otherwise up to no good. That is, if she really was into him.

"You going to be able to drive?" I asked.

"Yeah."

Oh goody. The man of a single word.

"Best get on it then," I said. "And welcome to the team."

He looked at me for a long moment, and then a faint hint of a smile curved his lips. "Yes, Ma'am," he said as he stood, hunching so didn't ram his head into the roof.

Leo and Jamie got off the floor and slid open the door. A rush of frigid air chased out the warm. I stepped out on the foot rail that ran down the side above the tracks. Price opened his door, putting the sack of artifacts on the floor between his feet. I climbed up on his lap as Patti eased back over the console to free the driver's seat. I looked in the back to see Dalton holding out a hand to help Taylor stand.

"I'm good here," she said.

He eyed her a moment, then shook his head and vaulted over the console and slid behind the wheel. Patti sat in the seat behind Dalton, which left Taylor with plenty of floor space. Leo and Jamie sat beside her. Jamie patted his lap.

Cass eyed him, then shook her head.

"Taylor's got the right idea." She sank down, sitting with her back against the door.

Dalton put the Snowcat in gear, and silence filled the cabin. I contemplated a nap. Price had his arms around me, and I laid my head on his shoulder.

We hadn't gone far when Taylor broke the silence.

"This might be an opportune time to talk about the fact that Tyrell had Riley's mom killed."

Chapter 29

Taylor

TAYLOR HADN'T planned to say the words, but they popped out before she could even think about them. Stupid, really, since Vernon's brain spider had revealed the truth and Vernon wouldn't remember telling her. Maybe he'd think she found out some other way. All the same, it was something Riley deserved to know. She deserved to be able to grill Tyrell about it, and she might never have another chance. For now, he was a captive audience. Literally. Of course, Taylor might have managed to say it more tactfully, though she wasn't sure just how.

As her words percolated through, everybody stiffened. Riley reacted like a scalded cat. She clawed her way up so that she could see Taylor.

"What?"

Taylor's voice softened. Even knowing all the shitty things Vernon had done, this was devastating to hear. "I'm so sorry, Riley. He had your mom killed."

Taylor wasn't sure what she expected Riley to do but was startled when her sister scrabbled up off Price, over the console, and over the back seat into the cargo area. Jamie and Leo managed to lean out of the way so that she didn't kick them in the head as she went over.

She stood over Tyrell, her breaths coming fast and hard, bright coins of red burning in her cheeks.

"You killed my mom?"

He didn't respond, and she grabbed his collar, jerking and twisting, the other hand clenching in a fist like she was going to pummel him.

"Did you kill my mom?"

"I did."

His cool reply shocked everyone, including Riley who just stood there, still gripping his collar.

"Why?"

"She stole from me. If it's any consolation, she lived far longer than she should have. I sent your father to kill her years before. He fell in love with her and convinced me to lift the order, on the grounds that she would no longer be a problem. But she was."

Riley swallowed hard. "How?"

"Your father began losing his . . . focus. His quality of work went down. I warned him. He failed to step up."

"So you *killed* his *wife?*"

Riley threw him backward. His head bounced against the window. She whirled to face Vernon. Tears streamed down her face.

"And you just *let* him? You kept working for him?"

"He killed the hitman I sent to take her out," Tyrell offered from behind her.

As if that was consolation.

Riley ignored him, her entire focus eaten by Vernon. Her eyes had gone huge, and her body vibrated with emotion.

"Why? Didn't you ever love her?"

Her voice broke, and Leo jumped over the seat and pulled her into his arms. Taylor stood, pulled up like a puppet on strings. She didn't know what she thought she'd do, but she was ready to back her sister.

Riley's body remained stiff in Leo's embrace as she stared at Vernon who seem unfazed by Riley's obvious suffering. Taylor's fist clenched. God, but she just wanted to punch him until he showed *some* sliver of emotion. She was so tired of his unrelenting dispassion. Like a sniper, never losing his cool, never letting anything color his resolve. Maybe that's where Dalton learned it from.

"I kept you safe," he told Riley quietly, his gaze flicking to Taylor and back.

Was that a glint of guilt? Taylor kicked herself for thinking it was possible.

"Your safety for my loyalty. That was the deal I made."

Before Riley could respond, Jamie pounced.

"And it wasn't enough that you gave your boss one hostage, you went and had another baby and got another wife," he said in a voice of cold rage. "Didn't you think you'd caused enough damage? Put enough people at risk?"

"Not to mention the mind fucking you did on Riley, Taylor, Mel, and probably the rest of us," Leo added, his voice gone lethal.

He'd kept his arm snugged around Riley but had shifted to stand beside her. In the crowded space, only inches separated them from Vernon. Taylor couldn't see Tyrell. Everybody was focused on Vernon, but she wouldn't forget that he'd been the one who'd ordered the murder.

Vernon ignored Leo and Jamie, continuing to focus on Riley. "I planned to tell you one day, but if you'd known, you'd have gone looking for revenge, and I couldn't risk that."

"Fuck you! You're a despicable manipulative coward and a miserable excuse for a father. Whatever you might have *planned*"—she put the word in air quotes-

—"you failed. You failed us. You betrayed us."

Her words hit Taylor in the chest like so many punches. She pressed her hand hard against her sternum as long-held emotions bubbled up, along with memories of growing up. Most of them were happy. Of him hugging her when she cried; of playing tag in the park with her whole family; of Christmas dinners and birthdays, building snowmen, skiing, playing practical jokes, and so many other moments.

Something crumbled inside her, and pain she'd pushed far down for so long geysered up. This man, whom they'd loved and believed in, had calculated everything since before she was even born. Had he even loved her? Wanted her? Or had she been some kind of piece on his game board? For revenge, according to the Spider, but how long could revenge actually take?

She made a low sound in her throat, and Riley jerked her head to look at her. Taylor could see her own anguish reflected in her sister's eyes. How many times did they have to lose their father before he was done hurting them?

Riley looked again at Vernon, her body tense, her neck taut with the force of the emotions she held in check.

"I'm done," she said. "I'm done trying to figure out what secrets are out there lurking that could explain your actions and redeem you. I'm done regretting, I'm done mourning for a life and father that never existed, and I'm done listening to your bullshit excuses. You're a parasite. You take and take and take, and you don't care who has to hurt or die so long as you get what you want."

She twisted around to look at Tyrell.

"We're not forgetting you. I promise we're going to make sure that we see justice for my mother's death."

Taylor could hear the amusement in his voice when Tyrell replied.

"Do you think any court will convict me? Men like me don't get tried, and if we did, we wouldn't lose."

"Who said anything about a trial? We'll deliver our justice ourselves."

The smirk remained in his voice. "You can try, but do keep in mind that I make a good ally and very bad enemy."

"Ally? The man who killed my mother?" Riley's voice rose.

"It would be a wise decision, and practical. You win nothing going to war with me."

Riley's back went stiff as a post. "Get me away from this piece of shit before I kill him right here and right now," she said, turning to squeeze past Jamie. Taylor grabbed her hand, unable to get any words past the knot in her throat. Not that she knew what to say.

What she'd suffered at the hands of Vernon didn't compare to what he'd done to Riley. If she felt like she'd been ripped in two, Riley had to be shattered.

Riley sat in the seat against the window and pulled Taylor down beside her. Patti claimed the last seat on the bench, squishing over to give Cass a place to sit. Jamie took the spot where Taylor had been sitting on the floorboards, wrapping an arm around Riley's lower legs. Leo remained in the rear, leaning back on the seat as he watched over Vernon and Tyrell.

Dalton had stopped as soon as Riley had clawed her way into the back, and now started driving again.

"We have Cass," Taylor murmured to Riley. "With her dreamer skills and Tyrell as our key to seeing the senator, we don't actually need Vernon. We could tie him to the bumper and drag him around by the neck."

Riley gave a little snort. "Don't tempt me."

"Why not?"

"Because I'm ready to gut him."

"I'm ready to help," Taylor said. "With great enthusiasm and panache."

"Panache?"

"Style is important when it comes to revenge."

"Why is that?"

"Because nobody remembers a boring revenge murder."

Riley actually laughed, and Taylor joined her. Pretty soon it bordered on hysteria, but neither cared. They leaned into one another, tears streaming down their faces, as they expelled the tension and hatred that had knotted inside them like tangles of barbed wire.

This, Taylor thought, *made their father's behavior worth it.* Without him, she wouldn't have Riley. Without him, neither sister would exist. For that, she could forgive him.

Right after they rolled him in a giant pile of panache and killed him.

AT SOME POINT Taylor dozed, waking when they stopped. She sat up, instantly alert. Price and Dalton opened their doors and climbed out, slamming them shut. A gust of cold wind and snow rushed through. Outside all she could see was white. Through the dense wall of blowing and falling snow, she could see it mounding in giant lumps over cars, bushes, signs, benches, and whatever else littered the sidewalk and road.

She knew that they were supposed to wait for the two men to locate Arnow and make sure they weren't walking into an ambush. All the same, she had to hold herself still to keep from following.

Riley had that faraway look she got when she was looking at trace. Taylor scowled, irritated at herself. She should do that, too. At least see what was what.

It took her several tries to find the mental trigger and release that allowed her drop into trace sight. Once again, everybody looked like human-shaped tree roots, some ultra fine, others thick. It was almost like seeing just blood vessels without any skin, bones, or flesh. But these were lit with brilliant colors and pulsing with life.

Before she could get hypnotized by the beauty, she looked for Dalton's and Price's traces. She stood, leaning over the front seat to pick up Dalton's.

It trailed out through the door, a rich mix of cobalt, orange, and red. But even as she watched, the color faded to nothing and disappeared.

Her heart jack-hammered. Price's trace was gone, too.

Her breath evaporated, her stomach sucking in like she'd been punched in the gut. How could they both just be gone? *Dead*, a quiet inner voice corrected her.

Taylor shook her head. No. They couldn't have just died. Just like that with no warning. Both were strong, skilled men, armed with both guns and magic.

But guns and magic didn't help if you walked into a sniper's bullet or a bomb. Dalton practically had x-ray vision, she reminded herself. No one could sneak up on him. But a bomb?

Wouldn't they have heard and felt the explosion?

With the muffling snow and the thick parking garage walls separating them from Dalton and Price, maybe they wouldn't have heard. Maybe they hadn't.

A noose slipped itself around Taylor's throat and she looked at Riley, expecting to see panic and grief. But her sister was relaxed and focused, still with that faraway look.

"Riley?" Taylor's voice sounded almost normal, though adrenaline pumped through her. "Everything going okay?"

"Dalton is coming back. Price is too far away to see what he's doing, but he's not in trouble."

Taylor didn't wait to hear any more. She grabbed the door handle and thrust it open, leaping to the ground. She landed in a waist-deep drift. She pushed her way through to the track Price had broken and followed it. She heard others follow, but she didn't look back to see who.

She jogged up the track, wishing she were armed. Trapped down in a snow trench, fighting would be tough.

She reached the entrance of the parking garage. A giant mound of snow blocked the entry. On the left side, she found a little notch and guessed Price had used his air talent to make it.

She stepped through and scanned the gloom. A lot of the parking spots were empty, but the garage was still pretty full. Which way had they gone? Up the ramp didn't seem reasonable, so she turned the other way, only to find Dalton coming around a broad support column.

He saw her and frowned, then hurried toward her even as his head whipped back and forth in a quick scan of the surroundings. Relief washed through her. Riley had said he was okay, but Taylor had needed to see for herself. She refused to think about why.

"Is Price okay? Did you find Erickson and Arnow?" she asked to cover her concern as Leo and Patti arrived behind her.

Dalton nodded. "Price's brother is there, too. And Tiny."

She'd never met Tiny, only heard about him. He was an up-and-coming Tyet lord from the Calavera neighborhood. He'd taken Price and Riley prisoner when they ended up in his territory, and then went to work for Gregg. Riley had said the two men were very alike.

Just what the world needed: a second Gregg Touray.

"Are they coming?"

Dalton shook his head. "Arnow wants to contact the senator from here. She said to bring back Vernon and Tyrell."

"We'll get them," Patti said, and she and Leo disappeared outside.

"You going to move the Snowcat?" Taylor walked deeper into the garage. She needed space between them

She wished she knew what she was feeling. She'd been worried when she'd lost his trace. Really worried. That suggested she had stronger feelings than she'd expected. Than she wanted? She didn't know. She was ping-ponging around and had no idea how to feel about Dalton or Touray, for that matter.

The whole situation irritated her. She didn't need the trouble of a relationship. She didn't want all the hassle and eventual heartbreak.

Doesn't need to end in heartbreak, her traitorous brain said. She told it to shut up. Even if a relationship with one of them could work out, there would be a lot of hurt. That came with the territory, and Taylor wanted nothing to do with that.

"It can stay there a bit," Dalton said in answer to her question about moving the Snowcat. "No one will bother it. Are you okay? That was a tough scene back there."

"I'm fine," she said, a response she fell back on whether she was fine or not. She felt stupid and ridiculous for maintaining a hidden hope that maybe Vernon hadn't been responsible for all the pain he'd caused.

Anyway, even if the blame all fell on Tyrell for the murder, that didn't absolve Vernon. He had plenty to answer for all by himself.

What had it been like for Riley's mom? Had Vernon told her that he'd been sent to kill her? That his boss wanted her dead? Had she felt safe with her little family? Had she trusted him?

Mel had trusted Vernon, and she was one of the smartest women Taylor had ever known. She had multiple PhDs, was a veteran FBI agent—well-respected by everybody she'd ever worked with—and she was a brilliant reader. She hadn't been able to read him, though, despite her powerful talent. She hadn't sensed his dishonesty and duplicity. Or rather, he'd made sure she couldn't.

Another thought struck Taylor, making her gorge rise. What was to say Vernon hadn't adjusted her brain to make her love him? Trust him? Had he turned her into his puppet, pulling the strings so she danced to his tune? Dear God, her mother had been a captive slave, not a willing wife.

Disgust and horror twisted in her gut, and she spun away from Dalton. She shuddered, and her stomach surged. Its contents splattered the floor, and it surged again. She couldn't stop her very visceral response. Her body didn't want to accept the truth, rejecting it with violent heaves.

Finally, she managed to choke back her response, drawing air in slowly as she fought to calm her short, panting breaths. Tears dripped down her cheeks. She wiped them away furiously. This was no time to cry, no time to lose her shit.

"What's wrong?"

She heard Riley's words and then her quick footsteps. Riley pulled Taylor upright, her forehead creased, her mouth pulled thin with worry.

"What happened?"

"I hate Vernon," she managed.

Riley nodded. "I know. We all do."

Taylor shook her head. "No. Don't you see? He had to have made my mother choose him. Made her blind to his deceit and messed in her head so that she trusted him. He could have done the same to your mom. They were his puppets. His toys. Once he got in their heads, he could make them do *anything.*"

Riley nodded, her face drawn. "I know. He's a psychopath. Scum. He doesn't care about anybody but himself, and we've all had to pay the price."

"I want him dead," Taylor said, voicing the thing that clawed at her. "I want to kill him myself. I have never in my life wanted to kill another person. Self-defense? Sure. War? It's necessary. But murder? Just the idea is despicable, and yet, if I could, I'd cut his heart out right now."

The tears were back, this time hot and full of hatred. She felt so much she couldn't hold it in anymore, and tears were her only relief.

"He made me feel this way," she said, "and I hate him for that, too. He's taken away everything I thought I knew. I can't tell what was real or fake with any of us. I don't know what memories are even true. He's a disease. A cancer that he's spread to all of us."

"I know," Riley said, and her eyes mirrored everything Taylor was feeling. She put her hands on Taylor's shoulders. "The truth is there will never be anything we can do to him that will equal the harm he's done to all of us. That doesn't mean we can't try, but it has to be later. Right now, we have to focus on the senator. Let's use Tyrell and Vernon to do something positive for once in their lives."

"At least Tyrell has been a philanthropist."

"Doesn't count if he's doing it to hide being a monster," Riley replied.

"Agreed." Taylor took a breath. "Go see Arnow. I need a minute, but I'll be okay," she said.

Riley nodded and turned away. Leo, Patti, and Cass had taken Tyrell and Vernon ahead, the knapsack of artifacts slung over Leo's shoulder. A minute later, Taylor was alone, except for Dalton who had remained behind.

She'd have told him to leave, but he wouldn't, and she didn't feel like arguing.

Instead, she centered herself, taking calming breaths as she focused on all her training and experience with flying and with being in a war zone. Survival depended on being able to compartmentalize and stay in the moment. You couldn't go into any sort of risky situation distracted. In a plane, you'd crash. In a war, you'd get killed. You had to become a robot and react quickly and efficiently, without any emotion.

She pushed aside her hatred and walled it off, along with any feelings she might or might not have for Dalton and Touray.

She pulled a blanket of calm around herself, letting go of everything else. It came with a sudden feeling of a relief that she hadn't expected, but she should have. She was so damned tired of feeling.

One last breath and she started down the ramp. Dalton fell in beside her.

"You going to be all right?"

She didn't respond, not quite sure what she wanted to say.

"Taylor?"

"Would it matter if I wasn't?" she asked, because it wouldn't matter. None of them had a choice.

"To me."

Since that response belonged in another compartment and could only be a distraction, Taylor brushed it away like a mental cobweb. "I'm fine."

"What's your definition of *fine*?" he growled, clearly dissatisfied by her answer.

"Am I capable of doing what needs to be done, when it needs to be done, and how it needs to be done? If the answer is yes, then I'm fine. You know the drill."

She hadn't served in the military, but she'd flown for several mercenary companies in Afghanistan and Iraq, and she understood the mindset. Lives depended on you, so all that counted was doing your job and doing it well.

His irritation radiated from him, but she ignored it. Another cobweb.

They went around the support pillar and found themselves looking down a roadway that ran to the other side of the garage, with angled parking edging along it on both sides. Halfway down was a crosswalk, with one side leading deeper into the garage, and the other side ending in a steel door.

The others had collected outside the door, waiting for Taylor and Dalton to catch up. She broke into a jog, as did Dalton.

"Inside," Arnow said, pulling open the door as the two of them joined the group.

Touray stepped up behind her and held the door. Arnow cast him an annoyed look and then strode inside, followed by Erickson.

He was the definition of grunge nerd. He wore his blond hair up in a manbun and had that pasty white skin of someone who spent most of his time holed up in a dark room hunched over a computer. Right now he had a backpack slung over his shoulders and wore a scuffed leather jacket that looked about fifty years old and a pair of Levi's.

A stranger stood on the other side of the doorway from Touray. Tiny, she guessed. Of course, with a nickname like that, he was anything but tiny. The man was about as wide as he was tall, and all of it was muscle. He was young, probably younger than Erickson, with dirty-blond hair and cold blue eyes. He scanned the garage behind them, an FN P90 held at the ready.

She looked Touray over as she approached. He'd lost weight, but that was to be expected, even though the coma had lasted only a few days. Otherwise, he looked the same. A bear of a man, with broad shoulders, thick black hair, intense black eyes, and a square face.

She couldn't help comparing him to Dalton who also had a pair of broad shoulders, but he was of a leaner build. His hair was long, down to the middle of his back, and he had a quiet way of moving that reminded her of shadows slipping over the landscape. Touray had a way of moving that was decisive and in-your-face.

He watched her with that penetrating intensity that probably cowed most people. Riley called them shark eyes. Cold, ruthless, uncaring. Mostly Taylor found the whole intimidation thing he had going on irritating. Maybe he should just relax and instead wear a big sign saying that his dick was bigger than everybody else's, so he got to be king of the dick mountain.

"You don't look too bad for having just been in a coma," she told him.

"I'll notify the press."

"And you're in such a good mood, too. You'd think with all that rest, you'd be less cranky." She gave a little roll of her eyes. What had she expected? The man was an asshole, a label he didn't mind wearing.

She gave Tiny a little nod and strode through the doorway, surprised when Touray said something she couldn't hear and then overtook her, Dalton and Tiny bringing up the rear.

"I'm sorry," Touray said as he came abreast.

She nodded. "Yes, you are."

"I deserve that."

"Yes, you do. Do you want a medal for admitting it?"

"Looks like I'm not the only cranky one," he said, and though she didn't look at him, she could hear the smile in his voice.

"Jackson Tyrell had Riley's mother killed. Vernon knew it and stayed working for the man. Then he married my mom and messed around in all our heads. So yeah, I'm feeling a little annoyed at the moment."

He didn't speak for a moment. "Fuck. I'm sorry."

He sounded sincere. Taylor didn't want to talk about it, so she changed the subject.

"I'm sorry you got nabbed by a brain-jockey."

"About that . . . I wanted to apologize for the Casanova routine. It was all I could come up with at the moment to break the jockey's hold."

"It's fine. It worked. No harm, no foul." She felt his gaze on her and resolutely didn't look at him. "Anyway, it doesn't matter. We've got bigger things to think about."

"As long as you know you can trust me."

It took all of her willpower not to laugh. Trust him? Maybe a little more than Vernon. Maybe not. Both men had an agenda and didn't much care who they had to run over to get there. Touray tended to keep Price—and maybe Riley—in the *do not touch* column, but anybody else? Free game. She had no illusions that he'd changed his spots since falling into the coma. It would be impossible for him to hit his head *that* hard.

"Well?" he asked when she didn't answer.

"Well what?"

"Do you trust me?"

"Are you kidding ?"

They reached the top of a set of stairs, and Taylor jogged down in front of him, ending their conversation. She could feel him smoldering at her answer, but she was fresh out of fucks to give.

Midway down a second flight of stairs, they overtook everybody else. Taylor fell in next to Cass.

"You look like someone stole your ice cream," the other woman observed.

"I'd say they peed on it."

"Ice cream's overrated anyway."

"Ain't it just," Taylor said. "I think I need to radically switch up my diet."

"Go vegan. No meat." Cass grinned. "Though I'm not sure how well that works when the steaks are chasing the dog." She glanced over her shoulder. "*Juicy* steaks."

"If I'm the dog in that scenario, then I am taking offense."

"Wolf. Steaks are chasing the wolf."

"Better."

"What are you going to do?"

"Ignore them and hope they go away."

"Do you believe in fairy tales, too?"

Taylor grimaced. "You have a better suggestion?"

"Tell them to fuck off?"

"Doesn't work."

"Well then, you've got a choice. Pick one, pick both, kill both, or kill yourself."

A laugh burbled up despite everything. "A ménage à trois with Touray and Dalton? Can you even imagine?"

Cass thought a moment, and then shook her head. "I have a fertile imagination, but those two having naked times together is beyond my abilities. Not even for a hot babe like you, which leaves you with the three other choices."

"Maybe I'll join a convent."

"You'll have to give up sex."

"It might be worth it."

At the bottom of the stairwell they passed through another steel door, then a fire door, into a long hallway. A half-dozen pipes and conduits ran overhead, with industrial lights hanging every twenty feet or so. The floor was sealed concrete, the walls beige-painted cinderblock.

Three-quarters of the way to the end, Arnow turned off through yet another door that fed into another industrial hallway. They twisted and turned through several similar passages until they arrived at another stairwell leading up. The stairs zigzagged back and forth. On the third turn, Arnow stopped on the landing between staircases. She motioned to Erickson. He put his hand on a conduit running up the corner of the stairwell. A second later, a section of the wall slid open.

Within was a small room not much bigger than an elevator and another fire door, Arnow waited until the outer door slid shut behind Dalton and Touray before she opened the other side.

"Welcome to the guts of our operation," she said, motioning everyone inside.

They stepped into a space that smacked of one of those super-secret computer rooms in movies. It had banks of electronics with a ton of blinking lights and two computer stations. With all the equipment, fitting was a tight squeeze and Taylor found herself squeezed up against Touray and Dalton. Cass snickered at her, and Taylor flipped her the bird.

"Erickson has managed to tap in and get a lowdown on the senator's location and his bugout team," Arnow said. "All that remains is to contact him and dangle the bait. Erickson has set it up so that calling from here will carry all the electronic and magical tags that indicate communications from a secured FBI line. He's hardwired a phone into the system from here."

Erickson preened, even as he watched Arnow with a sort of puppy-like longing. Taylor couldn't blame him. Riley called her an ice queen, and she looked the part. She was tall with ash-blond hair, blue eyes, and a face for the covers of beauty magazines. She was also smart, dedicated, and she didn't take shit. She'd eat Erickson for a pre-breakfast snack, if she noticed him at all.

Touray was more Arnow's type. Someone powerful, smart, and aggressive. A lion to Erickson's kitten.

At the thought of Arnow and Touray together, Taylor nodded to herself. They'd be good together, if they didn't kill each other first. As a mental experiment, she considered Arnow and Dalton together. A surge of possessiveness. *Crap.* She was so fucked.

Chapter 30

Riley

I WAS RELIEVED to see Arnow, which wasn't something you'd have heard me say a few weeks ago. In fact, a few weeks ago I'd have been happy to drop-kick her into the caldera. Apparently, like mold, she'd been growing on me.

She totally had a stick up her ass, usually turned sideways, and she was a pit bull when it came to doing her job. If not for her, Josh wouldn't have been involved in tracking the Kensington artifacts, and he and Taylor might even be married by now. Of course, if his tendency to want to kill me had been there all along, I suppose I should thank Arnow for pulling back the curtain on his real personality.

"I need everybody to keep quiet," Arnow ordered. "Bring Tyrell and Brussard up to the front in case I need to prove I have them."

Leo handed the bag of artifacts to Price and helped Jamie escort them forward, then looked at Erickson.

"Call," she told him as she slid on a headset that was plugged into one of the computer consoles.

We all fell silent.

"This is SA Sandra Arnow from the FBI," she said suddenly. "Put me through to the senator. I have information for his ears only."

The person on the other end spoke.

"Not going to happen."

Another silence, longer this time.

"Tell you what," she said. "You tell the senator I have a couple of high-level Tyet people in my possession that he's going to want to see personally. I'm not willing to go through regular channels for reasons that will be obvious. I'll give you fifteen minutes to call me back and then he loses the chance to have them all to himself."

She made a cutting motion across her throat and pulled off the headset, leaning back against the computer desk and folding her arms. "Now, we wait." She looked at Leo and Jamie. "Please do not entertain yourselves."

Price unzipped the bag he held and looked inside. His brows drew together, and he held it out for me to look inside. I saw three boxes. Three? We already had three artifacts. What the hell? Taylor caught our expressions and took a peek. Instead of surprise, she rubbed her hands over her face.

"I told you I had some things to tell you about those," she said as Touray, Dalton, then everybody else had a look.

Touray scowled. "That's not right."

"There should be five pieces and a key," Taylor said. "According to my new friend," she added with a meaningful look at me.

Kensington. I supposed he ought to know.

"What are you talking about?" Touray demanded.

Taylor shook her head. "I don't want Vernon or Tyrell hearing this."

"Not like they can do anything," Leo said.

"All the same."

"What do you want us to do? Have them stick their fingers in their ears and sing?"

"I've got it," Erickson said out of the blue.

He dug in his backpack and came up with a couple sets of earbuds. He plugged them into a little box and put them in each of their ears. When Tyrell started to shove him away, Tiny stepped closer, staring the man down.

Once the earplugs were in, Erickson set a finger on the box, then nodded. "That will do it."

Surprisingly, Taylor took him at his word.

"Kensington told me that there were five pieces and a key. He called it a machine, not a weapon, and he said it was for memory. So six pieces make sense.

And there's more—"

"Kensington?"

Everybody but Dalton echoed the name.

"*Kensington* told you?" Touray said into the following silence, his tone scathing. "Did you hit your head?"

Normally, that sort of comment would have pissed Taylor off, but she didn't seem to hear, her expression pinched with worry.

"Maybe this is another occasion for Cass to do her broadcast thing," she said finally. "Better you get the whole story straight from the source." She looked at me and seemed about to say something, then just shook her head and held out a hand to Cass.

"I'll try to be gentle," Cass said as she took Taylor's hand in hers. "Try to relax. If it's okay, while I'm in there, I'll have a look to see what your dad did."

Taylor nodded.

"You might want to sit down."

"I'm fine."

"Suit yourself."

With that, Cass dove in. Dalton shifted to stand behind Taylor, ready in case she collapsed.

I wasn't sure if Cass would start sharing the memories right away, or if she'd wait until she was done in Taylor's head. I braced myself just in case.

"It's going to hit hard," Cass said.

The memory came in like a missile, waited a moment, then detonated. It played across my mind like a weird movie, where I was the character playing Taylor. It didn't last long. I was thrown against a wall by the rupture made by the spirit world. I wondered why it had hit her so hard and hadn't affected Dalton at all. Because of her talent? Had it hit all tracer types that way? Or was she special?

I concentrated on the blob that was Kensington, ignoring the deep cold and the shuddering pain running through my fictitious body. As soon as Kensington vanished, the memory cut off. I rolled it through my mind again, focusing on his words. And the warning. I glanced at Price whose expression had turned plastic, like a doll. He turned away so I could no longer see his face.

"Holy shit," Tiny muttered. He sounded shaken. Not something he was used to.

"Can we trust that that was really Kensington?" Touray this time. He eyed Taylor speculatively.

I recognized the look. It was a *now that I know her talent, how can I use her* look. I couldn't help smirking. Let him try. He'd fair no better with her than he had with me.

"We've got six pieces. That lends him some credibility," Arnow said, sounding crisp as ever.

I swear she's made of titanium. The air in the room tightened. I inched toward Price and grabbed his hand. His tightened convulsively over mine. If it came down to using the artifacts, he'd lose me, Touray, and Cass in one fell swoop. We still didn't have a maker, though, so the whole possibility was moot. I said so. The air in the room loosened fractionally as that sank into his brain.

"You remember that artifact that was in the purple glass bulb?" Price asked suddenly. "The one that had been hanging over your kitchen sink when you were a kid?"

I nodded.

"What if that's the key?"

"Hiding it in plain sight so no one thinks it's important?" I considered. "Could be. Or maybe mom didn't even know what it was."

"They're calling back," Erickson announced.

We all went silent and looked at Arnow.

"Let Tyrell and Brussard hear," she said as she slid the headset back on.

Jamie pulled the earbuds out of the two men's ears and put a finger over his lips. Vernon looked like he'd eaten a lemon but also resigned to his treatment. Tyrell started to sputter, his face mottling red.

"I put up with your crap," Taylor told him, pulling a necklace out from under her shirt and showing it to him. "Now you put up with ours. Shut up now. The senator is on the phone."

If anything, he turned redder, but his lips snapped shut.

Arnow nodded to Erickson.

"SA Sandra Arnow. To whom am I speaking?"

Pause.

"I need confirmation that you are Senator Rice, sir," she said. "Can you tell me the name of your first mistress and the name of her child?"

My eyes widened. How the hell did Arnow know that? But then I gave myself a mental slap. Erickson. He no doubt had found all the dirt on the senator. If there was an electronic trail, he could probably find it. I'd known he had to be good as one of Savannah's lieutenants, but he was better than I thought.

Arnow waited longer this time, looking up at the ceiling impatiently. Finally, she spoke again.

"If you cannot or will not give me that information, then we're done," she said. "You've got two seconds."

A smug smile curved her lips, and she nodded. "Good. One more. What was the last medical procedure you paid for and who was the patient?"

Again she waited. After a moment, her eyes narrowed and hardened.

"That's incorrect. Senator Rice—if that is who you are—let me explain how this works. I don't have time for crap, and you don't want to lose what I am offering you. I can take this to my superiors and let the chips fall where they will.

"But I'm no fan of the Abbies, and I figure you'll make the most of this opportunity, particularly given what you've already been doing in the city. Therefore, I'd rather bring it to you, but I'm not going to risk blowing my career on some weasel who claims to be the senator and then stabs me in my back. Better for me to take this up the chain, in that case.

"I'll ask you one more time, what was the last medical procedure you paid for and who was the patient?"

This time he replied, and she gave a short nod.

"Very good, sir. Then you should know that I have Jackson Tyrell and his first lieutenant Vernon Brussard, aka Sam Hollis, in my custody, and I'm prepared to turn them over to you."

She listened and nodded again. "What proof would you like?"

Her eyes widened, and she glanced at Tyrell. "It could take a moment and a little convincing, sir. Please be patient."

She pulled off the headset and gazed at Tyrell. "The senator would like you to tell him what your talent is."

That had us all staring. Tyrell crossed his arms above his beer gut, getting a stubborn look on his jowly face. He didn't speak.

Arnow smiled. "I'm sorry, Mr. Tyrell, but this isn't an optional quiz. You'll tell me what I want to know, and you'll tell me now. If you don't, you're going to bleed, and I'll still get the answers I want. I'm sure the senator would love to hear me interrogate you."

He glared at her, and a lesser woman—a lesser human—might have quailed. But Arnow had seen too much and had too many run-ins with Tyet lords to be even a little bit fazed.

"Last chance, Mr. Tyrell."

"I'm a maker," he said finally, his mouth twisting as he practically spat the words.

I couldn't help smiling. It was more than delightful to see him squirm. And then what he said percolated through. I glanced at Taylor who was looking at me, her brow crimped. Now we had four of the five cardinal talents. Five if you counted Patti, who was a binder but nowhere near strong enough for using the artifacts. At least, according to legend. Of course, even if we could get Tyrell to help us, he was probably a dud maker. But we weren't going to need the artifacts. Our plan was going to work.

Famous last words. I ignored the snotty little voice in the back of my head and turned my attention back to the floor show. Arnow's brows arced, and she directed a condescending look at Tyrell.

"A maker," she repeated disdainfully. "You any good?"

"Maybe I'll have the pleasure of showing you one day," he said, his lip curling.

"You mean make me my own personalized dildo?" she asked brightly, clapping her hands like a kid on her birthday. "Oh, goodie! Can you make them in any color? How many speeds? I'd like mine bigger than, well, you appear to be. Even average would be okay."

He flushed almost purple, and I bit back a laugh. He probably had thought he'd heard it all, that he could predict people and control them that way, but Arnow was anything *but* predictable, as I'd discovered since knowing her.

She grabbed the headset. "He said maker, if you didn't hear." Pause. "Another one? Look, Senator, we're burning daylight here." Pause. "Fine. What is it?" She waited, then looked at Tyrell.

"He wants to know your boss's first name."

That caught all of us by surprise. He had a boss? But it made sense. Arnow had told me about the deepwater Tyets—huge criminal conglomerations that ran countries. She'd been running an off-the-books operation investigating something to do with them. What if Tyrell was part of one? If true, then his interest in Diamond City wasn't just about him.

More than that, if the Senator knew that Tyrell had a boss and also knew his name, that meant the Senator was tuned in to whatever Tyrell was up to. Which meant the Senator could be knee-deep in one of these deepwater Tyets, too, though how he could be and still be anti-magic, I didn't know. Then again, politics and corporate policies rarely made sense to me.

My stomach clenched as realization hit me. We had enemies we didn't know the first thing about.

We all looked at Tyrell, waiting for his answer.

His jaw tightened, his muscles knotting. "Hodan," he said finally.

"Hodan," Arnow repeated, her voice rising in a question.

I had the same question. What sort of name was that?

"Very good, sir," she said. "Where?" Another pause. She nodded as if she'd expected the answer. "I can. I'll see you soon."

Soon? How long was that? I expected him to be up on the Rim, which would mean hours of travel at least.

"Yes, sir. I have two other agents with me." Pause. "No, sir. They aren't Abbies."

He said more. Arnow nodded.

"I've had my fill of those self-important pricks," she said, disgust coloring her tone. "We're using nulls to keep Tyrell and Brussard contained, but me and my team are completely human."

She listened another minute and then signaled Erickson to cut the line, taking off the headset and dropping it onto the desk. She stared at it a second, then gave a minute shake of her head and looked up.

"Tiny can be one of the agents, and Patti the other," she said. "The rest of you are potentially recognizable as Abbies. Abnormals," she added, though we pretty much all knew what it meant. I hated the term as much as the untalented hated all the names given to them, "untalented" included.

"Erickson can give those two fake backgrounds that should stand up long enough to get close to the senator."

I didn't like it. I wanted to be there to make sure it all went as planned. I also didn't have a choice.

"As you've noticed, I didn't get on the senator's detail," Arnow said. "Not with the storm. But Erickson managed to dig out a lot of information on his team. The good news is that he's not far from here. He's at the Sedona House, which is a high-security hotel entirely run by Homeland Security for high-value targets."

I frowned. I knew just about every inch of the city. I had to in order to do my job and keep myself safe doing it. But I had no idea where this Sedona House was.

"Where?" Touray asked, and it made me feel better that I wasn't the only one who didn't know.

It looked like Homeland Security had done a good job of keeping its safe house a secret.

"It's on Magdaleine Court."

I frowned. "Never heard of it."

"Me, either," Price said.

"That's because it's hidden magically."

"Definition of ironic," Tiny said.

"For a man who hates magic, the senator sure uses a lot of it," I agreed. "Where is it?"

"Off Florence between Wall and George."

I pictured it in my head. "There's no court there. Just storefronts."

"Those storefronts are all run by Homeland. Above are apartments where agents live, and below is a private parking garage accessible over on South Warren. Those stores and apartments ring the block, but inside is Magdaleine Court, which is accessible through the garage as well as through a couple of the stores. As far as anybody knows, there's nothing back there but a big empty lot, thanks to a glamour."

"What's really there is a big mansion," Erickson inserted. "Senator's set up his headquarters there. He even brought his wife."

"How do you know?" Touray asked.

Erickson gave a sly smile. "Can't hide digital information from me. Eventually, I find everything."

Note to self: don't record secrets on any electronic devices. Not that I did. I wasn't big on computers. I was more like that ninety-year-old man who can't figure out that the reason his computer isn't working is that it's turned off.

"So, what's the plan? You three take Vernon and Tyrell to the senator and get control of him?"

Simple enough, but it wasn't easy. Not by a long shot.

"Once we guarantee your father won't turn on us." Arnow nodded to Jamie and Leo.

Snakes of thick steel cable wriggled up out of the floor, pushing back the industrial tile and winding around Vernon's body, holding him in place. Touray grabbed hold of Tyrell and pulled him out of the way.

Tiny stepped forward, and Arnow handed him something and gave a brief explanation of the poison and the biogel. He nodded and turned to Vernon. He put his fingers and the capsule up to the base of Vernon's neck. I heard a gasp, and Vernon swore.

Tiny stepped back. Blood smeared the tips of his fingers, but the poison pill had been inserted.

"What the fuck is that for?" Vernon demanded.

"You've got a habit of screwing people over," Leo said. "We're not letting you do that, this time."

"I already said I was on board for this."

"But you could easily decide to make the senator do things that suit you and not us, and we're not risking it," Jamie said. "You tried to have Cass shot."

"Ahem," she said. "He didn't just try. I *was* shot. I wouldn't be surprised if he was the one holding me prisoner."

"What about Tyrell?" Patti asked. "What's going to keep him from fucking us over. He's definitely pissed enough to do it out of spite."

"But not stupid enough to risk his own plans," Touray said. "He needs the senator gone as much as we do. Vernon's the wild card."

"Don't have another pellet anyhow," Leo pointed out.

"All right then. Now that that's settled, let's go," Arnow said, ending the conversation.

ALL OF US CROWDED back into the Snowcat, or more accurately, we crammed. Dalton drove again, and Price and I rode shotgun with Cass sitting on the console. Everybody else squeezed in the back. Dawn had broken. Not that it made much difference. We still couldn't see far in the snow.

What I didn't like about our plan was that Arnow, Tiny, and Patti would be tackling the senator on their own. The rest of us would be stuck waiting until they came out again, or the senator invited us in, which he would once Vernon took control of him. And what about the unknown jockey inside Vernon's head? Would that person then step out of the shadows to run the senator through Vernon?

So much could go wrong with this plan. So much needed to go right, and the universe didn't usually like to play that way. More like we were the walking definition of Murphy's Law: if it can go wrong, it will go wrong.

I let out a sigh, and Price tipped his head to look at me.

"You okay?"

"Define okay."

He smiled. "We're on the right side of the dirt, anyway."

"That's true."

He wrapped my hand in his. "It's tough to let people you care about go into danger without you."

I gave him a sharp look, but he looked sympathetic rather than smug that I'd be going through what I tended to put him through.

Don't take risks you won't survive. Promise.

I averted my eyes and squirmed.

"Hey." His fingers tipped my chin back up, his expression solemn. "It's going to work."

"Until it doesn't."

"Then we'll figure it out. We'll get through this."

"And then what? Fighting with Savannah's lieutenants? Going back to war with your brother? Fighting an invasion by a deepwater Tyet?" I scrubbed my hands over my face. "When does this end?"

As if it ever could. We'd be fighting this battle for the rest of our lives. A weight settled over me. This was going to be my life.

But really, was it so bad? Four months ago I'd been a loner, hanging out with Patti sometimes but mostly doing my own thing. I'd only been seeing my family a few times a month, and I'd been doing crap trace jobs in order to hide my abilities. Four months ago, my future had looked pretty craptastic, all things considered.

Now, even with all the endless maneuvering and fighting I had to look forward to, I also had Price. As hard as it was for me to believe, he wasn't going anywhere. Not willingly. He'd chosen me over everybody else in his life. I came first. That was new for me. My mom might have put me first, but I couldn't remember that. My father certainly hadn't, and I didn't let the rest of my family get close enough for them to consider it.

Speaking of whom, I was closer to my family than I'd ever been. Patti and I had always been tight, but I'd still kept her at arm's length with some things, and I wasn't doing that anymore. Cass and Arnow had become good friends, and even Dalton was in my corner. I'd gone from being a loner to being part of an obnoxious, strange, and wonderful family. I wouldn't change that for anything.

Price's chest rose and fell. "We could leave Diamond City. Live somewhere less . . . difficult."

I shook my head, startling myself that I didn't even consider it. "No."

The corners of his mouth flickered in a little smile. "No?"

"I can't believe you'd even suggest it. Our family is here."

His arms tightened around me. "Yes, they are."

There was a satisfied note in his voice that drew my brows together. "What?"

"You said *our* family."

"Duh."

"I wasn't sure you knew it."

I rolled my eyes. "You've made it pretty clear you're not quitting me, and I'm sure as hell not quitting you, so that means you're stuck with all of this." I waved in the general direction of the rest of the vehicle.

"Including my brother?"

"If he gives me any trouble, I'll sic Patti on him."

His brows rose in wounded surprise. "Not me?"

"All these years and you still haven't put him in his place. Clearly you're not up to the job."

"I never had a reason to."

"But you do now?"

He bent and brushed his lips against mine. "Maybe."

I glared. "Only maybe?"

He shrugged. "I haven't seen if you clean your hair out of the drain or leave your underwear on the floor. Could be dealbreakers."

"I supposed I could shave my head and stop wearing underwear," I mused. "Think I'd look good bald?"

He shook his head adamantly. "I changed my mind. I can live with the clogged drain, but I'm totally behind you going commando."

"Maybe the two of you should get a room," Cass said.

"You're just jealous," I said.

"Definitely. Love to have you rolling around in my bed with me."

I blushed, and Price shook his head.

"Sorry. You'll have to find someone else. She's mine."

"It's just pity. She feels sorry that you're an ugly asshole and decided to give you a little attention. Beauty and the beast."

He looked me, his eyes crinkling. "Is that so?"

I nodded. "You caught me, Beast-boy. It's all been pity."

"You do realize I'll make you take that back?"

I nodded. "But I expect you to make it worth my while."

"Oh baby, you can count on that," he growled.

Cass groaned in disgust as Price leaned down to kiss me.

All too soon we arrived. Or at least we stopped somewhere. It could have been exactly where we started for all we knew. Price wasn't feeding the storm's energy, but it continued to rage. Mother Nature didn't appreciate people fucking with her.

Tiny slid back the door, letting in a gust of wind and snow.

"Watch your backs," I told him, Arnow, and Patti.

"We'll be okay," Patti said, reaching over the seat to grab my hand. "We'll come get you as soon as we can."

"Try to be patient," Arnow said with a look that said she didn't think for one second we'd wait.

She was probably right.

"I'm always patient," I said with bright insincerity.

She gave me a sour look. "You're always a pain in the ass."

"Good thing you like getting your ass spanked, then."

"Do you now?" Tiny said, looking Arnow over speculatively.

She actually blushed. "Keep your hands to yourself, Junior," she said, pulling the bottom of her balaclava up over her mouth. "I eat boys like you for breakfast."

"You can have me for breakfast any time," he said with an easy grin. "And lunch and dinner and snacks."

"Focus," she said, grabbing Tyrell and pushing him out in front of her.

"I think she likes you," Patti said to Tiny, pushing Vernon out ahead of her.

"How can you tell?" Tiny asked.

"She didn't kill you," she said over her shoulder as she disappeared out into the snow.

"Don't let them get dead," I said to him as he started to shove the door shut. "Cells are working. Call if you get into trouble."

"Won't need to." He looked at Cass. "Want to ride with me? Be Overwatch? You'll know what's going on."

She looked surprised and nodded.

"Good." He flashed his cocky smile at me as if to say *see? I'm not all bad,* and then slammed the door and disappeared into the snow.

"I'm going to follow," Dalton said suddenly, opening his door. "Just in case."

He was gone before anybody could say anything.

Silence filled the Snowcat.

"I've got him," Cass said, staring off at nothing. "Tiny, that is. They are going in."

"Can you stay with them through nulls and binders?" Touray asked.

"Depends."

"On?" he prompted when she didn't say more.

"On me. You need to shut up now," she said and closed her eyes, bending over until her head touched her knees. "This is going to take some work."

Chapter 31

Taylor

TAYLOR FOLDED HER arms as a heavy silence fell inside the vehicle. Touray prowled back and forth in the short space along the sliding door. Cass concentrated on her link with Tiny. Leo stood with his arms crossed, face carved from stone. Jamie sat beside Taylor, staring up the Snowcat's roof, his jaw jutting, rolling a ball of liquid steel in his fingers. Erickson, whom Taylor had almost forgotten about, sat hunched in the back corner, his laptop open on his knees. He wore headphones, his fingers flying over the keyboard. Riley and Price sat in the front seat still.

It didn't surprise her when Price opened the door and stepped out, quickly disappearing into the snow. Riley pulled the door closed, brushing snow from her arm and shoulder.

"Where's he going?" Touray demanded.

"Stand guard," Riley said. "He can sense a lot more outside in the storm than inside. He'll know if a hit squad comes for us."

It was almost funny how casually she spoke of assassins. Taylor expected Touray's cool nod, given his line of work, but Riley was way out of her comfort zone. She had to be tough, though. They all did.

Touray brooded out the window at the endless white. He tapped his fingers, and the muscles in his neck pulled tight. Taylor sympathized. The inevitable hurry-up-and-wait period of any mission was awful. You sat twiddling your thumbs while quietly going out of your mind. Or not quietly. Some guys couldn't settle down and started singing or telling jokes or just about anything to deal with the tension.

She preferred to do something useful. Like give herself a crash course in her own magic.

Taking several deep breaths, Taylor centered herself, pushing aside everything else before she dropped into trace sight. It took a few seconds for her instincts to manage the shift.

Bright streaks of color appeared and wavered, blurring as if she were seeing them through wet glass. She focused on Dalton's trace, until it sharpened and she could see the way it overlaid the driver's seat of the Snowcat. But within a minute or two, it began to fade. Seconds later, she couldn't see it anymore.

What the fuck?

She twisted, gaze skittering across the interior of the Snowcat. Trace streaked through it, but even as she watched, several began to fade, like a flame burning along a fuse leaving nothing behind.

Understanding bloomed. *Damn.* Riley could see trace forever. Just Taylor's luck that she could only see very fresh trace. How long could she see it before it disappeared? Five minutes? More? Less? She'd have to time it. But that meant if she wanted to use her particular skill, she'd have to be quick enough to catch the target's trace before it disappeared.

The tension coiled tighter as they waited for Cass to relate what was happening. Everyone jumped when the driver's side door opened and Dalton climbed inside. That is, everyone but Cass and Riley. Cass was too focused, Riley was in trace sight and saw him coming.

Snow clung thickly to Dalton, turning him into a snowman. He jerked off his balaclava and gloves, shaking them off before stuffing them in his pockets.

"They got inside okay," he said.

"They just got in to see the senator," Cass said suddenly.

"Here we go," Leo said, rubbing his hands together.

"Did you see Price?" Riley asked.

He nodded. "He's wound pretty tight."

"Who isn't?" Taylor muttered.

"Yes, but if he loses his shit, he could wipe out the city," Dalton pointed out in a studiously reasonable voice.

"I'll go see if I can talk him down," Riley said.

"I'll do it," Touray said. "I could use some air." With that, he vanished into thin air.

Being a traveller had its advantages.

"What do you see?" Jamie asked Cass.

"They are in some kind of big lounge-style meeting room. There's a six-member Secret Service detail, the senator, his wife, and our intrepid heroes. They've done the introductions, and the wife is sending for refreshments." She snorted. "Like this is some kind of tea party."

"What are they saying?" Leo asked.

"Arnow's giving her spiel. Powerful prisoners, she wants the senator to reward her for bringing them in, blah blah blah. Senator is eyeing Tyrell like the cat with a bowl of deep-fried mouse balls. Smug bastard."

"Mouse balls?" Leo echoed. "And they are deep-fried?"

"Better than cream any day," Cass said.

"If you're a cat, maybe," Leo said, and Taylor noticed one hand drifted down to cover his own balls.

"Think about all the ball-less mice, running around," Riley said. "Has to be hundreds to fill a whole bowl."

"You can stop beating that horse, now," Leo said with a pained look.

"You guys are such babies," Taylor said, shaking her head but appreciating the moment of levity.

"Can we stay focused?" Dalton said. "What's happening?"

"Nothing. Refreshments and small talk about the storm. It's all very civilized," Cass said, her lip curling on the last.

"Are they nulled?" Riley asked.

"Went through a null wall to get in, but there's no magic suppression now.

"Stupid," Erickson muttered.

Taylor had all but forgotten his presence.

"In keeping with his whole 'magic is bad' thing, though," Jamie replied.

"Except for the null wall going in," Leo pointed out.

"Not his show, though, is it?" Dalton said, and everybody looked at him and he explained.

"He doesn't get to tell his security detail how to protect him. They know he's got magical enemies and that magic is the only good counter for magic. They'll accommodate his foibles as much as they have to, but they won't compromise his safety. He's stuck with whatever magic they choose to deploy."

"Wait. What the fuck?"

Cass's words froze everybody in place.

"What's going on?" Riley demanded when Cass said nothing else.

The dreamer held up her hand to *shush* her, shaking her head as she did. "I don't fucking believe it. What is that waste of skin *doing*?"

"What is *who* doing?" Touray demanded.

"Vernon. The asshat. He's telling them we're waiting out here. Just announced it. Shit."

"What's happening?" Riley asked, exchanging a furious look with Taylor.

Neither could help feeling responsible for the man, for involving the others in his machinations, and for risking their lives.

"Why would he do that?" Jamie sounded more exasperated than worried.

"What does he hope to gain?"

"Revenge, maybe," Taylor suggested. "For not trusting him and putting the capsule in his neck."

"No way. He's too much a psychopath to let his emotions get the better of him. I mean, he didn't go after Tyrell for my mom's death, and that seems a whole lot worse," Riley said. "He has to be getting something out of this. Or thinks he is, anyhow."

"The senator is sending people out to get us," Cass said. "He's told them how many of us there are and who we are. Jesus. He even said that Price is an elemental. How the hell does he know?"

"He was in my head back at Tyrell's. Maybe he found out then," Taylor said, her stomach churning. Price could defend himself, but elementals weren't just rare, they were practically unicorns. Just like Riley. And herself. The realization struck her hard. She'd gone from wishing she could do magic, to being able to do something unheard of. Given how much he hated magic, the senator would just as likely want to kill them all. They were too powerful to live.

"He's revealing all our talents," Cass said, shaking her head with disbelief.

"We've got to get you all out of here," Dalton said, gaze raking over Taylor as he reached for the door.

"No," Riley said. "Whatever Vernon is up to, it doesn't change what we have to do. Anyhow, this way we all get in the room. Gives us better odds, and we don't have to fight to get in."

"What about the artifacts?" Leo asked. "Should we hide them?"

"Do it," Riley said. "Outside somewhere, where it won't be obvious."

Even as she spoke, a portion of the floor separated, looking as soft as taffy. Jamie grabbed both Touray's and Tyrell's bags and tossed them in the hole. The floor curled over them and reformed. Wherever her brothers decided to put them, Taylor knew that nobody would find them.

"Might as well get ready," she said, standing up and stretching. "Who's going to warn Touray and Price?"

"Already did," Cass said, lifting her head and rubbing her temples. The white film that had slid over her eyes faded. "No point in keeping the connection with Tiny if we're going in."

"How long do you suppose we've got until they get here?" Jamie asked.

"They've got to scramble a team," Dalton said. He sat in the front seat, watching the rest of them in the rearview mirror. "They've got to armor up and figure out a plan. They'll be here soon."

Riley got that vague look that said she'd dropped into trace sight. "I don't see anybody yet."

"Good. That should give me plenty of time," Erickson said suddenly, tendrils of light uncoiling from his hands and dancing across his laptop like tiny tornadoes. They watched as he worked. After a little while, the light show stopped and he shut his laptop. "I set a virus in their system," he said smugly, stroking his fingers over the computer as if to reward it.

"What does it do?" Riley asked.

"Basically, they're going to start having some minor problems in their control systems. It'll start in the lighting and jump to the HVAC and then go into the water system and eventually security. It's not going to shut them out. It'll look like glitches in their system. With luck, they won't figure it's an attack until it permeates all their systems. They won't be able to stop it. It's going to sniff through all their electronics."

He grinned. "Electric toothbrushes, hair dryers, coffee pots—nothing's off limits that's plugged in or on Wi-Fi."

"Sex toys?" Cass asked, one brow arched.

Erickson blushed, and Taylor imagined if they pulled his socks off, even his toes would have been red with embarrassment.

"If they are plugged in." He hesitated. "*Do* they plug in?"

"Only the rechargeable ones," she replied with a perfectly straight face.

Leo and Jamie snickered.

Riley sighed. "You three are such children."

"Must be why I still like to breastfeed," Leo returned without missing a beat.

"And now I need my brain bleached," Taylor said.

"Or a frontal lobotomy," Riley said with an exaggerated shudder.

Silence fell then, and ten minutes or so ticked past.

"What is taking them so long?" Riley demanded

She looked like she was itching for a fight. Taylor could sympathize. She was strung so tight she twitched at every sound or movement. She just wanted to get this over with and get back to normal. Whatever normal was going to look like now that they'd taken tentative hold of Savannah's Tyet and they'd still have to deal with the fallout of handling the senator.

"Maybe they stopped to get a snack," Jamie offered unhelpfully.

"Or a potty break," Leo said.

"Can you see them, Riley? Or Dalton?" Taylor asked before her brothers could get on a roll.

Dalton answered. "Not yet. Touray and Price are on their way back."

Nobody asked how he knew, and a half minute later, the door slid open and the two men climbed in. Price had clearly protected them from the storm, and neither looked like they'd been out in the snow.

"We came back in so we could look like stupid sitting ducks," Price said. "Maybe they'll underestimate us."

"They're coming now," Dalton said, swiveling around to look out all the windows. His eyes were cycled from red to blue and back. "Looks like there's at least twelve of them. Pretty sure they're using infrared goggles, the way they're moving."

"Everybody ready?" Riley asked, pulling on her gloves and hat.

Everybody nodded with grim anticipation. Taylor flexed her fingers and drew a deep breath, steeling herself for what was to come. They had a plan and it should work. It *had* to work. Resolve hardened in her chest.

She'd already lost her mom. She wasn't going to lose a sister or any friends. If they couldn't get in the senator's head, she'd grab his trace and hold his life hostage until he did what they wanted.

And then she'd kill him so he couldn't take it back.

Chapter 32

Riley

THE SENATOR'S GOONS were clearly disappointed that we didn't put up a fight. They marched us through the nulled parking garage where they patted us down, handcuffed us, and then took us down through an also nulled industrial tunnel and back up into the hotel where they hung nulls around our necks on plastic-covered wire. The nulls themselves were padlocks.

The stupid thing was there was a gap in their null field. The room we entered upon leaving the tunnel was full of lockers, benches, and equipment, and the null field only extended about halfway inside. They put the padlock necklaces on us at the door leading out, which gave Leo and Jamie time to adjust our hand-cuffs. They might have looked secure, but we could break them apart in a heart-beat, a fact communicated to me by raised brows, rolled eyes, and a meaningful glance. We weren't allowed to talk.

From there they marched us through lavishly appointed and yet generically hotel-like rooms and corridors until we arrived at the one where the senator was holding court with Arnow, Tiny, Patti, Vernon, and Tyrell.

Arnow stood, radiating icy cold. Pretty much her usual. Tiny seemed as confident and relaxed. Patti had her legs crossed, her foot bouncing in irritation, her eyes thinned to angry slits. Given the chance, she'd be cutting throats. Agents from the FBI or Homeland or maybe Secret Service stood alert around the walls. Oh, and then there was the senator's wife.

She stood like a Stepford doll, with a small little smile, her body stiff. She wore a white turtleneck with a green skirt and a gold pin fastening the matching silk scarf around her neck. Her dishwater-blond hair was cut in a short bob that curled under at the ends. If I had to describe her, I'd call her frumpy.

My attention skipped back to the senator, who was stern-faced, his eyes sharp as flint. His expression arrested me. He looked like he wanted to be rubbing his hands together in wicked anticipation. That, along with the smug-ness dripping off him, said he was sure he was the winner in his twisted game.

A dozen more chairs had been brought in to accommodate us.

"Sit," the senator ordered, gesturing toward the furniture, which was set up in a semicircle around the others. As we went to our seats, his gaze hitched on Touray for a moment, then slid to Price.

Something about his look punched every one of my alarm buttons. Like a wolf eyeing a particularly plump and juicy chicken. It wasn't the look of a man who planned to disarm and disable a dangerous talent. He had other ideas for Price, and I was pretty sure they included using his talent for the senator's hypocritical benefit.

My fingers curled. If I could have got my hands around Vernon's throat, I'd have broken his neck and then strangled him just to make sure he didn't survive. Right after that, I'd do the same to Senator Rice, who had moved his gaze to Tyrell, not bothering to hide his smirking delight, reminding me of a skinny Jabba the Hutt. I'd probably kick him in the balls first.

"Welcome," Senator Rice said expansively, as if we'd had any choice about the matter. "I'm glad you could join us."

"He just needs a handlebar mustache to curl around his finger," Taylor murmured, and I stifled a laugh.

The senator's gaze darted to us. I gave him a wide-eyed innocent look. His brows drew together slightly, but he quickly lost interest and went back to gloating at Tyrell.

"Well, Jackson. It's finally over, and I think we can safely say that I've won," he said, gesturing around to take in the room. "I don't think you'll be weaseling out of this."

"Going to make me disappear?" Tyrell drawled. "Or scapegoat me?"

"Neither, I think. I'd rather turn you into a loyal soldier. The rules allow it."

Rules? What rules?

A ripple of fury and maybe fear ran across Tyrell's expression before it returned to disdain.

"No one will believe it."

The senator's triumphant smirk widened into a gloating smile. "Oh, I think they will. You'll make them believe. Dreamers are such useful creatures, aren't they? They can just take apart your mind and rebuild it however they want. It won't be long until you and I become great friends as you see the light and support my every move."

He laughed and looked up at his wife. "Won't that be delicious, darling?"

She tilted her head, looking down at him as if considering her answer, even though he'd stopped looking at her, clearly not interested in her reply. Poor woman. She looked like she was only there to fetch and carry, and no doubt stroke his ego whenever he wanted.

"Aren't you anti-magic?" Arnow burst out, looking confused. "I don't understand."

I wanted to applaud, she appeared so sincere.

The senator gave her an irritated look. "Of course I am. But it's a useful tool and one that must be kept in the hands of those who are best prepared to know how and when to apply it."

"Is that how you're selling your hypocrisy?" Tyrell asked with a surprising lack of heat, almost like he really cared about the answer. "Do you think people will fall for it?"

The senator shook his head. "Jackson, we both know how easy people are to manipulate. Given the situation here, with the explosions and corruption, it will be easy to believe that you saw the devastation and realized how dangerous the talented are." Rice smiled. "Even though you are among them. You may have to come out of the closet and reveal your talent. That would really show how serious you are about your conversion."

Taylor nudged me with her elbow, and I realized I'd become so involved in the exchange I had forgotten my job. Opening myself to the trace, I started unwinding the null I wore. It was solidly made and held enough power to keep most talents suppressed. I doubted it would hold Price if he shed control.

Elemental energy was a whole other level of power altogether. His would overload the null in seconds. It had been designed to absorb power, rather than to prevent power use. Generally, the effect was the same, but in this case, it allowed Price access to his power, which was a big mistake. It also made it easier for me to unwind the null, which I did in about two minutes while the senator and Jackson kept up their conversational jousting.

When I was done, I dropped into trace sight to consider the null setup in the room. Both the senator and his wife wore nulls. She had only one. He wore several, and more were embedded in the chair.

The security detail wasn't nulled, which seemed arrogant or stupid. Or they all had talents. All the same, it meant less work for me. The hardest part now was figuring out how to get close enough to the other nulls to destroy them. Because Jamie and Leo had ruined the handcuffs, all of us could remove our necklace nulls. I only needed to be concerned with the senator.

I eyed him. I couldn't believe there wasn't more than nulls creating a barrier between him and the rest of us. I should be able to sense a binder wall, even if I couldn't see it, but I felt nothing. Maybe some sort of pain curtain? Or something that worked as a physical block?

It just didn't seem reasonable that there wouldn't be more protection for him. Even with a dozen agents in the room, one of us could probably get to the senator before they could stop them. Senator Rice couldn't be so arrogant and stupid not to have protections. What *wasn't* I seeing?

I dropped out of trace sight, and my gaze swept the room. Nothing stood out. I rolled my eyes at myself. Unless it had a giant cartoon sign declaring it magical, I wouldn't know.

One of the ceiling lights in the corner flickered. It wasn't super obvious, but a couple of the guard agents took notice.

It flickered again and went out. The light in the room dimmed slightly, and the senator's wife looked around to see what had caused it. The senator just kept exchanging barbs with Tyrell.

A knock at the door caught everybody's attention. One of the two agents guarding it opened it while the other talked into his sleeve. A coiled wire running down from his left ear indicated he was probably talking to more members of the team.

The agent who answered the door stepped out, closing the door behind herself. The senator had paused to watch and wait. If anyone intruded on him, it had to mean something important was afoot.

The female agent stepped back into the room.

"What's going on?" the senator demanded.

"Sir, the fire alarm system has gone offline."

"So? They had to come here to tell you that? Why not just use the headsets? That's what they're for."

"A security check, Sir. To be sure you aren't compromised."

The senator made a huffing noise but didn't respond. Clearly, he thought the whole thing was unnecessary.

"Tell them I don't wish to be disturbed," he ordered. "Not for any reason short of a nuclear attack."

The female agent nodded and spoke into her sleeve. She looked like she'd eaten a spider.

The senator looked us all over, crossing his legs and putting his hands together. "Now then. What brings you all to see me?"

My brows furrowed. So Vernon had announced our presence but hadn't given away our plan. Why? What was he up to?

The senator flicked a look at Arnow, Tiny, and Patti. "Are you three really FBI agents?"

"Damned straight," Arnow said in her best ice-bitch voice. "I've been with the Bureau for nine years and have many commendations."

"Then how do you explain all this?" The senator's gesture took in all of us.

I almost wanted to wait to see what sort of explanation Arnow came up with, but we currently had the element of surprise on our side, not to mention the senator's distraction. I nudged Taylor with my left elbow, and Price with my right. I could sense the subtle movement as the message went down the line on either side.

Price and I sat in the center of our group. On the other side of him were Cass and Erickson and Touray. On the other side of Taylor were Dalton, Leo, and Jamie. I caught Patti's eye and gave a tiny nudge with my chin. She coughed delicately into her hand while tapping Tiny on the thigh with the other, though I expected Cass had already passed along the message directly into his mind.

Now all we needed was a distraction.

As if reading my mind, Tiny surreptitiously tipped over the delicate marble-topped end table next to him, the glass lamp on top of it thudding onto the carpet, the candy dish spilling its contents. Everyone looked at it.

A flurry of movement. I twisted my wrists, and the handcuffs cracked open. On either side of me, Taylor and Price did the same, then yanked off their nulls.

Dalton knocked himself backward. His chair landed with a heavy thud, and he somersaulted backward and flipped to his feet. Touray leaped to his feet having dispensed with his handcuffs and null. He disappeared, only to reappear across the room, shoving himself into the agents who'd been caught flatfooted and had only just begun to react.

A bolt of electric energy sizzled through the air, hitting the bookcase on the opposite wall. A charred splotch spread across the books and white-painted wood. Every one of my hairs stood on end. Another bolt sizzled, this time hitting right where Price had just been.

The chair exploded, sending splinters of wood flying through the air like porcupine quills. I caught several small pieces in the side of my face and one about the size of my finger through my calf.

Everybody was in motion. I couldn't see most of what was going on.

Then . . .

It was over.

Just like that.

I looked around. The agents were all trussed up, courtesy of Leo and Jamie. They'd also taken away the agents' ear pieces and comms units. With any luck, they hadn't had time to alert anybody.

"Put them all together, and we'll use the null necklaces on them," Touray said, and he, Price, and Tiny quickly shoved them together. A couple had been knocked unconscious, and I guessed that one of those was responsible for the electric bolts.

Taylor and Dalton collected the nulls, while Leo and Jamie fashioned an odd-shaped hoop that went around the entire group and then Taylor and Dalton fastened the necklaces to that, effectively nulling all of them.

"Trust you to be the only one to get hurt," Patti said, coming to stand beside me as she eyed the splinters sticking out of my face.

"Someone had to do it."

"Not really," she said. "But you couldn't let your track record be broken, could you?"

I tried not to smile. It hurt. My whole face throbbed. Blood trickled down over my jaw, and I resisted the urge to wipe it away. I'd probably shove the splinters in deeper. My calf screamed, but I didn't let on how bad it hurt.

Price caught sight of me, and his face went tombstone cold.

"Tiny! Fix Riley."

Fix me?

But I didn't have time to say anything because Tiny was there. He wrapped my wrist in one of his enormous paws and soothing numbness ran through me. He touched his fingers to my cheek, and that wiggly wormy feeling that always comes with healing squirmed under my skin and through my muscles and tendons. I started to pull away, but his grip on my wrist tightened and he pulled me back.

"Don't be a dumbass," he said.

"But I'm so good at it."

"That's for sure," Patti said. "One of the best there is at dumbassery."

"I deserve a trophy. A big one."

"We'll work on it," Leo said.

The splinters felt much worse going out than in, only because I could feel myself slowly squeezing them back out. I almost wanted to tell him to leave them in, the feeling was so revolting. I shuddered as they sprinkled down from my face onto my shoulder and chest. So gross.

"Don't puke," Patti advised. "You look kind of green under all that blood."

"Tell that to my stomach."

"Don't talk," Tiny ordered.

I bit my tongue to keep from sticking it out at him. My back was to the senator and his wife, and I had no idea what was happening. I couldn't see anybody but Patti, Price, and Tiny.

"What's going on?" I asked when Tiny let go of my face and squatted down beside my other wound. "What's happening?"

I twisted a little to get a look behind me. Bizarrely, Senator Rice remained seated, his wife behind him, still with a hand on his shoulder. He appeared tense, but like he wanted us to think he was perfectly relaxed. His wife continued to look like a Stepford robot. She didn't look alarmed or surprised. More like she was about to offer us some sweet tea and pie.

The wiggling sensation began again in my calf. Tiny clamped on before I could kick him away.

"Everything's fine," Patti said to me. "Get healed and we'll get to work."

"What about any alarms?"

Erickson answered from an easy chair in the corner of the room. He had his laptop open and was tapping furiously. How had he managed to keep anybody from taking it?

"Nobody got the word out, it looks like. Won't matter soon. System's about to shut down, but at that point, someone might come looking for the senator to see if he's okay."

Interesting that no one ever thought of checking if the senator's wife was okay. She was just an appendage. I hadn't even cared about her and still didn't. She might as well be furniture.

Not a nice assessment, but true all the same.

"We'd better hurry, then," I said.

The pencil-sized splinter squeezed out of my leg and dropped to the floor. I winced and looked away. It was one thing to know it was stuck in me and another thing to see it.

Blood dribbled down my leg, and by the time Tiny was finished, my sock was squashy with it. *Ew.*

At least it wasn't worse.

I turned and realized that all of them were waiting for me. Like I was in charge. Even Touray. I think hell must've froze over.

"Let's get to it," I said. "Are you up for it, Cass?" I sure as hell didn't trust Vernon.

She nodded. "I'd rather sit."

Dalton grabbed a chair that had tipped over and set it up beside the senator.

"What do you think you're doing?" Senator Rice demanded, his lip curling. If he was afraid, he didn't show it. "You know that this attack on me will only make things worse for you, for all the magically infected, don't you? Stop now, and you'll end up in prison. Otherwise, it'll be far worse."

"What's worse?" Leo asked sardonically.

The senator gave him a stony look. "Experimentation. Realize that with this crime, you have no rights anymore under the *Rice Act*," he said with a self-congratulatory smirk. "Anything we want to do to you is now on the table. You are nothing."

"For a smart man, you sure don't know how to read the room," Taylor drawled, arms folded.

Despite her stance, I could tell she wanted to rip his throat out.

"You're at our mercy," she added in case the senator missed her point.

"You won't hurt me," he declared with annoying confidence. "You made a serious miscalculation when you came in here. Your only play is to surrender. Otherwise, you'll be hunted down like the vermin you are."

His eyes glittered with something like excitement. Like he was getting off on the situation. I had to admit that I found that more than a little bit unnerving. He wasn't responding at all as I'd expected.

"You're right. We don't plan to hurt you," I said. "Just modify you a bit."

His eyes narrowed. "You can try. I'm protected against dreamers."

"Is that so? We'll see about that."

"He needs a new chair," I said to nobody in particular. "Nulls on his right wrist, left ankle, left front pocket, and the back of his neck."

Leo, Jamie, and Dalton pulled him up, shoving the chair aside and providing a new one. Tiny stripped off his nulls, all but the one on his neck.

"It's a tattoo," he said. "I can heal it, but it might not take off the null." He'd already suited actions to words by the time I spoke.

"I can remove the null."

I stepped over to the senator. The wife had stepped out of the way and stood watching, still with robotic impassivity. A chill rolled up my spine. She was beyond unnatural. Maybe she *was* a robot. The senator's own walking, talking sex-doll wife.

I threw up a little in my mouth, swallowing hard. I so did not need the image of him and her doing naked gymnastics in my head. Talk about nightmares.

The tattoo had vanished from the back of his neck, but the null, though weakened, still clung to its memory in the skin.

I looped my fingers through its power and quickly unraveled it. I did it so quickly I didn't have time to stop and consider its structure before it was gone. There was something odd about it. It wasn't an ordinary null. It was targeted somehow; specific in a way I couldn't identify.

"Let me see one of those," I said to Tiny who held the rest of the senators nulls.

He held them out and I picked one up. A watch. I pulled a small strand of the null free, dissecting it slowly.

One thing was certain right off. A powerful tracer had created it. As I pulled it apart, I realized that the oddity surrounded the fact that the null allowed certain magics past it. I couldn't tell what those were. I hadn't ever seen a null like it. I'd tried to create a similar one some years ago, without success, and decided it wasn't possible. Stupid. Just because I couldn't do it didn't mean it couldn't be done.

"What's wrong?" Taylor asked.

I shook my head. "Null was a little different than I expected. No big deal."

Likely the senator had had it made to allow him to have access to some magical tools while still protecting him from attacks.

"What are you going to do?"

We all looked at the wife in surprise. I felt a little bad that I didn't know her name. I'd no doubt heard it but had forgotten. It seemed rude, especially when clearly she was just part of his overall entourage. One of those wives whose entire identity was wrapped up in her husband and his success.

"We're going to tweak his brain and stop him from destroying the talented," Cass said. "Don't worry, he'll still be himself. Or enough. Maybe better."

She clearly didn't think much of the senator's attitude toward his wife, or what we'd seen of it, anyhow. I was pretty sure he'd be treating her a whole lot better once Cass was done with him.

I gave the wife a sympathetic look, so I saw the shift when it happened. It was like she changed into a new person. She straightened, her shoulders lifting, her entire body transformed from frumpy timidity to assertive confidence. Her eyes turned shrewd and calculating. The doormat disappeared, and in her place stood a take-control boss. It happened in the blink of an eye.

My mouth fell open.

"I'm afraid that won't be possible," she said, and even her voice changed. It was stronger, crisper, and decisive.

"What?" I know, a brilliant question, but my brain hadn't caught up with reality.

"I can't allow it," she said. "I've gone to such trouble, you see."

She cocked her head to the side, and I about jumped out of my skin when the senator started screaming and thrashing. I looked at him. He clawed at his face and body, eyes wide with terror.

Then he went totally still, frozen in the middle of his terror spasm.

Gunfire.

One shot, so close my ears throbbed and my skull vibrated.

I didn't have time to react.

The senator's head exploded. Bits of his skull and brain spattered all over the rest of us, the floor, the ceiling. He slumped and slid off his chair as all of us stared, shock freezing us in place.

"As I said . . ."

My body unlocked, and I turned to look at the senator's wife. She held a hand-canon. I didn't have any idea what caliber it was, but I was surprised she could even lift it. Where had it come from?

But then I realized she had a purse on the table behind her. More like a tote. Big enough to hold the gun, a couple of pizzas, and a car tire.

She set the gun down on her purse and faced us all again.

I'd begun to shake, a tremor that began deep inside me where my subconscious realized that the stuff stuck to my face, hair, and clothing were bits of the senator's head. I'd seen dead bodies, but never anything like this. Was that—? On my lips? I wiped my mouth across my sleeve and didn't look at what I might have left behind. I didn't want to know. Didn't want to think about it, not ever.

"Why the fuck did you do that?" Taylor demanded, being the first to recover her voice.

"He'd outlived his usefulness."

"And they call *me* a cold-blooded, ice-bitch," Arnow said.

"To be fair, you are," I said, still reeling.

Arnow gave a little shrug of agreement.

"He's your *husband*," Patti said to Mrs. Senator. "Didn't he mean anything to you?"

"Not particularly," was the dismissive answer.

None of us spoke for a long moment. None of us knew what to say. I was still frozen in place, not wanting to move in case I stepped on bits of senator.

"What are we going to do now?" Tiny asked. "Your plan won't work without the senator, and with him murdered, things will get worse."

He was right. And if we were going to fix it, we were going to have to act fast. *If* we could fix it.

"Why did you kill him?" Patti asked.

Mrs. Senator leaned back against the table behind her, then put her hands down and scooted up to sit on it, primly crossing her ankles. Her giant handbag with the hand-cannon sat beside her.

"I really couldn't have you prying into his mind."

"Why don't you just tell us what's going on," I said, foreboding coiling around my throat, "instead of playing games. You clearly have an agenda."

"But I like games," she said. "They make life so much more interesting. However, in the interest of moving things along and enlightening you as to your current situation, I will explain."

Enlightening us as to our current situation sounded more than a little threatening. I exchanged a look with Price who clearly thought the same. By the expressions on everybody else's faces, we weren't alone.

"All is not as it seems," she began.

Taylor snorted. "I think you made that clear when you blew your husband's head off."

"Amen, sister," Patti said.

"I'm speaking of the bigger picture. Of the way the world works. You think you know, but you don't. Powerful consortiums made up of wealthy and magically powerful people play chess with countries and people. Diamond City happens to be the current playing board, but the game is far more complex than even most of the players know."

"What does that even mean?" Touray demanded.

She glanced at him and away, clearly unimpressed by anything about him. That worried me. He was in full-on danger mode, and he even scared me. What did she have up her sleeve that made her so confident?

"My husband and Jackson"—she gestured at Tyrell—"have been vying for recognition and power in one of the consortiums. They wish, or rather, wished," she said, glancing at her headless husband, "to take over the leadership of the North American branch. They've both been jockeying against one another for years to prove themselves worthy of the opportunity, and recently the position has opened up. My husband planned to gain control over the talented by putting them into camps and recruiting those he had a use for. He'd build a talented army, while at the same time gaining power within the government as an anti-magic hawk and be a candidate for the next presidential election."

"That sounds like something straight out of a thriller movie," I said, trying to wrap my head around her explanation. "Next you'll be telling us Jason Bourne will be coming through the door at any moment."

She laughed. "I'm afraid not."

"What's all this got to do with you killing your husband?" Touray interjected.

"Yes, well, while Jackson and my husband have been squaring off, they overlooked the fact that others were playing the game, too. Arrogant, really. And stupid."

"Others?" Tyrell said suddenly. "Who?" He looked furious and more than a little consternated, though he tried to hide it.

She smiled, the proverbial cat eating the cream. "And the arrogant stupidity persists." She shook her head. "*I* will be assigned his seat in the senate for the interim," Mrs. Senator said. "I will be viewed as brave and heroic as I overcome this horrific tragedy and will gain sympathy with voters. When election time comes, I'll win."

"You shot your husband to get his senate seat?" Leo asked.

"I'd hoped to wait until he'd consolidated his power here and hamstringed Jackson. I wasn't expecting your interference. It appears I'm not the only one flying under the radar."

"He wasn't going to hamstring me," Tyrell growled. His face had flushed red, and his jowls tremored with his anger.

"Wasn't he? You would have been locked up in one of the internment camps and then you'd have disappeared." She blew on her bunched fingers and flared them out, like she'd blown away dandelion fluff.

He gave her a contemptuous look. "He couldn't have got near me."

Her smile would have scared a T-Rex. "No?"

Vernon leaped into movement before I could understand what was happening. He smashed his elbow into the side of Tyrell's head, then rolled around to straddle him and punched him. His blows fell rapidly. Bone crunched, and flesh pulped. Tyrell tried to push him off, but Vernon was dementedly strong.

Price and Touray dragged him off the battered man. Vernon's face was a snarling mask of rage. He twisted and howled, fighting against their hold with a violence that tested their strength.

Then, abruptly, he went still as a mannequin.

Tyrell moaned, his face swollen and bruised. His eyes had swollen nearly shut, his nose was clearly busted, and blood leaked from splits in his lips. It looked like his right cheekbone had been pushed inward, creating a divot where there should have been a little hill. He moaned and breathed raggedly through his mouth. I doubted any air could get in through his nose.

"You see," Mrs. Senator said. "*I* have been near you for *years.*"

"You're the spider," Taylor exclaimed. "Vernon's brain-jockey."

"Correct."

All of it took a few seconds to sink in. My brain scattered in different directions, trying to run down the ramifications. They seemed endless. All the things that she must know about Vernon, about me and Taylor and all the rest of us. About my mother, Tyrell, and his business. . . . It was impossible to imagine how deep her knowledge might go.

Wait. If she had control of Vernon, and Vernon had control of Touray, then she'd been responsible for the hits on Cass and his lieutenants. My brow furrowed. Vernon had seemed startled by the notion that he'd been Touray's brain-jockey. What if it *hadn't* been him? What if it had really been Mrs. Senator? A direct link the way she controlled Vernon. She clearly had the ability.

Which meant . . . what? She'd wanted control of Touray's operation? But why? To pit him against Tyrell? Then why cripple his power by killing off his senior people? Why attack Cass? So many questions and no answers. There had to be a reason, I just couldn't see it.

The answer was important. I could feel it all the way down in the marrow of my bones, and I had to figure it out *now*, or it would be too late. I didn't consider what exactly too late meant. I just knew it, like I knew about gravity and oxygen. Instinctive necessity.

Mrs. Senator wanted power in the Consortium. Big power. If she'd had her way, the senator would have become president with her having the power behind the throne. But once we showed up with plans to modify his thinking, that never would have happened. His new attitude would probably have turned off his voters, and he'd possibly have failed to get reelected. That would put a serious crimp in her plans.

She had absolute control of her husband, which meant she wanted martial law in Diamond City, *and* she wanted to lock up the magically talented, and she wanted Touray's organization in her pocket.

The questions continued to chase themselves around in my head, but I just couldn't put it together. Another worry crept in. She didn't see us as a danger to her getting everything she wanted. She'd put her gun down without ever being asked. She had an ace up her sleeve. But what?

Time? Sooner or later somebody would be coming to check on things when the senator was overdue for something, or when fresh Secret Service agents were ready to rotate onto their shifts. When they did, we'd have to fight again. She could be betting that we'd be blamed for the senator's murder. All the trussed-up agents could be her witnesses, once she adjusted their memories.

Erickson's virus might speed the outcome, if someone grew concerned about it being an attack and thought the senator might be in danger.

But why not use her talent to just reach out to someone and sound the alarm?

The answer hit me like a freight train.

Come into my parlor, said the spider to the fly.

Only *we* were the flies, and this was her parlor. She wanted us. Using her dreamer talent, she'd managed to have Vernon and the senator entirely under her control. Now she wanted to do the same to us.

We were all powerful weapons for her arsenal. We'd be her puppets. Her dreamer talent was strong enough to overwhelm any one of us, and with time, brain modifications, and drugs, she could make it impossible for us to resist her. Vernon was no easy prey, and if he hadn't even realized he had a jockey, her ability must be extraordinary. Especially if she'd been Touray's jockey, too. She'd managed to control both at the same time, plus her husband and who knew who else.

She didn't have much time to get us under control before the other agents arrived. When they did, she'd point to one or two sacrificial lambs and claim they murdered her husband. Then again, she didn't need to tamper with us to control us; she just needed us imprisoned in some fashion. She could work on our minds later. I just didn't know how she was planning to manage our captures.

That sense of time slipping away, of it becoming too late, chewed at my nerves. We stood in a trap, and we had to figure out how to get out before it closed on us. We'd gotten inside far too easily, and she'd known we were coming for hours—since Taylor had spoken with Tyrell and Vernon. She'd had time to make arrangements. The massive gun in her purse was proof enough of that.

And then something hit my brain like a meteor hitting a watermelon, and everything went black.

Chapter 33

Taylor

IT WAS SINGULARLY bizarre to be having a calm conversation while decorated from head to toe with a fine blood spray. Little globs of the senator's brain stuck to her clothing and hair. She could feel something on her face, though whether it was blood or worse, she didn't know.

The sound of Tyrell's thick and labored breathing filled the room, providing uneven syncopation for the unfolding revelations. Even though the senator's wife—Mimi or something like it—focused entirely on Riley, Taylor didn't doubt for one second that she was aware of everything else in the room. Ironic that she didn't know the woman's name. A testament to Mrs. Senator's skills. Given her mousey appearance and willingness to let her brash husband have the spotlight, no one would suspect she was the real power behind the throne.

Out of nowhere, a sledgehammer hit Taylor's brain and she collapsed, every muscle in her body going slack. Her chin hit the back of a chair. Her teeth clashed together, and she heard an audible cracking sound. Searing pain raveled up along the left side of her jaw, spreading through her nasal passages and into her eye sockets.

The side of her head bounced against the carpeted floor and she lay awkwardly torqued, her torso twisted to one side, her butt humped up in the air, and her knees spraddled.

Her eyes remained open. A trickle of blood escaped out the corner of her mouth, and she realized she'd bitten her tongue in her fall. Vaguely, she felt the pain of it, but it was nothing compared to her head.

Her skull throbbed like it was breathing. With every expansion, her skull stretched and splintered. If she moved, she thought it might shatter apart.

Adrenaline and urgency stabbed at her.

What had happened?

She heard slow footsteps on the carpet, and a pair of nylon-clad legs ending in sensible spectator pumps went by.

The senator's wife. So demur and beige in her demeanor and clothing. Only behind that Mrs. Rogers façade was a demon.

All she could hear was the ragged breathing from Tyrell whose nose was pulped, nothing from anybody else.

"All right, now, Vernon. Let's get to work and get everybody on the same page before the cavalry arrives."

The senator's wife sounded like a kindergarten teacher briskly talking to her class about learning to write their names, not butchering minds.

"I'll handle Mr. Touray. He may have escaped me once, but this time I won't give him the opportunity. I'll make him want to please me more than he wants to live. I'll take his brother, as well. Having my own elemental will be invaluable. You can start with your daughters. That's only fitting after all. Be careful. I want them in useable condition. The rest I'll give a little mental lobotomy for now so they'll be pliable, and deal with them later."

A pause and more movement. Vernon getting into place, no doubt.

Lobotomy? Oh hell no.

Taylor struggled to move, but she couldn't so much as twitch a finger. How she was still breathing, her heart still beating, she didn't know. The senator's wife had known exactly how to completely disable them all without killing them. It would be impressive if the bitch wasn't about to turn them all into puppets in her insane little version of *Sesame Street*.

The metaphor totally didn't fit, but Taylor didn't have time to think about it. As soon as the thought emerged, she was yanked into an icy-cold void.

Black surrounded her running on forever. Cold knifed through her clothing and to the marrow of her bones. A deep ache ran through her, agonizing and dull.

A hand on her wrist spun her around. Riley. Electric strands of neon light in various colors snaked over Riley's body.

"We're in the spirit realm," Taylor said and sounded bizarrely normal. There should have been an echo or some sort of vibration. "How come it's so dark? You said it was full of trace."

Riley frowned. "It is. Can't you see it?" She waved at the space around her with the hand not holding Taylor's wrist.

"No. Just the stuff that's on you and—" As she watched, some of it dimmed and started to fade. "It's disappearing. It did that before. In the Snowcat."

Understanding smoothed Riley's expression. "Your trace abilities aren't very strong, then. Doesn't matter. Here."

She turned Taylor's hand and laid a line of banded blue-and-white trace over her palm. Taylor bent her frigid fingers around it. It buzzed with hot vitality.

"That's Mrs. Senator," Riley said. "Stop her. Kill her if you have to."

Taylor jerked her gaze up and locked with Riley's. Never in her life did she think she'd ever hear those words from Riley. Not that she wanted to argue. This was about protecting their family. Riley would say it was also about protecting the city and the rest of the talented, but for Taylor it came down to what the senator's wife was about to do in that room.

Her fingers tightened on the trace. It was like squishing a handful of soft pasta. Just like that it separated into two pieces, and instantly turned gray.

She didn't have time to think about how sickeningly easy it was to kill.

"Now we have to stop Vernon. I still can't see his trace, and what Mrs. Rice did to us may still be in effect. I'm hoping that cutting her strings to Vernon will at least slow him down. If not—"

Riley's lips snapped shut, her eyes narrowing to slits. She gave Taylor a shove, and the next thing she knew, Taylor sprawled back onto the floor of the room. This time she fell on top of somebody else, her head banging off something relatively soft like a butt or a stomach.

She found she could move. She rolled stiffly over, her head swimming, her body sluggish from the cold and the fall. She clambered to her feet, standing wide-legged to keep her balance. Her gaze skimmed the room. She fixed on Vernon who stood as if startled. As she watched, his attention sharpened, and he bent purposefully, hand reaching out for Riley, who lay at his feet.

Taylor didn't think. Adrenaline surged through her like water from a broken dam. She lunged, plowing her shoulder into his side, tackling him into a chair. His breath exploded from him. She sank into trace sight, hooking his trace in her fingers. Without even considering, she crushed it in her fist and twisted.

Just as with the senator's wife, the trace turned instantly gray. The tension in Vernon's body slackened as everything inside ground to a halt. Taylor pulled out of the trace dimension and pushed herself upright, looking down at her father, whom she half sat on. His eyes stared blankly into the arm of the chair's nubby fabric.

Her gorge rose in her throat, her heart still jackhammering in her chest. She scrambled to her feet and took a step back, unable to look away from his body.

She'd killed her father.

No, this man wasn't her father. He hadn't been that in a long time. He was a sperm donor at best, and an enemy. He'd hurt her entire family for years. Damaged them all beyond repair, using them for his own twisted ends.

Her stomach twisted, lurching with uncertainty and guilt.

Or had those ends been his at all? How long had the senator's wife controlled him? What if he hadn't been to blame at all?

"Is he dead?" Riley had risen to stand beside her.

"Yeah."

For a long moment Riley said nothing. Then, "Good riddance."

"What if it was all her the entire time and he had no choice?"

Her sister considered, then slid her hand into Taylor's. "Even if he didn't, he was like a wolf with rabies. You stopped him from attacking me. Thanks to you, I'm not hurt, or worse." She pulled Taylor around to face her. "It was him or me. You did the only thing you *could* do."

Taylor nodded, though she wasn't sure she entirely believed.

Thankfully, their companions had begun to move, recovering from the paralyzing mental blow struck by the senator's wife. Price staggered upright, searching for Riley. His eyes had gone white.

Taylor helped Tiny. He looked like Elmer Fudd after Bugs had clanged him between two cymbals. Taylor half expected to see little stars and bluebirds flying around his head.

"You okay?" she asked as she helped wrestle him up so that he could lean back against a couch.

He rubbed his head with a meaty hand. "Tell the truth—I have a sword sticking out of my head."

"Maybe a small dagger."

She grinned and patted his shoulder before going to help Leo. She avoided Dalton for reasons she couldn't identify. Not that he needed help. He and Touray had gained their feet, and to look at them both, she wouldn't have known they'd just been nearly knocked cold by a psychic blow.

How nice for them.

She had a feeling she looked about as haggard as she felt. Of course, that might have something to do with killing two people.

"What happened?" Touray asked, sharp gaze darting around the room and pausing first on Vernon and then the senator's wife.

"They're dead," Riley said.

"How?"

She flicked a glance at Taylor who gave a microscopic shrug. They'd all find out eventually, so no point hiding what she'd done.

"Don't fuck with Taylor," Riley said by way of explanation and then immediately changed the subject. "We've got a serious problem. We no longer have Vernon, and the senator no longer has a brain," she said with gallows humor. "When it gets out that he's dead, whether we hide how he died or not, they'll send in the army to bring the city under control. Plus, they'll have another reason to hammer down on the talented. How do we fix this?"

No one spoke. Taylor glanced at Touray. He was always plotting. Surely he had an idea up his sleeve? He scowled at the floor, his arms folded, slowly shaking his head. Glancing around, she saw that no one else had ideas either.

"Come on. We have to be able to do *something*," Riley said.

"What if—" Leo broke off with a grimace. "No. It won't work."

"What about the artifacts?" Patti asked.

"We don't have a maker or a binder," Price pointed out. He looked at Patti. "At least not a strong enough binder."

"Sure, but if we did," Patti said, "what could we do with it?"

Taylor sighed. "It's for memory, according to Kensington. Can we erase memories?" Just the thought of it made her sick. She'd hated Vernon for brain-tampering, and here she was suggesting it.

"Presupposing we could make the machine work, what would we make people forget? And what kind of range does the machine have?" Touray asked. "If we were to wipe out people's memories of the senator's plans and get rid of the internment camps, we'd have to do it across the world. He's been on every news station on the planet. That's a lot of forgetting to make happen."

He wasn't wrong. At the same time, it wasn't like they had a lot of choices.

"All right. Presupposing, again, that we could put it together and make it work, and we could only reach the people of Diamond City, what could we do that would get us out of this mess?" Riley asked, looking around at everybody.

"I can manipulate digital footage," Erickson said. "We could create a new story and use creative video to reinforce it."

"You mean, use the machine to modify memories, and then spread around corroborating video?" Patti asked. "What kind of story?"

"Make him corrupt," Arnow said. "Connect him to Savannah and other Tyet lords. Get him taking bribes. Maybe connect him to the bombings."

"Then say that he was betrayed by one of his goons," Taylor said, nodding. "Could you create footage showing him getting killed by Vernon, maybe? Or another Tyet lord?" she asked Erickson.

He nodded. "I can. There's probably cameras in here, which will make it a piece of cake, but if not, we can restage a lot of it, and I can create the rest."

"Mrs. Rice needs to have died of an obvious cause," Arnow said. "One that the talented won't be blamed for. We also need to establish exactly how everything went down and make the forensics of the room match. That last will be tough if we have voids in the spatter patterns. Everybody is going to have to be accounted for so the science matches the scene. We just need a story to make sense of it."

"The senator comes to town to institute martial law and detain the talented, supposedly to clean up the corruption and make the city safe," Taylor began.

"He's dirty and is really after control of the diamond trade or political power. He plans to criminalize magical talent and use civil forfeiture to claim a lot of wealth, much of which will go to the US treasury, but he plans to skim off plenty for himself," Arnow added.

Patti took up the story. "But what he doesn't know is that his wife has collaborated with Vernon, a dreamer and Tyet lord, to control the senator's mind. She wants to be president and thinks the senator's death will help launch her there, so she organizes a meeting with known Tyet leaders and executes her husband, all the while planning to blame it on us." She frowned. "Is that too much of a stretch?"

"Not if we sell it right," Erickson said, not looking up from his manipulations. His fingers still continued to move madly, but he no longer touched the keyboard. Coiling snakes of white curled around him, matching the white of his eyes. "I'll lay in some dark web communications between her and Vernon and some others. Maybe toss in hints of physical abuse by the senator."

Riley nodded, then got a wicked look on her face. "What she doesn't know is that Touray's been working under cover for the FBI, and the rest of us just work for him. Patti can still be FBI. You can make all that stick, can't you, Erickson? Maybe she's a new transfer, or maybe she came in on the senator's protection detail."

"I've got you," Erickson said. "What else?"

Taylor jumped in. "When Mrs. Senator shoots her husband, Arnow kills her. When Vernon attacks in revenge, Patti shoots him." She eyed Tiny. "Can you make that work forensically? So that they both look like they were shot before they actually died?"

He gave a slow nod. "We just have to make sure the angles are all right and our stories line up as to where we all were in the room."

"It would be better if Riley, Taylor, Cass, Jamie, Leo, and Tiny were never here," Touray said.

"Why not?" Taylor demanded. "Why us?"

"Tyrell can be revealed as a secret talent, or he can just be here because Mrs. Rice blackmailed him into helping. Maybe she even offered to let him be her partner. Clay and I are known Tyet members working for the FBI, so it makes sense we're here. Dalton's been working with Vernon. I can have convinced him to work for me instead to take Vernon down. The rest of you don't have any good reason to be here."

"If we created that story, we wouldn't need artifacts," Taylor said, starting to feel hopeful.

"We stand a better chance if we do use them," Touray said.

Arnow nodded. "We could create memories of people working with the senator. Providing, of course, that that's something the artifact machine can do. Erickson could build electronic trails to reinforce the new reality."

"We don't have time to hunt down people for planting memories," Taylor argued. "And anyway, *we can't use the machine*."

"She's right," Riley said. "*Keep It Simple Stupid* is the smarter way to go."

"I disagree," Arnow said. "People will call the video a deep fake. We need corroboration."

"Tyrell's a golden boy—Cass can plant memories in him," Jamie suggested. "The networks would kill to get an interview from the reclusive zillionaire philanthropist. If he says it, nobody will have doubts."

"That'll help," Touray said. "I don't know that it's enough." He scraped his upper lip with his teeth as if considering his words.

That was a change. He was more the take-control-and-steamroll-over-everybody-else's-opinions.

"Can we risk failing?" he asked. "There's a lot on the line. If we do fail, the talented will have proven we're a serious threat. The senator will be vindicated, and they'll send an entire army to lock us down. It's just the excuse the government wants to take control of the mines and wipe out the talented community."

"That's worse-case scenario," Taylor said. "Anyhow, we still can't make the machine work."

"You know better than anybody here that we have to prepare for the worst and hope for the best," Dalton said softly behind her.

She stiffened, wanting to slug him, wanting to tell him to shut up, even if he was right. Maybe because he was right. She tossed up her hands. "Fine. Who are we going to implant these memories into, and what are we going to do for a binder and a maker?"

"I've been thinking about that," Price said, much to her surprise. She'd have thought he'd be first in line to stop this insanity. "Patti's not a strong-enough binder to pull in the magic she needs, or at least, that's my assumption. There's no reason to have powerful cardinal talents otherwise. She's a damned good binder, though." He gave her a little nod of acknowledgement.

"You bet your ass I am," she said.

"All she needs is the power, and the rest of us can provide it. Me, Dalton, Tiny, Leo, and Jamie can all feed power to her and anybody else who needs it. We've done it enough to know it works. And we can hope that with all of us pooling power, nobody has to die."

"That actually sounds reasonable," Jamie said. "What about a maker? We can't trust Tyrell and he's all we've got."

"He'll do it," said Cass. "I'll make his mind up for him if I have to."

"Are *you* up for it? You've just been through serious hell," Touray said, a scowl furrowing his forehead.

"I'll do what needs doing. Don't worry about me."

"I'm worried about *all* of us," Taylor muttered sourly.

"Me, too," Price said, his voice rough. "But if anybody can do it, it's gonna be us. Besides," he continued, meeting Riley's gaze, "your sister is too stubborn to fail, and I'll use every drop of magic in my soul to keep her and the rest of you alive."

Taylor couldn't help the surge of envy at the depth of emotion in his voice. What would it be like to have someone care for her like that? She could practically feel Dalton's eyes drilling into her. She had an uncanny feeling that he could read her mind and was annoyed at her thoughts. She shoved all that to the back of her mind, focusing on the here and now. She could deal with him later, if they survived to later.

"That takes care of one problem," she said. "Who are we going to implant memories into? How are we going to get to them?"

"I've got some suggestions," Touray said.

"So do I," said Arnow, and Erickson chimed in with a "Me, too."

"I'm pulling records of the senator's movements going back ten years," Erickson said, typing madly. Magic swirled and coiled around his fingers and wreathed his computer. "I can build a timeline that should hold up to ordinary scrutiny. The danger is that he's getting a blow job when he's supposed to be meeting someone and the sex worker pops up in *The Wall Street Journal* saying the senator couldn't have been out criming at that moment. He was busy getting his dick sucked. All right. I'm ready. Give me what you've got."

Touray and Arnow rattled off names and before long, the three of them mapped out a plausible story that required little of the senator's in-person presence but would have a carefully hidden electronic trail.

"He only needs to have worked with three or four key underworld connections. He'd want to limit how many could reveal his machinations," Erickson said as he worked. "That makes building a back trail easier. Savannah should be one."

"Has anybody considered how we'll target these key people? Or what memories we should instill?" Taylor asked. "We don't have their trace and no way to pinpoint them. It'll be like a needle in a haystack."

"I'm hoping that once we get Kensington's machine going, it'll help us do it," Riley said. "I know," she added, before Taylor could speak, "doing this by the seat of the pants is not just risky, it's insane. Trouble is, I don't see that we have much choice. We also have some smart, powerful people. If anybody can figure it out, it's going to be us."

"I guess we should fetch the artifacts," Leo said to Jamie. "Let's find a path for them to come to us."

Jamie went to a heat register on the floor and set his fingers on it, eyes closing as he used his metal sense. Leo did the same, though he chose a brass wall sconce.

"Now what?" Riley asked, looking around.

"What about the forensics? How are we going to make anybody believe we weren't here if our DNA is everywhere, not to mention blood voids and who knows what else.

"I'll handle it," Touray declared, like we should just take his word for it.

"How?" Taylor asked.

His lip curled. "I'll take care of it. That's all you need to know."

"I see the whole coma thing didn't do anything for your personality," Taylor said sourly.

He glowered at her. "Do you want me to waste time explaining just to satisfy your curiosity?"

She stiffened. He wasn't wrong, but she didn't have to like it. "I just want to be sure you know what you're doing."

"I do."

"We've got 'em," Leo announced as he dropped one of the artifact sacks onto a chair.

Jamie set down the other sack. "You weren't faster than me," he told Leo.

"Sure. You keep thinking that."

"You just got lucky with that conduit."

"Children, shut up and let the adults talk," Cass said. She sat on the couch with her legs pulled up.

"You know, our plan solves the problem of who killed the senator, but it doesn't mean our problems are over," Touray said. "We still have the soldiers and detainment camps. Government will just put someone else in charge."

"What are you suggesting?" Price's voice took on a rough edge.

His brother gave him an apologetic look. "If we're going to be using Kensington's machine anyway, we should see if we can use it to solve the other situation."

"What are you thinking?" Riley asked.

He rubbed a hand over his mouth. "Damned if I know, but there should be something useful we can do with it."

"We'll have to worry about it later," Arnow said. "The longer we're here, the better the odds someone's going to come looking."

"They wouldn't be here if we didn't have so much corruption," Tiny said. "They're here because of the bombings. Before that, they didn't have an excuse."

"You'd almost think they paid Savannah to do it," Taylor said.

"Now that they have an excuse to take over, they aren't going to be willing to just pull out," Price said. "The government and other entities have wanted to take control of the mines for years. Now that they've got a foothold, they won't give it up easily."

"Their only reason for being here is because the Tyets run roughshod over everything, and practically everybody in law enforcement and local government are on the take," Patti said. "Stop all that, and there's no reason for outside interference."

"Shouldn't be hard," Dalton said. "Blow the rest of the city up and voilà. Nothing to it."

"Or . . .," Riley began in that tone that said she was going to do something incredibly stupid. "We could make people hate corruption and want to do positive and legal things for one another. Increase empathy and generosity."

"For the entire city?" Price asked in a studiously calm voice.

"Why not? Then local government can meet with the Tyet lords, arrange to dissolve the Tyets or something like that. Have the city take over the mines and put those into a trust with money going to public works and city residents. Make it employee-owned so everybody gets rich here. Something to balance the inequity and make everyone feel invested. A lot of people join Tyets for protection and financial stability. Give them that and a piece of the mines, and they'll fight to make sure the Tyets don't come back."

"Even if you could do that, it could completely drain you," Price said. "And everybody else," he added.

"Besides, doing something like that will create a whole new set of problems," said Arnow.

"Problems that we can deal with later. They can't be worse than martial law and internment camps," Taylor said, hating that she agreed with Riley. Her sister didn't need encouragement on this risky road. At the same time, Riley would do whatever she thought was right, and Taylor had every intention of being right beside her. The more help Riley had, the more likely she was to succeed and come out alive. At this point, that was a hundred percent Taylor's goal.

"It's worth a try," Riley said with a stubborn look, confirming Taylor's thoughts.

"No saying you can do any of that," Dalton pointed out.

He leaned against a bookcase, arms crossed. He looked relaxed. Taylor knew better. He was wound up just as tight as she was. How did he feel about Vernon's death? They'd been close. Was he grieving?

A lump thickened in her throat as the memory of putting her mother in the ground slammed into her. She'd been dead only a month, and Taylor had made every effort not to think about her so she wouldn't have to feel the loss.

A stray thought wandered across her brain. With both of her parents dead, she and Riley were orphans.

She snorted at herself. *Bitch, please. An orphan at your age? Get over yourself, already.* Anyway, she was supposed to be thinking of Dalton's feelings.

He studiously did not meet her gaze, the muscles in his jaw flexing, his eyes glinting metallic silver. Maybe he hated her for killing Vernon.

Her brows drew together as she tried to sort out how she felt about that. Anger, resentment, defiance and . . . hurt. A lot more of the latter than the first three put together. Her fist clenched. So much for him wanting a relationship. Guess she wasn't the woman he'd thought she was.

Asshole.

"True enough," Touray said in response to Dalton.

"We're talking about using the machine to tell Tyets to disband. Why don't we just tell the FBI and police to quit being corrupt?" Jamie asked. "Tell the corrupt ones to resign and leave town, or turn themselves in, or hell, have them take a swan dive into the caldera." He glanced at Price. "No offense."

Price barely flicked him a glance before returning his attention to Riley. Like he thought she might disappear right before his eyes. Which, to be fair, she easily could.

"None taken."

"Clay was a *good* cop," Touray declared. "He refused to come work for me, as you very well know." This last he directed at Riley.

"He did when you threatened her," Patti said. She gave Price a gentle look. "Not that he had a choice." She turned back to Touray. "For future reference, you don't fuck over family that way."

Taylor gave a sharp nod of agreement.

Touray's face flushed, his mouth twisting into a snarl.

Arnow jumped in before he could respond. "Don't rewrite history. He did jobs for you," she told Touray coldly. "He just wasn't full time on your payroll."

Arnow and Touray didn't have a happy history. Taylor didn't know any details, just that the two had run into each other when Arnow worked for Savannah, and whatever had happened between them had pissed her off. Of course, Touray was highly skilled at pissing people off, so to be fair, Arnow's dislike could be over something relatively small.

Taylor doubted it. The blond FBI agent's icy gaze dripped loathing.

"Let it go," Price told his brother, ending the argument.

Riley nodded. "We've got a narrative. We've got a plan to use the artifacts. Let's figure out how to make them happen."

In the next few minutes, Tiny worked on the bodies and everybody else wiped away fingerprints and got rid of whatever evidence might undermine their story.

"What about them?" Patti asked, motioning toward the captive agents.

"I'll adjust them after we finish," Cass said.

If she was still alive. Taylor glanced at Riley who looked desolate, no doubt thinking the same thing. Taylor squeezed her hand. "It will be fine," she mouthed, determined to make it true.

Riley nodded and squeezed back. She lifted her chin and her expression turned confident.

Fake it till you make it. Taylor had done it many times.

When they were confident they could do no more to set the scene, they turned to the table where Jamie and Leo had emptied out the bags containing the artifacts.

She knew from what Riley had told her that the larger box—no bigger than a shoebox—contained two artifacts. Beside it, a small glass jar contained a metal object that looked like a butterfly with a circular, elongated body. Beside it lay a filigreed vial of blood with a red wax stopper. Someone had cleaned it so the copper filigree gleamed. Three more containers sat beside those.

One was a squat round box made of what appeared to be lead with metal straps holding it closed. It had been dented and scraped up and looked about as old as it probably was.

The next was made of oak and shaped like an octahedron, tipped to sit on one of its triangular sides. Taylor couldn't see how it opened. The third was the largest of those that had come from Tyrell. Made from dark-blue glass, it was about the size of a small loaf of bread. It looked completely solid.

Cass pushed the lead box with her finger. "Does anybody else feel like we're about to open the Ark of the Covenant and our skin and flesh is all going to melt away like candle wax under a welding torch?"

"We're not the Nazis," Leo pointed out. "Indiana Jones came out just fine."

Jamie nodded sagely. "Good guys always win."

"Last time you opened them, you took a couple big hits," Price said to Riley, and his taut expression indicated how hard it was to hold his emotions in check. "You can't afford that. Not if you want to be on your feet to use them."

"To be fair, I'd also just been shot and healed," she pointed out. "So I was coming at it while I was still pretty weak."

"To be fair, you still got hit with a couple magical sledgehammers, and this time we don't have nulls to take the edge off."

"Good point," Riley said, moving over to the shelf where a small Remington bronze of a horse and a cowboy inching down the side of a very steep slope sat. "I'll just whip one up real quick."

Taylor actually felt the surge when Riley started pouring magic into the statue. She shifted uncomfortably as every hair on her body prickled and stuck up on end. She glanced at the others. No one else seemed to feel anything at all.

"Will it be enough?" Taylor nudged her chin toward the statue when Riley set it on the table.

"We'll find out."

"Very reassuring."

"I aim to please."

Riley flashed a smile. It had a reckless edge that worried Taylor. Riley was making this up as she went along, and she was more likely to sacrifice herself than not. She had before and nearly died. Had died.

Glancing around at the others, Taylor saw she wasn't the only one who thought so. Price looked like his teeth were going to crack, he was clenching them so hard, and his eyes were pure white. Jamie and Leo, who ordinarily had a lock on being stupidly reckless, wore identical grooves between their brows as they scowled at Riley. Patti and Cass just looked resigned.

"Let's get to work, then, shall we?"

Riley took the lid off the jar containing the small tube with its butterfly wings and turned it over in her fingers. "Could be the key Kensington told you about." She handed it to Taylor.

It vibrated in her hand. Excitement ran through her, and she clutched it tight, meeting Riley's questioning gaze. "I think you're right."

Riley blew out a soft breath and picked up the octahedron box. "I don't see any way to open it. No latch, no lid."

"Maybe the boxes are keyed to a particular talent," Cass said.

"Or maybe the key could do it," Patti suggested.

Riley handed the box to Taylor who trailed the hollow end over it, but nothing happened. She returned the box to Riley. Once again Taylor felt a surge of power. It subsided and Riley shook her head and handed it to Touray.

"You try."

Taylor couldn't feel his magic. Interesting. He shook his head and passed the box to Cass. This time the box lit up, the artifact inside turning scarlet red and glowing through the thin panels of wood. The facets of the octahedron slid back, fitting inside each other to expose the thing within.

The light softened, revealing what amounted to a crystal ball, but the light swirled and coiled inside like a knot of eels. Looking at it made Taylor queasy.

She averted her gaze. Jamie caught her eye and tipped his head. He walked a few steps away from the rest of the group and waited for her to join him.

"You okay?" he asked, putting an arm around her shoulders.

"Why wouldn't I be?"

He gave her an impatient look. "Because you killed Vernon and Mrs. Senator?"

"I don't plan to lose any sleep over it," she said, shrugging.

"Road to hell is paved with good intentions," Leo pointed out, having followed along. "Doesn't actually answer the question, either."

"So take a hint and drop it."

"Nah, don't think so. I know you've been in situations overseas where you've killed people, but this isn't the same," Jamie said.

Leo nodded. "It's up close and personal, and Vernon was your dad, even if he was an asshole. If you don't feel guilty about that, then I'm guessing you're feeling guilty about it being too easy to kill him. Am I right?"

"What are you, a shrink?" Taylor rolled her eyes at him, annoyed that he'd hit the nail on the head.

"I'm just smart," Leo said.

"Smart-ass, is more like it," Jamie said

"That, too," he agreed. "But I'm not wrong, am I?"

Taylor sighed. "No," she said grudgingly. "Not that it matters at the moment. Looks like they got the other boxes open."

"Show time," Jamie said, expression hardening, eyes flat with determination.

Leo fell in behind him as they returned to the others, with Taylor bringing up the rear, doing her best to ignore the foreboding growing like a thornbush in her heart.

They'd either snatch victory from the mouth of defeat or they'd all go down. But at least they'd be together. No one left behind to live or grieve. Her mouth curved an ironic smile as a sense of fatalistic amusement settled over her. What a stupid thing to take comfort in.

Chapter 34

Riley

ONCE CASS HAD opened her box, each of us quickly found our own. The wooden box from my original find in Josh's office belonged to Touray. He didn't have any trouble opening it. Nestled within, looking just like it had when Price and I had opened the box was a long, thin piece of metal covered in delicate silver whiskers. They shifted and moved with liquid grace, like they were underwater.

Before I could warn him, Touray pulled it out of the box. When I'd brushed it delicately with a finger, it had combed through my skin like tiny scalpels. Not Touray. The whiskers lengthened, stretching out to curl lovingly around his hand.

Next was the tin cylinder. It seemed to like Tyrell. Tiny had healed him up, though he'd left some bruising and swelling, just to remind Tyrell he wasn't in the driver's seat on this bus. Not that he looked like he was in danger of taking over. He had a sunken, diminished look, like all his hopes and dreams had caved in, leaving him a shell of a man. Which, to be fair, was mostly true, though I couldn't scrape up the slightest bit of sympathy for him.

He unscrewed the top of the cylinder and tipped the contents into his hand. The turquoise piece was just as ugly as I remembered. It looked like a weird, abstract flower. About five inches long, on one end it was dully rounded. At the other was a flat, wheel-shaped flower with a round center and nail-like petals.

Connecting the two ends were three interwoven strips carved in varying shapes. One looked like a string of square beads strung haphazardly. The second looked like knotted string, and the third was knobby, sort of like a diseased tree trunk but really small.

I waited for it to do something the way Touray's had, but it remained inert. Did that mean something? Like Tyrell wasn't as strong as he needed to be? I chewed my lower lip and focused on the last two boxes.

"Which one do you want to try?" I asked Patti, trying not to let my worry for her color my voice.

She was a minor binder. It was entirely likely she couldn't do what the artifact machine would need. What if trying killed her? My stomach knotted so hard it hurt. I couldn't tell her not to try. We all got to make our own choices, and we all had to live with the consequences.

Patti eyed the two remaining boxes, shrugged, and reached for the lead box with the metal strapping. She picked it up, and I felt a surge of magic. The straps separated as if cut. Both curled up like springs but remained attached. Patti removed the lid.

Inside contained a nest of straw. Nestled into it was some kind of wheel. Patti lifted it free. It was no bigger than the palm of my hand, with notches around it that almost looked like gears, but not quite. The interior contained little geometric cutouts with no pattern I could discern.

"Now you," Cass said, gesturing toward the blue glass block.

I ran my fingers over the smooth top. I could see through it. Whatever was inside was either invisible, the same color blue, or translucent. I was strangely reluctant to find out. It felt like the point of no return. The fact was we'd passed that when Mrs. Senator had blown her husband's head off. I shuddered at the memory of the spattered blood and brain and the way his skull looked like it had exploded. I had a feeling I'd be seeing that in my nightmares for a long time. Worse, we were all wearing part of him. I shuddered and forced my mind back on task.

Aware that everyone was waiting, I fed nulling power into the block. I wasn't prepared for the results.

In the blink of an eye, it melted and stretched out tentacles, latching onto me, Cass, Patti, Touray, and Tyrell. It wrapped each of our wrists and burrowed into our skins into our veins. It didn't stop there. I could feel it traveling through me like a virus, reaching into every vein, every artery, every capillary. It happened so fast, I barely had time to gasp or notice the trickle of blood running down over my palm.

More than half the block remained, and it quickly expanded and spun into ribbons, reaching out to snatch the other artifacts and move them into place. Into Cass's gear piece went the flower petals of Tyrell's turquoise piece. The dull bottom end of the turquoise nestled into a pocket in the glass. Now the thing really did look like a flower.

A straw of glass shot up the middle to serve as a stem, while the three stringy-looking bits separated from the base and curled up to insert themselves the gear's interior holes. They pushed through and reconnected above the crystal ball and clamped it in place on the point formed from four shoots of glass that had come through the four equidistant holes on the gear, closing together like the corners of a pyramid.

More glass rose around the entire construction in a mesmerizing, twisting shape, coming together six or seven inches above the crystal ball. Touray's piece was the final bit of the puzzle, its rod fixing itself into the top of the glass and hanging down to just above the ball.

All that happened so fast I didn't even have time to panic.

As soon as the last piece locked into place, the whole thing began to spin. As it did, a spiraling light lit the crystal ball, flinging scatters of light over us. The fine metal whiskers of Touray's piece lengthened and surrounded the ball, the tips curling inward to rest on its surface.

An unexpectedly low whine sounded through the room. It made my bones ache with relentless, dull pain. From the sounds the others made, I wasn't the only one. I could feel the glass floss inside me vibrating like harp strings.

To say it was freaky would be an understatement.

Seconds dribbled past as we tried to sort through what had just happened.

"Are you okay?"

Price sounded like an enraged bear, his voice low and rough, more a growl than speech.

"Uh-huh," I managed.

"What's happening?" This from Jamie who stood behind Cass, arms folded, fingers tapping.

"I don't know." It was hard to form words.

"It's waiting for something," Touray said. With the blue veins in his eyes and the blue tint to his skin from the glass, he looked scarier than usual. Like some kind of alien-zombie-demon creature.

"We should feed it power," Tyrell said.

His eyes had gone wide, and his face was slack. He leaned away from the spinning machine, but the glass around his wrist and running through his body held him fast.

"On three," I said. Then counted. "One . . . two . . . three."

The light in the crystal ball brightened so much I had to squint, but nothing else happened.

"Stop," I said, after it was apparent that our combined magic wasn't the key to starting it up.

Wait. Duh. Key.

"Where's the other piece? The key?" I asked.

"Here." Taylor held it up.

"See if there's a spot for it."

She leaned in between me and Patti, scrutinizing the glass base from which the tentacles holding each of us emanated. It was the only thing not spinning.

"I don't see anything."

She moved around to the other side and checked there.

"Nothing."

"Maybe it sits on top," Patti suggest. "Like the finial on a lamp."

"Feel free to hurry. I'm not exactly comfortable," Cass added

She was so thin that the blue of the glass running through her was visible everywhere I could see skin.

"Not the top either," Taylor said trying it. "Maybe someone else has to do it."

I shook my head. "I don't think so. Use your talent and see what happens." Kensington had sought Taylor out. Her power was akin to his. That meant something; Riley could feel it all the way to her toes. Taylor was the metaphorical and literal key.

Taylor gave a little shrug and directed power into it, gasping as the crystals inside turned to iridescent smoke. It swirled out the hollowed tip and wove through the spinning blue glass spindles.

Light flared. Power exploded. I almost couldn't breathe. Pressure squeezed me from all sides.

The glass filaments inside me began to move. Horror made my gorge rise as they wriggled out from beneath my skin like thousands of tiny worms. They lengthened, stretching through the air, reaching for the filaments that had grown out of the others. In seconds we were all connected, sewn together within a web of spun-glass threads. I didn't dare try to move.

Light pulsed and red poured out of the interior ball. It dripped down to the ribbons extending out to each of our wrists, and then flooded into and through each of us, turning the candy floss stitching us together crimson, then it all turned gold.

Everything went still. I couldn't hear anything beyond my own ragged breathing. Panic slammed me as my claustrophobia triggered. All my instincts screamed at me to break free, to run.

My breathing grew shallow. Dizziness made it hard to think. Shudders ran through me, and I ran cold, then hot. Oddly, I didn't feel any pain from the skewering glass, and I couldn't feel any trickles of blood.

"You're hyperventilating, Riley. Breathe slower. Count."

Price spoke from behind me. He touched the back of my neck. He kept talking, and I held on to his voice and gentle touch. He sounded calm. Like a hostage negotiator talking down a terrorist wearing a bomb. Which was closer to the truth than not.

I forced myself to breathe evenly and deeper, until the dizziness receded.

"That's it, baby," he said. "You've got this. You've done miracles before. You can do it again. Don't let me down."

Sure. Absolutely. If I had the vaguest idea what to do now. How did we make the machine work?

Before I could try to come up with an idea, something *shifted.* I felt a tugging. Not on my flesh, but deeper. My astral-self. Then it was like something uncorked. Magic flowed out of me in a fast-flowing stream.

Not just me, I realized. The machine was sucking power from everybody. The space inside the glass floss filled, and the tug turned to a heavy drag, the pressure increasing by the second.

Was this supposed to happen? Should we be fighting it? Should we be figuring out how to use the machine's power? We were doing this by the seat of our pants. Maybe this was working exactly right. It didn't matter. However things were *supposed* to happen, I had to deal with what was actually happening.

So now what?

Lacking any better idea, I reached out for the power. It leaped into me as if it had been eagerly waiting.

Magic coursed into me like water through a broken dam, but it didn't overwhelm me. I was a bottomless lake, able to take as much as it threw at me. I'd never felt so powerful in my life. Practically like a god.

Now what did I do with it? Cass was the dreamer. She was the one who knew how to change minds. How did I tell her to do it? Another thought struck me. With all of us connected, our magic flowing through the machine, could I borrow their talents?

Trouble was, even if I could use their powers, I didn't know how. Just like someone getting a hit of Sparkle Dust and getting a temporary talent. I was more likely to blow myself up than not. I had to try something, though. I didn't know how long all of us could continue to feed power into the machine.

With all their collected power feeding into me, theoretically, there shouldn't be anything I couldn't do. Every non-cardinal talent was a mix of the others, so in reality, I had command of every possible talent. Only I had no idea what to do.

You also had no idea you could do some things with your own talent and you just decided to make it work for you, didn't you? Stop whining like a baby and get on with your job, already.

My crabby inner Susie-Cheerleader voice wasn't altogether right, but I *had* done some pretty wild and unexpected and up-until-then impossible things.

So do it now. Think outside the box.

Fast.

Chapter 35

Riley

I EXPECTED THAT the power would start to overwhelm me and burn me alive, but for once it didn't. I just felt exhilarated, like I could do anything I wanted to do. At the same time, I could sense a softening deep inside. A tiny rotten spot in a piece of ripe fruit. Nothing big—yet—but a reminder that I was running out of time. We all were.

Instinct drove me to start with my own power. First thing on the to-do list: Find three or four Tyet lords who could have conspired with Senator Rice. But how? Erickson. I reached out to his trace and slid easily into his mind. I didn't think about how I was doing this. I could figure it out later. Now I just needed to get my job done.

Give me the names of those who should conspire with the senator. I should have asked before we started in with the artifacts. Stupid mistake. I had to make that my last one.

Surprise and wariness suffused Erickson at my intrusion, then he quickly focused on the question. Savannah, of course. Ibrahim Deneli. Morgan Pilferan. Alex Ruffinach.

Savannah was dead. We could attribute all sorts of things to her. But how did I find the others?

I could travel.

As soon as I thought it, I found myself sliding through dreamspace and into a luxurious bathroom. A man stood peeing into a marble toilet. I grabbed his trace and sank into his mind, pushing deep. I forged memories, erasing any glimpse of myself. I repeated the process with Morgan Pilferan, finding him in bed with a boyfriend. Alex Ruffinach rode a stationary bike while watching a video of mountain scenery skimming past. I quickly implanted the memories. With all of them, I added in doubts about their professions. Couldn't hurt to encourage them to change jobs.

Once I finished, I travelled back. Had my physical body gone anywhere? Or had the glass floss kept me tied in place? Probably the latter. I needed to be plugged into the machine to access other powers.

Now for something harder. I had to influence every person in the city. I had to create an intolerance of corruption, plus convince everybody the mines should be turned over to the city and owned by the people. I had to create a surge of empathy and generosity that wouldn't fade.

I should have been disgusted at manipulating their minds the way my father had mine and my family's. For our own good, according to him. In this case it was a last resort. It didn't mean I didn't feel guilty, but I could live with that. I didn't know how else to protect the people of the city. This might not work, but it was our best shot. I just hoped I could do it.

How do you touch an entire city? What an idiotic idea. I'd had a lot of those in my life. Idiotic didn't mean impossible. I'd make this work whatever I had to do.

I began by gathering all the bits and pieces of trace clinging to me, left behind by various people. I pushed my awareness out along those threads, finding the owners, which included everybody in the room. I picked up the trace clinging to them, then let go of my companions. I didn't want to change their minds. I continued stretching myself farther, grasping every line of trace I touched.

It felt blazing fast, and it surprised me how easy it was to hold them all. The further out from myself I went, the slower I got. Like pushing a rock uphill. Sensations, thoughts, and emotions traveled back to me through the ever-growing bundle of trace that I held. I'd never experienced that before. An effect of the machine, I supposed. It made it difficult to concentrate, to remember who I was and what I was doing.

At this rate, it would take days to reach everyone. By then, my brain might have melted. Who was I kidding? I'd be a pancake. I had to do this faster.

If only—

The instant I thought of it, I'd already begun to make it happen. I didn't know how. Maybe because I was tied to everyone else, and their instincts were mine.

I shifted halfway into the dreamscape. Touray could pop in and out and show up wherever he wanted, wherever he thought to be. I went a different route, combining our powers so that instead of going where I wanted, I sent my awareness of trace everywhere in the city, skimming quickly, one foot in the real world, one in the dreamscape.

The more trace I picked up, the harder it was to keep myself separate. To suddenly grasp it all was like getting hit by a stone wall. Thoughts and emotions boiled up inside, fragmented, overlapping, manic. My brain skipped from one to the next like a hummingbird on crack.

I sank under the maelstrom. Panic gripped me. Or seemed to. I couldn't keep hold of myself long enough to know anything. I was awash in thousands upon thousands of disembodied feelings and confetti of thought that felt like mine and yet were alien. No context for formulating a coherent thought, for understanding anything. Just an endless pastiche ratcheting into me.

I lost my sense of time. I clutched the trace tighter, terrified I'd lose it before I'd figure my way out of this mess.

Suddenly, it stopped.

I was blessedly alone in my head.

You're okay. You've got this.

Cass.

Relief choked me. I wasn't so alone after all.

Are you okay? I asked.

Just hurry.

She vanished, and I was alone again.

The weakness inside me had grown. I felt it now, a heaviness that weighted me down. I had no idea how much time we had left before one of us died. I had no intention of finding out how long that might be.

The hard part of this project loomed before me. I'd already done one semi-impossible thing by gathering up the city's trace. Now to do the actual impossible thing.

Dreamers could create fake memories and rearrange brainscapes, so I knew that dreaming power would be part of this. But I also had to make those memories stick and feel real. *Be* real. Dreamer power could do that, too, but I had to make these impossible to separate from the real memories, so that no one would ever know they'd been manipulated. For that, I needed binding power. More than that, I needed Taylor's power to bind this inside their trace, inside their astral selves.

Even as I made the decision, I pulled on the power and pushed out into minds and trace of every person in the city.

I stuttered and slowed. I was pushing through frozen molasses. It clung to me, holding me back. The weakness in me, in all of us, dragged on me.

I didn't have the strength.

I drew harder, caught between desperation and the knowledge that taking the power would inevitably kill the others.

My chest tightened; my throat knotted.

I didn't have a choice.

The extra energy let me reach farther but soon petered out. I kept pulling. There wasn't much left.

I made an inarticulate sound, though I couldn't have said if it was anger, desperation, or apology.

Power surged into me, like I'd been plugged into a fresh battery. More came pouring from the others.

Price, Leo, Jamie, Tiny, and Dalton.

I grasped the extra power, and the thick sludge faded. I extended myself to the limits of the trace I held.

Letting instinct guide me, I used dreamer power to extend myself into the minds of the populace, then gingerly took up Taylor's talent. She'd killed easily, snapping apart Vernon's and Mrs. Senator's traces with hardly any effort. I didn't want to cut through any that I held and accidentally slaughter huge swathes of people.

I could feel null resistance and kicked myself. How had I not thought they wouldn't be using them? How many had I overlooked?

Stupid.

I turned my attention back to the city's tangle of trace and searched for blank spots that indicated nulls, then set about blowing through them. With the magic pouring into me and my ability to tear them apart, they didn't give me much trouble, but it took time. More time than I could afford.

Urgency drove me as I shredded them. I couldn't leave any behind.

By the time I was done, my body pulsed with the effort. On top of that, just holding the trace and all that power had begun to eat at me. I wasn't meant for so much power. It chewed at my muscles, bones, and nerves. It gnawed me from the inside out. Exhaustion and a deep, excruciating ache pulled at me, weighing me down, making me flat.

I fought against it, once again extending my consciousness into the minds of the populace. Minutes or hours ticked past as I carefully inserted myself into the giant bouquet of trace, praying I wouldn't cut any apart. I refused to hurry.

Too many people could die.

At last I'd merged with both minds and trace. I trembled, inside and out. If I hadn't been fixed in place by the web of glass, I'd have collapsed. As it was, I felt like I might melt to the ground. My entire body felt like it was disintegrating. Like all my puzzle pieces had smooth edges and nothing to hold them together.

Still, I wasn't done. People would hear about the senator's dealings on the news, but I primed them to believe all that would be said. Next, I needed to change the leadership of the FBI and police, and I needed to get the Tyets to shut themselves down. It would be easier if the Tyet soldiers and leaders *wanted* to turn themselves in. They had to think it was a good idea, noble even, and believe it was fundamentally important to keep Diamond City free of martial law and protect its citizens. Time for the corrupt to start giving back. Like community service, except they'd want to do it. Call it reparations for all the harm they'd done over the years.

I built the narrative in my head, giving cops the option to turn themselves in or go straight, but they all had to confess to what they'd done. Their new bosses could decide if they were worth keeping after that.

Despite my exhaustion and my growing pain, I smirked. I couldn't wait to see how those new bosses liked their jobs.

When it felt firm, when the details felt firmly fleshed out and real, I pushed it out into people's brains, using the dreamspace to speed the process, and used Patti's binding power and Taylor's talent for manipulating trace to insert it and bind it so everybody would feel its truth, all the way down into the very core of their beings.

I started to withdraw and then realized there needed to be more. Something concrete. Something physical to reinforce it all, especially for the vultures in far off Washington DC, waiting for a chance to swoop in.

The idea that popped into my head was perfect.

If I could pull it off.

I took a deep breath. Or at least I tried. My lungs barely expanded, and I heard a weird gurgling. My chest hurt, my head spun. Something dribbled from my nose, onto my lips, and into my open mouth. Blood.

My stomach heaved, and bile rose in my throat. I couldn't cough, could barely swallow it back down. My vision had gone cloudy.

I'd better hurry. I picked up Erickson's trace. *Help me.* I showed him what I wanted. His instant agreement startled me.

Go ahead. I'll guide you.

I deepened the connection to his mind, melding us together so he could help me do what I needed to. Summoning Tyrell's maker power, we went to work. It didn't take long to create incriminating footage of the senator talking to his wife alone, before our arrival. Erickson could have done that without me. I added the rest in. Small pieces of evidence that would reinforce the story we'd fashioned. In his room, a safe containing a handwritten journal. A coded list of secret bank accounts. Real ones that Erickson had uncovered. And then . . .

DNA and fingerprints. We sprinkled the senator's liberally in the homes and offices of Savannah and the Tyet lords we'd targeted.

Next, I gathered up all the blood and tissue that had splattered on us and turned it into dust.

What else? The words came sluggishly. Exhaustion lay thick over my mind.

It's enough, Erickson said. *Better pull out now before you can't. And just so you know, any time you need something from me, just call. I like you, and I like what you want to do for the city.*

I didn't answer. I had to save what energy I had left to free us all from machine before it killed us. If it would let us go.

Chapter 36

Taylor

THE INSTANT SHE'D activated the last piece, opalescent smoke poured from the tip and wound through the spinning ribs of glass of the machine. Blinding light flared. In the same moment, the butterfly wings of the piece wrapped her hand, and dragged her forward. Pain exploded in her palm as something stabbed through it. A split second later, that was overwhelmed by blistering heat scorching her hand and arm. Taylor tried to yank away, but her hand was stuck. Movement below her palm suggested that she was somehow skewered on top of the machine above the crystal.

Then something speared up her wrist and broke apart, pushing through like thousands of needles tugging and pulling long threads.

Glass threads.

It took every last speck of self-control to keep Taylor from fighting against the invasion. When they burst out of her skin, sticking through her eyes, nose, mouth, scalp, and every other part of her, she let out a sound, half scream. Panicking, she tried to twist away, but the threads held her fast, weaving through the floss now piercing everyone else. The horror of it was almost more than she could stand.

As if she had a choice.

Taylor made herself breathe. She couldn't swallow, couldn't blink, and her vision had become fragmented, like looking through drops of blue water. She had no idea how her heart managed to keep beating or her lungs to keep breathing.

She struggled to hold back her magic as it started feeding into the machine but stopped herself. If this was the way it was supposed to work, she had to make herself cooperate. She just hoped it wasn't an insane mistake. It didn't help that she had no idea what was happening.

She had no sense of time, just the constant drain. Then it became a suctioning draw, like someone was pumping the power out of her. Hope flickered. That had to mean somebody was doing something, that the machine was working.

She began to feel thin, like paper. Like all the vitality leached out of her. If not for the glass, she'd have slumped to the floor, or curled up like ash and been blown away. As it was, she thought she might start to crumble into dust.

Then came an influx of power as someone fed it into her. It spread through her like water over dried ground, soaking into parched tissues and brittle nerves, giving them back their elasticity.

"You're too fucking stubborn to let this thing beat you. Goddamn you, *stay alive.*"

Dalton's words sounded low and furious, his fingers pressed against the sides of her neck, between the strands of glass. He was the one feeding her power. She'd thought it was Leo or Jamie.

His words made her prickle with indignation, as no doubt they were supposed to do. If she could, she would have rolled her eyes at herself. So predictable. So annoying that Dalton knew just what buttons to push to piss her off. *Asshole.*

Still, she was grateful for the power he poured into her, and to know she wasn't alone. Inwardly, she snorted at herself. *Alone?* Hooked up to five other people with her brothers, Price, Tiny, Dalton, Erickson, and Arnow in the room? *Dumbass.*

She frowned. Why had the machine pulled her in? Had it always required six people and Kensington had opted to leave that fact out?

Before long, she began to feel weak and wobbly. Dalton didn't stop pouring what he had into her. She had no way to make him stop. What was he trying to do, sacrifice himself? Then they'd both be dead. What was he trying to prove?

We need to shut it down.

Taylor started when Riley's voice ribboned through her mind, sounding ragged.

How? Taylor wondered.

Fuck all if I know.

How are you talking to me?

I'm talking to all of you. Borrowing Cass's power.

That made sense, Taylor supposed. But that didn't answer the real question, which was how to shut this down—without killing them. That would be good.

It would be good, Riley agreed.

Anybody have any ideas? Taylor asked.

No. We think you must be the key. Your piece turned the machine on. I'm hoping it can turn it off.

How?

No clue. I don't know how you ended up in the glass matrix anyhow.

That's helpful.
You're welcome.

Taylor considered the situation. Damn but it would be nice if Kensington were here to answer a few questions. Too bad she had no way to contact him.

Unless . . .

Got any ideas on how to summon Kensington? He could tell us. If he hadn't disintegrated after talking to her.

Silence.

Riley?

Trying to pick up his trace. From the vial of blood.

Silence.

Got him. Smug triumph.

The temperature dropped. Taylor's bones ached.

He's here.

I told you not to put it together. Kensington's mental voice was a mix of accusation and irritation. *Now you're going to die.*

We'd rather not, Riley said dryly.

How do we shut it down? Taylor asked.

Kensington's reply was less than helpful. *You don't. It runs until it has no more energy, and then it stops.*

You didn't put in an off-switch? That's about the dumbest thing I've heard, Riley said.

Taylor agreed. *If that's true, how did you survive?*

Hesitation. *I did not become part of the circle.*

How? It needed someone with your talent—our *talent*—*to turn it on.*

I took precautions.

What kind?

Does it matter?

It could. Much as she wanted to scream at him, she kept her mental voice calm.

Another hesitation. Longer. *I had a twin.*

It took a second for Taylor to internalize that. Riley was faster.

You set your twin up to die? What kind of asshole are you?

A pause. Then, grudgingly. . . . *We drew straws. It was necessary for the city,* he added, and Taylor could feel his guilt and grief.

So you get why we had to do this, she said.

Kensington's response came whiplash fast. *No. This city deserves to die. My brother and the others sacrificed their lives, and for what? You're back doing the same thing again. How long will it last? Who will have to die next time? Diamond City is and will always be corrupt. People don't change. They don't deserve to be rescued from themselves. They certainly won't be grateful.*

Taylor agreed, at least in part. A lot of people in the city weren't worth saving. Like the Seedy Seven. But even so. . . . *Too many good people would have been hurt if we didn't try.*

And now you will die for them.

Not if I can help it, Taylor said.

You can't. You're all dead. You just haven't stopped breathing yet. No point in me hanging about watching.

Taylor had the impression of him dusting his hands together.

Riley ignored his hint to let him go. *When all the energy dries up, the glass filaments just retract and the machine can be taken apart?*

Correct.

Maybe Price could use his talent to pull out the key, Riley suggested. *He wouldn't have to touch it.*

It's embedded in my hand, Taylor said.

Embedded?

Yep.

Okay, then. Different strategy.

If it's the only choice, then we have to do it. Better if I lose a hand than everybody dies.

It won't work, came Kensington's voice. *The machine has to reverse and reel in the diamond floss. If you try to stop it before it retracts, the magic keeping it from killing you will no longer protect you.*

Diamond floss? The glass wasn't glass at all? Taylor wanted to ask questions, but she was getting colder by the second, and she had no idea how long before she'd just fall asleep and freeze to death. She smirked inwardly with bleak humor. The cold and the machine were racing to see who would kill everyone first. Plus, the more of their energy that the machine ate, the less they had to stop it with.

You're the only one who could do it, Kensington tacked on grudgingly. *If it could be done.*

Who? Riley asked. *Me or Taylor?*

Taylor.

Oh goodie. She had to do something impossible without a clue of what to do or how, with a talent she'd just learned she had, not to mention she had to do it quickly. No pressure.

Taylor had always been good in tough situations. When flying overseas in a war zone, she'd been able to compartmentalize and go cold, not letting anything get to her. It had been a matter of survival—hers, the members of her team, and those she was picking up or dropping off.

Now the universe wanted to test that ability. Challenge accepted.

She took hold of her fears and squashed them down into a tiny mental box and sealed it up tight. Everything snapped into laser focus, and she felt her inhibitions, doubts, and anything resembling self-preservation fall away. If she was the only one who could stop the machine, then she would damned well do it, no matter the cost to herself.

Kensington was so sure every possibility hinged on her. She'd literally been the key to starting it. It had responded to her and not to Riley. So the fact that they could both see trace wasn't the reason for its connecting to her. It had to be because she could physically manipulate trace. That suggested that she needed both that talent and the key to fix things.

She gave a mental shake of her head. She still didn't have any idea what to *do*. A thought occurred to her. She shook her head, rejecting it. It couldn't be that simple. But the idea wouldn't let her go.

Was she overthinking? Was everybody overthinking? Was the answer more literal than metaphorical? The power was *inside* her; the talent was *inside* her. The key was *inside* her. The diamond threads were *inside* her. Could it come down to them all being inside her at the same time?

If so . . .

Hope tightened her chest. She knew what to do, or at least she knew what to try.

She reached out to her talent.

Chapter 37

Taylor

SHE COULDN'T SEE anything of the machine, just the swirl of the glow it put off. Touray and Patti stood across from her, both equally unable to move. Was that a flicker of panic in his eyes? Or just reflections of the machine's light? She couldn't imagine him afraid. Even possessed by the brain-jockey—the senator's wife—he'd been focused and angry, but not scared.

Somehow his fear calmed Taylor's nerves. She let herself sink into her talent. Touray and Patti turned shadowy, their complex patterns of human-shaped trace brightening until she could no longer see their physical forms, just Patti's lacy tangle of pale green and lavender and Touray's black and yellow.

The diamond floss twinkled with sparkling blue-tinged brilliance. The light rippled, energy coursing along each fine thread. Taylor drew inside herself. She felt her own trace spreading through her like an extensive root system. She wished she could look at it and see better what she was doing.

She became aware of the pulse of energy along the floss inside her and the throbbing energy in her right hand. More than that, she could feel the machine. She felt its beating heart. Or maybe that was her own heart.

Taylor focused on her hand. Her mental fingers ran over the floss. It felt soft as silk, tangling with her trace, but not piercing it. Interesting. The odds were that it should have put a hole *somewhere* in her trace. That meant it had avoided it.

She slid her awareness down her arm to the hand connected to the machine. This part was confusing. Fiery energy crackled up along the floss but ignored her mental touch. She pushed into it, and it enveloped her in liquid heat that flickered and streamed around and between every strand and fine filament of her trace. The pulse and shimmer and flowing energy reminded her of the northern lights.

She pushed further. The energy turned into a wind tunnel, shoving back hard against her. Taylor dug in to her trace and used it to pull herself against the flow. Prickles ran throughout her body, under her skin, across her scalp, through her intestines, down into the marrow of her bones.

Though she knew she was getting closer to her destination—the place where her hand, the key, and the machine all came together—it was slow. Too slow.

She dragged herself harder against the flow, digging deeper into her trace to anchor herself. The prickles turned to embers and flared white hot. She shuddered at the pain but didn't stop, didn't slow down.

At last she reached the center of the flow. A bright energy pulsed at the intersection of her hand, her trace, the diamond floss, the key, and the machine. The key's light was hard and silvery. It pierced her trace and ran down into the machine. Coming up through its hollow center was a core of twinkling blue. It broke apart into filaments, spreading through her blood vessels and outward to join the thread cocoon stitching them all together

What was intriguing was that the key had penetrated her trace, and with it, the diamond floss. Did that mean something?

Kensington said the machine had to reverse. That suggested she needed to get it spinning in the opposite direction. But how?

She focused her attention on the junction of her hand, the key, her trace, and the diamond floss, touching it with her talent.

That tiny touch against the juncture made her entire body spasm,. Her heart stumbled and then raced. A jolt sizzled along her trace. It was worse than getting hit with a taser.

If she could have moved, the powerful *zap*! would have sent her reeling. Her body twitched and shivered as much as it could in the machine's grasp. Her vision clouded and spun with bright halos. She smelled burned hair. *Suck it up, Buttercup. It's only going to get worse. Deal with it.*

She gathered herself. She might have only one shot, and she needed to go in with all the strength she could scrape together. It wasn't much, but hopefully sheer stubbornness would fill any gaps. Mule-headedness always seemed to work for Riley.

This time Taylor reached out boldly, the same way she had when she'd awakened the key's power.

It was like plugging into a nuclear reactor. Power dragged on her, hauling her into a vortex of violent magic. It felt primordial, unformed, like it was waiting to be forged into something. It battered her, tossing and churning and boiling. She was aware of pain, but it was too vast to comprehend. Like every molecule of her body started separating from the rest, the bonds stretching and fraying as they pulled against one another.

She was going to die.

The certainty could not be denied. Not the way her body screamed. Not the way the magic chewed through her like she was caught inside a jet engine. Not the way she felt pieces of herself peeling away.

Fine. She'd pay the price, but not until she saved everybody else.

She thrust herself deeper inside the vortex. She could feel the junction of herself and the machine like a black hole that both sucked her in and repelled her.

Just like her relationship with Josh. *Come here, get away, come here, get away, come here. . . .*

Maniacal laughter bubbled up from nowhere. Because her love life mattered so much at the moment. The burst of coherence, of remembering herself enough to laugh at her own idiocy gave her the impetus to drive forward.

Abruptly, the force shoving her away dissolved. She turned liquid, sliding down through the key into the heart of the machine.

The pressure pulling her apart abated. Her spirit self coalesced in the stillness at the center of the whirling power. She thrust herself out into it, imagining herself like a thick oak branch jamming into the spinning spokes of a wheel.

A hurricane slammed into her. Pressure like nothing she'd ever experienced pushed at her, demanding she give way. She felt herself skidding sideways. She pushed back with all the strength of her talent. She reached out for whatever extra energy she could summon and levered herself forward.

It was like pushing a square six-ton boulder up a mountain.

She strained with all her being, wondering how long she could maintain such effort. She couldn't rest, couldn't fall back and regroup. If she did, she'd be flattened.

She felt like she was tipping back and forth on the point of a pin, and if she could just lean a little farther, push a little bit more, she'd manage to push the machine in the other direction.

Instinct made her grasp the opalescent light winding through the glass spindles. She drew up all the energy she had left and shoved back against the rotation.

At first she thought nothing was happening, but then she realized it was starting to slow. Exultation drove her to dig deeper. Maybe, like a top, it would start spinning in reverse as it slowed down. Then maybe she could keep it going long enough to let everybody go.

You are going to die. You are almost dead.

Kensington's voice in her head startled her, and for a moment she lost concentration, her grip slipping. As she did, she saw that her trace was transparent and the scarlet and gold had washed out, fading nearly to gray.

Not before I free everybody.

She grabbed hold again, redoubling her efforts, gritting imaginary teeth.

Something closed around her. Energy ran up over her, feeding her, boosting her strength. She pushed harder, and the spin of the magic slowed to a stop. The machine wobbled on its base. It needed to spin to stay upright. Taylor shoved, trying to restart it and get it up to speed before it toppled.

Relief crashed over her as it finally began to turn.

Let go. You need to back out. I'll finish.

She understood instantly that he meant to stay and sacrifice himself. The machine needed to feed on something. He was giving it his energy so it could reel itself back in.

Why?

I resolved to stay as long as the machine remained, to prevent its use. I feared unscrupulous people would use it. I tied my spirit to the bottle of my blood.

Is that how you got out of the spirit realm?

She could sense a smile.

No. That was the work of your sister. You are both extraordinary.

Yeah, that's what you said. We're unicorns.

In more ways than you think. I was always tempted by the machine's power. To crush enemies. Always in the name of good, of course. But we can always find justification for anything we want to do, no matter how heinous, can't we? My twin brother was beguiled by its possibilities and had he survived, I believe he and I might have done terrible things. I realized this and knew that I had to protect the machine from those who would misuse it, especially me. I'd created a thing of evil, and I couldn't let it be loosed on the world again. If your sister had not given me the means to escape the spirit realm, the machine would have pulled me into this dimension as soon as you started putting it together.

But now you don't think it needs protecting?

Taylor watched the spindles as they sped up and blurred together with the opalescent smoke.

I can trust you to do so. You were not tempted by the power. You were not tempted to save yourself alone. You and your sister will not misuse it, nor will you allow it to be misused. I am content. Now go, or you will not survive.

He somehow gathered her up and squashed her into a ball, launching her toward the key. She willed herself to go through and return to her body.

Luckily, nothing seemed to want to stop her. She slid easily back up through and slammed into her body.

Instantly, she felt faint. A gray haze fuzzed her vision. Her body remained numb from the cold. At least, she hoped it was the cold.

She felt the diamond floss retract and pull out of her hand. The key pulled free of her palm, but its wings didn't let go. Instead, the key slid higher, the wings wrapping around her arm just below her elbow.

The instant she was free, her body melted. Someone caught her and laid her on the ground.

"What do we do?" Arnow demanded, sounding full-on ice bitch.

"*I'm* going to keep them alive," Tiny said in his slow, methodical way.

Them. That meant she wasn't the only one still breathing. Thank God. Thank Kensington. Without his boost of energy at the end, she might not have succeeded.

"How can I help?"

"Stay out of my way."

Normally, Taylor would have expected Arnow to just gut the man or rip his head off, but she remained silent. Taylor could hear her fuming, though.

"*Can* you keep them alive? Tinkers can't fix magical drain."

"Then go find me some batteries."

And by batteries, he meant cooperative donators of magic. Trouble was, giving magic wasn't all that easy. There was a learning curve, according to Leo and Jamie. They'd been doing it for each other for years, though, so they were pretty much experts.

"I can help."

Price sounded ancient. Taylor tried to open her eyes to see him, then abandoned the effort when it was clear she needed to concentrate on breathing.

"Right," Tiny said. "Then I'll just end up having to keep you alive."

"I don't give a shit. Give Riley whatever she needs."

"I am. Go sit your ass down before you fall down."

It occurred to Taylor, then, that she didn't hear anybody else. Not Jamie, Leo, or Dalton.

Worry almost gave her enough juice to pry open her eyelids, but the effort was more than she could manage. Instead she lay there, stewing.

Hands touched her head.

"You're awake," Tiny said.

Little jets of energy flowed into her. He was clearly providing battery power.

"Stop," she managed to gasp, twitching in his grip.

He didn't let go.

"Look . . . after . . . the others," she managed to whisper. Her lips were parched, and her tongue felt huge.

"Shut up and let me work."

"How is . . . everybody?"

"Alive. Passed out."

"Brothers?"

"Did I stutter? Passed. Out."

"Dalton?"

"Shut up," Tiny said, the thin veneer of his patience peeling away to reveal worried strain. "Trust me."

"I don't know . . . you."

Thanks to the energy he gave her, she was able to open her eyes. He was bent over her. She wrinkled her nose.

"You could use a mint."

"I could use a whiskey," he said.

"Fair enough."

He pulled his hands away and stood up in a single graceful move that should have been impossible for an anvil like him.

"You'll make it for now," he said. "You need to warm up, though."

With that, he moved away out of sight. She was on her own for getting warm, but at least she wasn't in imminent danger.

Taylor sucked in a breath and rolled onto her side, groaning softly. She felt like she'd been beaten with barbed wire. Looking at her hand, she saw that the wound in her palm had been healed, though it ached dully. Tiny had fixed it, she supposed. She hadn't felt a thing. Strangely, a dime-sized white scar remained on the back of her hand and palm. Was that because he hadn't bothered with fixing the scars? Or he couldn't?

She gave a mental shrug. Didn't matter.

Pushing all the way over onto her stomach, she struggled onto her hands and knees. It took a minute for her to reach her feet. Her head spun and she staggered.

Someone caught her arm.

Dalton.

He looked wasted, like he'd lost seventy pounds. His clothes hung loose. His cheeks had hollowed, and his eyes looked bruised, like he'd taken a couple of hard punches. He swayed, and Taylor wasn't sure if he was holding her up or the reverse.

"You all right?" She still couldn't scrape up more than a hoarse whisper.

"Still on the right side of the dirt," he said, though she had to strain to hear.

His gaze dropped to her chest and she saw his eyes cycle through their various colors. His brow pinched together.

"What?" She looked down at herself.

Tiny holes pocked her clothing where the diamond floss had poked through. That surprised Taylor, since the filaments had barely been the size of a strand of hair. But the holes were distinct and many.

"Are *you* all right?"

"Tiny seems to think so. Says I need to warm up, though."

Dalton turned, his body stiff and ungainly. Odd for a man made of grace.

"Sit on the couch. I'll pile pillows over you."

As much as she wanted to argue, the thought of sitting was suddenly very appealing.

She sank down onto the cushions, and Dalton piled throw pillows on her, then collapsed beside her.

Taylor watched Tiny work, moving from person to person. He'd clearly triaged who needed help soonest. She couldn't figure out if she'd been in that number or if he'd done a quick healing while triaging her. Erickson had come to put a hand on Tiny's shoulder, lending him energy.

Riley lay across Price's lap. He looked about as wiped as Dalton. He'd burst blood vessels in both eyes and appeared slightly demonic. He bent down over Riley and said something. Taylor was relieved to see that she responded.

Her gaze moved to where Tiny worked on Cass. Before, she'd looked anorexic. Now, she looked like a mummified corpse. Touray, Jamie, and Leo all knelt touching her. They didn't look like they had much left to give. Jamie and

Leo looked like pallid sacks of bones, their eyes and cheeks sunken, their skin pale and papery.

Dalton's hand found hers under the pillows and clasped it in a firm grip.

"She's going to be fine."

Taylor wanted to believe it, but she lived in the real world. "You don't know that."

"They won't let her die. Trust them."

Her gaze roved over the ruthlessly determined expressions of her brothers and stopped at Touray. He wasn't altogether there. His eyes were white, and he was transparent, as if he straddled the line between the dreamspace and the real world. He spoke to Tiny, who didn't look up but gave a short nod.

"He's channeling energy from the dreamscape," Taylor said, too tired to be surprised. Not that she should be. He treated Cass like family.

"He's not going to let her die."

"I could—"

"No," Dalton said, tightening his grip on her hand.

"You don't even know what I was going to say."

"Doesn't matter. You've done your share, and they can handle the rest. Tiny won't thank you for adding to his job."

"Rude," she said, when she couldn't think of a good response.

"Yep," he said, unconcerned.

They sat in silence and watched the others work on Cass. At last, color started to return to her ashen skin.

"See?" Dalton said.

"No one likes a know-it-all."

"You do. Come out to dinner with me."

Taylor blinked and turned to look at him. "Dinner? As in a *date*? You're asking me out? *Now?*"

"Thought we should work it in before you go starting another war or have another near-death experience."

"I'm not Riley," she said, insulted, though she didn't quite know why.

"No, you are not. Answer the question."

"Aren't you still pissed about me killing Vernon?" She tried not to sound hurt, mostly successfully, she thought.

"I was never pissed at you."

"Sure. You wouldn't even look at me, after."

"I was pissed I let it get that far. That you had to be the one to put him down. Killing your own father, even one as crappy as him, had to hit you hard."

"You liked him."

"He was good to me. Didn't make him a good man. Didn't make him a good father. He let me see one side of him, and I could respect that side."

"What about after you found out what he'd done to us? To me?" She was surprised at how important the answer was to her, though she wasn't entirely sure what she wanted him to say.

Dalton was silent a long moment, then finally, "He was a dead man walking."

It didn't take a lot of brains to translate that into Dalton planning to kill her father. She wanted to know more. When, for instance. And what exactly had been the tipping point. But now wasn't the time.

"You going to answer the question?" he prompted when she remained silent.

"I'm considering." She counted to ten, sure she was going to regret her answer. "Okay. Fine."

A brow rose. "Such enthusiasm."

"Are you complaining?"

"Just observing. When?"

"When?" She rolled her eyes at herself. She sounded like the village idiot repeating everything.

"Yes. When are you available? Tonight?"

"I don't even know what time it is. What day it is. Plus half the city is shut down. And we just went through a wood chipper. How about in a week or two?" Maybe she'd regain her sanity by then and cancel.

"There are restaurants open, or I'll cook for you. Doesn't matter what time it is. Breakfast, lunch, or dinner, I don't care. Any is good. You survived. It's worthy of celebration. And you need to eat."

"It's hard to say when I'll be free. I've got a couple of things going on." She gestured at the scene in front of them.

"Squeeze it in."

He'd pulled her hand onto his lap and began running a light finger over her palm.

"We both need rest." She was running out of excuses and fast.

"You need to eat before you sleep in order to recover. Using magic requires calories."

"I'd be shit company. That, or I'd fall asleep on my plate."

"You can be however you are. That's how I like you. If you fall asleep, I'll make sure you don't suffocate in your dessert."

At the talk of food, her stomach had begun to make comments, and at the word "dessert," it growled hungrily. Dalton heard and smiled smugly down at her hand.

She sighed dramatically. "I guess we can eat after we get out of here. But not until I shower." She sniffed. She didn't smell rank that she could tell, but she probably was. "And change clothes."

"Done."

Silence fell between them. Taylor gave a little shake of her head. How far they'd come. She'd gone from hating Dalton's guts to kissing him, and now a date. She was living in Upside-Down World.

"This *is* a date," Dalton said.

She glanced at him. "I got that."

"I just wanted to make sure you understood my intentions."

"I don't have a clue about your intentions. Never have."

He eyed her a long moment, then gave a little shrug. "I hear mystery spices up a relationship."

"It's a date, not a relationship," Taylor said.

"Sure."

She shook her head and fell silent. Arguing wouldn't make a difference, and she wasn't entirely sure she wanted to. She didn't know if she wanted to be in a relationship with anybody, much less Dalton, but she'd certainly like to get back to having ordinary days where choosing what to wear on a date was the hardest thing she'd have to do.

Unfortunately, she had a feeling that those days would be a lot fewer and farther between than they used to be. They'd taken responsibility for Diamond City and the people in it. Just because they'd hopefully fixed the current problem, didn't mean there wouldn't be more.

She knew for a fact that Riley would always try to protect the city: an unknown, unsung hero. Taylor would always be by her side. So would Price, Jamie, and Leo. Maybe Dalton, too. A motley crew of dysfunctional superheroes. She'd have to get herself a cape.

Chapter 38

Riley

I PASSED OUT. Or I think I did. I didn't remember much after I'd done my thing. The last thing I remember was talking to Kensington, but the details were fuzzy.

Wait. I'd fallen down. The diamond thread had reeled back out of me, and I'd dropped like a bad habit. I'd landed. . . . No, Price had caught me. Now he held me, my head in his lap as we sat on the floor. He said something. The roaring in my ears didn't let me make sense of the sounds.

My brain throbbed. Who was I kidding? All of me throbbed. And ached. And prickled, like my circulation had stopped and had just restarted. I felt like I'd been picked up by a tornado in Colorado and dropped in China. My mouth tasted like copper pennies. Oh, right. Bloody nose.

I licked my lips and winced. My lower one was fat. Had I bit it? Probably. Just to add insult to injury.

"Riley?"

Price's hands tightened slightly where he held me, and his head dipped close. His breath fluttered against my cheek.

"Yeah," I croaked. Pretty literally. Bullfrog city. If Johnny Cash was a bullfrog with a really bad cold.

"You're okay." He made it a statement, rather than a question.

"Alive, anyway. How's everybody else? Taylor?" Terror flashed through me. Clearly, she'd succeeded in freeing us from the machine, but that didn't mean she'd survived the effort.

I struggled to sit up. My muscles tensed, and I lifted myself for a bare second and collapsed. I didn't have the strength of a roadkill rabbit.

"She's okay," Price said, stroking a hand over my hair.

"Patti? Cass? Touray? My brothers?"

"They're working on Cass. Patti's unconscious but okay. Gregg is helping Tiny."

Relief lumped in my throat, and if I hadn't felt as dry as a desert, I might have cried a little. "What about Tyrell?" I asked, finally remembering him.

"Alive. Also Arnow is climbing the walls."

"I'd better talk to her. Help me sit up?"

He lifted me and turned me so that I sat between his legs and leaned back against his chest. He slid his arms around me.

"You okay?" I asked, feeling like the worst girlfriend for not asking earlier.

"Alive, anyway," he said, and I could feel his lips curve into a smile as he repeated my words back to me. "Tapped out, though."

"Of magic?"

"Yep. For now, anyhow."

"Thanks."

"For what?"

"Loving me. Not giving up on me."

His arms tightened. "I could say the same."

"Just don't forget it in the next few minutes."

He stiffened. "What did you do?"

Before I had to answer, Arnow stomped over and squatted down.

"Tell me everything," she said in a clipped voice. "What do we need to do now?"

Before I could answer, she interrupted, answering her own question.

"We need to move you out of here as soon as possible. You don't need to get caught here. Erickson has been monitoring the system and herding agents away from here. Locking up doors, shutting off the elevators, and such, but we can't bet on it lasting much longer. We have to pack up the machine's parts. They all came apart. We need them to disappear, ASAP."

"I'll take care of the pieces," Taylor said. Throw pillows cascaded aside as she rose from the couch. Dalton had been holding her hand and reluctantly let it go, standing beside her.

She looked about as crappy as I felt. "How? The pieces only go willingly with the people of the right talent."

She grimaced. "I'm pretty sure I can handle them."

"'Pretty sure' could get you killed."

She grinned. "Could. We'll soon see."

Then she winked and went past me. Winked. Who even does that? Arnow snapped her fingers in front of my face.

"Earth to Riley. We're burning daylight."

"I got it all done. Ask Erickson about the other evidence we created." I yawned widely, unable to stop it.

She stared and then swore, lunging to her feet. "We've got to get you all out of here. Now."

The sharp edge of her voice had everybody looking at her.

"Don't just sit on your asses. Get up and move! Everybody who's not part of the story needs to get out." She whirled to look at Erickson. "Make a path out of here. Get these idiots to safety. You, too."

She glared at me when she said "idiots." Little did she know.

A book-case-cabinet combo swung open in the wall to our right. A door hid behind it. I was in a James Bond movie.

Arnow waved at us to get up and get moving.

"Come, on! Riley, Taylor, Cass, Tiny, Leo, Jamie: time to hit the road. Get into the passage. Erickson will lead you out."

We all started moving. Tiny carried Cass, flanked by Jamie and Leo. Taylor and I followed. I'd have liked to say we went fast, electrified by Arnow's urgency, but we shambled like geriatric marathon runners after running uphill twenty-five miles while wearing leg shackles.

I turned around just inside the cinderblock tunnel, my gaze shifting to Price. He was helping a groggy Patti to her feet. I didn't like leaving any of them, but especially those two. Both were out of magic and worn to the bone.

"We'll meet with you later," Arnow said, grabbing the door to swing it shut.

"There's more I have to tell you," I said, putting up a hand to block it.

Arnow twisted her head and scowled. "Company is coming. It's going to have to wait." She pushed against me, and I fell back a step.

"It can't."

My words bounced back at me as the door clicked firmly shut. A lock clicked into place.

"Shit."

"What's the matter?" Taylor stood beside me. She carried the two bags containing the artifacts. Apparently, packing them up had given her as little trouble as she'd expected. The others had continued ahead, following Erickson up the dimly lit corridor.

"I might have done something," I said, digging my phone from my pocket. It was full of tiny holes and refused to turn on. "Shit."

Taylor pulled hers out and held it up with a grimace. "Same as mine."

"I guess they'll have to figure it out, then," I said, starting after the others. Taylor fell in beside me.

"Figure what out?"

"We never talked about who should take on running the FBI or the police department."

She eyed me. "Yeah?"

"We need someone we can trust in those positions. Trust them to clean up the corruption in Diamond City's law enforcement and keep the city corruption free."

"Okay. Sure. What did you do?"

"I mean, Arnow, Touray, and Price all hate the corruption and want the Tyets out. The only reason Touray even started his own organization was to take down the others and protect the city, right?"

"Riley, what did you do?" Taylor asked in an excessively patient tone.

"It's possible Arnow's boss is about to resign and highly recommend Arnow and Touray to take up running the local FBI office. As co-directors, or agents in charge, or whatever they're called."

"You didn't."

"It's also entirely possible that I asked Erickson to beef up Arnow's commendations and build Touray a bulletproof file all about his undercover work in the Tyets."

Taylor chuckled. "One or both of them is going to kill you."

"Not if Price gets a chance first," I said.

It had all seemed like such a good idea at the time, and sure, funny, but I really thought putting Touray and Arnow in charge was a good idea. They'd balance each other out, and they both were on the side of good. Most of the time. Having someone with talent and someone without would make people on both sides trust them. But Price—

I sighed. Chances were he'd really hate what I did. He'd feel compelled to take over Chief of Police job, if only to make sure he cleaned house and established anti-corruption policies.

"He's not going to kill you," Taylor said when I'd explained. "He'll make your life hell for awhile, but you'll deserve it."

"True enough. You and Dalton, huh?"

I think Taylor blushed.

"We're going on a date."

"He's nothing like Josh," I observed.

"Not even a little bit. Anyway, it's just one date. We'll probably argue, I'll tell him to fuck off, and that will be that."

"Maybe." Dalton didn't seem the type to give up easy, and Taylor was worth working for. "What are you going to do with the artifacts? Maybe we should find Kensington's workshop and hide them there."

Taylor dug in her pocket and held out her hand. The filigree vial of Kensington's blood—or at least, that's what I think it had been—sat in her palm. Now it was just a charred hunk of melted metal and glass.

"I'm betting his trace is gone," she said.

I was too tired and drained to check, but I couldn't help myself. I dropped into trace sight. I staggered, and Taylor caught me by the arm to steady me.

"No trace at all. But that can't be right," I said, coming back out of it. Even though it was a minor use of magic, doing it seemed to double the weight of my exhaustion. It took work to scrape up the energy to just breathe. I was ready to sprawl out on the floor and take a nap. Maybe hibernate for a year or two.

"He helped me escape," Taylor said. "Kept the machine going so we could all get free. I think it must have destroyed what was left him. He said he was tied to this vial. Makes sense it would be destroyed, too."

"That surprises me. He didn't seem like he even wanted us to use the machine."

She nodded. "I thought the same, but it turns out he worried we would use it for our own personal benefit. We surprised him when we didn't. And he was bitter about how the city hadn't really changed since they first used the machine. He thought their sacrifice had turned out to be worthless."

"You convinced him otherwise?"

"No. I just said there were too many good people here to give up on them, and then I pretty much ignored him until he decided to help."

"Thank goodness he did," I said, sliding my arm around hers and squeezing her close.

She squeezed back. "Amen."

THE SUN WAS coming up when we made it outside again. Everybody else took the Snowcat and headed for Taylor's house. I probably should have gone, too, but I needed time to myself. I needed to decompress and be alone in silence for a little while. Plus Price would look for me at home.

They dropped me near the entrance of Karnickey Burrows. The storm had let up considerably. Snow still fell steadily, but it wasn't a blizzard. Maybe Price had siphoned energy out of it to help us. If that was even possible.

I had to walk about a half mile, part of that up the narrow trail that led steeply up over a high ridge. Luckily, I'd long ago had spells laid on it to melt snow and ice, so while exhaustion made the climb slow, I didn't have to contend with breaking a trail. Walls of snow and ice towered up on either side, at least ten feet above my head. Some had collapsed here and there, but what was left still hid me quite well from prying eyes.

Not that anybody was looking.

By the time I opened my front door, I was ready to collapse. I stripped down to my underwear and headed for the kitchen where I put on coffee. I then headed for the bathroom where I didn't dare sink into the hot-spring-filled natural tub. Instead, I stepped into the shower and let the hot water sluice over me for awhile before washing and wrapping up in a robe.

I poured coffee, added sugar and cream, and then foraged for something to eat. Lucky for me, there was a lot of food left, and I made a ham and cheese sandwich with a side of pickles and corn chips.

By the time I was done, I was beginning to feel alive again. I cleaned up and went upstairs. I eyed my bed longingly but didn't let myself sleep. Not yet.

I dug in my small closet for the big canvas duffle bag buried under a pile of summer clothes I really needed to fold and put away.

I unzipped the bag and started grabbing clothing. Underwear, bras, shirts, pants, socks—enough for at least a week. I pulled open my "delicates" drawer. Unlike Taylor, I didn't tend to invest in pretty lingerie or lacy underthings. All I had was a semi-sheer blue, thigh-length nightgown with spaghetti straps. It still had the tags on it. I couldn't remember when I'd got it. I shoved that into the bag and eyed my underwear.

I usually dressed for comfort, not sexiness, but it would be nice to surprise Price. So far he'd mostly seen the grungy, just-shot, almost-dead me. He seemed to like that all right. How would he like sexy Riley?

Maybe enough not to kill me for putting him in charge of the Diamond City Police.

Not that he had to take it, I reminded myself. I almost wish he wouldn't. We'd said we'd take two weeks and go somewhere just the two of us when all this was done.

Well, I was sure as hell done. I wanted my two weeks with Price. But if he took the job of Police Chief, he'd be chained here for a good while with no chance at vacation and probably a whole lot of overtime.

I made a disgusted sound. I'd shot myself in the foot with that one.

Sighing, I looked for something sexy I could wear underneath the nightgown, but I had nothing. Commando it was, though the idea of Price peeling a lacy thong off me with his teeth gave me shivers.

I guess I was going to have to do some shopping, and soon.

I shoved some toiletries into the bag, and anything else I thought I might need, then zipped it up. I had no idea when to expect Price. I tried not to worry. I'd done everything I could think of to sell our story. He shouldn't be in danger.

I chewed my lips, tempted to go downstairs and check what the TV was saying, but decided that was far too much work and instead crawled into bed and was asleep in moments.

"RILEY. WAKE UP, Baby. Come on, now."

Something cold trickled down my neck, and I woke with a start. My heart thudded as I shot straight up.

"Hey, easy. It's just me."

Price sat on the edge of the bed. Though he'd shed his coat and boots, snow clung to his hair and pants. He wore a worried look.

I wrapped my arms around his neck and pulled myself onto his lap, totally ignoring the chill and damp of the melting snow between us.

His arms came around me, and he kissed me slow and deep, like we had time. It was . . . erotic. I hadn't had a chance to really savor being with him, to explore him the way I wanted.

He must have felt the same way because he pushed me back from him and grabbed the back of his shirt, pulling it over his head.

Hot damn. He'd lost weight in our ordeal, but it only revealed his muscular, sexy body. He pushed my robe down without untying it so that the collar held my arms prisoner. He made sounds of approval when he saw I was naked beneath, and then began exploring. I wriggled to free myself so that I could touch him, but he only chuckled and pushed me back so he could straddle me and pin my wrists under his knees.

Then he kissed and licked and bit and sucked and turned me into a raving bundle of eager desperation. He refused to let me free or go any faster, though I bucked my hips, searching for satisfaction.

He quit his teasing and kissed me for awhile. I thought I'd explode. Then he returned to my neck, chest, and stomach. This time, though, he studiously avoided my breasts. Like they didn't even exist. They ached for his touch, and I was pretty sure I begged him to suck them, but he pretended to be deaf and continued his sensual onslaught.

I swear if he'd so much as breathed on my nipples, I'd have exploded. I was so wet and ready.

"So, you decided I should be Police Chief," he said as he swirled his tongue in my belly button, then nipped his way up to the hollow between my breasts where he repeated the gesture.

I was having trouble being coherent. I answered with a groaned affirmative.

"I also see you're packed. Planning a trip?"

Again with the groan as he ran his tongue up the side of my neck and nibbled my ear.

"Were you planning to tell me or just take off without a word?"

I wasn't sure if he really doubted me or was just using the opportunity to punish me in an incredibly delicious way.

He lifted his head up, staring down at me, waiting for my answer.

I guess he was serious.

"Where are you going?"

Part of me wanted to play the "wouldn't you like to know?" game, but the rest of me was a tangle of throbbing nerves, desperate for him to fulfill the promises he'd been making with his mouth.

"Depends," I said.

On black brow lifted. He had a dangerous glint in his eye. "On what?"

"If you take the job, I figure we'll have to live closer so we can make the most of your free time. If you don't take the job, then you owe me two weeks of one-on-one time, and I aim to collect before another disaster hits."

He gave me a long look as if weighing my answer, and then he shifted back into action. Only this time he wasn't teasing.

He pulled my robe wide and stared down at me, then he was on top of me, hot and hard. He apologized to my breasts for ignoring them, sucking and licking until I broke apart from the intensity of it. He was smugly delighted that he could get me off without getting anywhere near my clit. I yanked on his belt, but he ignored the hint and instead moved down to my feet then made love to every bit of me until he reached my hips again.

I was on fire. I wanted him inside me like I'd never wanted anything before, but he appeared determined to prolong my pleasure—and agony—for as long as he could.

He blew on my clit and I had to admit I flung myself wide open and pulled on his shoulder with one hand, while trying to work my hand into the top of his pants with the other. He pulled away and then he was down there, his tongue working magic, and I was pretty sure I died. At least once, but who knows? The pleasure kept rolling through me, and I couldn't tell if it was just one long orgasm or a dozen.

He slid his fingers inside me, hooking them to touch my g-spot. I'd been spiraling down, but that shot me off again. I was making incoherent noises, and my body was jerking around like I'd been hit with electricity.

I hardly realized when Price pulled away, but then he was back. He slid inside me without any more teasing, and it was enough to make me come again. He rolled us over so that I could ride him, playing with my breasts and looking at me like he planned to devour me all over again.

I started moving my hips, wanting to give him back some of the wild pleasure he'd given me. I flexed my inner muscles and rose slowly until he was just barely touching my entrance, and then lowered down, equally slowly. I closed my eyes to savor the sensation.

Price flexed when I bottomed out, pushing in as far as he could go. I gasped and clenched as tight as I could. He moaned, his hands falling to my hips. He ground against me, holding me fast.

We repeated the sequence I don't know how many times. I wanted to speed up, to have him drive into me with all the power of his hard body, but I also wanted to draw the pleasure out, to feel his solid heat inside me.

At last it was too much. He rolled me over and thrust, his mouth on mine. We didn't last. My body spasmed around his as every nerve ending in my body fired with electric pleasure. My mouth fell open, but I couldn't make a sound. All I could do was feel wave after wave of pleasure rolling through me.

When the orgasms subsided, Price rolled onto his back, pulling me on top of him. I sprawled there, out of breath and unable to move.

His heart beat fast beneath my cheek, and sweat coated both our bodies. I ran my fingers over his ridged muscles and toyed with his nipple. He sucked in a breath and grabbed my hand.

"Careful. You're not going to get much rest if you keep that up."

I lifted my head to look at him. "Who said I wanted a rest?"

He shook his head and looked up at the ceiling. "Fuck. You're going to be the death of me."

"But what a way to go, right?"

I wiggled my hips against his cock, delighted that it hadn't gone soft in the slightest .

"Besides, you seem ready to go again."

He smiled. "I'm never not going to be ready when it comes to you." His expression turned serious "Do you really want me to go back to being a cop? To running the show?"

And here I'd been hoping he'd be so high on sex endorphins he wouldn't want to talk about it for awhile.

I sighed and laid my head back down on his chest. "No. Yes. I don't know. Who else would clean up the corruption and make sure the cops stayed on the up and up?"

"It means a lot of hours. A lot of overtime for who knows how long."

"I know."

I didn't say anything else. I might be able to talk him out of it, but Price wasn't the kind of man who shirked his duty. Nobody would do as good a job as he would. He'd be fair, and he cared about the people of the city. The minute he was offered it, he was destined to take it, whether he knew it or not.

"What about you? What will you do? Keep tracing?"

I hadn't thought about it. "I guess. Maybe I'll become a consultant for the local cops, or the FBI. I'm pretty sure my references are good." An idea occurred to me. An awful idea. A wonderful, terrible, awful idea. "Better yet, I might ask Taylor, Leo, and Jamie to start a business with me."

"That sounds like trouble waiting to happen. What kind of business?"

"Private investigators. Bet we could bring Erickson in. Maybe Dalton. I wonder if Cass would want to."

I lifted my head to look at Price, my eyes dancing with excitement. "We could specialize in kidnappings and missing persons. Together we would be a force to be reckoned with."

"Undoubtedly," Price said dryly.

I frowned. "You think it's a bad idea?"

"I think you'll save a lot of people."

"But?"

He sighed. "But I have a feeling you're going to be working worse hours than I am and we'll never see each other."

He had a point.

"I won't let that happen," I promised. "And once you get things squared away, you can quit and join the family business."

His eyes darkened, and he rolled me over, holding me caged between his arms.

"*Family* business? Is that a proposal? Because I damned well plan to marry you as soon as you'll let me, but I was going to wait awhile for you to come around to the idea. If you're already there, then I say we make a date, and make it soon."

He was serious.

I opened my mouth, but no words came out. My brain felt scrambled. Price waited, and though he looked patient enough, his entire body was rigid with what? Anticipation? Fear of rejection?

Don't overthink this, Riley.

"I don't have any pretty underwear."

He blinked. "What?"

"A girl needs pretty underwear for her wedding, doesn't she? And I want a honeymoon. So you'll have to make sure you have time off—"

He started kissing me again, and we didn't come up for air again for a long while.

I was curled up against Price, feeling like I could sleep for a year.

"How much time do you need?"

"For what?"

"Planning the wedding?"

"Me? That's Taylor's department."

"Fair enough. How much time does she need?"

"How much time do we want to give her?"

"Is twenty-four hours enough?"

I giggled. "If you've got a death wish."

"A week then."

"You don't want to wait until spring or summer? Or at least until the snow melts?"

"I don't want to wait, period. If you do, I'll deal."

I didn't see any point in waiting. "How about two weeks, and then you can take me somewhere private and warm with waterfalls where we don't have to wear any clothes if we don't want to?"

"Will that give you enough time to buy pretty underwear? A lot of it? Because I really want to see you in it, but chances are I'm going to end up ripping it off you."

Caveman Price ripping my underwear off me sounded hot.

"Pretty sure I could buy a warehouse full by then."

"Then two weeks it is. I'll arrange our honeymoon and you deal with Taylor and planning the wedding."

"Okay." I snuggled closer, deciding that Taylor could wait a few hours. If I told her now, she blow up my phone with questions and plans. Or I'd ruin her date with Dalton. Either way, no thanks.

"And, Riley?"

"Mmhm?"

"Do you think you can manage to avoid getting involved in any apocalypses or extinction level events until after our honeymoon?"

"Depends."

"On what?"

"On how pissed Taylor gets for having only two weeks to plan a wedding, and how much trouble Leo and Jamie give her in the process."

Price was silent for a long moment. "Maybe we should elope."

"Who would kill us first: Taylor or your brother?"

"Shit."

"We don't have to get married." Even saying it gave me a pang. I *wanted* to be tied to Price in all the ways possible. Who knew I was so sentimental?

"We're getting married, and we are having a family, and we are growing old together," he said forcefully, the arm around me tightening. He hesitated. "Do you want kids?"

"Maybe I should start with a fish." It wasn't that I didn't want kids. I hadn't really thought about it. Mostly, I was terrified I'd screw them up.

"You don't think you'd be a good mom?"

"I think I have a crap record keeping plants alive, and if not for Patti, I wouldn't eat regularly."

Price chuckled, his chest rumbling beneath my cheek. "And yet you can save a city full of people, practically single-handed."

"Uh, no. I had a ton of help, as you very well know. I've managed to figure out I can't do things all on my own, which is why we need to let our families plan our wedding. They'll want and need to be involved."

"Same with raising kids."

"Jamie and Leo would have a field day. They'd teach our kids all kinds of things we don't want them to know."

"Like you'd let them get away with anything," Price scoffed.

I lifted my head to look at him. "I guess that means you want kids?"

"I do. But if you don't, then we won't. You matter more."

I was hit with a mix of panic, and a longing to see him holding a baby. Our baby. "Do I have to decide now?"

"No."

"Good, because it's freaking me out a little." Or a lot.

He stroked a hand over my head and pressed a kiss to my forehead as he snuggled me closer. "Forget I mentioned it. Last thing I want to do is freak you out. You do crazy things when you're freaked out."

"I do not. And the chances of me forgetting are slim and none."

"You do, too. But I can think of one way to get your mind off it." He trailed a finger down my cheek and around the curve of my breast.

I sucked in a breath and caught his hand. "I thought we were going to actually sleep?"

"I don't remember agreeing to that. Besides, we're talking now. We could talk and enjoy ourselves, too."

"Aren't you tired?" I gave a deliberate yawn, even though I wasn't at all against the idea of having another round of Riley-goes-out-of-her-mind orgasms.

"I think I've got a second wind," he said pulling me up and sliding on top of me. He was hard against my slick heat.

"Second? I believe this might your fourth or fifth. Not that I'm counting. Or complaining."

He smiled down at me, flexing his hips. "I'm never going to get enough of you."

I gasped, and started to say something snarky, but he rested a finger over my lips, his sapphire gaze earnest.

"Seriously, Riley. Never. I don't know by what miracle you decided you could put up with me, even after you found out about my brother and all that shit with Shauna, and after I killed your stepmom—"

I pushed his hand away. "That wasn't your fault. You weren't responsible. The FBI was. Them, and the senator for passing that stupid, bigoted law, and everybody else including Vernon, Tyrell, Savannah, and even your own insane mom."

He shook his head at my vehemence and brushed my lips with his. "And that's why I love you. When you go in, you're all in. I'm the lucky bastard who gets to have you."

I shook my head. "Pretty sure I'm the lucky one. How many times did you choose me over your brother, over everything else? Even when I told you to go away and leave me alone?"

"Wasn't a choice. Was just a fact."

My forehead scrunched. I had too many feels going on, and changing the subject seemed like a really good idea.

"Do your brother and Arnow hate me?"

"Gregg is amused. Arnow, less so. If she wasn't afraid of leaving the fox in the henhouse, I'm fairly certain she'd have hunted you down and given you an earful by now. As it is, she's watching Gregg like a hawk."

I gave a little shake of my head. "Who'd have imagined she and I would be friends? I hated her so much. Or that you and I would be getting married? When we started, I was faking being a two-bit hack tracer, anonymously finding kidnapped kids, and you were part-time cop, part-time enforcer for your brother—a major Tyet kingpin intent on running all of Diamond City.

"Now he and Arnow, who I'd have gladly dropped into the caldera on more than one occasion, are going to be running the local FBI office, and you're going to be heading up the police. *And* Arnow is probably going to be one of my bridesmaids. Meanwhile, everybody on the planet knows I'm a whole lot better tracer than I pretended to be. Oh, and you're also a wind elemental.

"How did all that happen? I mean, a few months ago you hired me to do a trace on that guy—Corbin Nader. Next thing I know, we're taking over Savannah's organization and literally rewriting history and cleaning up the corruption in Diamond City. What's next? Visiting Mars?"

"Next is a normal life. Well, as normal as anybody can have in Diamond City, anyway."

I smiled. "White picket fence and all that? That's—"

I shook my head, feeling close to tears. "I never thought that was even possible for me. No husband, no kids, either. I always thought I'd have to be alone, off the grid. That was always going to be my life. I was happy with that. I thought I was happy with that, anyway. Then you came along and I wanted more. But are you sure you want to be with me? I'm a lot of work, and Cass couldn't fix me all the way. A lot of what my father did to me is still in my head. I could wig out over nothing. You'll never know what to expect or if you can count on me."

Price drew a deep breath, and rolled off me onto his side, propping his head on his elbow as he looked down at me, tracking my cheek with his fingers.

"That's what your father wanted you to think, but you're stronger than he imagined. Your father wanted you isolated, but you refused. You had Patti, and your family, and you fell in love with me. You've fought his programming your whole life, and you won. Cass might have helped you get to the other side, but it never would have happened if you hadn't broken through first."

He cupped his hand around my face. "You don't have to be afraid of yourself or anything you want to be or do. Look what you were willing to do for your sister, to find Josh for her. Look what you were willing to do for me. You literally *died* for me. You've risked your life over and over, for your family, for me, hell, for the entire fucking city. Your father's dead, and good riddance. You get to start your own life on your terms. I trust you. I always will. I know I can count on you, even if you wig out. You won't let anything like that get the best of you."

A rush of relief and love knotted my throat. "Well, when you put it that way . . ."

He gave me a dirty smile. "Makes you want me again, doesn't it?"

I rolled my eyes. "You're so full of yourself."

He lifted himself on top of me again, nudging my legs apart. "I bet you'd like to be full of myself, too, wouldn't you?"

He practically purred.

They say pick your battles. I'd picked mine and I'd won. I'd won them all. I got the hot guy, I conquered a city, and I killed the bad guys. I figured I could let Price have this one. Besides, losing this one was going to feel so, so, good.

The End

Acknowledgements

I started *Scatter of Light* shortly before Covid hit. At the same time I was dealing with some other life issues, and the book quickly turned into a giant knot of yarn that seemed impossible to untangle, much less knit into something pretty and coherent. I'd have settled for coherent, really. The fact that you are holding this book is a little bit of a miracle.

Everything you like about it can be attributed to the wonderful people in my life who've supported me, including you! Because without them and you, I think I'd have potentially crawled under the covers with my dogs and just hibernated for as long as it took to wake up in a happy world. I also lost one of my boys during the writing, and that was gutting.

First and foremost, I'm grateful to my family for supporting me. And by support, I mean ordering takeout as necessary, cheering me up, taking on household responsibilities, and generally taking care of me when I was crawling up walls and hiding under the bed and primal screaming into my pillow. I tried primal screaming at the computer, but strangely, that only upset the dogs and did nothing to convince the computer to make words for me. Strange.

Good friends near and far have carried me a long way in my life and career, and especially through the last couple of years. Devon Monk, Jeff Howe, Christy Keyes, Megan Thyagarajan, Melissa Sawmiller, Melissa Marr, RJ Blain, Faith Hunter, Cynthia Porter, Jean Harvey, my Rainforest friends, my Word Warriors friends, my Miscon friends—too many to name, but know that even if I did not mention you here you are precious to me and I thank all of creation for putting you in my path.

I have the best editor. She's kind, generous, sweet, and sharper than a katana. Deb Dixon has been a rock in all sorts of ways. I'm so grateful for her insights and encouragement.

And to Teri Sullivan, copy editor extraordinaire. She caught a lot of typos and misspellings and other problems. Any left are my fault. Not every manuscript can be perfect, in fact not every manuscript is perfect, but she got me a lot closer than I could have on my own. Thank you, Teri!

More than anything, I am grateful to readers who continue to read my work, who care about me, who want more. . . . You are everything. Thank you for letting me into your homes and lives and sharing my love of these gloriously messy characters.

The title of this book comes from Gerard Manley Hopkins's poem, "God's Grandeur."

The theme for the past two years can be summed up in The Grateful Dead's song, "Truckin'": What a long, strange trip it's been. I hope this book gives you escape and joy.

About the Author

Diana Pharaoh Francis is the acclaimed author of more than a dozen novels of fantasy and urban fantasy. Her books have been nominated for the Mary Roberts Rinehart Award and *RT Magazine*'s Best Urban Fantasy. Find out more about her at www.dianapfrancis.com.

Made in the USA
Monee, IL
10 August 2022

11161304R10187